HAVENWOOD FALLS HIGH VOLUME SIX

A HAVENWOOD FALLS HIGH COLLECTION

ALI WINTERS   ROSE GARCIA   LIZ FERRY

ABOUT THIS BOOK

Three novellas (books 17-19) in the young adult paranormal fantasy series Havenwood Falls High, Home of the Dragons – and vampires, wolves, fae, and much more.

Saving Infiniti by **Rose Garcia**

Infiniti Clausman is determined to make her senior year one to remember, but when she travels from Houston to Colorado for the holiday break, she finds her world turned upside down. Joe Greg will never forget the injured girl he and Kase Kasun found on the side of the mountain in 2012, when he was only twelve. When he sees the girl again in 2018, she looks exactly the same. He figures out that she's time-traveled to his present, with a reaper on her heels and a mystery to unravel. Drawn to protect her, he's hell-bent on standing by her side. Even if it means his death.

Willful by **Liz Ferry**

Celeste is used to getting her way—it comes naturally. Now that she's coming of age, she's about to learn why things turn out in her favor so often, and find out some hidden truths about her own identity. Jonathan has been on the run for as long as he can remember. He and his mom hope Havenwood Falls will be a safe haven for them and the secret they protect. But they may have run right into the hands of their enemies. When Celeste sets her sights on Jonathan, she may be in for her biggest challenge yet. He can't afford a distraction like dating. But every time their paths cross, they're drawn closer together. Let the battle of wills begin.

Cast in Moonlight by **Ali Winters**

After Clarke Price and her mom end up in the ditch while moving to Havenwood Falls, Clarke wakes up to find her mom in a coma. She's never felt so alone as she grapples with impossible truths about the town, her family, and the unbelievable realization that she's a witch. She keeps running into a stunning guy with gorgeous eyes who turns her into her least favorite cliché. But can Clarke trust this handsome stranger, or is he responsible for the accidents that have nearly taken her life—twice? And what about the nightmares that feel like a dire warning that something bad is coming?

HAVENWOOD FALLS HIGH BOOKS

Written in the Stars by Kallie Ross

Reawakened by Morgan Wylie

The Fall by Kristen Yard

Somewhere Within by Amy Hale

Awaken the Soul by Michele G. Miller

Bound by Shadows by Cameo Renae

Fata Morgana by E.J. Fechenda

Forever Emeline by Katie M. John

Reclamation by AnnaLisa Grant

Avenoir by Daniele Lanzarotta

Avenge the Heart by Michele G. Miller

Curse the Night by R.K. Ryals

Blood & Iron by Amy Hale

Shadows & Spells by Cameo Renae

Falling Deep by J.L. Weil

Saving Infiniti by Rose Garcia

Willful by Liz Ferry

Cast in Moonlight by Ali Winters

Promise the Moon by Kallie Ross

Blurred Lines by Daniele Lanzarotta

Ascending Darkness by J.L. Weil

Finding Infiniti by Rose Garcia

Unicorn's Lament by Megan Linski

Paper Bird by Amy Richie

Predestined by Valia Lind

Rediscovered by Morgan Wylie

Ashes of Fate by Apryl Baker

Stay up to date at www.HavenwoodFalls.com

SAVING INFINITI

ROSE GARCIA

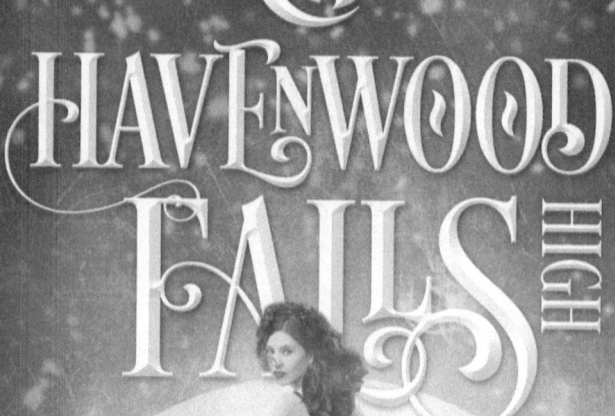

HAVENWOOD FALLS HIGH

Saving Infiniti

ROSE GARCIA

~ A Havenwood Falls Young Adult Novella ~

ALSO BY ROSE GARCIA

To everyone who believes in one true love.

CHAPTER 1

*F*leet ran his fingers through his dark hair before tilting his head toward the night sky. He eyed the top floor of the Houston skyscraper Tavion had called home since tracking Dominique and her protectors to the oversized Texas city. A cool December breeze swept through the streets, kicking up the stench of trash from a nearby dumpster. Fleet hated all the concrete, all the glass buildings, but mostly he hated taking on the role of being one of the Tainted and on Tavion's side against the Pures. He had accepted the directive for the greater good, but the passing of so many years had started to muddle allegiances in his brain. All sense of right and wrong had started to merge. Too good at his job, he found himself alone and sure of nothing but the perpetual clench in his gut.

Fleet closed his eyes. He tried not to picture the horrible things he had done in Tavion's name while tracking Dominique, but had a hard time suppressing the images. His only solace was knowing that in this life, her final life, Dominique had no recollection of any of her prior lives. Even if it meant forgetting him forever, Fleet hoped Dominique's memories would never return. There was too much pain and suffering for anyone to have to recall, let alone someone he secretly cared about.

Fleet banged his fist against the glass wall of the downtown apartment building. "Get your shit together, man."

Pressing his palm against the cool surface, he held his breath, then let it trickle out between clenched teeth. He had built a brick wall around his true feelings for Dominique and the Pures ages ago, vowing not to let anyone ever see that side of himself, especially Tavion. He had a job to do and was determined to see it through no matter what. To hell with what anyone thought of him.

"Don't let anyone in," he muttered, while strengthening the fortress of his mind. With his vulnerabilities hidden, he turned his focus to Tavion's directive: find Dominique and prepare her for death.

"I got this," he whispered to himself. "I can do this."

With his emotions in check, he jerked the heavy door open. He nodded at the security guard behind the holiday-adorned lobby desk. The guard peered at him from over his computer screen.

"Hey, Fleet. Your boss is in quite a mood tonight." He whistled. "Quite a mood."

Fleet knew exactly what sort of mood Tavion was in. Starving for death and destruction, he displayed hatred like a neon sign. But some days his harsh light shone brighter than usual. Today must have been one of those days.

"Thanks, Sammy."

Sammy said something else about Christmas spirit and holiday joy, but Fleet ignored him. Joy didn't exist for him, hadn't in a long time. And it wasn't likely to ever return.

Pushing the button for the top floor with his key card, Fleet repeated his mission over and over in his mind, drowning out the doubt that lingered in the darkest corners. With a ding, the steel doors opened. He loathed interacting with Tavion and mostly operated on his own, but every now and again Tavion would call him in for a status report.

Fleet steadied himself. He cleared his mind. He stepped into the all-white foyer of the sprawling penthouse. Thick silence and heavy foreboding sucked the air right out of the space. He knew this meeting, like all the others, was going to suck.

Windows lined the long L-shaped living space that looked out on the sparkling buildings of the massive city. The dark sky outside blended in with the shadowy room. Only the soft light from the gleaming neighboring structures gave any indication of life in the space. An oversized brown leather chair facing the view was the lone piece of furniture in the entire apartment. It was Tavion's favorite spot.

Tavion extended his arm over the armrest. He waved Fleet over.

"Come."

Fleet's boots thudded against the marble floors, the echo of each step bouncing all around him like a lonely symphony. He took his place next to Tavion and clasped his hands behind his leather jacket. Glancing at Tavion, he saw that he was dressed in his usual black suit. His profile revealed a deep scowl.

"How may I help you, sir?"

Tavion moved his long skeletal fingers to his pale face and started rubbing his chin. "Dominique Wells," he said, letting the *s* trickle out of his mouth as if he were a slithering snake. "I've been thinking of her final life, and the differences here as compared to our other lives, and I do not like it. The events of late do not sit well with me. This year in particular, 2012, is fraught with too many unknowns."

Fleet remembered a time when Tavion's appearance was hardy and robust. Tavion had once stood on the side of right, but over time, a deep-seated hatred toward mankind pulled him away. Tavion detested humans and blamed them for the gradual destruction of the natural world. His departure split the Transhumans into two factions: the good became known as the Pure. The evil became known as the Tainted, and Tavion became their leader. He eventually marked Dominique for death in an attempt to get back at the Pure. With each passing decade, Tavion's hate grew in his heart and in his body, reducing him to his current death-like appearance.

Yet Fleet knew Tavion was right. Things in this life were way different, mainly with the involvement of first lifers Trent Avila and Infiniti Clausman. Friends of Dominique's, Fleet suspected they'd play a role in Dominique's quest for survival. It seemed Tavion shared the same sentiment.

Testing his theory, Fleet asked, "What do you mean?"

Tavion let out a low growl. "Do not pretend that you know not of what I speak." He stood and faced Fleet. "Or are you keeping something from me?"

Hiding his surprise at the threatening move, Fleet eyed Tavion with matching menace, a look he knew Tavion respected. Tavion resided in perpetual paranoia, forcing Fleet to work overtime to keep Tavion's trust secured.

Fleet raised his chin. "I assure you, I am not keeping anything from you, sir. Nor would I make pretense."

Fleet waited for Tavion's response, wondering if Tavion had somehow discovered the conflict within him. Fleet curled his fingers behind his back, ready to form an energy ball and strike Tavion if needed. Luckily, Tavion's face softened. He placed his hand on Fleet's shoulder.

"My apologies, Fleet. I should not be so angry with you, especially since you are the only one I've been able to count on all these very long years."

Fleet relaxed his fist, but his body remained tense. "It's okay, sir."

Tavion eased back down on his chair. He returned his gaze to the twinkling lights of the downtown buildings. "Dominique keeps eluding us, but I know she's close. I can feel her fear, can practically smell her blood. Her parents cannot hide her forever. Eventually there'll be another break, and we'll find her. In the meantime, I want you to follow this one."

Tavion let loose a dark mist from his palm. It gathered into a swirl, forming a large oval shape. The mist thinned out, revealing an image of Infiniti Clausman, Dominique's neighbor and friend. Petite with small features and long dark hair, she danced around her room while packing a suitcase.

"This first lifer is important," Tavion said. "I can sense it."

Just as Fleet suspected, she *was* important. He thought of the other first lifer.

"What of Trent Avila?"

"Leave him to me." Tavion jabbed his finger at the floating image. "But this one is leaving in the morning with her mother on a holiday trip, and I want you on her heels. You will follow her to Colorado. I want to know everything about her. Understood? What she eats, what she drinks, what she loves, what she fears. All of it."

By the look of her room and the way she carried herself, she seemed like an average teenager of the time—interested in parties, music, and all things superficial. Yet something about her had struck a chord with Tavion. Fleet, too. There had to be more to her, but what?

"Understood, sir."

Tavion whisked the image away. He dismissed Fleet with a wave.

"Go."

A sinking feeling grew in the pit of Fleet's stomach as he rode the elevator down to the first floor. He'd never been away from Dominique before. He didn't want to risk Tavion finding her while he was gone, yet he also didn't want Tavion to know about the conflict within him. Should he abandon Tavion's directive? Or should he follow Infiniti to Colorado and trust that Dominique would not be found until he returned?

Back outside, Fleet paced up and down the sidewalk, his mind on overdrive. Everything had repeated perfectly from lifetime to lifetime, but in this life nothing was the same. Nothing! And it was driving him crazy.

"It's better that way," a small voice said.

Fleet whipped around and saw a young girl. No more than five years old, she wore a long white dress that matched her long hair. She studied him with oversized green eyes.

"What's better?" he asked.

"That everything is different in this life."

A million things raced through Fleet's mind. Before he could say anything, the girl went on.

"You need to follow her. She will need you."

"The first lifer?"

"Yes. Infiniti. She will need you in Colorado."

A pink shimmery hue radiated from her body. Recognizing the young girl as part of the spirit world, yet sensing something familiar about her, he peered at her with questioning eyes. He moved closer.

"Who are you?"

The girl lifted her skirt off the floor with dainty hands and gave an old-fashioned curtsey. "I am Abigail. It's nice to meet you." Her innocent face flashed with remorse. "I used to be like you, but then I died. I had to in order to help save Dominique. Her friend is my friend, and Infiniti is important. Everyone in this life is. So you see, that's why you need to follow her. You need to help her."

Fleet latched on to her statement about being like him, but had no idea what she meant. Before he could ask her to explain, she stepped forward. She held out her hand, as if she wanted to touch him, but then dropped her arm. She lowered her head, her shoulders sagged, and she looked as if she might burst into tears.

"I am so sorry about what you are going through. I really am."

He looked about to see if anyone was around to witness the conversation he was having with the spirit girl, but the streets were empty. When he turned back to Abigail, she was gone.

"Hey! Come back!"

Desperate to ask the girl more questions, he waited a few minutes for her to return, but she didn't. He clasped his hands behind his neck. He walked up and down the sidewalk. He had no idea what she meant about feeling sorry for him, but figured it had to do with him joining Tavion's ranks. Shit, even he felt sorry for himself. He eyed the night sky that had begun to lighten to a soft gray. If Infiniti was important enough to garner Tavion's attention, then she probably would need his help.

"Guess I'm going to Colorado."

CHAPTER 2

*I*nfiniti clutched the armrests of her seat as the plane from Houston to Denver bobbed up and down. Glancing next to her, she saw her mom's usual scotch and soda splash over the edge of the plastic cup as she struggled with puckered lips to get the liquid into her mouth. Infiniti wished she had a drink of her own.

"Maybe I'm being punished," Infiniti said to her mother, her anxiety on overload. Streaks of light shot through dark clouds. Rain pelted her window. Rumbling thunder shook the plane. "Maybe we should've left on Friday instead of today. Maybe I should've stayed for that dumb test."

"Fin, no one is being punished. Okay? Your teacher said the test was optional. Leaving on a Wednesday will give us more time with the cousins." Infiniti's mom sipped her drink. "Relax."

Infiniti's gut twinged because her teacher hadn't exactly said that. Pushing aside her guilt, she fished through her backpack, searching for her pack of gum. Finding the cinnamon sticks, she unwrapped them and shoved three into her mouth. Terrified of crashing, Infiniti's mind raced with all things she hadn't done yet with her life—graduate, get a tattoo, go to college, backpack across

Europe, fall in love. She hadn't even had her first kiss yet. Her stomach twisted tight with fear and regret.

"We can't die. We just can't."

"We're not dying, Fin," her mom admonished between each hard-earned sip. "It's going to be fine. It's only turbulence."

With a sharp drop, the drink tumbled out of her mother's grasp. Luggage careened from the overhead bins. Oxygen masks released overhead. Infiniti wanted to yell, but her voice was strangled in her throat.

Infiniti's mom flew into action mode. She grasped Infiniti's arm with one hand, hollered commands Infiniti couldn't hear over the shouting all around them, and yanked at the masks. She slipped hers on with frantic motions.

Infiniti knew she should be doing the same, but couldn't move a muscle toward the life-saving plastic bag. Her mother swooped in. She snatched at the mask in front of Infiniti. She wrestled with the cords, like a woman possessed.

Images of death and wreckage blasted through Infiniti's mind. This was it. Game over! She burned with the sudden need to confess all the crap she'd done, because there was no way they were going to survive this.

She stopped her mom from slamming the mask on her face. "Mom, I'm sorry about all the sneaking out, smoking weed, skipping school, and throwing parties every time you went out of town! I'm sorry for all of it! And I lied about the test being optional!"

The plane leveled out. The blinking emergency lights turned off. Infiniti's mom tore off her mask.

"Really?" Her mom narrowed her eyes. She sat back in her chair, both masks dangling before them now. "Dammit, Infiniti Marie."

Infiniti gulped. She spotted the wad of gum on her pant leg, wondering when it had dropped out of her mouth. She scooped it up and slipped it between her lips.

"Mom, we were—"

Her mom cut her off with a raised finger. "That's your one get-out-of-jail-free card. Got it, young lady?"

"Yeah, got it. But—"

"Infiniti, stop. Not another word."

Feeling like a crappy daughter, and debating whether she should beg for forgiveness despite her mom telling her to be quiet, the pilot saved her with an announcement.

"Ladies and gentlemen, apologies for the rough ride. The skies have not been very friendly today, and I've received word that the Denver area is taking a beating right now. We'll be landing at Montrose Regional Airport instead. Personnel will be at the gate once you deplane to assist with connecting flights and answer any questions you may have. My apologies once again, folks. Flight attendants, prepare for landing."

After a bumpy landing, Infiniti and her mom managed to find a room at a small inn not far from the airport. They were even lucky enough to secure a rental car in case the airport became backlogged due to all the rerouted and canceled flights. Snuggled in their beds for the night and grateful to be alive, Infiniti whispered to her mom.

"Mom, I'm really sorry."

"I know, honey. I am, too. But we're alive, and all is good. Now let's get some sleep."

Infiniti tossed and turned while visions of fiery crashes cluttered her mind. She rearranged her pillow at least a hundred times, hoping to find the perfect level of fluffiness for her head. She shifted her legs from tucked up to her chest to splayed out. It took forever for her to fall asleep, and when she finally did, she was jarred awake by her phone alarm. She grumbled at herself for not remembering to turn it off, but it was too late. She was awake again. She brought her phone close to her face and saw that it was eight in the morning. How long had she actually slept?

Not exactly wanting to be awake yet, and finding it hard to

breathe because of the high altitude, she decided to go ahead and get out of bed. With a groan, she trudged her weary bones to the window and opened the curtains of their small first floor room. She couldn't believe her eyes. Snow was piled all the way to the top of the glass. It was as if their room was nestled inside a giant sno-cone. A wave of cold air seeped into the room with the fabric pulled back, even though the heater was cranked.

"This is crazy. Mom, come over here." Infiniti held her hand up to the window. "I'm not even touching the glass, and my hand is freezing."

Infiniti's mom rubbed her eyes. "Really?" she asked with a yawn. She put on her glasses and joined Infiniti. They stood together eyeing the white snow. "Oh, no. Looks like we may not make it to Breck this holiday." Sensing Infiniti's disappointment, since missing out on Breckenridge meant not seeing their cousins who were already there, Infiniti's mom tacked on, "But who knows? Maybe it'll clear out soon."

Infiniti perked up. "Yeah!" Then her stomach growled. "But whatever we do, we need food."

"Yes, we do," her mom said, rubbing her forehead. "And electrolytes. My head is killing me, and I'm having a hard time breathing."

"I'm feeling it, too," Infiniti said as her mom set up her laptop on a small desk in the corner of the room. "Why don't you stay here and search for flight information while I find us some drinks and food."

"Good idea," her mom agreed.

Infiniti quickly got dressed. She studied herself in the mirror. Dark jeans, a red sweater, her favorite black boots with fur at the top. She thought her outfit looked pretty cute. She ran her fingers through her hair, trying to revive the curls that had flattened without the humidity. They refused to bounce back to life, but she didn't mind. She liked how long her hair was when it was straight.

She dotted some concealer on the dark circles under her eyes, then puckered her lips and put on some gloss. She wanted to look decent in case she ran into any hot guys while exploring the inn. Boy crazy for as long as she could remember, keeping an eye out for hotties was her favorite hobby, especially when she was out of town. Plus, she had her senior year bucket list to keep in mind, with the number one item being to fall in love. Or deep like. Or anything close. Really, she just wanted a kiss.

She wrapped her wallet strap around her wrist. "Be right back!"

Stepping into the hallway, she caught a glimpse of someone coming her way. She backed up to her door so she wouldn't run into anyone, but when she faced the direction of the passerby, nobody was there. Her spine tingled. Her stomach dropped.

"What the?" she asked herself in a whisper, swearing she had seen someone in her peripheral vision.

Examining the red-carpeted hallway and the dark wood walls, a crazy notion dawned on her. Maybe the inn was haunted. Shivers raced across her arms. The decor certainly matched the spooky vibe. She loved all things supernatural but had never come face to face with a ghost or anything. She had a Ouija board at home, a new deck of oracle cards from her spiritual neighbor Jan, and a penchant for watching scary movies, but nothing otherworldly had ever happened to her.

Panic mixed with excitement stirred in her. She stepped away from the door and into the middle of the hallway.

"Um, hello? Anybody there?"

She waved her hands out in front her, as if she could touch a ghost if one had been near. With no response, she shook her head, dismissing the idea of paranormal activity. She looked around to make sure no one had witnessed her waving her arms in the hallway like a crazy person. She blew out a heavy breath, relieved to not see anyone. A fresh rumble in her stomach reminded her of her food-gathering task.

"Come on," she muttered to herself.

She made her way down the hall with a brisk stride. Turning

the corner, she emerged into a quaint woodsy lobby. With their late arrival the night before and chaos from the small crowd checking in from the airport, Infiniti hadn't had the time to scope out the place. With the dawn of the new day, she was able to take it all in.

The inn could've served as a location for a sweet and cheesy holiday movie. A roaring fire crackled in a massive stone fireplace in the middle of the room with gorgeous hand-knit stockings hanging from the chunky wooden mantle. An assortment of animal hides adorned the dark wood floors. Antlers and pictures of scenic landscapes hung on the wood-paneled walls. A short and stout Christmas tree stood by the front door. Infiniti couldn't help but feel merry and hopeful. But what made everything even better was the scent of cinnamon coffee that wafted her way. Her mouth watered.

Scanning the area for the source of the goodness, she spotted a small café on the other side of the twinkling tree. A handful of people hovered near the counter. Taking her spot in line, she overheard their conversations. Most were chatting about the big snow storm, how they had other destinations to make, and how they'd been hounding the airlines for updates. When it was her turn to order, she was lucky enough to get coffee for her and her mom, and two small croissants. All the other breakfast items were sold out.

"The roads have all been plowed in the area if you want to venture out for food," the nice grandma looking lady behind the counter suggested.

Sipping the warm liquid, Infiniti thanked her for the tip. With her coffee and food in hand, she went back to her room.

"I've got coffee and two small croissants. But the lady at the café said the roads were clear and suggested I go out for food. Is that cool with you?"

Her mom had buried herself in something work-related on her laptop. She took a few seconds to answer. "Yeah, yeah, that's fine. I've got this matter to handle real quick anyway."

"Okay," Infiniti answered. "Text me if you need me."

Wearing her new puffy black coat, she hurried out of the inn and to the parking lot. Expecting the car to be piled high in snow, she found it had been scraped and cleaned off.

"That was cool," she said, thinking someone from the inn had done it, because all the cars looked the same.

Infiniti cranked the heater in the beige four-door rental. Waiting for the car to warm, she scanned the radio stations for music. Finally finding some decent tunes, she rolled out of the inn parking lot and headed down the street.

Mounds of snow lined both sides of the small road, but that didn't intimidate her. She'd spent several holidays driving around Breckenridge in the snow and sleet; she could definitely handle a freshly plowed road. Eyeing the gray skies, she took the lack of falling snow as a good sign.

"Yep, everything's gonna be all right, all right, all right."

Passing by cute cottages, most of which were decked out with Christmas wreaths and other holiday decor, Infiniti finally came upon an intersection. A small grocery sat on the corner, nestled behind a row of magnificent blue spruce trees. With her stomach on hunger overdrive, she parked and dashed inside the store. She maneuvered up and down the aisles with speed. Finished with her shopping spree, she eyed her cart, thinking she probably had too much stuff, but didn't care. She was starving, and she was pretty sure her mom was, too. The food would not be wasted.

Back in her car, she fished through the grocery sacks. She pulled out a sports drink that promised a high percentage of electrolytes and a bag of Flamin' Hot Cheetos. With one hand on the wheel and the other on her favorite snack, she moved the bag to her mouth and ripped open the top with her teeth. A cluster of Cheetos poured into her mouth.

"Oh my God, yes," she moaned with each crunchy bite. Setting the bag down, she chugged her drink.

Feeling a ton better with food and drink in her stomach, she decided to take a quick, self-guided tour of the town. Since her mom hadn't called or texted yet, she figured she had some time to spare. She loved new places, and the mountain town was too cute to not explore. Passing rows and rows of the most adorable homes, she eventually found herself on a two-lane road. She admired the majestic mountains, the snow-blanketed terrain, and the enormous trees that hung on to clumps of white.

Driving around and digging into a second bag of Cheetos, Infiniti was totally caught up in the sights when she noticed a shadowy movement from the corner of her eye. Her stomach dropped, her hands shook, and her Cheetos bag fell from her hands. She wondered if a ghost had followed her from the inn.

She lifted her foot off the accelerator and coasted for a bit. She held her breath. She eyed the space to the right. She looked at the backseat through her rearview mirror. Not seeing anything, she let the air trickle out of her mouth. A nervous laugh escaped her lips.

"Stupid altitude. Now I'm hallucinating."

She started to speed up again when a hard shudder passed through her body. Every light inside the car started flickering. Blaring static took over the music. She slammed on the brakes, screeched to a stop, and hopped out of the car.

"What the hell!"

Her heart slammed against her chest. Her body shivered, and not just from the winter cold. She peered into the car through the open door.

"If there's a ghost in there, go away!" She thought of some of her favorite horror movies, trying to recall the correct words to use against an evil spirit. She made a cross sign with her fingers. "The power of Christ compels you!"

She dropped her hands, thinking she probably sounded crazy because she knew she did. She looked up and down the road, hoping someone would drive by and help her, but the roads were empty. But then she wondered what she'd even say to someone passing by. "Uh, excuse me, there may be a ghost in my car. Can you help?" Yeah, that would go over well. She mustered up her courage and moved closer to the rental, ready to take on her ghost by herself.

"I'm getting in the car now and driving back to the inn," she declared. "And you'd better leave me alone!" She added for good measure, "You are not welcome here!"

Easing herself back onto her seat, her hands shaking like crazy, she turned the car around so she could haul ass back the way she had come. Suddenly, she became aware that her mom hadn't called her. In fact, her phone hadn't made a sound in a long while. How much time had passed anyway?

She picked up her phone from the cup holder and brought it to her face. No service.

"Uh oh," she muttered, wondering how long her phone had been like that, knowing full well that her mom was probably going out of her mind. "She's gonna be so pissed."

She accelerated to a high speed while trying to call her mom over and over with frantic fingers, hoping she'd hit a pocket of cell service. She lifted her phone up in the air while at the same time pressing the redial button, but her phone tumbled from her grasp and onto the seat next to her. She let out an exasperated grunt. She stretched her fingers for it, but the phone was out of reach. She scooted over and made a lunging grab. Her fingertips barely made contact with the device. She scooted the phone closer with a flick and scooped it up.

"Yes!" she proclaimed.

With her phone in hand, she brought her eyes back to the road and saw that she had veered into the wrong lane.

"Shit!"

She jerked her wheel to get her car back over, sending the car into a fishtail. The sedan spun out of control. She took her foot off the pedal, her hands off the wheel, and started screaming.

Flashes of snow and trees whirred before her. Her mind raced with crazy thoughts of how she had survived a near plane crash only to die here on this stupid mountain. Alone. Never having been freakin' kissed. Also, her mom would never forgive her!

Her body lifted off the seat. Her seatbelt engaged, holding her down with a tug. A lone red Cheeto sailed across her line of sight. Her hair flew about her face. And that's when she realized the entire freaking car had plunged off the side of the road.

She sucked in her breath. She closed her eyes. She squeaked out an "eep" as a roar sounded in her ears.

CHAPTER 3

*F*ocusing on his energy, Fleet let loose a stream of gray mist from his hands. The warm haze seeped over every inch of him, turning translucent and covering his body like a second skin. The mist rendered him invisible and would stay there until he willed it away.

Staying close, he followed Infiniti and her mom. From the backseat of their car to an empty seat at the rear of the plane, he studied the seventeen-year-old like a hawk, trying to figure out what was so important about her. And when the plane took a nosedive and the pilot managed to right the aircraft, he wondered what role death played in her life. Even as he waited all night outside her hotel room, he couldn't fathom her significance and how her life had intertwined with Dominique's.

Infiniti stepped out of her room early in the morning. Fleet watched her press her back against her door, as if trying not to bump into anyone. But no one was there. She stood in the middle of the hall and called out. She waved her hand before her, as if whisking away a ghost. Fleet narrowed his eyes. Had she caught a glimpse of his energy source? He moved in. He snapped his fingers in front of her face, testing if she could detect him, but she didn't.

He followed her to the lobby for coffee, then into her car to get groceries. He crossed his arms in the backseat and waited for something to happen. He could sense an event was near, but didn't know what kind it would be.

"*Save her,*" the spirit girl whispered in Fleet's head.

Fleet sat forward. *Save her? From what?* He scanned the road ahead of them and behind them. He eyed the trees, the snow, and the mountaintops. Nothing. Yet alarm grew inside of him. He needed Infiniti to get back to the inn. She'd be safer there than on the road. He focused on the electrical system of the car, willing it to short circuit. With lights flashing and static blaring, Infiniti screamed. She slammed on her brakes.

Turn around, he thought. *Go back to your mom. Right the hell now.*

Infiniti hopped out of the car, staring at it as if it had come alive. With his help, it kind of had. And as much as he didn't want to scare the small-framed teen, he needed her to reverse course.

She crept closer to the car. She warned whatever ghost she thought was inside to go away. She slowly got back in the driver's seat. She turned around and started back for the inn, just like he wanted. She reached for her phone, looked at it, and started calling her mother over and over and over until she accidentally dropped the phone.

Dammit, Tiny, come on, Fleet thought, as if he could will Infiniti to get her shit together.

Beyond frustrated with the girl, Fleet sat back. He leaned his head against the seat. Staring at the roof of the car, he was thinking of bailing on her and going back to Houston when the car spun out and plummeted off the highway.

"Son of a bitch!"

The car barreled through branches. Metal creaked and crunched. Glass shattered. He zipped into the seat next to Infiniti. He slammed his hands on the dashboard. He poured every ounce of energy into the car, slowing the plunge as best as he could.

Gritting his teeth, sweat pouring down his forehead, he thought they were almost to the ground when a pop and swish sounded. The strap of Infiniti's seat belt whipped away. Her small frame smashed through the windshield. Fleet catapulted after her. Arm outstretched, he made contact with the back of her wool coat. Clutching the fabric, he pulled her to him. He wrapped his arms around her limp body. With her cradled close in his arms, they slammed against a surface of snow-coated rocks and skidded to a rest.

He clung to her as he caught his breath. He gently eased her on her back. What he saw shocked him to his core. Blood caked her face. A tree branch lodged in her chest, right under her collarbone. Shards of glass were embedded in her neck.

"No, no, no," he whispered.

He placed his fingers under her ear to see if she was alive. Pressing harder, he detected a faint thumping. The spirit girl had said to save Infiniti, that she was important, and right now she was dying. He flung off his leather jacket and got to work.

"Come on, Tiny. Stay with me."

He untangled her legs and arms so that she lay straight. He rubbed his hands together and held them over her face. A stream of sparkling mist oozed from his fingers, coating her face like a liquid mask. Leaving the substance to work on her injuries, he opened her coat all the way and tore her sweater more than it already was, so he could work on her unobstructed. He hovered his hands over her neck and chest and closed his eyes, surveying the damage. He detected broken ribs, bruised lungs, and severe internal bleeding. Although the tree branch sticking into her chest missed any major organs, death appeared imminent.

"Not if I can help it," he seethed.

He released another burst of energy to coat her upper body, taking the time to pour everything he had into healing her. Wiping his brow, he sat back and eyed the unconscious teen.

"Come on, Tiny. Fight."

Fleet eyed her mangled body while an overwhelming sense of guilt flooded him. He had let this happen, and he was pissed at himself. Suddenly, at that moment, nothing else mattered but saving Infiniti.

"She's mine, you know."

A tall guy with short dark hair appeared on the other side of Infiniti. He was leaning against a tree with crossed arms. "The doll's gonna die no matter what you do, Transhuman."

"Not today, reaper."

"The name is Shade. Shade StormIron. You may have heard of me."

Yeah, he'd heard of the reaper, but didn't want to give him the satisfaction. He ignored his unwanted guest and kept watch over Infiniti.

The reaper let the silence stretch out for a bit. "And you are Fleet, Tavion's right hand. Must suck working for a monster like that. The leader of the Tainted. How can you stand it? Or maybe you love it?"

Fleet's jaw clenched at the thought of Tavion. He couldn't stand it one damn bit, but had resolved to play whatever part was necessary in the war between the Tainted and the Pure.

"Get the hell out of here."

"Hell?" The reaper laughed. "Yeah, I know a thing or two about that place." He moved closer to Infiniti. He watched her for a few seconds before sauntering back over to Fleet. "Seems your efforts have patched her up for the time being. But rest assured, cupcake, her soul is calling for me. This doll's number is due." He licked his lips. "And I'm rather partial to petite brunettes."

Fleet started for the reaper, but he disappeared, leaving Fleet alone with the healing Infiniti. Spent from the exertion, he watched his efforts at work. The tree branch dissolved. The shards of glass disappeared. The blood on her face dissipated. The deep gashes over her forehead, face, and neck started closing. Fleet moved closer to check her pulse when Abigail appeared.

"You did it," Abigail said with a smile.

Fleet picked up his jacket and slipped it on. "Not without a whole hell of a lot of effort. And with that behind me, I'll be heading back to Houston now."

"It's not over," Abigail said.

Footsteps and snapping twigs sounded in the distance. Abigail looked over her shoulder, then back at Fleet. "She'll be transported to a medical center, but she'll be in the wrong time." She reached for Fleet's arm, but her small hand passed right through him. Her Pure energy tingled through his jacket. "She needs to go to 2018. You need to help her get there for something she needs, and then bring her back here to 2012."

Fleet tilted his head. He gazed into her face. "You're a Pure?"

Before he could ask her anything else, the spirit girl disappeared. Two guys burst onto the scene. One had tan skin with short cropped hair. The other had fair skin and blond hair. They couldn't have been much older than thirteen or fourteen. They hurried over to Infiniti and crouched down beside her. Still cloaked by his energy field, Fleet watched to see what they'd do, ready to jump in if needed.

"Oh my God," the guy with blond hair said. "Is she d-d-dead?"

The kid with dark features edged up closer to Infiniti. He put his hand under her nose. "She's alive, but barely." He eyed the wreckage. "It's a miracle."

From his vantage point, Fleet could see Infiniti's wounds were still healing. But with her tattered clothes and the blood that had oozed all over the snow, it made sense for the guys to think she was a lot worse than she was.

"Listen, Joe," the darker kid said. "You need to stay with her while I get help, okay?"

Joe's eyes grew big. "What? Why me, Kase? Why not you?"

"Because I'm faster, that's why."

"B-b-but, Kase, what if she wakes up? What do I do?"

"Keep her calm. She probably won't come to anyway, but I gotta get our dads and Nicholas." Kase put his hands on Joe's shoulders. "I'll hurry, I promise. Okay?"

"Yeah, okay."

"If only I could shift, this would be a lot easier," Kase said, before dashing off through the trees. "Be back soon," he hollered.

Shift? Fleet had no idea what the kid was talking about, but wondered if by chance he was referring to a paranormal shift, one of an animalistic nature.

Fleet scanned the area. Instead of Breckenridge as planned, he and Infiniti and her mom were in the Montrose/Telluride area. After crashing her car, two guys came up from who knew where and one of them talked about shifting like it was no big deal. Suddenly, Fleet knew exactly where they were. He ran his hands through his hair.

"Fucking Havenwood Falls," he muttered to himself.

They were on the outskirts of town, yet close enough for trouble. Transhumans, especially Tavion and the Tainted, were not welcome. The people of the area wanted no part of their civil war. So Transhumans kept their distance. Being here was not good. He knew he'd have to work overtime on his invisibility shield to prevent the supernaturals living in the town from detecting him. He hoped he and Infiniti could get in and out of the area without any problems, because without a doubt the help that would be coming would be from Havenwood Falls. And Havenwood Falls wanted nothing to do with him.

CHAPTER 4

*J*oe was freaked about being left with a bloodied car crash victim, so he decided to keep busy. If he could keep busy, he wouldn't think about her dying. As a supe, and a descendant of a wolf shifter family, he'd seen a lot of stuff, but nothing like this. But what to do?

He spotted the nearby wreckage and wondered if the girl's stuff was in there. Since his dad was a police officer, Joe figured he should look for evidence. He hoped his dad wouldn't be mad that he and Kase were roaming about outside the Havenwood Falls borders, but he knew he would be.

Walking around carefully, he found grocery items. A package of bagels, cream cheese, bananas, a box of chocolate chip cookies, bottles of water, sport drinks, and several bags of Flamin' Hot Cheetos. Trudging through the snow, hoping to find the girl's purse or phone, he came across the brown sack from the store she must've gone to. He picked it up and inspected it, finding it still intact and without any rips. He thought it strange the paper had come out of the rubble in perfect condition.

Sticking with his distraction plan, he re-sacked the groceries. He put the heavy stuff on the bottom and the lighter stuff on the top. Finishing off with the Cheetos, he thought of his little brother, Boris. He loved Cheetos, too. Joe was glad Boris hadn't joined his and Kase's afternoon hike. Boris was only eight and still somewhat sheltered from the wolf shifter life. The wreckage and the blood probably would've traumatized him.

With everything he could find in the bag, Joe studied the girl from afar. He gulped, eyeing her still form, thinking she looked lifeless. Her dark clothing and hair stood out in sharp contrast against the snowy background. His heart raced with fear. He wondered if she was dead and thought he should probably check. He had never seen a dead body before and didn't want to, but had to get close. He came from a family of protectors and needed to step into the role.

"Please be okay," he whispered.

Puffs of vapor came out of his mouth as he moved next to her. He had noticed her sweater was torn open the second he and Kase burst onto the scene, but had quickly looked away, because he didn't want to be disrespectful. Plus, her body was covered in blood. Now close to her, he struggled to keep his eyes away from her chest as he held his hand under her nose. Without meaning to, he found himself staring at her black lace bra.

"What are you doing?" he asked himself in horror, his face flushing and his heart thrumming wildly. But then he noticed something. He could actually *see* her bra. He had thought earlier there was too much blood to really see anything. But now, the blood didn't look as red or thick. In fact, it was almost all gone. Or were his eyes playing tricks on him out of stress? He didn't know, but needed to find out.

He leaned in. He examined her chest. He could definitely see her bra and her white skin. He tore his eyes away as a fresh wave of heat gathered in his face.

"Don't be a perv," he said to himself. At almost thirteen, he knew all about that puberty stuff. Sometimes it was a struggle for him to keep his eyes where they needed to be whenever a pretty girl was around. But this was different. He needed to make sure the girl was still alive.

He drew in a series of deep breaths. "Be cool and help," he said to himself.

He brought his attention back to the girl and waited for movement. Her chest rose ever so slightly, then fell. "Thank God," he sighed with relief.

He studied her face. Even though crisscrossing cuts laced her cheeks and forehead, he thought she was beautiful. Petite, with delicate features and long dark hair, she was probably one of the most gorgeous girls he'd ever seen. He wondered where she was from and how the heck she had crashed her car off the side of the mountain. He also couldn't believe her injuries didn't look as bad as when he and Kase first saw her. Or maybe most of her injuries were internal. Or maybe she was a supe. No matter what she was or how she got there or what may or may not have been happening to her wounds, his worry over her condition elevated with each thought.

"Please don't die, okay?" he said with a nervous laugh.

He reached for her coat with trembling hands, wanting to cover her up, when she stirred. A moan came out of her. Her eyes fluttered open. A series of groans escaped her lips as she tried to sit up. He put his hands on her shoulders in an effort to steady her.

"It's okay. You're okay. Try not to move."

Easing back down, she looked about in a daze before she noticed him. She blinked, forcing herself to bring his face into focus.

"Who are you?" she asked.

While he was locked in a stare with her, a feeling struck Joe in the pit of his stomach. Strange and unfamiliar, it grew inside of him. He tried to make sense of the sensation while at the same time trying to form words to answer her.

"Where am I?" the girl asked. She tried to move, and a yelp escaped her lips.

Joe steadied her again. "My name is Joe. You were in an accident. My friend and I found you. He went to get help and should be back soon."

He watched the girl look around, dazed and out of it.

"You really shouldn't move," he warned, concern for her safety taking over his thoughts. He took her hand and held it. It was delicate, small, and cold. Since he hadn't had his first shift yet, he couldn't warm her skin with his own. He hated that he still hadn't made the change, but knew it would come soon. At almost thirteen, he looked more like fifteen or sixteen. If only he could help her somehow.

He thought of pulling off his sweatshirt and draping it over her for extra warmth. He'd started to release her hand when she gripped him with surprising strength. She held him in place.

"Don't leave me," she pleaded.

"I'm not," he blurted, wanting to comfort her, his protective instincts kicking into high gear. "I was gonna take off my sweatshirt and put it over you. It'll help keep you warm. Is that okay?"

"O-k-k-kay," she managed to choke out.

He carefully moved her hand to the ground, as if it were made of glass. He tugged off his sweatshirt in one fluid motion. He spread it out over her chest and arms.

"There," he said. "Is that better?"

Her eyes had welled with tears. She couldn't speak, so settled on a nod.

He scooted closer. "I'm right here and I'm not—" His sentence cut short as his voice pitched low and then high again. *Damn puberty*. He cleared his throat. "I'm not leaving you."

He thought about the time he broke his arm when he was little. He was climbing a tree and lost his footing on a high branch. He had hurtled to the ground and snapped his arm in two. Kase was there to calm him until his dad arrived and took him to the medical center. Kase told him funny stories to occupy his mind throughout the ordeal. He thought of doing the same with the girl, but didn't know what to say.

"So, uh, what's your name?" She didn't respond, her eyes looking freaked out and panicky. "Where are you from?"

Her eyes darted around the area, taking in the mangled car and downed trees. Tears spilled down her cheeks. It was as if she realized for the first time what had happened to her.

"I crashed." And then she whispered, "Cheetos."

"Cheetos?" As crazy as it seemed, he wondered if she wanted some. "Are you hungry?" He eyed the grocery bag not too far away. "Do you want me to—?"

She gripped his hand. She pulled him close. He stared into her big brown eyes, wanting nothing more than to wipe away her tears and tell her everything would be okay. And then he thought of her bra, and her skin. He pushed the image of her exposed chest from his mind, trying to focus on helping her.

She brought him in with a desperate and scared look on her face. "I'm dying."

Blood had oozed into the snow, forging a path through the white terrain like a liquid fire. With so much blood on her clothing and around her, he thought she might be right, but didn't want to say so.

"No, you're fine."

"There's so much I haven't done yet. And now it's too late." Fresh tears flooded her eyes. She looked away from him for a second before looking back at him. "Joe, I'm going to tell you I love you, and I want you to say it back."

"What?" A wave of emotion he'd never felt before enveloped him. His skin tingled. His palms grew sweaty. His stomach dropped. The image of her skin and bra popped in his mind.

"Please," she said, propping herself up with a groan. "Do this for me before . . ." Her lip trembled. "Before I go."

"Uh, okay," he agreed, feeling immense sorrow for the beautiful girl and wanting to do whatever she asked.

"I love you," she breathed out.

Everything around him amplified. He saw her more clearly than ever, his senses sharpened like never before. Deep rich brown hair and eyes, perfectly fair skin that reminded him of milk. Even the hue of her cuts looked fluorescent and magical.

"I, uh, love you, too."

His muscles tensed. His jaw clenched. Every internal organ started throbbing. He dropped the girl's hand. He backed away.

"Oh, no," he uttered.

Starting with his feet and cascading all the way up to his neck, his bones broke, then healed, then broke again. His teeth grew to razor sharp points, slicing through his gums. His fingernails jutted out, forming thick nails that could kill with a swipe. With a yell that turned into a howl, fur replaced his skin until he was on all fours.

A wolf now, he felt beyond incredible. Strong, energized, and electric. He considered running away from the girl because he didn't want to scare her, but he also didn't want to leave her alone. He had to protect her until Kase and the others arrived.

"Stay!" she called out, helping him make up his mind. She was propped up on her forearms, taking him in with astonished eyes. She held out her arm. "It's okay."

In this truest form of himself, he found her beauty magnified. She even looked as if the cuts lacing her body had started to fade, though he thought it was impossible. Maybe his new wolf vision was playing tricks on him. He approached with caution. Head slightly down, tail swishing back and forth, he came to a halt beside her.

"J-J-Joe? You're a w-w-wolf?" she asked between chattering teeth, the cold taking over her reflexes. "A b-b-beautiful w-w-white w-w-wolf? Or am I d-d-dying and s-s-s-seeing things?"

He nudged his head under her hand, letting her know he was real. Sensing she was relaxed and at ease with him in this form, and feeling how freezing she was, he curled up next to her to share his body heat. She moved her hand slowly down his back, working her fingers through his thick fur. He detected her skin warming, her muscles relaxing. She nestled next to him. The vibration of her heartbeat settled into a strong and steady beat until she finally fell asleep.

After what seemed like forever, but couldn't have been more

than an hour, Joe detected movement in the brush. Ears in the radar position and snout in the air, he sensed his dad, Sheriff Ric Kasun, and EMT Nicholas Jordan approaching, their usual stealth mode overtaken by the dragging and banging of something in tow.

Faint at first, the din grew louder until two wolves—his dad and Sheriff Ric—and a mountain lion—Nicholas—emerged onto the scene. Nicholas pulled behind him a stretcher with a bag strapped to the middle. The three morphed to human form.

"Well," Nicholas said. "Look who made the change."

Joe huffed but stayed by the girl's side. He watched his dad, Sheriff Ric, and Nicholas put on the clothes that had been stuffed in the pack and tied to the stretcher. His dad walked over to him and the girl.

"Son, that must've been a pretty intense experience." He patted Joe firmly on the head. "You've done good work here, but now you need to step aside so Nicholas can do his job."

"Thanks, Ivan," Nicholas said.

Joe knew his dad was right. He got up and moved away, but stayed close and in wolf form. Sitting back on his haunches, he kept a keen eye on his charge.

Nicholas removed Joe's outstretched sweatshirt from the girl. He made a visual assessment with a furrowed brow.

"This doesn't make sense," he muttered. "Ric, Ivan, you too, Joe. Come look at this."

Everyone moved closer to see what Nicholas meant. Joe tried not to stare at the girl's plunging lace bra and instead focused on the spot where Nicholas pointed.

"There's clear evidence of a wound here," Nicholas explained. "Right below her clavicle. The skin is red and bruised. There's blood everywhere. But there's no puncture."

"An injury with no injury?" Sheriff Ric rubbed his chin. "That doesn't make sense."

"Maybe she's a supe," his dad suggested.

Nicholas kept a perplexed look on his face. "Maybe. It does

seem as if her wounds have been . . . healed? Or were never there?" He eyed Joe. "Did you see actual punctures?"

Joe huffed and nodded his assent. He had seen the cuts, and remembered her looking way worse when he first came upon the scene.

His dad and Sheriff Ric kicked into officer mode. They scanned the forest, peering about. Joe wondered what they were looking for.

"You see anything, Ivan?" Sheriff Ric asked his dad. "Anything to indicate anyone else could have been here?"

His dad swept the landscape with laser focus. "Nope, I don't." He went up to Joe. "Son, do you see anything?"

In wolf form, Joe would be able to see and smell things the others couldn't in human form. He perked up his ears. He pointed his nose in different directions and sniffed about. He moved in a circle studying every inch of the woods around them, but didn't detect anything. He huffed and shook his head no. He was as confused as they were about the girl's miraculous recovery.

Nicholas dragged the stretcher over. "Whatever is going on, we need to get her to the med center, and quick. The temps are dropping fast. We can figure out more when we get her there."

Joe watched his dad pick up the sack of groceries. He poked through the contents. "No phone or purse?" his dad asked him.

Joe shook his head.

"I'll bring the evidence," his dad said to Sheriff Ric.

"Nicholas and I have the stretcher," Sheriff Ric responded.

On three, Sheriff Ric and Nicholas carefully lifted the girl and set her on the portable stretcher. Nicholas went to his pack and pulled out a thick blanket. He covered the girl from her feet all the way up to her chin.

"Alright," Nicholas said. "Let's get her out of here."

Joe watched Sheriff Ric and Nicholas carry the girl away. His dad followed behind with the grocery sack. Joe filed in after them. They painstakingly carried her up the bank and to the nearest road, where Nicholas's ambulance was parked. Joe watched as the three slid the girl in the back.

"We'll see you at the clinic, son," his dad said, leaving him to follow them to Havenwood Falls on all fours. "Make sure you get out of these parts and back in the city limits quick. We'll talk later about why you and Kase were out here in the first place."

At that moment, breaking the rules and hiking outside of Havenwood Falls didn't matter to Joe. As the flashing lights faded away, Joe could only think about the girl and the emotions she had stirred in him. She said she loved him because she thought she was dying, and he had said it back. He wondered if it was the words that prompted his shift, or her skin, or her lace bra. Probably it was all of it. Either way, he vowed never to talk about it with his dad or Kase or anyone. They'd never understand.

CHAPTER 5

$\mathscr{F}$leet didn't want to witness Infiniti's emotional interaction with the kid, didn't want to hear her pour her heart out because she thought she was dying, so he kept his distance. And when the pack of supernaturals, two wolf shifters and one mountain lion shifter, arrived and morphed into human form, he moved even farther away.

Still cloaked and crouching down near a cluster of snow-laden bushes, he kept a keen eye on the group. After a quick inspection, and talk over Infiniti's missing wounds, they strapped her to the stretcher, wrapped her in a blanket, and loaded her into an ambulance. Only the kid remained, still in wolf form, but he soon raced off after them.

Finally alone, Fleet stepped out onto the road. He examined the space all around him. He looked up at the gray sky.

"Now would be a really good time for you to show yourself."

He waited for the spirit girl to appear, but she didn't. Her words repeated in his head.

She needs to go to 2018.

He thought of what Tavion had said back at the penthouse.

She's important.

He faced the direction the ambulance had driven and started

formulating a plan. Lock on to Infiniti's signature, go to wherever the ambulance was taking her, whisk her to 2018, and hope the spirit girl would appear and tell them what to do. He just hoped he could do whatever needed to be done before any supes in the town could figure out what was happening. The last thing he needed was to start something deadly with the locals.

Moving from the road to a nearby cluster of trees, he waited a bit to make sure Infiniti would have plenty of time to arrive at her destination. With her wounds more than likely gone by her arrival, she'd be placed in a room and kept there until she would awake. He needed to time his arrival perfectly, or everything would be for naught.

Eyeing the setting sun, he thought of Infiniti. He feared for her safety, but he also felt something else—sorrow. She didn't deserve to get caught up in his mess. At seventeen, she had so much to live for, yet here she was, fighting for her survival, and she didn't even know it. He was tired as hell at all the death in his life but resolved right then and there to get Infiniti out of Havenwood Falls alive.

Stars started sprinkling the wintry sky. He thought enough time had passed for Infiniti to be in an optimal location. He doubled his cloaking efforts to avoid detection in the town. He rubbed his hands together, blew into them, and placed them on the snowy ground. He pictured Infiniti—long dark hair, big brown eyes, petite features, and important.

"Go to her," he whispered.

Gray vapor poured out of his hands. The warm tingling mist pooled around his feet, swirling beneath him like a whirlpool. He slipped into weightlessness, then found himself on solid ground.

Crouched down, he surveyed his new surroundings. He appeared to be in a small dark hospital room. He rose to his feet and spotted Infiniti. She was lying on a twin-sized bed tucked under a white sheet, fast asleep. Her face and hair had been cleaned. He could see that she still wore her red sweater, but it wasn't ripped or bloodied anymore. He thought someone in the clinic must've magically repaired her clothes. A light nasal snore filled the air. He spotted a bag on a chair in the corner of the room and recognized the fur from her boots peeking over the edge. He grabbed the bag and placed it on her legs. He put his hand on her shoulder.

"Okay," he muttered. "Let's see what's in store for us in 2018, Tiny."

Focusing on the exact same place, but a different year, his energy stream oozed out like a fog. It swirled around them like a slow-churning funnel cloud. The phenomenon picked up speed, and Fleet felt the floor drop from below him. A few seconds passed before he met solid surface under his feet.

He looked around and saw that he was in the same place with Infiniti, but he could sense they were in a different time. The walls were the same plain white; the bed and side table identical. Only the chair in the corner had changed from the one that had been there six years earlier. Fleet studied Infiniti's sleeping form. He placed the bag back on the chair. He stepped back. He waited for her to wake up, wondering what would happen next.

CHAPTER 6

*I*nfiniti heard a soft whisper. It floated around her head like a breeze. Cool and inviting, it comforted her while she slept, until, eventually, it didn't want her sleeping anymore.

"Wake up," the voice urged. "Now!"

She swatted at the source, irritated at being woken up, yet peeled her eyes open anyway. "Okay, okay, sheesh. I'm getting up."

Rubbing her head, she was wondering how late she had overslept and what test she was going to miss when she noticed her walls weren't purple anymore. Even her black comforter had been replaced with a flimsy white sheet. And that's when reality gripped her. She wasn't home. She hadn't overslept. She wasn't going to be late to school. She was in Colorado, she had been driving, and . . .

She sat up with a jolt. The sudden motion rocked her head. Stars littered her vision. She moaned, easing herself back down. When the twinkling faded, she sat back up with caution.

"Holy shit," she whispered to herself.

The overpowering smell of hand sanitizer and bleach invaded her nostrils. She scanned the small room. She was on a twin-sized bed with raised bed rails. To the right was a closed door, to the left was a small window, and in the corner was a chair with a plastic bag. No one was around, so who was telling her to wake up? Or was the voice part of some weird dream?

"Where am I?"

A tray next to her held an oversized plastic cup with a lid and a straw. Seeing the cup prompted her to realize how dry her mouth was. She took the cup and sipped, yet nothing came out of the straw. She lifted the cup and shook it, but it was empty.

"Really?" she mumbled.

She set the cup down with shaky hands and swallowed but didn't have enough spit to coat her throat. Feeling drained and empty, she sat there for a second while her brain processed her situation. Then realization hit her like a brick. Her car had swerved, she lost control, but what had happened after that?

She rubbed her head, trying to piece together the events from the swerve to now. She thought she must've crashed, but couldn't remember any of the details. Her body ached all over, and her muscles felt sore and stiff. She wondered how bad her injuries were. She brought her fingers to her face, moving them around inch by inch, but her skin felt fine. She patted her arms and then her chest and thighs. There was no indication of breaks or anything like that, even though she felt as if she'd been run over by a train.

"Mom," she whispered to herself. Her heart lurched at the thought of her mom at the inn, worried and scared. Her eyes met the bag on the chair. Her stuff had to be in there, including her phone.

She pushed down on the bed rail, forcing it to collapse, and then peeled off the white bed sheet. She examined her clothes. She was wearing the same outfit she had put on back at the inn. Despite a few wrinkles here and there, her clothes looked fine. She swung her legs over the side of the bed and stood. She shuffled over to the bag. Peering in, she saw her boots and nothing else. No wallet. No phone. She patted the back pocket of her jeans, hoping to find it there, but didn't. There wasn't even a phone in the room.

"Great."

Thinking she needed to get out of there, she pulled on her boots. She stepped out into the hallway, discovering she was in what looked like a house converted to a clinic. An empty clinic. A little spooky, even. The lights were dimmed, and not a sound could be heard.

"Hello?" She waited for a response. "Anyone here?"

Making her way down the hall and out the door, she stepped outside. A cold blast hit her face. Snow flurries floated around her. She crossed her arms and held them snug to her body, wondering what had happened to her new coat. She loved that coat.

Turning back around, she faced the building and saw that she had stepped out of a white house with blue trim. A sign over the door read *Medical Center*. As she surveyed her situation, a yummy smell of greasy goodness drifted her way. Her stomach growled. Her eyes followed the scent. Down the street she spotted a shopping center with a fast food restaurant in front of it. Outside a vintage neon sign blinked *Burger Bar*.

"Oh, thank God."

She hurried for the burger place, hoping she'd find someone to take pity on the lost girl from Houston who was starving and needed to use a phone.

The cute restaurant with a black-and-white-checkered floor bustled with activity. Lively Christmas music played from an antique-looking jukebox. Christmas decorations adorned each wall. She made her way to the back so she could scope things out. Eyeing the crowd, she wondered whom she should approach for help. Her attention landed on the TV in the back of the room. The news was on. The reporter was talking to the obnoxious rich guy with the hideous comb-over from *The Apprentice*. The guy that fired everyone.

"Huh," she muttered to herself. "Wonder what that wacko is up to and why he's in the White House."

She was trying to make out the interview conversation when someone tapped her shoulder. She turned around and saw a guy her age. Tall and slender, he had short-cropped blond hair and piercing hazel eyes. He sported a blue letterman's jacket with white and silver accents. He tilted his head to the side and stared at her with a slightly parted mouth.

"You're the girl."

"I'm the girl?" She had no idea who he was or what he was talking about, not that she minded too much. He was gorgeous.

His eyes scanned her face, roamed her body, landed on her boobs, and then returned to her face. Astonishment mixed with joy took over his expression.

"You're okay. And you're . . . here."

"Yes, I'm here, and I seem to be fine."

She relaxed her stance, grateful to have found a friendly person who must've seen her being brought into the medical center. A hot person at that. He was sure to have a phone she could use, and money to buy her some food.

"Do you happen to have a—"

"How did you get here?" He got up close, as if her answer was some sort of secret. "Where have you been?"

She gave him a curious look. She pointed in the direction of the medical center. "Well, um, I've been at that medical center house down the street, and I walked over here."

Eyeing the guy, she thought maybe there was something wrong with him, especially since she had a history of attracting weirdos. She started backing away.

"Excuse me," she said, clearing her throat. "But I need to go."

Before she could turn away, a memory blasted through her. It shook her through to her core, rooting her in place. She was lying on the snowy ground, bleeding. A guy was with her. He looked like the guy before her. Same blond hair, same hazel eyes, but younger. She thought she was dying. She had asked him to say he loved her. And then he had transformed into a white wolf.

Her mouth dropped. A wave of goose bumps dashed across her skin. She backed away a little. He was the same guy, but older.

"You're . . . the . . . the . . . the wolf." Tears sprang to her eyes. "I thought I was dying. You stayed with me, and I asked you to—"

"Shh," he said. His warm hand took her cold one, and he pulled her into the nearest empty booth.

Heat filled her cheeks as she remembered every second of her encounter with him. She was horrified, embarrassed, and freaked out all at the same time. How was she okay? How did he look older? Was he really a wolf? And why the hell had she asked him to say he loved her?

"I can't believe it's you," he whispered.

A guy with tan skin and dark hair came up to them. "Dude, Joe, there you are. I was looking for—" The guy took a good look at Infiniti. He dropped his phone, and it clanked on the metal table. "Holy shit, the girl."

The guy across from her said again, "Yeah, the girl."

Coming completely unglued, she said, "Yeah, I'm the freakin' girl!"

This time both guys shushed her, looking around to make sure no one had heard them.

"Somebody'd better tell me what the hell is going on before I start screaming!"

The blond guy held up his hands, as if to calm her down. "I will, I promise." He eyed his friend. "Give us a sec, okay?"

"Yeah, sure," the dark-haired guy said, getting his phone and leaving with a shocked look on his face.

He returned to a group by the counter, but Infiniti didn't pay them any attention. She couldn't. Her mind reeled at the pieces of her ordeal filtering back into her memory. Throbbing pain. Splattered blood. Shards of glass. The guy looking younger and transforming into a wolf. What the hell was happening?

"Who are you?" the guy whispered.

"I'm Infiniti. I'm from Houston. Who are you?"

"I'm Joe, and I'm from here. Havenwood Falls."

"Havenwood Falls?"

"Yeah." He leaned over the table. "The town close to where you crashed. You were transported to the medical center." He moved in even closer. "You disappeared."

She stared at him in disbelief. She pressed her back against the booth. It took her a minute to find her voice. "I what?"

"You vanished. We searched for you for days. Months, even. With no leads, we had to give up."

Her hands folded and unfolded on her lap. Her mind raced. "I crashed. I woke up, and I walked over here."

"You woke up? As in, just now?"

"Yes."

"*Now* now?"

"Yes. Like ten minutes ago now."

His brows stitched together. He rubbed his chin. "So what happened to the last six years?"

Six years?

She examined his face. He most definitely looked six years older, but her car crash had happened that day. So that would be impossible. But then she thought of all the sci-fi movies she'd seen, and all her supernatural paraphernalia at home—her Ouija board, the spiritual cards her neighbor Jan had given her. She was a believer in all things unexplained, but had something otherworldly really happened to her? As in, for real?

Her hands trembled. She shivered. "It's 2018?"

"Yeah, it's 2018."

Her gut clenched. Every sound in the restaurant faded as horror and shock crowded her senses. Panic soared through her veins. "Give me your phone."

"What?"

"Your phone. Please. Give it to me."

He handed her the sleekest phone she'd ever seen. She pressed the home button, desperate to call her mom, but nothing happened. Staring at it, she had no idea how to get it to work. He motioned for her to give it back.

"I need to put my thumb on there."

"Your thumb?"

She held it out. He placed his thumb on it and the device sprang to life.

"Holy shit, I am in the future. I really am."

She stared at all the bright apps, not really sure how to make a call, or even if she *should* make a call. She had wanted to call her mom, but her mom was in the past now, and she was in the future, and there was the whole time-space-continuum thing to consider. She had no idea what to do. Her throat clogged with tears.

Joe slid out of his side of the booth and scooted in next to her. He put his arm around her and held her close. "Hey, it's okay. I'm here. I'm not gonna leave you."

She pulled away and stared at him. Every moment on the mountainside came back to her in a whoosh—the bitter cold on her face, the pain in her body, the blood trickling from her wounds. All of it.

"You said those words to me on the mountainside, when I thought I was dying."

She didn't want to lose it in front of a stranger, but a lone tear slipped out onto her cheek. He wiped it away. "I know. I meant it then, and I mean it now. I will help you, I promise."

His reassuring words started to comfort her but fell short. She was stuck in a time and place she didn't belong. And even though she had a gorgeous guy by her side, all she wanted to do was go home.

CHAPTER 7

*J*oe couldn't believe his eyes. The girl from the crash who had said she loved him was standing in Burger Bar. The last time he'd seen her was six years ago. He remembered every second of their encounter because it had sparked his first shift. He had even felt called to her, but was so young at the time, he didn't realize it. Her long dark hair, her bloodstained clothes, her fair skin, her lace bra, every word she had spoken—it had repeated in his mind at least a million times over the years. And now, miraculously, she stood in the back of his favorite burger place, chewing her bottom lip and staring at the TV. An overwhelming sense of needing to protect her had kicked in back then, and stirred again inside of him.

How is she here?

He and a handful of friends had finished their last final and were celebrating with burgers and shakes when suddenly nothing mattered but the girl. He left his friends at the counter and went to her. With each approaching step, he marveled at the fact that she looked exactly the same, minus the injuries. She even wore the same clothing, yet her wardrobe wasn't torn or stained anymore.

Fumbling for what to say, and resisting the overwhelming urge to wrap her up in a bear hug, he settled on an awkward intro.

"You're the girl."

Talking to her, he found out her name was Infiniti and that she was from Houston. She remembered the crash and that he had shifted into a wolf. But what took her awhile to understand was that the crash and his transformation had happened in 2012.

Her hands trembled. She shivered as if she'd been standing outside in a blizzard.

"It's 2018?"

"Yeah," he said, wanting to help her but not knowing how. "It's 2018."

Sitting in a booth at the back of the restaurant, she asked to borrow his phone so she could call her mom. It was the strangest thing to see her stare at the device, completely unable to use it. A beautiful girl, out of time, and all alone. Doing his best to comfort her, he sat next to her and hugged her, saying he wouldn't leave her, but what could he do? She didn't belong in Havenwood Falls, let alone 2018. And then he thought of the wards. Her presence was sure to trigger them. He was about to tell her they should get out of there when his phone beeped. It was a text from his dad.

Dad: Sheriff Kasun has reinstated the APB for the girl from the crash who went missing six years ago. If you see anything strange, let me know ASAP. And come home right after you eat. Something is not right in the town.

Crap, this wasn't good. Not at all. He didn't want to be rude to the girl, especially since she looked like she was seconds from breaking down, but he needed more info from his dad.

"My dad is texting," he said to her. "Gotta text back real quick."

Me: Huh? Not right with the town?

Dad: Lyra Beaumont and others in the Luna Coven have recognized an energy shift, same as the one they felt when the girl went missing in 2012. Probably nothing, but stay sharp, ok?

Joe's heart hammered against his chest as he read his dad's text a few times. The message, combined with his dad's recent overprotectiveness, made his gut tighten. He replied with a simple *OK*, then stashed his phone in his back pocket. Scanning the faces in the restaurant, he thought he should get the girl out of there before they were spotted. There were too many people around, and he wanted to protect her from whatever minions the Court of the Sun and the Moon would surely be sending her way. Even if it meant his ass, he wanted whatever time he could get with her. His dad would have to get over it.

"Let's go someplace where we can be alone and talk."

He started to get out of the booth, but she pulled him back down. "After we get some food and drink, if that's okay. I'm starving."

He was starving, too. "Good idea," he said, thinking her hunger meant she was calming down a bit.

He spotted Kase getting his order, and an idea came to him. "Hold on a sec," he said to Infiniti.

Joe approached the counter, grabbed a to-go bag, and started stuffing Kase's usual double order in the bag. Two burgers, two fries and a bottle of soda. Perfect for him and Infiniti.

"Dude," Kase whispered, so focused on the girl he didn't even mind his food being stolen. "What is going on? I just got a text from my dad."

"I know. I got a text from my dad, too. You didn't say anything, did you?"

"Nah, wanted to talk to you first." Kase peered over Joe's shoulder. "How is she here?"

"I don't know, but I'm gonna find out."

Kase pulled him close. "I see it in your eyes, dude." He lowered his voice even more. "Are you called to her?"

Deep affection for the girl had budded in him back when he was twelve and never left him. Back then, he didn't know what it was. He had also never mentioned it to anyone, and didn't plan on it now. He held up the bag of food. "I'll pay you back for this."

"That's fine, but Joe," Kase looked around the place, "we need to tell our dads that she's here, before the Court gets involved, and we're grounded for life."

"I know, and I will, but I want to talk to her first." He eyed his best friend for a few seconds, giving him the *I'm serious* look. "Okay?"

"Yeah, okay," Kase said with an exasperated grunt. "May as well warn her about the interrogation that's sure to come. If our dads know something is up, then Addie must be losing her shit right now. She's been on the warpath with everything going on, you know, with that Harper girl being missing and everything."

Joe clasped Kase on the shoulder. "Good idea. I'll give her a heads up."

Joe went back to Infiniti, still not believing she was right in front of him. "We're all set with food for two." Eyeing her outfit, he took off his jacket and handed it to her. "But you're gonna need this. It's really cold outside." As a wolf shifter, he didn't need protection from the elements like regular humans. She slipped it on, and it engulfed her petite frame. He smiled. "It's a tad too big on you."

The lighthearted moment erased the worry lines on her face. "It's perfect. Thanks, Joe. But why are we leaving? And where are we going? And just so you know, I'm trying really hard not to lose it," she said with a nervous laugh.

His heart swelled with tenderness and sympathy for the girl, and he knew right then and there he'd do anything for her. His mind scrambled to figure out where they could go when he spotted his high school through the window. It was late, so nobody would be there, except maybe the janitor. He thought he could find an unlocked door pretty easily.

"I know the perfect place. Come on."

With the bag of food and drink in one hand, and Infiniti's dainty hand in the other, they left Burger Bar.

"My school is right over there." He indicated with his chin the three-story red-brick building with an arched doorway. Luckily, a few lights were still on. They hurried to the front entrance, rushing to get out of the snowfall, and found the door unlocked.

Stepping inside, Infiniti looked around the dark hallway.

"Why does it feel like we're hiding?" she asked in a hushed voice.

He continued down the hallway. "I'll explain as soon as we get to the room." He stopped at a door at the end of the hall. He peered through the glass panels to see inside and saw that it was all clear. Once inside, he turned on a small lamp at the back. "This is the art room. We can hang here while we figure things out."

He sat at a long wooden table and watched Infiniti roam about for a few seconds, eyeing the hanging artwork.

"Are you an artist?" she asked.

"Me? Nah. I picked this room because of the tables. I'm into sports."

She sat across from him as he emptied the contents of their to-go order on long sheets of drawing paper. He kept watching her expressions, thinking she was probably in shock or something. Keeping quiet, waiting for her to process everything, he started eating. She did, too. He stopped himself from gulping his food down like he normally did, and chewed at a slow pace. He was searching for the right thing to say to her when she started the conversation.

"I . . . time traveled." She set her fry down. "And you . . . are a wolf."

"A wolf shifter," he explained. "There's a big difference."

"A wolf shifter," she repeated in a low voice. She moved her food around on the paper, as if trying to figure out if she still wanted to eat. "Is this for real? Is this really happening?" She stared off in the distance. "Maybe I'm in a coma." She pinched her arm.

"You're not in a coma, I promise." Images of her fair skin and black lace bra entered his brain. He forced himself to focus on her big brown eyes instead. "And yes, this is really happening."

"And the wolf thing?"

"Wolf shifter thing," he clarified. He thought of the prime

directive of Havenwood Falls to keep all things supernatural hidden. But since she was a time traveler, and had already seen him shift, he thought it best to be honest with her about the town.

He rubbed the back of his neck. "This whole town, Havenwood Falls, is filled with supernatural beings."

Her mouth fell open, closed, then fell open again. "Stuff like that isn't real," she finally said. "I mean, if it were real, people would know about it. Like, this place would've been all over the news."

"I can assure you, it's real. This town is a safe haven for us. And when people leave, they forget everything." A pang of sorrow at the idea of her leaving and forgetting him shut his brain off for a second. He paused for a few seconds before going on. "It's the way the town and the people living in it are protected. It's how we stay hidden." He waited for her to say something, but she didn't. He decided to continue so he could prepare her for whomever the Court of the Sun and Moon would be sending their way. "And when people come here without being registered, there's an investigation."

Her eyes took on a spark of recognition. "Someone is going to come investigate me?" She swallowed. "So I'm like in trouble or something?"

"No. I mean, yes, but it's not bad. That's why I brought you here, so I could tell you, and also, you know, so we could talk."

He wanted to tell her so much more, but didn't know how to begin or what to say. She had been a part of his life for six years. He had been called to her, and the idea of her being in any kind of jeopardy had him on red alert. Secretly he hoped she wouldn't be able to get back to her home. He wanted her to stay.

Feeling a pull toward her, he moved closer. "Infiniti, back at the crash when you said you loved me, I felt something for you." He waited for a bit before continuing. "I know I was young, and it may sound unbelievable, but—" He stopped short of revealing his attachment to her and instead said, "You're special."

Infiniti blushed. "I am?"

"Yes, you are."

She gazed at him for a while. "It doesn't make any sense at all, but I kind of feel something for you, too," she said. "It's like our experience on that mountain bonded us in a way."

"I know," he said.

He reached across the table and took her hand, wondering if his bond with her sparked some sort of return in affection. He hoped so. He stared into her sweet and innocent eyes. Without even knowing what he was doing, he leaned across the table, and she did, too. Their lips almost met when Joe's spine tingled with alarm. The air in the room changed. He jumped to his feet, ready to shift, when a guy materialized out of thin air. Tall, with dark jeans and a leather jacket, he held a ball of light in his hand. He aimed it straight at him.

"I'm not here to hurt you," the menacing stranger said to Joe before he could shift. "But I need Infiniti."

Infiniti was on her feet now, looking at the guy with shock. "Uh . . . I don't know who you are, but I'm not going anywhere with you."

Joe moved Infiniti behind him. "I suggest you get out of here," he growled, "before I—"

"Shift to wolf form? I've seen it. Six years ago at the wreckage when you came upon Infiniti."

"What?" Infiniti whispered. "You were there?"

Joe's mind picked apart the afternoon he had stumbled upon Infiniti. He had combed the area in wolf form. His eyes, ears, and nose hadn't detected anyone around. Even his dad, Nicholas, and Sheriff Ric hadn't sensed anyone.

"If you were there, I would've known."

The stranger looked impatient. He gritted his teeth. "I don't have time for this. Someone is coming, and I need to get Infiniti out of here. Now step aside or I'll have to make you." The stranger kept his energy ball at the ready, his eyes narrowed with determination. "You don't want me to make you."

Joe's phone beeped, interrupting the deadly face-off between himself and the stranger. Over and over it dinged with messages. It even rang. Joe knew the guy was right. Something was happening, and someone was trying to warn him.

Assessing the guy with his heightened senses, he quickly came to the conclusion that he meant them no harm. He relaxed his stance, but stayed close to Infiniti. He took her hand, lacing his fingers with hers.

"If you take her, you're taking me, too."

Boots pounded down the corridor. Joe detected the stride of Sheriff Ric and two females. Still gripping Infiniti's hand, he went up to the guy. Unafraid of him or his weapon, he growled, "Those are my people coming, and you'd better not hurt them."

CHAPTER 8

*E*ven though Fleet thought he could trust the wolf shifter, he wasn't so sure the people coming down the hallway would trust him. One look at him, and they'd know he was one of the Tainted, Tavion's second-in-command, because he had played the role for over a century. Supernaturals the world over knew him, feared him, and kept their distance. Yet here he was, in the hidden mecca of supernatural suburbia where supes lived with humans. He wondered why the spirit girl wanted him and Infiniti to come here.

The energy ball warmed his hand and sizzled with power. If seen as the aggressor, he'd be attacked and would have to respond. The last thing he wanted to do was kill innocents. Plus, he knew the lovestruck kid standing before him would pounce. He sensed the protectiveness he had for Infiniti.

Footsteps thudded closer. He could hear the swishing of clothing. He cursed under his breath, then let the power in his hand dissolve. He eyed the kid glued to Infiniti's side.

"Listen up, Joe. I'm not going to hurt them. Trust me on that. But we do things my way. Got it?"

Before Joe could formulate a response, the classroom door swung open. Fleet zipped in front of Infiniti and her newfound defender. He let loose a stream of energy at a man and two women. The gray mist shot out like a laser beam, freezing the trio in place.

Infiniti covered her mouth. "Holy shit," she mumbled through her fingers.

She and Joe approached the mannequin-like bodies. Joe waved his hand in front of the faces of the frozen.

"Are they okay?"

Fleet came up beside Joe. "They're fine. Who's in charge?"

Joe pointed at the dark-haired man. "That's Sheriff Kasun. He's kind of in charge."

"Kind of?"

"Well, it's complicated."

"Who's everyone else?"

Joe pointed at the older woman with shoulder-length brown hair dressed in gypsy attire. "That's Lyra Beaumont." He pointed at the younger woman next to her. Wearing dark-rimmed glasses and dressed like she could be in a rock band, she resembled the taller woman. "That's her daughter, Addie." Joe looked worried and guilty. "I guess they're looking for me." He eyed Infiniti. "And you."

"Me? They don't even know me or that I'm here."

Joe ran his fingers through his hair. "They had an idea. My dad is a police officer. He texted me while I was in Burger Bar. He wanted to know if I had seen you, the missing girl from the crash six years ago."

Infiniti shot him a look. "Why didn't you tell me?"

Before Joe could explain, Fleet cut in. "It doesn't matter. We're here, and this is happening. And I need to talk to the sheriff."

Joe pulled Infiniti, and together they backed up a little. "Okay, but he's not gonna be happy."

"Well neither am I," Fleet muttered.

Fleet approached Sheriff Kasun. He laid his fingers on the man's forehead. A spark connected at his skin, and Sheriff Kasun sprang to life. With a blink, he went for his gun, but Fleet beat him to it. He drew it from the holster with lightning speed.

"Sheriff Kasun, my name is Fleet, and I mean you no harm." Fleet showed him the gun, then slowly handed it back as a sign of trust. "But I will fight back if I'm attacked, and I don't want to do that."

The sheriff narrowed his piercing blue eyes at Fleet. He took the gun and put it back in its place. "I don't want you to do that, either." He scanned the still bodies of Lyra and Addie before examining Joe and Infiniti. "Joe, are you and your friend okay?"

"Yes. Her name's Infiniti, and we're fine," Joe answered.

Satisfied there was no immediate threat, the sheriff walked up to Fleet. He raised his chin. "You're in my town and you've got my people in a spell. You'd better start talking, and fast, or there will be hell to pay."

"Did someone say hell?" Shade StormIron appeared in the back of the room, wearing a cheeky smile.

Fleet hadn't seen the reaper since the crash, and he wasn't at all happy to see him now. He moved closer to Infiniti, unsure about the reaper's motives and why he had appeared, since Infiniti was clearly alive. Or was something about to happen to her? He rubbed his fingers together, ready to act if needed.

"Can someone please tell me what's going on?" Infiniti called out.

"Allow me," Shade said, eager to join the group. "Shade StormIron here. Reaper and comedian extraordinaire. Good looking, too." He winked. "Listen, doll. Time's ticking on that soul of yours. No matter what the year, 2012 or 2018, it's all the same to me. This Transhuman here is the bad guy in this scene. He's a member of the Tainted, after all. Fleet by name, Fleet by nature. Right, cupcake?" Shade sneered at Fleet, and Fleet glared in return.

The reaper moved closer to Infiniti. "You crashed, and he saved you, taking work from me, which I don't appreciate. You see, I'm on a tight schedule, doll, as are you." He slapped his hands together, causing them all to jump. "Anyway, here we have Princess and her mother, both witches. Well, one's half hellhound. These guys are wolf shifters. It's like the Count's birthday party in here. Want to know anything else?"

"You're a reaper? Here for me?" Infiniti gulped. Her face transformed from shocked to freaked out, and then to pissed off. She put her hand on her hip and stuck out her right foot. "Well, take a damn number, because I'm not dying anytime soon."

Smiling on the inside, proud of Infiniti and her spunk, Fleet added, "Tiny has a point. Get the fuck out."

The reaper chuckled. "Fine. But I'll be back, doll. Let Princess know I swung by. She'll be sad she missed me." His attention zeroed in on Infiniti. A deadly expression erased his playfulness. "You can't cheat death."

A blast of wind shot through the room as the reaper disappeared. Thick foreboding crowded the air as the reaper's words sunk in. Fleet knew damn well there was no escaping a death sentence.

Joe held Infiniti closer to him. "Don't listen to that asshole."

Sheriff Kasun shook his head. "Enough of all this. Now release my people so we can figure this whole damn thing out."

Fleet thought he could trust the sheriff, but needed reassurance first. "We are in agreement that I'm no threat?"

The sheriff rubbed the back of his neck. "We are. For now."

With a nod, Fleet flicked out a burst of energy, reviving Lyra and Addie.

"What the hell?" Addie said.

Sheriff Kasun quickly defused the situation. "It's okay. Everything is under control. Joe has found our missing person with this Transhuman named Fleet. He says he means us no harm."

Lyra stepped forward. "A Transhuman? In Havenwood Falls? So that's what Addie and I, and the rest of the coven, were feeling." Lyra looked from Addie to the sheriff. "Back in 2012, I wrote in my journal about the energy shift I had detected—a shift I thought was caused by the girl." She approached Fleet with a look of wonder on her face. "But it was caused by you—a member of the Tainted and a henchman of Tavion's. Your presence has caused quite a stir."

"I'd say calling it a stir would be an understatement," Addie added with crossed arms, summing him up. "I've heard of your abilities to travel through space and time. But why would you do that? Now? With this girl?"

"I'd like to know, too," Infiniti said, her head tilted to the side a little, as if taking it all in but unable to figure it out yet.

With the school closed for the holiday break and the heater turned down, cold air had started to fill the room. Fleet watched the supernaturals with keen interest, wondering why the spirit girl had wanted Infiniti to come to this place, and in this time. He also wondered when she'd appear again, because he had no intention of waiting too long.

"Explain," Addie commanded in a voice that vibrated with witchy strength. "Before we declare you an enemy of the town."

Fleet laughed. "I could kill all of you in a second, before you even knew what was happening, but that's not why I'm here."

Sheriff Kasun stepped forward. "Then why are you here?"

"Yeah," Infiniti interjected. "Why *are* we here?"

Fleet had no idea if he could explain, because he didn't completely understand Infiniti's purpose and why the spirit girl had sent them to Havenwood Falls. And where to start? Should he go into the conflict between the Tainted and the Pure? Explain how their war was linked to the survival of the human race? How Tavion sensed Infiniti had a role to play in Dominique's quest for survival? And that a spirit girl had told him to bring the teen to this place and in this time?

He didn't know the supes in the room, but he knew damn well that secret truths were never kept secret. And his dealings with Tavion were none of anyone's damn business. Instead of going into detail, he settled on offering the most basic of answers.

He pointed his chin at Infiniti. "I brought her here from 2012 because she's important for the survival of the human race. There's something here in this time she needs. I just don't know what yet."

"Whoa," Infiniti whispered as she moved closer to Joe. Lyra and Addie shot each other questioning looks. Even the sheriff had no response.

Addie broke the silence. She kept her stare on Fleet, but addressed her mother. "Mom, should we have Elsmed meet us here?"

The elder woman tapped her chin. "Let me check his aura real quick. If he's clear, we can move this conversation to my house."

"Okay," Addie said.

Lyra approached Fleet with caution. "May I?"

"Have at it," Fleet answered, confident he'd pass whatever scan the woman was about to conduct, because he meant the town no harm.

Lyra held her hands up, palms facing Fleet. She kept them like that for a few long seconds, then lowered her arms back to her sides. "His aura is clear enough for us to go to my house and have Elsmed meet us there."

"Elsmed?" Fleet asked.

"Yes, Elsmed," Lyra responded. "He'll be the one to verify your story."

Everything Fleet had said was true, so he didn't mind any verification procedure. Plus, if he wanted the supes to help him, he needed to cooperate.

"Fine."

"I'll let Elsmed know to meet us at my place," Lyra said.

Sheriff Kasun pulled out his phone. "I'll cancel the APB on the girl."

Even Addie started texting. "I'll notify the coven and the Court that we've got everything under control."

Fleet leaned back against the table as he watched everyone take to their tasks, except Infiniti. Standing with Joe, she kept her gaze down. Her brow knitted together in worry. And when Joe said he'd be right back and left her to say something to the sheriff, her expression switched to one of despair.

He sidled over to her. "It's gonna be okay, Tiny."

Her big brown eyes glistened with tears. "How do you know?"

He smiled. "Because I'm here, and I've got your back."

"So you're a bad guy, but you're really a good guy?"

Fleet paused, thinking of all the things he'd done for Tavion, but quickly pushed those terrifying memories aside. He had learned long ago to compartmentalize his feelings, and right now the girl needed him.

"Something like that. And I'm not gonna let anything happen to you. I got you here; I'll get you home."

"What about that reaper?"

Fleet knew reapers never lied when it came to souls they had to reap. So if Infiniti's number was up, then it was up. He just didn't know when or how. But he did know that she didn't need that laid on her.

"Pfft. Reapers don't know shit."

The worry lines on her face relaxed. She let out a breath she had been holding in.

"Thanks, Fleet."

Joe came back to Infiniti and took her hand. Fleet dropped back, letting everyone do their thing. He thought it funny how the sheriff thought he was calling the shots, when in actuality everyone was doing what Lyra and Addie said. He wondered if the sheriff even knew.

With the plan in place to go to Lyra's, Fleet, Joe, and Infiniti climbed into the sheriff's oversized truck. Darkness engulfed the town as they drove. Except for a few traffic lights from the roads and nearby holiday decorated buildings and homes, the only constant color came from the white snow falling down in sheets.

Following Addie and Lyra, they entered a neighborhood with impressive mansions. Weaving through the streets, they came to a smaller home in the back of one of the estates. Once inside, Lyra set fresh logs in the fireplace. She stacked some kindling underneath and lit it with a match. A small, red flame came to life. It spread quickly, and soon the logs crackled with warmth.

Fleet stayed quiet. He studied every inch of the home while Joe comforted Infiniti, saying her mom would be okay, that they shouldn't try to contact her, and that they'd do everything to help her. Not long into their conversation, the doorbell rang.

"That must be Elsmed," Lyra announced.

Fleet tensed. He eyed the front door. Lyra had said Elsmed would verify his story, but he wasn't sure who Elsmed was or how he'd verify anything, though he guessed it would involve mind reading. Expecting a commanding figure to waltz in, he saw a man of at least a hundred years. Tall in stature for someone so elderly, the slow-moving fossil made his way into the room with the aid of a wooden cane.

"Is this everyone?" the man asked Lyra, scanning the faces with frosty blue eyes.

"Yes, it is."

The old man rested his cane against the couch. He breathed in deep, then let out a slow trickle of air. When he did, his ears took on an arrow shape, growing until they poked through his silver hair. The wrinkles lining his face smoothed out. His nose flattened, his long chin dropped until it almost touched his chest, and he grew to a slender but towering size of well over six feet. He huffed, and looked directly at Fleet.

"So, you are the Transhuman, one of the Tainted, villains by any standards. Yet you say you come here in peace to help this young lady." He motioned at Infiniti with long and skinny fingers. "Is that right?"

"That's right."

"Who sent you?"

"A spirit girl named Abigail."

"Interesting," Elsmed whispered. "And you're aware that I'm here to authenticate your story by reading your mind?"

"Pretty much," Fleet answered, wondering if he was making a mistake by letting the old fae probe his mind.

"I'll only look at what I need," Elsmed added with wise eyes. "Nothing more, nothing less."

Fleet raised his chin. "Well then, let's do this."

"Wait!" Infiniti called out. She went to Fleet's side. "Be careful with him, okay?" she said to the fae. "He's sort of like my ride home."

Elsmed tilted his head at her. "Young lady, I am always careful."

"Good." She gave Fleet's arm a reassuring pat, then went back to Joe. "Go ahead," she said to the fae. "Resume."

Elsmed lifted a brow at her before giving Fleet his full attention. "Now," Elsmed instructed in a serious tone, "be still. This will only take a few minutes."

Fleet locked eyes with the fae. He directed his energy to his mind, guarding the pieces he didn't want Elsmed to see, leaving the barest relevant truth available.

I'm here to help Infiniti, sent by a spirit girl named Abigail, and I mean no harm.

Holding the thought, he felt a warm tingle spread across his scalp. Subtle and light, it traveled from temple to temple, swirling around his head.

"Very good," Elsmed whispered, as if signaling completion of his job.

Fleet expected the fae to break his connection, but he didn't. Instead, the fae's eyes narrowed. His nostrils flared. Fleet felt the fae probe deeper, pressing against his barriers in an effort to seek hidden truths.

"*That's none of your damn business,*" Fleet said with his mind.

Elsmed blinked. He stopped the telepathic interrogation. He stepped back. "I suppose you are correct," he conceded. "But I had to try." Elsmed eyed Lyra and Addie. "What the Transhuman says is true. He is no threat whatsoever to the people here."

"Not even from the Collector?" Addie asked.

"The Collector?" Fleet asked.

"A person of interest," the sheriff answered.

"And if you don't know who it is, then it's not your business," Addie added.

Elsmed retrieved his cane. "Correct, not even from the Collector. But I recommend the Transhuman complete his business and move along quickly. His kind always leads to trouble."

"Trust me, I don't want to be here any longer than I have to," Fleet agreed, thinking he needed to hurry and figure out what Infiniti needed to do in this time before Tavion could catch on that something was up. The last thing the peaceful town needed was a madman like Tavion coming for a visit.

Elsmed engaged his glamour, his body morphing back into a regular old man. "I'll let you all get on with it. Reach out to me should you need me again, Lyra."

With the fae gone and the night stretching out, Lyra decided everyone had had enough for the evening.

"Infiniti," Lyra said, "you can stay with me while we sort this whole thing out."

"That's fine with me," the sheriff said, looking tired and worn out. Fleet wondered who the Collector was and what kind of threat he posed to the town. He could sense it was bad, but didn't ask. The last thing he needed was to be pulled into another battle.

"Me, too," Addie said. "My plate is full with other—" She paused, as if finishing the sentence would reveal some sort of secret. "Projects." She turned to her mom. "Unless you need me on this."

Lyra picked up the metal fireplace poker and stirred the fire. "The town is plagued with threats of late. If I can take this piece of worry away from you and the others, then I'm happy to do it. Besides, our time travelers mean us no harm. I'll help them find what they seek, so they can be on their way."

"Yes," Infiniti cut in. "Please. I just want to get home."

Fleet's sentiments echoed Infiniti's, because back in Houston in 2012, Tavion was still hunting Dominique. He needed to accomplish whatever needed to be done, and get back before too long.

"It's settled then," Addie announced. "Infiniti will stay here. And Fleet will stay—"

"I don't need anybody arranging my accommodations."

"Suit yourself, tough guy," Addie said with an eye roll.

Fleet made his way to the door, itching to be alone. "I'll be fine on my own. Be back in the morning."

Outside in the cold, Fleet shoved his hands in his pockets. He started walking to the back of the neighborhood. Finding a dark place surrounded by trees and shrubs, he crouched down. He put his hand on the snowy ground. He thought of transporting to Houston in his proper time so he could check on things, but knew Tavion would detect his presence. So instead, his thoughts went to the Boardman River in Michigan, the place where he used to live before Tavion marked Dominique for death. He loved it there—magnificent trees, the peaceful river, the fresh air. He spent a lot of time there thinking and getting away from things.

Eyeing Lyra's house, he thought Infiniti would be fine with her for the night as he used his energy to go home.

CHAPTER 9

*I*nfiniti felt safe in Lyra's cozy and quaint home, but when Fleet left and Sheriff Kasun and Addie followed, she didn't feel so safe anymore. Feeling a pull toward Joe, and not wanting him to go, she watched him leave, too.

Alone and scared, she wished to be home with her mom. And then she wondered if she'd even make it home. A sinking feeling settled in her gut. She thought of her house, her comfy bed, the giant purple *I* painted on her door, her friends and relatives. A feeling of homesickness the size of Texas settled deep inside her, prompting an aching pain in her heart.

When she left Houston for Colorado, she had high hopes for a great time with her cousins, and possibly even a holiday romance. But when she and her mom got on that plane and they almost crashed, it was as if the bad luck from that event followed her. Staring at her hands, missing Joe's warm and comforting touch, she thought about their almost kiss in the classroom. So far, meeting him was the only good thing to come out of her ordeal.

"Dear," Lyra said, pulling her back to the moment. "Would you like something to eat or drink?"

Her stomach churned with anxiety, but her head still

throbbed. "Something to help with my headache would be great. Thank you."

"Altitude getting to you?"

Infiniti rubbed her forehead. "Yeah, a little. I haven't acclimated yet."

"I've got the perfect thing for that," Lyra said with a comforting smile. "Come on."

Infiniti followed Lyra through the living room and to the kitchen. The creamy beige walls and wood floors were perfect for the peaceful Colorado home. She sat at the small round table while Lyra busied herself in the kitchen. She eyed her clothes. She had slipped them on that very morning, in the inn with her mother. For her it had only been hours, but for everyone in Havenwood Falls, six years had passed. She wondered if her mom was okay, and what her life looked like now that Infiniti had been gone for so long.

She was distracted from her somber thoughts when Lyra set a mug in front of her, along with a plate of cookies.

"I've made you a drink with some special herbs that will help your head. The sweets should do you good, too."

"Thank you," Infiniti said. She sipped the floral-smelling water, then helped herself to the food. With each drink of the liquid, she started feeling better. The lingering aches and pains in her body from the car crash began to fade. The clench in her gut released. She even noticed her shoulders relaxing.

Realizing the effect the concoction was having on her, she marveled at her host. "Wow. I don't know what you put in that drink, but I feel so much better."

Lyra chuckled. "I agree, it's good stuff."

Infiniti leaned forward. "Can you show me how to make it?"

"And give away the secret family recipe? I don't think so." Lyra smiled and sat across from her with her own mug in hand. "But I do have an endless supply, should you need another serving."

Together they drank and ate. As the seconds turned into minutes, Infiniti started feeling like her old self. With her worries in manageable mode, and her body relaxed, she asked, "What now?"

Lyra thought for a moment. "How about a good night's sleep? That's what. We can face our worries in the morning." Lyra reached for Infiniti's hand and squeezed. "Everything will work out. It always does."

Lyra reminded Infiniti of her mother—boldly optimistic despite mounting odds. She liked an outlook like that, and was glad her mother had raised her to believe in the impossible. A feeling of hope grew in her. She smiled and put her hand on top of Lyra's.

"You're right. I'm here for a reason. I can feel it. We're gonna find out what it is, and everything will be okay."

Lyra nodded. "Indeed."

After finding some of Addie's pajamas that were small enough to fit her petite frame, Infiniti took a long hot shower and settled into the queen-sized bed of the first floor guest room. Laying on her back, she stared at the ceiling. With her fear in check, her thoughts drifted to Joe.

"Joseph Greg," she said out loud to herself, liking the way his name sounded. He was the first normal guy to show interest in her. Except, he wasn't exactly normal. Tall, gorgeous, with sparkling hazel eyes and chiseled features, he was perfect . . . for a wolf shifter. Oh, and one not in her same time.

She grabbed her pillow and slammed it over her face, thinking she had the worst luck with guys. She let out a groan when she heard a tapping sound coming from the window. She slid her pillow off her face. She strained her ears. The tapping sounded again, but louder. She sat up, got off the bed, and tiptoed to the window. She placed her shaky fingers on the thick curtains, and paused. She wasn't in Houston suburbia, but supernatural crazy town. Visions of deadly creatures lying in wait on the other side of the glass popped into her mind. But then another thought came to her. What if it was Joe? She grabbed a candlestick from her bedside table to use as a weapon, just in case.

"Please be Joe," she whispered to herself.

She pulled the curtain to the side. She peered into darkness before noticing Joe. He was crouched down, as if keeping out of sight. He smiled when he saw her, and a host of butterflies exploded in her stomach. He pointed to the lock on the window and mouthed the word open.

Placing her weapon on the floor, she moved her hands to the lever. She popped it to the other side, and then pulled the window up. A surge of frigid air swept through the room. She shivered with cold as Joe hurried through the opening and closed the window behind him. He swept clumps of snow off his shoulders.

"Hey," he smiled. "Hope it's okay that I came by to check on you."

She combed her hair back behind her ears, trying to hide her excitement at seeing him. "Yeah, sure. It's great."

A knock sounded on her door. She sucked in her breath. Her eyes grew wide. Joe's eyes darted around the room, looking for a place to hide.

"I don't mind visitors," Lyra called out, "as long as they're announced and seen in the living room."

Infiniti cleared her throat. "Sorry, we were—"

"Going to the living room, right now," Lyra commanded. "And Joe?"

"Uh." He cleared his throat. "Yes, ma'am?"

"If your parents don't know you're here, please tell them."

Joe grinned like a kid caught with his hand in the cookie jar. Infiniti thought he looked so cute like that. "Yes, ma'am."

She stifled her laugh until Lyra's footsteps faded away. "We just got busted."

Joe flashed her a sheepish grin. "Sorry."

She pulled the blanket from her bed and wrapped it around her shoulders. "Come on. Before we get in even more trouble."

They made their way down the hall and to the living room. The logs in the fireplace had reduced to glowing embers. The fading light cast the room in dark shadows, making everything look slightly sinister. Infiniti shivered. Joe must've thought she was cold, because he went to the fireplace right away.

"Here," he said. "Let me stoke up the fire."

He took fresh logs from a stack on the hearth. He placed two chunks of wood on top of the dying ash. He shifted them around with the poker until flames caught in the middle.

"There," he said, sitting next to Infiniti on the couch. "Better?"

The glow of the revived fire and the warmth from Joe calmed her instantly.

"Yes, much better. Thank you."

He pulled out his phone and started texting. "Gotta let my dad know I'm here."

She waited, worried his dad wouldn't let him stay. After a quick exchange, Joe set the phone on the coffee table. "All good. I can stay."

She hid her relief and played it cool, not wanting to show too much excitement about him staying.

"So . . ." she said in a nonchalant tone, searching for the right thing to say.

"So . . ." he repeated.

A nervous laugh escaped her lips. She stared into his dreamy eyes, thinking she could get lost in them.

"Infiniti Clausman," he said with a smile. "From Houston, Texas. I still can't believe you're here. In the flesh. Next to me on this couch." He took on an expression of wonder. "It's crazy."

She angled her body toward him. "I know. Right?" She looked around the room. "This place, this town, the people." She pictured him in wolf form, remembering how he had fallen over onto the snow, his body contorting as he transformed. "I can't believe you're really a wolf shifter."

"Yeah, I really am."

"What other kinds of people live in Havenwood Falls?"

"You mean, what other kinds of supes?"

She pictured a town where all kinds of paranormal people

walked around freely. Like Halloween, but every day. "Yeah, supes."

"Well, we've got vampires, ghosts, fae, gargoyles, demons—"

She grabbed his arm and squeezed. "Demons?" A hard shudder moved through her body. "As in, evil spirits that kill people?"

He took her hand. "It's not like that. We live in peace together. We're not killing each other."

"Peace? With a demon? Seems hard to believe."

"We do have some crazy stuff that happens from time to time, but yeah, we pretty much live together in peace." He started playing with her fingers. "There's nothing to be afraid of in this town. I promise."

As they sat close, staring into each other's eyes, the rest of the world seemed to fade away. It was just her, a gorgeous guy, and a romantic fireplace.

"I feel like I've known you forever, even though it's only been a really long day," she said in a low voice.

He took on a serious expression. "It hasn't been a day for me, Infiniti. For me, it's been six years of thinking about you. Six years of wondering who you are and where you went. Six years of longing to see you again." He traced the side of her face with his finger. "It's hard to understand, but for six years you've been in my mind. In my heart. Not once have I stopped thinking about you."

She melted inside. Her heart hammered against her chest. She had never really believed in love at first sight, until meeting Joe.

"Really?"

He stared into her big brown eyes. He brought his hands up to her face. They felt strong and warm against her skin.

"Yes, really."

Like magnets, their bodies moved closer. Their lips parted. Infiniti closed her eyes, ready for her first kiss, when a crashing bang rocked the house. She let out a gasp as Joe jumped to his feet.

Lyra rushed into the room. She flicked on the light. "What was that?"

"I don't know," Joe said. "But it sounded like it came from the front door."

Lyra moved quickly to the front of the house. Infiniti and Joe followed. Shaking like a leaf, wondering what the noise could be, Infiniti envisioned a horrible monster coming for her. Or maybe even that creepy reaper.

Joe placed his hands on the door. He took in a series of small sniffs. "All clear."

Lyra moved her hands around, as if sifting through the air. "Agreed. There's nobody there."

Lyra opened the door. On the ground was an oversized rock with a note tied to it. A huge indention marred the wooden door. Lyra frowned, eyeing the damage.

"Spirits," she whispered.

"Want me to sweep the area?" Joe asked, working his jaw with determination.

"That won't be necessary. But thank you, Joe."

Lyra picked up the rock, stepped back inside, and shut the door behind her. She slipped the parchment out from the brown string. She unfolded the paper. The note read in all caps:

THE GIRL AND THE TRANSHUMAN MUST GO

Infiniti covered her mouth. Her spine tingled with fear. The scrawled print screamed anger and hate. "I'm not safe here," she said between parted fingers.

Fleet appeared behind her. "You are as long as I'm around."

He stomped past her and Lyra and opened the front door. Clumps of snow fell from the sky. A wintry wind whistled in the air. Joe joined him on the porch.

"See anything?" Fleet asked Joe.

Joe narrowed his eyes and scanned the area. "No. You?"

"No."

Back inside, Lyra held the note in her hand. She furrowed her brow. "I need to tell Addie about this. Please excuse me." Before she turned and left the room, she added, "Gentlemen, if you wouldn't mind staying the night, I'd be most appreciative."

"Me, too," Infiniti whispered.

"Yes, ma'am. Of course," Joe said.

"Sure," Fleet added.

Infiniti watched Lyra walk to her room. The expression on the woman's face told her things were bad. She moved up close to Joe and slipped her arm around his.

"I'm so freaked right now."

"It's okay. I'm here with you, and I'm not leaving."

Fleet worked his way around the room, as if securing the place. "Same here, Tiny."

The warning on the note struck fear in her, but having Joe and Fleet around definitely made her feel better. Resolving her will, she decided her best course of action was to stay near them. Going to sleep in her room, alone, was the last thing she wanted to do. Still clutching the blanket around her shoulders, she eyed the couch and the two oversized cushioned chairs up against the wall.

"I think we should all stay in this room tonight. Together. You know, safety in numbers and all that."

"Good idea," Joe said. "You can take the couch, and Fleet and I can make do on the chairs." He looked at Fleet, who was still moving about the room. "That cool with you?"

"Sure."

Relieved at their plan, Infiniti went back to the guest room to collect the pillows. With her arms full, she remembered the basket she had seen earlier. It was overflowing with blankets. She clutched the pillows in one arm and grabbed a few blankets with the other. Armed with slumber party supplies, it occurred to her that she was about to have a sleepover with two super hot guys. The circumstances could've been a lot better, but she'd take it.

Back in the living room, she saw Fleet standing near one of the windows. Arms crossed and leaning against the wall, he kept a steady lookout. He looked tense and deadly, but in that moment she saw something else in him. Something that resembled loss. Maybe even heartache. She wondered what his story was, and if she'd ever find out.

Joe went over to help with her supplies. Together they tossed everything on the couch. Joe indicated with his thumb at Fleet.

"I don't think he's gonna need any of this stuff."

"Maybe not, but there's plenty for him in case he's interested."

She put a pillow and a blanket on one of the chairs for Fleet, then handed a pillow and a blanket to Joe. She made herself comfortable on the couch, finding the cushions a lot cozier than she imagined. Joe moved his chair closer to her.

"Do you mind if I prop my feet up by yours?"

Her heart fluttered. "I don't mind at all."

He tugged off his boots. Sitting back in his chair, he kicked up his feet by hers. At first, she scooted her feet over, but as they talked about anything and everything into the night, their feet ended up intertwined.

Talking with Joe felt like a dream, as if her brain had imagined the most perfect guy and made him come to life. He loved Cheetos, sci-fi movies, all things chocolate, and amusement parks. He laughed at her jokes and understood her perfectly.

"Tell me about your life back in Houston," he said.

"Well," she said. "It's the regular boring stuff. School, homework, getting ready for graduation, hanging with friends. You know."

Joe didn't say anything for a while. "Does the hanging with friends part include a boyfriend?"

She stopped her foot from rubbing against his, nervous because she had never had a real boyfriend or even kissed a guy before and didn't want to say so.

"No, no boyfriend."

He nudged her foot with his. "Good."

A moment of quiet descended on them. Fleet had long disappeared to another part of the house, and Lyra had been asleep in her room for hours. With the fire out, the only light in the room came from slivers of moonlight through the blinds from the nearly full moon outside. With their feet snuggling against each other, Joe said, "I really like you, Infiniti."

Her heart leapt. A pleasing tingle swirled around in her stomach. They had almost kissed twice, and each time had been interrupted. She thought of getting up from the couch, sitting on his lap, and finally meeting her lips to his. She could almost feel her hands working their way up his neck and her fingers working their way through his hair. Heat filled her body, and suddenly she knew what people meant by needing to take a cold shower.

She drew in a deep breath and told herself to calm down. "I really like you too, Joe."

Somewhere between talking, laughing, and foot flirting, Infiniti fell into a deep and peaceful sleep believing somehow everything would work out.

CHAPTER 10

*J*oe stayed up all night watching Infiniti sleep. He loved the way her mouth slightly parted, the way her long dark hair covered half her face. She made a light snore every other breath, and sometimes her petite nose would twitch. He could look at her for hours and never get tired.

"Does she know?"

Fleet came into the room and sat on the other chair. He leaned over and placed his elbows on his knees. Joe had a feeling he knew what Fleet meant, but asked anyway.

"Know what?"

"That you're called to her."

When wolf shifters were called to someone, it was for life. He had suspected his attachment to her was more than a crush, but didn't know for sure until he saw her at Burger Bar and his heart sang to hers. He hadn't said anything to anyone about it, and wondered how Fleet knew.

Joe slid his feet off the couch. He turned to face Fleet all the way. "No, she doesn't."

"Good," Fleet said. "She doesn't need to know, got it?"

His heart ached, because he knew they could never be a thing. He loved her with everything he had, and no one would ever compare. Eventually, she'd find whatever she needed in Havenwood Falls and go back to her proper time and place. What good would it do for her to know how he felt?

"Yeah, I got it."

"As soon as we figure out what she needs from this place, we're gone."

"I said, I got it," Joe shot back with intensity.

"Okay, then," Fleet said, getting up and leaving the room.

Joe exhaled. He eyed Infiniti. As much as he didn't like it, Fleet was right. He had to let her go, no matter how much it would suck. And he couldn't let her know how he felt. Not ever.

Somewhere between watching Infiniti and worrying about her, Joe fell into a restless sleep.

THE SAVORY AROMA of bacon tickled Joe's nose. It registered in his brain and traveled all the way to his stomach, waking him with a rumble.

He eyed the couch and saw that Infiniti had already woken up. The room was empty. He got to his feet and stretched, then made his way to the bathroom. He splashed water on his face and toweled it dry. He stared at his reflection in the mirror and said, "You have to let her go."

His head hung low as his directive lingered in the air for a bit before he went to the kitchen. Infiniti and Lyra were working on a spread of scrambled eggs, bacon, and hash browns.

Infiniti lit up when she saw him. "Good morning."

He tried not to sound too excited to see her. "Good morning."

"Sleep okay?" Lyra asked.

"Yes, thanks," he lied, joining them at them stove. "You all need any help?"

"Sure," Lyra said. "If you could pour juice in the glasses, please."

Joe eyed three glasses on the set table. "No Fleet?" he asked.

"No," Lyra said, placing the cooked food on the table. "He's out, trying to make headway on how to get Infiniti home."

His gut twisted at the idea of losing Infiniti, but he pushed it aside as he went to the refrigerator for the juice. He poured the orange liquid into the glasses and sat down. He thought of the note and how Lyra had retired to her room with it in her hand.

"Did you figure anything out about the note?"

Lyra sighed. "No, and I tried all of my tricks. Whoever wrote the note and threw the rock did a good job concealing their identity."

"But I'm not in any danger here," Infiniti chimed in. "Lyra and I already discussed that."

"Correct." Lyra motioned about with her hands. "My home is secure."

They ate for a bit in silence when Joe thought of the Cold Moon Ball. It was in one day, and it was the event of the year. He'd been helping his mom prepare for weeks. As much as he wanted to stay all day with Infiniti, he knew his mom would need him back home to finish preparations.

"Today is Friday," he said out loud.

"Yes, it is," Lyra responded.

"I told my mom I'd help her finish preparing our offering for the Cold Moon Ball." He eyed Infiniti. "The ball is tomorrow."

Infiniti set her fork down. "A ball? Called the Cold Moon Ball? What kind of ball is that?"

Joe always had mixed emotions about the ball. He was never too thrilled about having to get dressed up for it, but he loved all the food and always had a fun time with his friends. "The cold moon is what the full moon is called in December. It's called the cold moon because the weather is so cold."

Lyra wiped her mouth with her napkin. "The ball celebrates the legend of protective spirits that keep the residents of Havenwood Falls from freezing to death during the harsh winter months. It starts at sunset with an elaborate feast in the town community center known as the Annex, then moves to a large ballroom in the Mills mansion."

"Wow, a ball," Infiniti said with wide eyes. "I've never been to a ball."

Suddenly Joe felt as if he and Infiniti were the only ones in the room. Nothing else mattered but spending as much time with her as he could before she had to leave. To hell with playing it safe.

"Do you want to go with me?"

"Wait a minute," Lyra said. "It may not be the wisest thing—"

"Yes!" Infiniti interjected. "I'd love to!"

"Great," Joe said with a grin. He faced Lyra. "My family will be there. So will the whole pack. She'll be safe."

Lyra looked from Joe to Infiniti. Joe could tell she knew how they felt about each other. But would she allow Infiniti to go to the ball?

"If you were still in town," Lyra said to Infiniti, "I was going to stay home with you during the ball." Joe's heart dropped. He could see the matching disappointment on Infiniti's face. "But," Lyra continued, "if you'll still be here, and since you have a date with someone who knows a thing or two about protection, I don't see why you can't go. Some of the Luna Coven and I will be there too to watch over things."

"Oh, thank you!" Infiniti said, beaming with excitement.

The tense mood that had lingered in Joe's gut since his conversation with Fleet changed to an outlook filled with possibility. Leaving Infiniti with Lyra, feeling confident in Infiniti's safety with one of the wisest and most powerful witches in Havenwood Falls, and knowing Fleet would appear if needed, Joe set out for home to help his mother.

Joe told his parents he was taking Infiniti to the ball. Since his dad was a police officer and was there when she crashed in 2012, he already knew all about Infiniti and had filled in his mom, but they had a ton of questions anyway. Joe told them everything, leaving out the part about being called to her, because it didn't matter. One way or another, she'd be leaving Havenwood Falls, and he couldn't change that. But if he could have one amazing night with Infiniti, he was going to take it.

When he finished doing everything he needed to do at home, he hurried back to Lyra's to have dinner with Infiniti and watch a movie. Like a couple who'd been dating forever, they laughed at the same stuff and finished each other's sentences. And before he even realized it, it was almost midnight. He would've stayed all night if he could've, but his dad had ordered him home by the stroke of twelve. He didn't show up again until it was time to pick up Infiniti for the ball.

Dressed in his tuxedo, he waited a few seconds in his car outside the house before going to Lyra's front door. His heart was going bonkers. His hands were a sweaty mess. He wiped them on his pants and gripped his knees.

"Be cool," he said to himself, exhaling one last time before getting out of the car and going to the front door.

He rang the bell. He shifted from side to side. Finally it opened, and there stood Infiniti. She was wearing a purple dress fit for a princess. Long and flowy, it—and she—looked magical. He noticed his mouth was open, and he forced himself to close it.

"Wow. Infiniti, you look beautiful."

She smiled. "Thanks, Joe. You look incredible, too. So handsome."

He held out his hand. "You ready?"

"Yes."

Lyra came up from behind Infiniti. She draped a long black coat around Infiniti's shoulders.

"See you two there," she said.

Joe tried to act cool walking Infiniti to the car, but it was like he couldn't think. He fumbled with the door handle. He dropped the keys. He even sat in his car for a few seconds forgetting how to start it.

Infiniti laughed. "You okay?"

"Yes," he said, pulling it together and finally driving away from the house. "Actually, no. You have an effect on me."

"I do?"

He shifted gears. "You most definitely do."

Infiniti folded and unfolded her hands on her lap. She even started twirling her long hair as if she didn't know what to do with her hands. He smiled to himself, knowing she felt the same way about him.

"So where are we going exactly?" she asked.

"The Cold Moon Ball starts with a dinner at the Annex."

"The Annex?"

"It's an old warehouse complex that's been updated to connect the buildings. Havenwood Falls has a lot of functions there. There'll be tons of food and even some games for those who don't mind braving the elements." He gazed out the window. "And tonight seems like a great night. Cold, but clear. Great for moongazing."

Infiniti peered up at the sky. "Does the full moon, you know, do anything to you?"

"No." He smiled. "My pack's not like that. For us, we're stronger during a full moon, but that's all."

"Oh, I see," she said. A few seconds passed, and Joe could tell she was processing everything. "And after the Annex, then what?"

"We'll be escorted by wagon to the Mills mansion for the dance."

They pulled up to a parking spot. Joe turned off the car and faced her. He lost his words for a second, her beauty nearly taking his breath away. He even thought of going in for that kiss, but thought it wasn't exactly the right moment.

"You ready?"

The whole town had been abuzz about the girl from 2012 who had suddenly reappeared at Burger Bar. Joe knew all eyes would be on them, but he didn't care. All he wanted was to be with her as long as he could. Make every moment he had with her count.

"Yes," she said, looking nervous and excited. "I'm ready."

Staying close and holding hands, they worked their way through the crowd. Joe introduced Infiniti to his parents and his little brother, Boris. A few friends from school even came over for some introductions. He hadn't seen Kase or his family yet, and figured they were running late. But his favorite part of the evening was watching Infiniti ooh and aah over the extravagant holiday decorations.

"It's pretty phenomenal, isn't it?"

She squeezed his hand. "It sure is. Thank you for inviting me."

Bells started chiming, signaling everyone to make their way to the eating area. Joe directed Infiniti to the long tables. Not wanting to be in the middle of the action and having lost sight of his family, he chose a semi-secluded table at the far end of the room. They sat across from each other, and as soon as they did, waiters approached from the sides of the rooms. They draped napkins on their laps, filled their glasses with water and tea, and set down plates piled high with food.

Infiniti's eyes bulged. "This is like Thanksgiving on steroids."

Joe took his fork and knife and started cutting into the turkey. "You could say that."

After the guests had eaten as much as they could, the servers appeared again. This time they whisked away the dinner plates and set down trays of every dessert imaginable.

"I don't think I have enough room in me," Infiniti groaned.

Joe waved his fork around the delights. "There's no room for cookies, pies, cakes, and brownies?"

She laughed. "No, there's not."

Joe set his fork down. He could've devoured the cake, but didn't want to stuff his face too much. At least not while wearing a tuxedo and sitting in front of the most beautiful girl he'd ever seen.

With their settings cleared, Joe found himself leaning over the wooden table to get closer to Infiniti, and she did the same. Entranced with each other like that, they laughed and chatted while the party went on all around them. After a while, they began to notice the quiet in the room. They looked around and found the space practically empty.

"Oops," he said. "We'd better get going so we don't miss the last wagon."

"Sure. But I need to go to the ladies' room first."

Joe walked Infiniti to the restroom. Standing outside and waiting for her, he spotted a young girl on the other side of the room, all alone. She was wearing a long white dress and had long fair hair. She started walking over to hm.

"Hey, are you lost?" he asked when she got near. He crouched down so they could be at eye level. "Where are your parents?"

"You have to help save her," the little girl said.

Joe did a double take. "What?"

"Saving Infiniti is the only thing that matters right now. Understand?"

"The last wagon is leaving in five minutes!" someone called out.

Joe looked in the direction of the voice and gave a wave. When he brought his eyes back to the girl, she was gone. Stunned, he knew she had to have been the spirit Fleet was looking for, the girl he had said was named Abigail. Flustered, he wondered how he could get in touch with Fleet, when Infiniti came out of the bathroom.

"I'm ready," she announced.

Joe rubbed his hands on his pant legs, making a quick decision not to tell her about the girl. He knew it would freak her out.

"Uh, yeah, okay. Let's go."

Glued to her side, and scanning the area around him with every step, he led Infiniti to the area where the last wagon was lined up. He helped her up, and then joined her on the bench. They sat close together, and Joe put his arm around her. The wagon rolled away from the Annex and started its slow-moving trek through the town.

They passed lit and decorated businesses before turning into a neighborhood with lit and decorated mansions. Joe had thought the wagon ride would be the perfect spot for that kiss he'd been longing to give her, but now he was on red alert, eyeing every passerby on the street and investigating every shadowy corner with his heightened vision.

Infiniti put her hand on Joe's knee. "Hey, you okay?"

"Yeah," he said, hiding his worry. "I'm great."

The wagon came to a halt before Infiniti could say anything else. Joe hopped out first and then helped her down. He let Infiniti take in the sight of the exterior of the mansion before ushering her to the door.

"It's like a fairy tale," Infiniti whispered.

Joe watched her marvel at the impressive concrete stairs that led up to the front door of the enormous house. Lights adorned every inch of the façade. Lively symphonic music drifted in the air. He was so used to coming to the Mills mansion, he hadn't really thought of how an out-of-towner would react to seeing it.

"Now *that's* a mansion," she said. She lifted her skirt before taking her first step, then she spotted two large stone statues. She pointed. "Are those dragons?"

"Yes," Joe said, thinking he'd skip the explanation that old man Mills could shift into a frost dragon. Right now he needed to get her into the house and find Fleet. "Those are dragons."

He matched her stride up the stairs, stopping himself from hurrying her along. The last thing he wanted to do was scare her. Besides, he had already decided on his course of action. Get in, make a beeline for the backyard, and figure out a way to summon Fleet.

Once they were inside, an attendant checked Infiniti's coat. A few more steps in, Infiniti held Joe in place.

"Wow," she whispered, admiring the grandeur of the ballroom. "I've never seen anything like this. Look at all those candelabras."

He pushed away his fears over seeing the spirit girl, especially since they were in a safe place surrounded by supes he trusted. "If you think this room is impressive, try looking up at the ceiling."

He watched her gaze roam upward to the sprawling skylight. Crystal clear glass took up every inch of the ceiling. Majestic moonbeams of the cold moon poured through the glass, bathing the space with soft light.

"Incredible," she whispered.

He squeezed her hand, thinking the light of the moon on her dark hair and fair skin made her glow like an angel.

"You're incredible."

She looked up at him, her eyes telling him everything he needed to know about the way she felt for him.

"Do you want to," she half shrugged her shoulders, "dance?"

He wanted nothing more than to get up close to her, to feel her body pressed against his, but his senses were telling him something was up. And it wasn't just the encounter with the spirit girl. He needed to find Fleet right away.

"Why don't we go out to the backyard first? The back patio offers the best view of the moon."

Her eyes widened with delight. "Okay."

He scanned the room, looking for the nearest door to the backyard. He spotted Kase with his family. Not far from them were Lyra and other leaders of the Luna Coven. And then he saw his mom and dad. They were looking at him and Infiniti without really looking. Acknowledging them with a nod, he spotted the double doors he was looking for.

"Come on," he said, taking her hand and making his way outside.

A huge garden sprawled out to the right. To the left was a paved porch with a blazing fire pit in the middle. Everyone must've been inside dancing and eating, because the area was empty. Joe led Infiniti to the fire. Instead of trying to reach Fleet right away, he decided to open up to her. He thought that if something was going to happen, and if she was in danger, he wanted her to know how he felt about her.

Really know.

They sat on the stone seating around the warm blaze. They angled their bodies so that they were facing each other. Their knees touched.

"Infiniti, you—"

She placed her cool and delicate fingers on his lips. "Joseph Greg, I think I might die if you don't kiss me."

Every worry on his mind faded away. There was only him, Infiniti, a warm blaze, a majestic moon, and the calling for her that spread throughout his body like wildfire.

He caressed her face with his hands. He leaned forward. Infiniti parted her perfect lips. She closed her eyes. He was inches from meeting his lips to hers when a rustling in the nearby bushes pricked his senses.

He dropped his hands. He rose to his feet. He issued a silent warning to Infiniti not to make a sound as he moved her behind him. He eyed the darkness that hugged the shrubbery of the garden. His senses analyzed the area—whistling wind, the rustling of leaves, and the menacing padding of animal paws.

Shit, Joe thought to himself, as four wild and hungry-looking wolves emerged from the garden. They were crouched low with teeth bared and saliva dripping. The pack approached with stealth.

"Please tell me they're with you," Infiniti said in a low voice, her words laced with fear.

"They're not."

Joe made a quick assessment of the situation. He needed to shift so he could protect Infiniti, but first he needed to get out of view of the ballroom windows. He couldn't let anyone see him turn into a wolf, especially the humans at the dance. Shifting in public could get him banished, but he was willing to take that risk to protect Infiniti if need be.

"Back up to the shadows," he urged, moving in that direction and increasing the distance between them and the wolves. "When I say now, you get away from me."

"O-k-kay," she whispered, taking Joe's hand in a death grip.

Joe backed out of view of the ballroom with Infiniti pressing up against him. The wolves followed them, matching each step away from the patio. The moonlight highlighted the approaching predators, but then faded as they stepped into the shade of the forest.

Encased in darkness, Joe released Infiniti's hand. "Now!"

Infiniti broke away as Joe's neck cracked. His muscles bulged. His bones broke again and again as his clothes ripped to shreds. He fell to all fours as claws formed. Fangs jutted out of his gums. Fur replaced skin. In full wolf form, he issued a low menacing growl. He crouched down, matching the stance of the predators that were approaching. He readied for their attack, the spirit girl's warning to save Infiniti ringing loud in his head.

CHAPTER 11

*F*leet walked around town in cloaked mode, hoping to trigger something to make Abigail appear. His senses had been tingling since he arrived, and he was starting to have a hard time locking on Infiniti's signature through all the supernatural energy in the air. He needed to find Abigail, and fast. The longer Infiniti was in town, the more at risk she was.

"Come on, where are you?"

He spent a day and a night looking for the young spirit girl. He combed the streets. He searched the woods. Frustrated and angry, he decided to change his tactic. Instead of continuing his search, he thought it'd be best to stay close to Infiniti. If the young girl wanted to show up, she would.

The town had been preparing for a big event, a ball celebrating the cold moon. Peeking in on Infiniti at Lyra's, Fleet saw that she was getting ready. He instantly felt sorry for her. If a reaper was on her tail, then death for her was certain. She'd never be able to be with Joe.

"Poor kid."

Letting her have her time with Joe at the dinner, he made one last sweep of Havenwood Falls before making his way to the mansion where the dance was being held. Almost to the home, his spine tingled with intensity.

"Son of a bitch," he seethed, knowing Infiniti was in danger.

He crouched down. He placed his hand on the ground. He focused on Infiniti's energy signature. He fell into weightlessness. When his boots hit the ground, he found himself on a back porch. A pack of wolves had pounced on Joe in wolf form in the shadowy edge of the forest. They were tearing each other to shreds. Fleet gathered his energy in his hand and threw it at the largest attacking wolf. The bolt slammed into the back of the animal, sending a shriek into the air. Stunned, the beast backed up. The others did, too.

Fleet tossed out another blast. "Get out of here!"

The pack scurried away as the back door swung open. A small group started running toward him. Fleet recognized Joe's parents. Sheriff Kasun followed with a woman in a red dress with long red hair at his side.

Fleet held his hands up to make sure they knew he was helping. "It's okay. They're gone."

Infiniti fell to her knees. She wrapped her arms around Joe's bloodied neck. "They came out of nowhere, and Joe protected me," she said between tears.

"I like to come out of nowhere, too." It was Shade StormIron, appearing before them. He eyed Fleet. "Listen, cupcake, this is twice now you've taken my kill from me. First with this doll whose soul was calling out to me after her crash; and now with this wolf shifter who was moments from certain death. Why do you treat me so badly?"

Fleet fisted his hands at his side. He clenched his teeth. "Their souls aren't calling you anymore, so get out of here."

Shade laughed. "Well, his isn't. But the doll's soul still wants me. I can feel it. I'll be back in due time. Lucky you."

Shade disappeared, but his words lingered deep within Fleet. How could he save Infiniti if that damn reaper sensed her soul was still running out of time? Where was the spirit girl when he needed her?

Joe's mom rushed to Joe's side. Sheriff Kasun and Joe's dad started securing the area so no one inside the mansion knew what was going on outside. The last thing they wanted was a panic at the Cold Moon Ball.

While they bustled about, Fleet ran his fingers through his hair. His body shook with frustration. He'd had it. Pissed and ready to kill something, he hollered, "Show yourself!"

His words echoed all around them. They bounced off the forest trees and nearby mountains. When his voice faded, he saw that everyone was looking at him. He started to offer an apology to the group for his outburst when a hazy white glow came into view. It hovered near them and grew in sharpness and clarity until it formed into the girl.

"I'm Abigail, and I've been waiting for you."

Fleet followed Abigail's line of sight. She was looking at the redheaded woman standing by the sheriff. The woman put her hand on her chest.

"Me?"

"Yes, you," Abigail said. "I didn't know it was you that Infiniti needed until you came into her space. What's your name?"

"I'm Rose. Rose Howe."

Fleet eyed the woman named Rose as she approached Abigail with curiosity. "How can I help you, Abigail?"

Abigail pointed to Infiniti. "We need to save her, so she can help Dominique."

"Who's Dominique?" Rose asked.

"Wait, what?" Infiniti asked, still next to Joe. "Dominique? My friend and neighbor?"

Fleet wanted to interject and explain how Dominique had been hunted by Tavion for lifetimes, but he held his tongue. Abigail needed to explain, because she was the one calling the shots. Besides, the group didn't need all the details.

"Yes, your friend and neighbor. She's important to mankind,

and needs to live," Abigail said. "You are vital for her survival, Infiniti. She's going to need you as she faces off against Tavion for the last time."

Stunned, Infiniti had no response.

Fleet thought he should offer some clarification. "Tavion is the leader of the Tainted, and he's been after Dominique for a long time. And if Tavion isn't stopped, he'll kill her and then move on to killing others."

Infiniti stared at Fleet, as if trying to understand. "And I need to help her?"

"Yes," he said. "Apparently, you do."

The lively music from inside trickled to the outside, offering a sharp contrast to their talk of death. Fleet couldn't help but think the world was one messed up place.

"Wow, okay," Rose piped in. "I'm more than happy to help," she said to Abigail, eyeing the group for a second. "What can I do?"

"You need to help Infiniti become a void, so Tavion and his evil forces can't harm her," Abigail said.

Infiniti and Joe moved closer to the conversation. Blood had marred Joe's white coat, and he moved with a heavy limp. He stayed close to Infiniti's legs, pressing up against her.

"Evil forces are trying to get me?" Infiniti asked.

Joe huffed and then growled, signaling his anger at hearing that Infiniti was the target of anything evil.

"Yes, but Miss Rose can help you," Abigail said. "Right, Miss Rose?"

Rose put her hand on her chin. "Are you sure you want me? There are way more powerful witches in Havenwood Falls who can help."

Abigail drifted closer to Rose. She looked up at her with hopeful eyes. "They don't have what you have."

"What I have?" Rose repeated back.

"Yes, what you have."

"What I have," Rose muttered to herself.

"Maybe something at your shop?" the sheriff offered.

Rose squeezed the sheriff's arm. "That's it! The Howe witches date back centuries. I bet there's something in my shop unique to Tavion."

"See? I knew you could help," Abigail said with a smile.

A frosty wind blew through the trees. It swept down onto the back patio, taking Abigail's ghostly form with it like dust in the wind.

Nobody spoke for a while, until Fleet kicked into action mode. "If you can really help Infiniti," he said to Rose, "then we need to get on it, like yesterday."

"Agreed," the sheriff added. "The sooner we help these two accomplish what they're here for, the sooner they can leave."

"Let's do it now then," Rose offered. "Everyone is here at the ball, so there'll be no distractions. Sound good?"

"Sounds good to me," Fleet said.

"Me too," added the sheriff.

"I guess," Infiniti whispered with a faraway look on her face. Fleet could tell she was about to lose it, but he needed everyone to finish with the plan before he could go to her.

"It's settled," Rose announced. "Meet at my shop in one hour. Okay?" She focused on Fleet and Infiniti. "It's called Howe's Herbal Shoppe."

"I know exactly where that is," Fleet said, relieved to finally be getting somewhere with their mission. "Infiniti and I will be there."

Joe's parents left with Joe, so they could patch him up. Sheriff Kasun decided to stay at the party to run interference in case anyone caught on about what was happening at Rose's shop.

For the first time since the crash, Fleet and Infiniti were alone.

Fleet approached the petite teen with caution. Her brows were knitted together. Streaks of blood lined her arms from where she'd been holding Joe. She started shivering and looked like she was in shock. Fleet took off his leather jacket and draped it over her shoulders. She turned into him and started crying against his chest. He patted her back, letting her spill out her tears. Her sobbing slowed down until it finally came to a stop.

"I hate that reaper," she mumbled against his shirt.

Fleet smiled. "So do I, Tiny. So do I." He pulled her away and looked at her tear-streaked face. "Are you okay?"

Infiniti nodded. "I think so."

"Good, because I need you to be strong." He waited for her to answer, hoping she'd have the courage to go on now that they knew what they were there for.

"I'll try."

"Trying is the first step. Now let's get you to Lyra's so you can change and get cleaned up. We've got a witch to meet in an hour."

Infiniti wiped her face with her hands. "Okay."

Letting the revelations of the night slowly sink in for Infiniti, and letting her pull herself together, Fleet waited a few minutes before he summoned his Transhuman skills to transport the two of them to Lyra's place.

Using a key that Lyra had given Infiniti, they went inside. Fleet stayed in the living room while Infiniti fixed herself up. He stared at the clump of ash in the fireplace. He thought about Rose and wondered whether she really had something of Tavion's that could help her fashion a spell. Was it possible that Tavion had somehow exposed himself to one of the Howe witches in the past? He'd spent over a century with Tavion and didn't recall Tavion with a female, let alone a witch, but then again he wasn't glued to Tavion's side either. If Abigail had sensed it, he thought Tavion must've encountered one of them at some point. The dumb bastard.

When Infiniti came back out, she was wearing the same clothes from the crash—dark jeans, a red sweatshirt, and black boots with fur at the top. They were about to go full circle, and Fleet was ready. He was ready to get back to Houston and 2012.

CHAPTER 12

$\mathcal{A}$ feeling of weightlessness came over Infiniti. It disappeared when she found herself transported with Fleet from Lyra's house to a sidewalk in a quaint square-shaped shopping area.

"This is it," Fleet said, indicating an antique door with a glass panel in the middle that read *Howe's Herbal Shoppe* in big cursive letters. A shade had been pulled down to prevent seeing inside, but the glass façade to the right of the door showcased a display of soaps, candles, teas, and vials of oil. A dim light shone from the rear of the store, casting a soft glow in the wood-paneled shop filled with wooden shelves.

"You ready?" Fleet asked.

Infiniti thought of Abigail's words, that she needed to become a void so she could help her friend, Dominique. The idea of being caught up in some sort of good versus evil struggle terrified her, because she believed in evil, really and truly believed in it. Even though she had always put up a good front when it came to seeing scary movies with her friends, oftentimes the images on the big screen would plague her for nights. Goose bumps lined her skin. She looked up at Fleet.

"Why me?

Fleet shoved his hands in his pockets. "I ask myself that question all the damn time."

"You do?"

"Yeah, I do."

"And what's the answer?"

Fleet thought of everything he'd been through, and imagined what was still to come. "Because I can take it." He flashed Infiniti an encouraging look. "And you can, too."

She let his words work their way through her. She wanted to match his strength and determination, no matter how freaked she was.

"Damn straight, I can take it."

"Now let's try this one more time." He put his hand on her shoulder. "Are you ready?"

She drew in a deep breath. "I'm ready."

Fleet tapped on the door. It swung open right away, revealing a battered Joe. Stitches lined his forehead and cheeks. One of his eyes was swollen and bruised. A crutch was under his right arm.

Infiniti gasped. "Oh my God, Joe."

She knew his injuries were bad, but couldn't really tell before, with all the fur. Now that he was in human form, she could see all the damage.

"It's okay," he said, ushering them in with a limp. "It looks a whole lot worse than it feels. Really."

"Man, sorry, Joe," Fleet said. "I got there as soon as I could."

"I know, and I'm glad you did. You saved my ass."

"What was up with those wolves anyway?" Fleet asked with a furrowed brow. "Why did they come out and attack like that?"

Joe shook his head. "I don't know. They looked on the hungry side, but my dad thinks someone may have spelled them or something, to get them to come out like that." Joe shrugged. "Maybe the same person who wrote that note and threw it at Lyra's."

"Son of a bitch," Fleet whispered under his breath. He eyed Infiniti. "Guess it's a good thing we're leaving, then."

Guilt at what happened to Joe gripped her. "I guess."

Fleet looked around. "Where's Rose?"

Joe pointed behind him. "Back room."

Fleet went to the back, leaving Infiniti alone with Joe.

Infiniti's lip quivered as she eyed the injuries on Joe's handsome face. She lighted her fingers on his cheek and stared up into his striking hazel eyes. "This is all my fault," she said, her throat clogging over with tears. "You could've been killed because of me."

He took her hand and moved it to his lips. He kissed her fingers. "None of this is your fault. And I'd do anything for you, Infiniti. Anything. Including risk my life."

Standing there with Joe, with the moonlight trickling through the window, she thought him the most amazing person she'd ever met—beautiful in every sense of the word. Everything about him filled her heart, and if soul mates existed, she knew hers was meant for his. But destiny was cruel, and soon she'd be going back to her proper time, with every memory of Havenwood Falls erased.

"I don't want to lose you," she whispered.

He sighed. "I don't want to lose you either."

Moving closer, Joe finally brought his mouth to hers. His lips were soft and smooth, his tongue was velvety, and his breath mixed with hers sent her head into the clouds. He dropped his crutch and held her tight as their mouths connected over and over and over, neither of them wanting to break apart from the other, knowing their first kiss was going to be their last.

Their lips slowly separated, yet they stayed close together, catching their breath.

Joe gazed at her with passion-filled eyes. "I don't know how, and I don't know when, but I'm going to find you, Infiniti Clausman."

Infiniti brushed her lips against his. "You promise?"

He kissed her again, nice and slow. "I promise."

They parted as Fleet came into the room. If he noticed their moment, he gave no indication. "It's time."

Infiniti handed Joe his crutch, and together they went to the back room of the herbal shop. If the smell of herbs permeated the front area of the store, then it was crazy powerful in the back, and with good reason. The walls were lined with wood shelves filled with jars upon jars of twigs, roots, leaves, and powders.

"Wow," Infiniti said. "An earthy candy shop."

Rose was still wearing her long red ball gown. She smiled at her collection with pride. "Impressive, isn't it? I call this back room my office. I keep the popular herbs in the front of the store—sage, rosemary, and vanilla. You know, common stuff. Back here is where I keep the hard-to-find resources. Only supes would know to ask for these products."

Infiniti got up close to the shelves and read some of the labeled jars. "Brahmi, lobelia, woad, and horehound?" Infiniti snickered. "What does horehound do?"

Rose laughed. "Horehound is used for treating respiratory infections. And by the way, none of these are named by me."

Infiniti continued studying the room. A brown antique desk sat in the middle of the space. Books crammed the shelves behind. Some looked modern and new, while others appeared worn and ancient.

"This is so amazing," Infiniti said, marveling at everything around her.

"It is indeed, and this," Rose held up a small leather book, "has the perfect spell for you. These words, combined with the ingredients I've already gathered and mixed, will accomplish what we're after."

Infiniti gulped. She squeezed Joe's hand. "It will?"

"It sure will."

"And the ingredients include something of Tavion's?" Fleet asked, his words laced with disbelief.

Rose nodded. "I cannot share what I have, or how it was acquired, but yes, I have something of Tavion's. The Howe witches have gathered a wide variety of objects and materials over the centuries, especially items belonging to the powerful. As the spirit child suggested, my Howe collection contained something of Tavion's. I had actually all but forgotten I had the item. You may check my potion if you'd like." Rose set her book on the desk. She lifted a small bowl filled with a dark liquid. She held it before Fleet. "Here you go, but please don't touch the contents."

Fleet took the bowl with one hand. He placed his other hand over the top, hovering his palm inches from the rim. He closed his eyes. He face took on a look of concentration as a glowing light shone from his palm. The radiance saturated the bowl, bathing it with his stream of energy. He powered down and handed the bowl back to Rose.

"Tavion's essence is in there, all right," Fleet said. "I'd know it anywhere."

Infiniti found herself pressing against Joe, squeezing his hand in a tight grip. She envisioned all kinds of things of Tavion's that could be in that bowl—blood, hair, pieces of skin. Joe put his arm around her, letting her know everything would be okay.

Rose moved the small bowl to one hand. She picked up her book with the other and tucked it under her arm. She eyed Fleet.

"This Tavion has quite the complicated emotions."

Fleet rubbed his face. "You could say that."

"Well, now that we've got that all established," Infiniti said nervously, ready to finish what they had started before she chickened out, "now what?"

"Now we step into my treatment room."

Infiniti didn't like the sound of that, but followed Rose anyway. The red-haired woman led the group through a door that Infiniti had assumed went to a closet or bathroom. Instead, it connected to a small room like the ones used for massages. There was a long exam table, a small table for supplies, and a chair.

Rose patted the table. "Have a seat right here, Infiniti, and I'll explain the procedure. Everyone else, file in."

Trying not to show any fear, Infiniti got up on the table. Joe stood by her side, still holding her hand. Fleet closed the door and leaned against it.

"While you all were getting here, I came right on over and started researching." Rose flipped through the pages of the book, found her spot, and tapped the page. "This spell prevents harmful energy, either natural or manmade, from reaching you."

"Reaching me?"

Rose set the book down. "You can't prevent someone from trying to harm you, but you can prevent whatever they are sending from reaching you. This spell will do exactly that by creating a sphere-shaped invisible shield around your person."

"Come again?" Infiniti said, confused by it all.

Rose tapped her temple. "Think about it this way. Let's say someone wants to cast a spell that makes you sick. If you are inside a protective shield, like a telephone booth for example, the spell will bounce off. It won't reach you."

Infiniti thought of the TV show with the guy that went into the telephone booth and transported through time. She imagined herself standing inside one of those and someone blasting a laser of death at her that bounced off the glass.

"Nothing can get me while I'm in the booth."

"That's right," Rose nodded. "After you drink my potion, the spell will be specific to Tavion and anyone associated with him."

Infiniti shuddered. She was pretty sure she'd need to drink the goo, but actually hearing Rose say it made her stomach turn.

"This will work against Tavion's cronies, too?" Fleet asked.

"Correct. This spell should be effective against anyone following Tavion's directive," Rose explained.

"So this Tavion guy and his people can't hurt her?" Joe asked. "After you're finished?"

"That's right."

Fleet rubbed his chin. "How long will it last?"

"That part I'm not sure of," Rose admitted. "But hopefully indefinitely."

"What about the spell around the town that makes people forget this place when they leave?" Joe asked. "Can you do something about that?"

Infiniti gripped Joe's hand and pulled it close, hoping for a way to return to this place and in this time. But Rose's face told her there was no way.

"The spell is only effective against Tavion and his harmful influence. Besides, the wards are designed to help, not hurt. So like all people who leave, Infiniti won't remember us or any of her time here." Rose placed her hand on Infiniti's shoulder. "I'm sorry."

"It's for the best, Tiny," Fleet said.

"It really is, my dear," Rose added.

Speechless, Infiniti couldn't say anything. All she could do was hold on to Joe's promise that somehow he would find her, though deep down she knew it was impossible.

Rose got to work. She handed Infiniti the bowl filled with the dark liquid. Infiniti warily eyed the thick substance.

"Is this gonna taste disgusting?"

"Probably," Rose answered, lighting a white candle.

"Great," Infiniti muttered. She held her breath and closed her eyes, pretending she was at a party about to take a shot. She put the glass to her lips and chugged the grossness with one swig. She shuddered. "God, that was awful."

With the goo traveling down her throat, Infiniti watched Rose light an incense candle. She waved it around Infiniti. Burning smoke trailed the air while a heavy woodsy aroma wafted about her.

"I actually love incense," Infiniti said, thinking of her sticks of incense back home.

"Ah, you're a young lady of nature?" Rose set the burning stick on a wooden holder, then took the bowl and set it aside.

"A little," Infiniti said, feeling peaceful and relaxed, thinking Rose had slipped some sort of calming element to the drink. She wondered if it shared some of the same ingredients as the drink she had at Lyra's. Or maybe the calmness came from the pleasing smell of the incense. She wasn't sure, but she was glad for the soothing effect.

Rose rubbed her palms together. "Infiniti, close your eyes.

Visualize a circle forming around you, in front of you, and moving all around you completely. And then, above you, behind, and all around you. Essentially, you are enclosing yourself in a sphere. The sphere is permeable. Good energy can come in and bad energy stays out. Especially energy from the Tainted leader known as Tavion and those aligned with him."

Infiniti closed her eyes. Staying with Rose's analogy, she pictured herself standing in an all-glass telephone booth. She immediately felt safe inside, as if nothing could harm her within the enclosure.

"Do you see it?" Rose asked.

"Yes, I see it."

"Are you safe?"

Infiniti felt as if a warm sun was shining on her. "Yes, actually. I feel very safe. Kind of peaceful, even."

"Good, now keep your eyes closed and hold the image while I cast the spell."

Infiniti tightened her eyes. Rose began speaking in a language she couldn't understand. Flowy and almost musical, the words floated around in her head like an ancient rhyme. Believing in their power, Infiniti also started believing in something else—her love for Joseph Greg.

"Okay," Rose announced, pulling Infiniti out of her trance-like state. "It's done."

Infiniti opened her eyes. She looked at Rose. "That's it? I'm protected now?"

"You are."

A quiet hush fell on the group. Fleet broke the silence. "Sorry to say this, but it's time for us to leave, Tiny. Mission accomplished."

Infiniti gulped. "Right now?" For some reason, Infiniti thought she'd have more time for goodbyes, more time with Joe.

"Yes, now."

"I have to agree," Rose chimed in. "You two are not naturally from this time or place. The sooner you can get back to where you belong, the better."

Infiniti exchanged a lovesick look with Joe. "Can I have a minute with Joe?"

"Sure," Rose said. "Fleet and I will wait for you in my office."

Alone with Joe, and still sitting on the table, she pulled him close. She wrapped her arms around his neck, and he kissed her sweetly. They kissed with love, with heartache, and with sorrow, holding on to each other with desperation before they slowly parted. Joe nestled his face in the crook of her neck.

"Please find me, Joseph Greg," she whispered. "Please."

He pulled away and studied her. He traced the side of her face with his fingers. "I will."

He looked down for a second, and then looked back at her, as if struggling to find the right words for something he desperately wanted to say. Infiniti's mind took her to that moment on the mountain when they first met, when she had asked him to say he loved her.

"Joe, tell me—"

"I love you—" he said. "Really and truly, with everything I am, I love you."

She pulled him in and kissed him again, thinking she could kiss him forever, telling him she loved him back. Slowly and reluctantly, they finally separated.

She and Joe joined Rose and Fleet in the other room. Fleet put his hand on Infiniti's shoulder.

"You ready to go back to 2012, Tiny?"

She hesitated with her answer, suddenly consumed with ideas of time travel and alternate time lines. "Will I be the same when I go back? Like my life and my family and my friends? Or will everything be . . . bizarro world?"

"There'll be no bizarro world," Fleet explained. "Time travel doesn't have to be wholly disruptive. What has happened here is a splintering of events. We'll go back to our original timeline, and what has happened here in Havenwood Falls will remain intact in its own timeline."

"Oh, okay," she whispered, confused by it all but trusting Fleet.

Although she was ready to see her mom, she was not at all ready to lose Joe forever. Plus, there was the whole whatever was going to happen to Dominique thing. There were so many scary unknowns in her future, but she refused to let fear or doubt rule her. Like Fleet said, she could take it. And somehow or another, she believed in her heart of hearts that everything would work out and Joe would find her.

"I guess I'm ready."

She and Fleet backed away from Joe and Rose. Wispy gray tendrils oozed out of Fleet's hand. The mist wrapped around her arm, spilling down her body until it formed a small churning circle of vapor beneath their feet.

She kept her eyes on Joe until he slipped out of view and was replaced by the windshield of her rental car. She slammed on the brakes. She screeched to a stop on the side of the road. She looked all around and found herself alone. The radio blared. The smell of Flamin' Hot Cheetos hung in the air. She stepped outside the car and into the cold air. She spun around searching the space around her.

"Fleet?"

She waited for him to appear with his deadly good looks and bad attitude, but he didn't. She was alone. Her thoughts turned to Joe. She wasn't sure when the magic of Havenwood Falls would kick in and erase her memories, but she figured it'd be right away.

Frantic determination seized her. "Joseph Greg, Joseph Greg, Joseph Greg," she repeated as she hopped back in the car and snatched her phone. She opened her text to send herself a message, but was so flustered she dropped the phone. "Dammit."

She scooped it back up, and it rang in her hand, giving her a small heart attack. She looked to see who it was and answered right away.

"Mom!"

"Fin, are you okay? You've been gone a while."

"Oh, Mom! It's you!"

"Of course it's me. Is everything all right?"

"Uh . . ." Her brain scrambled with what to say. "I started driving around to check out the area and lost track of time. I'm so sorry. I didn't mean to worry you."

"It's okay. Just get back soon. I'm starving."

"I will."

She ended the call, then opened up her messages and went back to her text. She stared at the device, searching for the name she had been repeating right before her mother called. Her hand moved to her lips. Suddenly she remembered the tingling from Joe's kiss.

"Joseph!" She typed, *Joseph Greg*. She stopped, her fingers lingering over her phone while she racked her brain for the name of the town.

"Havershire," she said out loud, but thought it didn't sound right. "Nope, that's not it. Havenshire." She slapped her hands against the steering wheel, knowing that was wrong, too. "Maybe it's not with an H. Maybe it's with a W. Woodenshire, Woodhaven."

She grunted with frustration, when a horn honked behind her. A car pulled up next to hers and stopped. It was an elderly couple. They had their window rolled down. Infiniti rolled hers down, too.

"You need some help?" the lady asked.

Infiniti raised her phone. "No, I'm okay. I was just taking a call. Thanks, though."

"Smart girl," the lady said. "This pass is known for people driving off the cliff."

Infiniti smiled and waved. "Oh, got it. Yeah, I'll be careful."

She rolled up her window as the couple drove off. She stared at the side of the road that edged up to a sharp drop. She shuddered, thinking a plunge off the side of a mountain would totally suck.

And then she realized her phone was in her hand. She looked

at it. She noticed an open text to herself with the name Joseph Greg. Nothing more.

"Huh," she mumbled. "Who's Joseph Greg?"

She watched the letters of the name disappear as she pressed the back button. She eyed the blank screen for a second, feeling as if she was forgetting something. She brushed it off, then set her phone in the cup holder. She fiddled with her radio, found a good song, and headed back to her mom and the inn, hoping they could somehow make it to Breckenridge for Christmas.

EPILOGUE

*J*oe stared at Infiniti. He studied every detail, desperate to imbed her image in his brain before she vanished, because he didn't know if he'd really be able to find her once she left Havenwood Falls. Long dark hair, ivory skin, the most beautiful face he'd ever seen. A gray mist oozed out of Fleet's hands. It spilled down to the ground and formed a swirling vapor around their feet. Infiniti's lips parted, as if she wanted to say something, before she plunged from view.

"Infiniti!"

He dashed to the spot where Infiniti had stood with Fleet. He glanced around, as if she'd reappear, but she didn't.

Heartbreaking silence filled the room.

"I'm very sorry, Joe," Ms. Howe said in a low voice.

His heart crumbled. A lump the size of a football lodged in his throat. He felt as if a piece of him had been ripped away, and he didn't know if he'd ever get it back.

"I'll let you have a minute," Ms. Howe added, leaving the room.

Joe couldn't remember the last time he had cried, but seeing Infiniti disappear brought tears to his eyes. He rubbed them away with the back of his hands, forcing himself not to lose it. Not here, anyway.

He put his crutch under his arm and hobbled out of Ms. Howe's office and to the front of the herbal shop. He kept his gaze down, not wanting to make eye contact.

"Thanks for everything, Ms. Howe."

"Sure thing, Joe."

He fumbled with the keys in his pocket as he painstakingly made it out of the shop and into his car. He sat there for a minute, thinking how hours earlier Infiniti was sitting next to him, dressed like a princess for the ball, and now she was gone. He leaned his head against the headrest, thinking of their amazing kiss and the promise he had made to find her.

Could he really do it?

He started his car and headed home. He was driving through the quiet streets of the town when a memory exploded in his brain. A few months after Infiniti had vanished back in 2012, he had a series of dreams of horrible things happening to her, incidents that all resulted in her death. Another car accident, being swept away by a tornado, drowning in the ocean, even catching on fire. He shuddered as the feeling of horror mixed with intense loss worked his way through him.

He thought of that damn reaper and his words.

"But the doll's soul still wants me. I can feel it. I'll be back in due time."

Had they sent her back only to die?

Had they made a horrible mistake?

Joe screeched to a halt. He made a U-turn in the middle of the street and hauled himself back to the herbal shop. Rose was emerging from the front door. He hopped out of his car and rushed over to her.

"It didn't work!"

She huddled into her coat and wrapped her arms around herself. "What do you mean?"

"We sent her back to 2012, and she's going to die there. I know it."

Rose looked away for a second, as if contemplating the possibility. "Listen, Joe. I don't know if you're right or wrong, but I do know a thing or two about destiny, and I can tell you that destiny cannot be changed. Ever." She stared up at the sky. "It's like telling the moon not to be bright. It simply can't be done."

He looked down at the sidewalk, racking his brain for a response, because there was no way he was going to give up on Infiniti. Finally, an idea came to him.

"Okay, fine, I get that about destiny, I really do. But what if her coming here was another type of destiny? A way for the right destiny to counter the wrong destiny?" He stopped, thinking his words weren't making any sense and sounded a little crazy, but he went on anyway. "I mean, we didn't bring her here, yet she showed up needing our help. Maybe, just maybe, she needs our help again."

He hobbled forward, waiting for the red-haired witch to give him some sign of hope.

She nodded with a pensive look on her face. "Maybe she does, Joe. But let's get through the holidays first, okay? And we can take up this conversation later."

"Okay, yeah," Joe said. "I'll come by after the new year."

Her offer to help was encouraging, but he couldn't wait until after the holiday break to do something about finding Infiniti. Back home and in his room, he texted Kase, knowing he'd be up at midnight.

Me: Dude.

Kase: Yeah.

Me: Need your help.

Kase: About the girl? Did it work? My dad told me.

Joe wasn't surprised that Sheriff Ric had said something to Kase. And he didn't mind. Kase was his best friend.

Me: Yeah. She's gone.

Kase: Sorry.

Me: It's ok. But I have an idea. Come over tomorrow. I'll fill you in.

Kase: Is it a crazy idea?

Me: Maybe.

Kase: Cool, I'm down. See you then.

Joe set his phone on his bedside table and lay on his bed, exhausted and feeling like crap. But more than anything, he was determined to find Infiniti Clausman. And no one could stop him.

∽

Thank you for reading!
Infiniti & Joe's story continues in
Finding Infiniti.

ABOUT THE AUTHOR

Rose Garcia is the author of the critically acclaimed Final Life Series. The saga features gut-wrenching emotional turmoil and heart-stopping action with a diverse and dynamic cast. A lawyer turned writer, Rose has always been intrigued by science fiction and fantasy. More recently, she's been intrigued by a blend of science fiction and reality and the idea that some supernatural events are, indeed, very real. Just ask her about the ghost she used to share a house with. Rose lives in Houston with her husband, two kids, and two dogs. Luckily, there are no ghosts in her current home. For information on Rose's new releases and appearances, sign up for her newsletter at www.RoseGarciaBooks.com/newsletter. You can learn more about Rose at www.rosegarciabooks.com.

ACKNOWLEDGMENTS

I have so many incredible people to thank for helping me bring *Saving Infiniti* to life! First and foremost, I want to thank the amazing Kristie Cook. A visionary like no other, Kristie Cook is the creator and publisher of Havenwood Falls. When I first heard of her project way back when, I knew right away that I wanted to be a part of it. And when I pitched the idea of bringing Infiniti and Fleet from The Final Life Series into the world, she was on board!

To all the Havenwood Falls authors who helped me breathe life into my story: Kallie Ross who shared many of her characters with me including Joseph Greg and his family, Sheriff Ric and Kase of the Kasun pack, and Rose Howe; Justine Winter who let me set her cheeky reaper Shade StormIron on Infiniti's heels; Kristie Cook who let me use the wise and caring Lyra Beaumont and Lyra's daughter Addie; E.J. Fechenda who let me use her mind-probing fae Elsmed; and Tish Thawer who educated me on all things witchy. A special thanks to Regina Wamba for my amazing cover and Liz Ferry for her eagle eye editing! And really, the entire Havenwood Falls author family has been beyond helpful, and I'm so glad to have them in my life!

To my amazing beta readers and critique partners who've been a part of my writing journey for many years: Heather Elliot, Jessica Ramirez, and Wade Moriarty, and my teen readers Olivia and Jake. You guys ROCK! I seriously don't know what I'd do without y'all! And, of course, to the PR professionals who've helped me so much: Amber Garcia and Marya Heidel. Also, a special thanks to my PA Kellie Kortright who helps me so much with my FB fan page! For those wondering where *Saving Infiniti* fits in The Final Life Series, it's an expansion of a scene in *Final Life*, book one in the series. *Finding Infiniti*, due out summer of 2019, will fit into the series after *First Life*, book four in the series.

WILLFUL

LIZ FERRY

HAVENWOOD FALLS HIGH

Willful

LIZ FERRY

~ A Havenwood Falls Young Adult Novella ~

For my willful child

PROLOGUE

JONATHAN

*I*t was a bright, sunny day when it happened. If it had been rainy, we would have stayed home, and they would have caught us. But it was cool and crisp, and Mom wanted to take a stroll down to the open-air market to pick up some fresh vegetables. She usually went with Mrs. Viegas, our neighbor, a nice old lady who'd lived in the small mountain town for her whole life, but today she asked me to walk with her, and I did, because I was bored.

We walked along the cobblestone streets, Mom drilling me on history facts, dodging kids playing and women sweeping their stoops. At the market, surrounded by the earthy smells of farm-fresh produce, we picked up tomatoes and cucumbers, onions and potatoes, celery and cabbage. At every booth, Mom stopped to chat with the farmers, asking about their children, their harvest, and their health.

On our way back from the market with a bag full of vegetables, we ran into Mrs. Viegas hurrying down the road. She stopped us with waving arms, but lowered voice. She spoke into my mother's ear for a minute, and I watched my mom's expression turn to panic, matching the old lady's, as her hand came up to clutch the gold pendant she wore. My mother started nodding rapidly, then shoved the bag of vegetables into our neighbor's arms and grabbed my hand.

"*Obrigada, obrigada,*" my mother thanked Mrs. Viegas, then turned and ran, dragging me along with her.

I was surprised at the speed with which we were able to leave town. Apparently, Mom had set up contingency plans for getting us out if—when—we needed to run. We ran to Mr. Mata's garage, where my mother pulled him out from under a car and told him she needed her keys. He ran to the office and handed over a set of keys, then pointed to the back door of the shop. Within minutes, we were out of town and speeding down the road to Lisbon.

About half an hour after we left, I looked out the back window to see a thin plume of black smoke rising into the sky above the town that had been our home for the last three years. I hoped Mrs. Viegas was okay.

CHAPTER 1

CELESTE

"Celeste! Finally," Margaret said as she opened the door. Her mass of black curls was held back with a thin pink headband, which matched her chiffon dress.

"That's what you're wearing?" I bypassed polite greetings and got straight to the point. "No, no, no. Come on, we still have time," I continued, marching through the front door and up the stairs to Margaret's room, with my friend trailing along behind me.

"What's wrong with it?" asked Margaret. I could tell she was already resigned to the fact that her pale pink party dress from Dress Perfect would be spending the night back on its hanger.

"Well, first, you wore it to Christine's birthday party six months ago. And second, it's . . ." I trailed off, looking the dress up and down, trying to find a way to tell her it would send her crush entirely the wrong message. Catching Margaret's disappointed expression, I softened my tone. "It's just not flirty enough. Tonight's not just the Sweetheart Dance, it's your first date with Xavier. You've got to show off those curves! Remind him how lucky he is that he landed a date with you."

"Oh . . . yeah, I guess you're right," Margaret conceded,

looking to her closet worriedly and adjusting her glasses. "But what will I—"

"Where's that little black dress we got at Callie's?" I interrupted, impatiently flipping through the hangers in the closet.

"Behind the door, but—"

"But what?" I asked, turning to pull the dress, still wrapped in its plastic cover, off the back of the closet door.

"It's so . . . short," Margaret admitted, her eyes glued to the hemline.

I looked at my friend and closed the mirrored closet door in front of her. "Margie," I leveled in my best no-nonsense voice. "Look at those legs. Hike up that long-ass skirt you're wearing and look."

Margaret obliged, shrugging.

"You've got gorgeous gams, girl! You can't not show those things off."

"Gams?" Margaret laughed. "Who says that?"

I giggled. "I couldn't resist. Look at this fantastic flapper dress! I'd be dying to wear this! It's perfect for tonight."

Margaret held up the vintage twenties gown, complete with black fringe and crystal beading. It really was beautiful, and Callie had sworn it was authentic.

"Okay," Margaret caved. "Find me some shoes."

Suppressing a squeal of glee, I dove back into the closet in search of footwear while Margaret changed, and came up with a pair of strappy black heels that were hidden under a mountain of flats. I helped pin her curls into a stylish twist on top of her head, watching her transform from awkward teen to sophisticated young woman before my eyes.

"Perfect!" I exclaimed when Margaret stepped into the shoes and twirled, the fringe floating around her. "Xavier's going to melt, you're so hot."

"Speaking of hot," Margaret said, grabbing her extra-long coat, "I'll need this so I don't turn to ice—and to make it past my dad."

We laughed our way back down the stairs arm in arm,

Margaret's shoulders loosening with every step, then freezing when the doorbell rang.

"It's him," Margaret said.

We made it through the obligatory stern looks from Margaret's dad and piled into Xavier's car. Even though it wasn't far to the Annex (nothing was really *far* in our little town), it was too icy to walk more than a block or two in heels.

By the time we got to the Annex, my mood had turned from giddy to glum. I walked into the building wondering why I was even there. With no sweetheart to bring to the Sweetheart Dance, why bother? As I watched Xavier's eyes nearly bug out of his head when Margaret slipped out of her coat, though, I remembered, and I couldn't keep a smile from my lips. My friend had been pining after the object of her desire for months, and I was happy to finally see them on the right track.

Handing my own coat over at the coat check table, I smoothed my hands over my silver sheath dress and looked around. Now that the important part was over with, I'd have to make the best of the evening.

The space inside the Annex had been rearranged to accommodate the event, and I had to admit the decorating committee had done a great job. The stage at the far end was set up for one of the better local bands, the Mountain Monsters, but just now the DJ, on a separate dais to the right, was playing upbeat music and taking requests for slow dances later on.

I turned to my left and headed for the refreshments table. As I turned back with a plastic cup of pink punch, someone walking in the door caught my eye. Someone new.

I watched as he stopped short of the dance floor and appeared to scan the crowd for a familiar face. His shaggy blond hair shone in the multicolored lights, and long lashes framed pale blue eyes. He was in a sleek black leather jacket and dark jeans. As I watched, he ran his fingers through that hair, sending shivers down my spine.

"Are you going to stand there like a statue all night, Celeste, or come show us your moves?" A voice beside me shook me out of my guy-ogling reverie.

"Emma, you're here!" I said a little too loudly. "Just hydrating before dancing," I covered, raising my cup to my lips and hoping she hadn't seen my eyes glued to the hottie.

"Well, finish that and come on! We need you in our girl circle of power," Emma said, her long light brown hair pulled into a sleek braid down her back, with curled tendrils framing her heart-shaped face.

Nodding, I drained my cup and turned to put it on the table behind her, surreptitiously taking another peek toward the entrance. A steady stream of people now flowed in through the door, but the new guy was nowhere to be seen.

I let my friends drag me out to the dance floor and tried to put the guy out of my mind. I hadn't found one yet who had held my interest past the first conversation. No doubt this one would be the same. I reminded myself to live in the moment and enjoy the night out, and to stop searching the crowd for a leather jacket.

"DAD, I'M HOME," I called as I walked in the door. I lived with my father in a modest two-bedroom house on Third Street, a short walk from both the high school and Miller's Plaza, where my dad's office was. He was a business accountant, keeping the books and doing taxes for several of the small businesses around town.

"You're home early," Dad replied, coming out of his study, where he spent most of his evenings during tax season. "How was the dance?"

"Oh, fine, just the same kids I see at school every day all dressed up," I said, hanging my coat by the door. Looking up to see my father's eyebrows pinched together, I quickly readjusted my own expression into a believable smile. "Fun. It was fun."

His face relaxed into a mirror of my own, and he gave a quick nod. "Good, well, there's lasagna in the fridge if you're hungry. I've got some more forms to finish up," he said, heading back toward his desk.

I went to my own room, getting ready for bed while I pondered a set of blue eyes framed by long lashes.

~

EVEN THOUGH I absolutely intended to sleep in on Friday, since we had a four-day weekend for Presidents' Day, I was up as usual at six in the morning. Unable to fall back to sleep, I got ready for my day. Emma, Gianna, and I had plans to go skiing later, but I had a few hours to kill, so I left a note for my dad, whom I could hear in the shower, and walked toward the town square. The sun was out, and the mountain air was fresh and mild. It would be a great day to hit the slopes.

I walked into Broastful Brew and ordered a coffee and a muffin, then settled in at my favorite corner table. It was a busy weekday morning, but early enough that most of the high school kids were probably still in bed. The town square was decorated with an explosion of heart decorations in pink and red. A beautiful woman with long black hair strode through the park in heels, still dressed in her slinky gown from the night before. I liked the peaceful, quiet vibe in the coffeehouse. I occasionally went to the other coffee shop in the square, Coffee Haven, if I happened to be shopping nearby, but I could have sworn I caught Willow giving me strange sideways looks whenever I went in there. It gave me the creeps. Mabel, the owner of Broastful Brew, always had a smile and a kind word for everyone.

As I gazed out at the square, I tuned out the conversations around me, until Irene Beckett's voice sounded from the table just behind me. She was a little old lady who used to teach at the high school decades ago and still thought she had the right to tell everyone how to live.

"Is that Tasha Young doing the walk of shame this morning?"

I glanced over to see her breakfast companion, Sybil Carson, who was always an eager audience for Mrs. Beckett's gossip. Usually they hung out at Coffee Haven, but I guessed they were here gathering information on someone or another.

"It looks more like a walk of pride to me," Sybil replied with a smile.

"Well, it's too bad she was never my student," Irene said, "or I'd have talked some decency into her. Look at that dress! It's fit for a—"

"Can I get you ladies anything else?" Mabel broke into their conversation just as Mrs. Beckett was about to lose her composure. I hid a giggle behind another bite of my muffin.

"No, thank you, dear," Mrs. Beckett said with an edge in her voice. "Have you seen the new woman in town yet? She's got a teenage son—it's just the two of them—and they just arrived this week."

"No," Mabel sighed, "they haven't been in here. I heard they're staying with Mrs. Walsh, so they probably go over to Coffee Haven for their caffeine."

"Well, don't you worry about that," Mrs. Beckett said. "One bite of those cookies, and they'll be hooked!"

"Why, thank you, Irene. Now I'd better get back to the counter. Let me know if you need anything!"

I focused back on my coffee. A new family in town, just this week. Could it be the guy I had spotted at the dance last night? I had kept an eye out for him the rest of the evening, but hadn't seen him again. I was beginning to think he was just an illusion.

Shrugging off the thought, I cleared my dishes to the counter and waved goodbye to Mabel. If he was at the dance, he'd be at school, and I'd find out soon enough who he was. But I had more important things to worry about. Like getting my ski on.

CHAPTER 2

CELESTE

*I*t seemed like half the high school was out on the slopes already as I rode the ski lift up Mount Mae with Emma and Gianna.

"So are you ready for Hell or High Water, Celeste?" Gianna asked, referring to the double black diamond trail on the slope we were ascending.

"I want to warm up on a blue square first, then we'll see," I said. "It's been too long since I was out here. Not like you two ski bunnies. How about starting on Renae's Way?"

My friends looked at each other and nodded. "Sure," they said in unison. I loved how easygoing they were.

"How late did you guys stay at the dance last night?" I asked, watching Emma stifle a yawn.

"Oh, they shut it down at eleven. But we went to Gianna's afterward and watched *Thor*." She got a dreamy look in her eye. "I wish I knew some movie stars."

This prompted a giggle from Gianna. "Look around, Emma. There are plenty of beautiful people in town. Some of them are even our own age!"

She pointed to the group of skiers waiting for a turn on the slope as we reached the end of the lift. I looked over and spotted

Laurel Alverson chatting up Brice Blackstone, and Samuel Milton sneaking glances at Aurelia Petran.

"Yeah, but they're all so . . . ordinary," Emma whined. At this, Gianna burst out laughing, and didn't stop until we reached the top of the trail. She did tend to have an odd sense of humor at times.

I took the first run, and met my girls at the bottom to board the ski lift again, after which we proceeded to ski the black diamonds for the rest of the afternoon. We had all grown up in Havenwood Falls, where skiing was one of the few available pastimes in the winter, so we had all become rather good at it, if not quite experts.

It being Friday, there weren't many adults on the slopes, but there were a few couples who had taken a long weekend and were being all lovey-dovey in the crisp mountain air. Mesmerized, we all watched Rusty Higgins zig and zag as he descended the mountain. Sherry winked at us when he turned out of sight and smacked her lips as she prepared to follow him down.

After the sun was long past its peak, we were lined up at the top of the Hell or High Water trail for what would be one of the last runs of the day. Emma was telling us about her plans for spring break—she was going to Maui with her family—and the woman in front of us kept looking back.

"Do you girls think you're ready for this trail?" she finally asked.

Gianna, Emma, and I looked at each other, stunned at this woman's gall, and burst out laughing.

"Yeah, I think so," I managed to get out after the hilarity died down a bit, "since this is our fourth run up here today."

"Well, maybe you should spend more time focusing and less time chattering," she snipped. "This course requires focus, and you'd do well to respect it."

I gaped. Who did this woman think she was? I put on my sweetest smile. "We are so glad that tourists like you are here to educate us on our slopes. Oh, look, it's your turn. Best focus on your skiing, now. We wouldn't want you to have an accident."

She harrumphed—really!—and turned around to descend the slope. We watched her in stony silence as she collected herself and then took off down the side of the mountain. I narrowed my eyes, cursing her in my head, watching for some flaw in her technique I could taunt her about when we ran into her at the bottom. Were her legs too far apart? All of a sudden, her left foot shot out, the ski catching a stray patch of ice and sending her tumbling toward the tree line.

Everyone gasped as she crashed into a tree. Judging by the force with which she hit, she definitely broke an arm, maybe a rib or two as well.

An employee from the ski resort arrived and called for paramedics. We watched sadly as he then closed off the run for the day.

"Sorry, folks," he said. "Head down that way for the next run." He pointed across the mountain to the next trail, and we all tromped off toward it.

I shot a glance back at the woman crumpled against the tree and found her glaring at me. As if *I* was responsible for her mishap. Shaking my head, I continued on after my friends. *Some people will blame anyone but themselves.*

"Well, I'm done," Gianna said when we reached the end of the next run. "I've got a family dinner to go to tonight, and I'll catch hell if I'm late."

"Are we still on for tomorrow night?" Emma asked, taking off her hat and combing fingers through her straight hair. We had made plans to meet at Margaret's house for a movie marathon and sleepover.

"Yes, definitely," Gianna said. "I'll bring the popcorn."

Emma grinned at me as we made our way back to the parking lot. She loved getting the girls together at every opportunity, and this weekend was like a dream for her.

I arrived home to a dark house. Even though it was almost six, my dad was still at his office. He would be working for another hour or two, so I went in and turned on all the lights, to make me feel less alone. The truth was, though, I needed some time to myself. Spending all day with my friends was fun but draining. Funny as it may sound, I felt as though I was constantly monitoring their moods and making sure they had a good time. It was like I'd been directing traffic for hours. I shook my head to clear the strange feeling and refocus, then warmed up some leftover lasagna and settled in on the sofa to watch TV.

I woke with a start when my dad arrived home, slamming the door behind him and muttering something about motorcycles and not respecting traffic laws.

"Hi, Dad."

"Hmm." It was more a grunt than a response. I tried again.

"Everything okay at work today?"

"One month until business taxes are due, and I still don't have receipts from half my clients. Half!" he began to rant. "You know they'll all magically come up with them a week before the deadline, and I'll be stuck working around the clock to get everything done on time."

"Life of an accountant?"

He scoffed. "Yeah, well, it gets older every year. Why can't people be more organized? I'm not a machine!"

"I know, Daddy. People are the absolute worst."

His face softened as he looked at me. "Ah well, without them, where would I be, eh?" He nodded at my empty plate, still on the living room coffee table. "Sorry I didn't make it home in time for dinner, Celeste."

"Oh, it's no biggie. I was famished after spending all day up on Mount Mae."

"Ah, I forgot you were heading up there today. How was it?"

"Fine. Go on and put your briefcase down, Dad. I'm going to go to bed. I am wiped."

He bobbed his head and went into his office. I hoped he'd at least take a break to eat and relax a bit tonight, instead of picking right back up working again.

I filled the next day with homework, wanting to get my English Lit assignment done so I could enjoy the rest of the weekend. It was a comparative essay on *Brave New World* and *The Hunger Games*, and it would not do to have it hanging over my head for the next three days.

~

I HAD a bounce in my step the first day back at school after the long weekend. On Saturday night, we got the play-by-play of Margaret's dance date with Xavier, including their first kiss. She was still so giddy, and it made me happy to see my friend all aflutter. On Monday, I put my headphones on and took a walk out to the falls, then returned home, built a cozy fire, and spent the rest of the day reading.

I had gotten my fill of solitude and was ready to return to society. As I walked into English Lit, I turned in my paper to the box on Mr. Zander's desk. Taking my seat, I looked up to see the guy I'd noticed at the dance walking into the classroom. His eyes swept the room before he turned and introduced himself to Mr. Zander, who pointed him to a seat near the door.

As the guy strode toward the desk, Mr. Zander began the class without mention of the new student. I tried hard to focus on the class discussion, but my eyes kept straying to the corner desk. I was lost in thought, trying to will his blue gaze to turn my way, hearing only the jumbled sound of tuned-out speaking.

"Celeste?"

Oh no. What did he just say? I tried to replay the last ten seconds in my mind, but all I got was something about a leather jacket. I was sure that wasn't Mr. Zander's question.

"I'm sorry?"

"Sorry for what, exactly?" Mr. Zander mocked me.

"I'm sorry I didn't hear the whole question. Could you please repeat it?" I gave him my best innocent look.

The teacher sighed at me. "Please explain the role of the utopian dream in *Brave New World*."

"Oh. Um. Well, Huxley uses the idea of utopia to extend our claimed ideals to their extremes and show that what we think is best for us will ultimately imprison us," I said, parroting the paper I had just turned in.

"Aha, and . . ." he said, running his finger down his clipboard, "Margaret, what does Ms. Atwood have to say about the dangers of taking our ideals to their extremes?"

I breathed a sigh of relief as my friend explained the premise of *The Handmaid's Tale*. I refocused back on the discussion in case I was called on again, which was all too likely to happen in our small class. I was glad when the bell finally rang, and began to put my notes away. When I looked up, the new guy had already slipped out the door and was gone.

"Are you studying in the library during tutorial today, Celeste?"

I turned to see Margaret putting her bag on her shoulder. "Yeah, I'll be there. Hey," I said, lowering my voice to a near whisper, "do you know who the new guy is?"

"New guy?" she repeated, looking around. "I don't see anyone new."

"He was sitting in the corner. You didn't see him come in?"

Margaret shook her curls. "No, I was trying to finish my Trig homework. I was a little busy this weekend . . ."

I chuckled. "A little busy making out with your new boyfriend, you mean?"

Pink infused Margaret's face. "Celeste!" She swatted me on the arm. "Well, maybe," she conceded. "He's so sweet, C, you don't understand . . ."

I tuned out as she babbled on about Xavier. She was right about one thing. I didn't understand. Boy-crazy was not in anyone's description of me, ever. But I'd be lying if I said the mystery of this new guy wasn't starting to drive me a little mad.

As we walked to our lockers, I scanned the hallway. He was nowhere to be seen, but Emma was coming our way in a hurry.

"Oh. My. God. You guys won't believe what just happened. Gary Smithson tried to pick a fight with the wrong guy. Come on!"

Margaret and I glanced at each other, then took off after Emma, who flew down the hall in front of us. We rounded the corner and saw a small circle of students surrounding two boys facing off. One of them was the mystery guy.

I gasped as Gary lunged at the taller boy, knocking the wind out of him with a shoulder to his middle. But tall, blond, and elusive was quick to recover, twisting to let Gary's forward momentum sail past him and straight into the lockers behind him. Gary rammed head-first into the lockers, and a trickle of blood ran down his forehead.

"Break it up," commanded Mr. Friske, striding purposefully around the corner. Students skittered away to avoid getting caught up in the principal's gaze, which was casting about for likely witnesses. My feet were sluggish, though, as Margaret tugged on my arm.

"Go on to class," I muttered to her, not even turning my head. My eyes were glued to the scene in front of me.

I saw her shrug out of the corner of my eye as she said, "Okay," and turned toward Ms. Wells's classroom.

Mr. Friske examined Gary's cut, then helped the bully to his feet and turned to face the new guy. "Mr. Burns," he said sternly, "I don't know how it was where you came from, but this type of behavior will not be tolerated in my school."

His only response was a cool stare.

"Go wait for me in my office while I take your sparring partner to the nurse."

"It wasn't his fault," I found myself piping up.

All eyes turned toward me.

"Did you see what happened here, Miss Long?" Mr. Friske asked.

"Uh, not all of it, but I heard that Gary started—"

"You heard, did you, Miss Long?" Mr. Friske cut me off. "Well, hearsay won't hold up in a court of law and it won't hold up in my determination either. Why don't you get to class before you earn yourself a tardy." It was not a question.

I turned to go, but not before I caught those bright blue eyes fixed on my face. I shivered and fast-walked to Bio lab, trying to dispel the blush crawling up my cheeks.

~

JONATHAN

I WAITED in the principal's office while he took that bully to the nurse. This was exactly why I didn't want to come to this school. I preferred to mind my own business and for others to mind theirs. Having a jackass for a locker neighbor was not in my control.

"Well, Mr. Burns," the principal said, entering his office and closing the door behind him. "Let's start from the beginning, shall we? Tell me why you were fighting with Mr. Smithson."

"I wasn't fighting. I didn't throw a punch."

"Well, why were you there?" he asked. I was asking myself the same thing.

"My locker is there."

The principal picked up a folder from his desk, the same one that the secretary had leafed through this morning when she gave me my class schedule and locker combination. "Locker 246?"

"That's the one."

He pulled another page from his desk drawer. "And Mr. Smithson is at—" he ran his finger down the page—"247."

He looked up at me. I looked back.

"Did you say something to Mr. Smithson?"

Of course words were exchanged. But Friske didn't need to be apprised of them. I really didn't care what Jackass thought of my haircut. I shrugged. "I might have said hi."

Friske narrowed his eyes at me. "And how did he hurt his hand?"

"His punching form could use some work."

The principal raised an eyebrow. "So why aren't you the one in the nurse's office?"

I shrugged. "He didn't land many."

"Are you hurt?"

"It's nothing serious." Never mind that he *had* landed a few punches. My jaw would bruise, even though no one would see it, and my internal organs were still feeling the impact of that shoulder.

"Maybe you need to go see the nurse, too."

"I'm fine," I said. I had no desire to run into that buffoon again today.

The principal heaved a big sigh, as if I was keeping him from something important. "So how did he end up with his face cut?"

"He charged me." I shrugged again. "I moved."

Friske looked at me sideways, like he didn't believe a word of it. But he clearly didn't have anything on me, because he said, "As this is your first offense *and* your first day, I won't suspend you. Detention for the remainder of the week, and see the secretary for a new locker assignment."

"Yes, sir," I said, standing to leave.

"Mr. Burns," Friske said, stopping me as I headed for the door.

I turned back. "Yes?"

"Let's make this the last offense, shall we?"

"Yes, sir," I repeated, and got out of there before he ran out of stern looks.

～

MAN, it sucked being the new kid. I didn't know my way around town yet, and most of the people I passed seemed friendly, but I could tell they were watching me like hawks. That's why I kept my guard up most of the time. Technically part of my glamour, it allowed me to go unnoticed by most people. It didn't exactly make me invisible, just created a sort of blind spot around me that it took extra attention to penetrate, unless you were right on top of me. Like Jackass was when he decided to pick a fight.

At least the place we were staying was close to the school, so I didn't have to walk through the center of town every day. Mrs. Walsh was living in the spacious house pretty much by herself, with her parents in a separate apartment over the garage, since her daughter Makenna had gone off to college. She was kind enough to take in my mom and me when we arrived less than two weeks ago, and I think she was glad for the company.

"Hi, Mom. Hi, Mrs. Walsh," I said, spying them in the kitchen sipping tea as I walked in the door.

"Jonathan," my mother said, "we need to talk."

Shit. She was mad. Of course the principal would have called her. I dropped my bag by the door and joined them at the high counter separating the kitchen from the dining room.

"How was your day?" she began, causing me to sigh inwardly. *I guess we'll be taking the long way around, then.*

"First day at a new school. I'm still trying to get my bearings."

"Did you make any friends?"

I glanced at Mrs. Walsh, who had turned and was pretending not to hear us as she rinsed off some dishes.

"It's all right," my mom reassured me. "Helena knows how we came to be here."

I nodded, continuing more quietly nonetheless, "No, I kept to myself, like you said."

"Then why did I get a call from Mr. Friske today about a fight?" she asked, anger creeping into her voice.

"Because the locker next to mine belonged to a bully," I

snapped back. I was already tired of being blamed for shit that was not my fault.

Taken aback, my mom sat straighter on her stool and held my gaze for a long moment before taking another sip of tea and clearing her throat.

"I understand the other boy was injured, but not seriously. Did you hit him?"

"Not once, Mom. Defensive maneuvers only."

She nodded. "Okay. He's been suspended for two weeks."

"And my locker's been moved," I added.

"Good. Do you think you can steer clear of him after he comes back?"

"Yeah. He's a senior, so I don't think I have any classes with him."

She picked up her teacup and saucer and took them over to Mrs. Walsh at the sink. "All right. Let's go, then. I've made an appointment for you at the medical center."

What? "Why?"

"Mr. Friske suggested you get checked out, even though you said you weren't hurt."

"I'm fine."

"Okay. Let's go."

"A human doctor won't see anything, Mom. It's a waste of time."

"The doctor's not human. Next argument?" She picked up her car keys and walked toward the front door.

Rolling my eyes at my mother, I picked up my bag and followed her out the door, returning Mrs. Walsh's wave bidding us goodbye. I knew it was no good to argue with Mom once she had her mind made up. I was glad to see her acting like her old self again, though. The past month had been tough on both of us, and maybe getting used to life in a new town was just what we needed to distract us.

We had come to Havenwood Falls from another supposed haven, which proved to be not so secure, halfway around the world. It seemed no place was safe for us. The war raged on in Faerie, but its ramifications were felt in this world too. My father had fallen victim to it, but my mother was determined to keep us out of harm's way. I wasn't so sure that this new sanctuary was going to protect us, but it was probably as good a place as any to hide. We would just have to get better at hiding.

CHAPTER 3

CELESTE

*A*fter school, I walked across the street to my dad's office. I helped him out with filing and scanning a few times a week during the busy season so Polly, his office assistant, could concentrate on contacting clients and making sure all the deadlines were met.

"Hi, Polly," I said as I walked in.

"Hi, hon," she replied, looking up just long enough to smile before the phone started to ring. Her expression quickly flashed to annoyance before the smile returned so she could answer with a cheery "Long and Associates."

The space had three offices for accountants, though only two were occupied. The third office was half filled with boxes of old files and a desk with a computer and a scanner. That was where I worked, scanning receipts and other documents that clients brought in with their tax forms, and filing away originals we needed to keep.

My dad's door was shut, meaning he was in a meeting with a client, and the second office was dark. An independent accountant, Hunter James, rented the space from my dad and met with clients there, but he was seldom around.

I got to work and wasn't at it long before my dad knocked on the open door to get my attention. I turned, surprised to see he had someone with him.

"Hi, sweetie," he said. "Good day at school?"

"It was fine," I replied, keeping an eye on the man behind him.

"Good. I don't know if you've met Elsmed Fairchild before," he said, moving aside and gesturing to the man, who looked to be about a hundred years old, but stood upright in a suit and tie. "He was . . . a friend of your mother's."

"Oh," I said, a bit stunned. My mother did not often come up in conversation. "Hello."

The man's steely gaze seemed to chill me where I sat, and I shivered. "Good afternoon, Miss Long. May I have a few moments of your time?" Though he looked frail and walked with a cane, his voice was smooth and commanding.

"Of course, please come into my office," I tried to joke, but it came off empty as my growing unease made my voice shaky.

Unsmiling, he strode to the empty chair on the other side of the desk and sat, those eyes on me the whole time.

Polly came to the door and slipped a note to my father, probably letting him know a client was waiting on him.

"Excuse me, Mr. Fairchild, I've got to take this call. I'll be back in a few moments."

"No rush," said the old man. "I won't take too much of your daughter's time."

My father nodded and then abandoned me to this stranger.

I gave my best attempt at a smile, waiting for him to speak, because he clearly had an agenda.

"How are you doing, Miss Long?" he asked, making it sound less like a polite greeting and more like a therapist concerned about his patient.

"Fine?" I said hesitantly. *Who is this guy, and why is he asking me how I am?*

"As your father said, I knew your mother, and, well, her family, and I thought it was about time I checked in on you."

After fourteen years, he thought now *he needed to check on me?* "Oh. Well, I'm fine," I repeated. *Was this guy senile or something?*

His eyes seemed to flash a moment, and he heaved a sigh. "Any mood disturbances lately? Anything strange happen to you? Or around you?"

"Uh . . . no," I said slowly, not sure what he was getting at.

"And your father's been around? Not working too hard, is he?" the man asked.

What is this, an interrogation? "My father's around plenty," I snapped. "And in case you haven't noticed, I'm old enough to take care of myself." I'd had about enough of this weird guy and his weird questions.

He reared back, as if *I'd* said something to offend *him.* "Well, perhaps you should try keeping a lid on that temper, Miss Long," he had the nerve to say to me. "It won't go well for you if you continue to take it out on innocent people."

I felt my face flush instantly, whether from mortification or anger I wasn't sure. *Is he threatening me now? Who the hell is this guy to come in here and tell me how to act? He didn't even know me before today.*

"I've had my eye on you from afar for quite a while, Miss Long," he said, as if in answer to my unspoken question. "But your father has done an excellent job of caring for you, and I have not heretofore felt it was necessary to check on your well-being."

"But you feel it's necessary to do so now?" I retorted, trying to restrain the spitefulness from my voice.

"Well, as you pointed out yourself, you are nearly ready to strike out on your own," he said, adopting a conciliatory tone, like he was trying to soothe me. "I thought it wise to make sure you had everything you needed in the way of support."

Ha! This guy, supportive? I took a breath, about to give this old man a piece of my mind when my dad appeared back in the doorway.

"Sorry about that. I've been trying to get that client on the phone for weeks. Have you told her about the internship yet?"

My focus darted from my dad back to the old man. "Internship?"

"Ah, no, I was just getting to that." That piercing gaze settled on me again. "I came to see if you would be interested in interning for me. I would provide training, and you can help me with various errands that I need done."

"What kind of training?" I asked, too curious to reject the offer out of hand.

"Mr. Fairchild is a very important member of the community," my dad interjected. "He can teach you all sorts of leadership skills."

"What kind of errands?" I asked, letting suspicion creep into my voice.

He chuckled, though I wasn't sure what was so amusing. "Nothing too strenuous, I promise. I won't have you scrubbing floors or fetching coffee."

That wasn't much of an answer.

"My dad needs my help here," I began to decline this shady offer. "I couldn't leave him shorthanded during the busy season."

"Nonsense," said my father. "I've been thinking about hiring some part-time help for filing. You need to get some experience doing something more meaningful. Think of how it'll look on your college applications!"

I could see he'd already been sold on this idea. Filing *was* awfully boring. Maybe I could give this internship a chance, just to humor him. I could always quit if it wasn't my thing.

"Can you start tomorrow?" said Mr. Fairchild.

"I haven't said yes yet," I answered, then kicked myself mentally for admitting I was going to accept.

"Well, let's get on with it. I haven't got all day," he said.

I almost narrowed my eyes and glared at him, but I knew my dad respected this guy and would be upset if I lost my cool.

"I can start tomorrow, if you're sure you don't need me, Dad," I said, turning to my father again. He was practically beaming.

"No, no, she's all yours," he said, crushing my last hope of getting out of this bad idea.

Mr. Fairchild rapped his cane on the floor and rose. "Tomorrow, then. Meet me at City Hall after school."

Without waiting for a response, he walked toward the door, my father thanking him for the opportunity. I turned my back on them so they didn't see my massive eye-roll.

THE NEXT DAY, I trudged through the snow from the high school to City Hall after school. Mr. Fairchild was nowhere to be seen outside, so I went in the front door and looked around the large atrium. There were a few people bustling to and fro, but no old men with frosty stares.

I went to the security desk and asked a uniformed guard, who looked me up and down, as though wondering what I was doing asking after Mr. Fairchild. Finally, he said, "Down that hallway," pointed to a hall leading toward the back of the building, and turned away.

Raising my eyebrows at the curt response, I proceeded across the atrium and found a hallway with several offices for city and courthouse business. I walked past the Finance Department's office, the City Comptroller's office, and the Planning & Building Department's office before I found a series of doors bearing names, but no titles or departments. I came to a dark wood door with a frosted glass window pane that was embossed with the name Elsmed Fairchild in gold letters. I listened for a moment, but heard nothing. I couldn't tell whether anyone was in the office or not, try as I might to peer through the glass. I took a deep, steadying breath and knocked.

"Come in!" a distant voice called.

I turned the knob and stepped inside. There was a desk, though no one was sitting behind it, and some filing cabinets occupying the corners of the small room. Another entryway stood to my left, the door open.

"Mr. Fairchild?" I asked the empty space.

"In here," his voice called from the open doorway, and I stepped toward it. Elsmed sat behind a large desk piled high with papers and file folders, in front of which sat two upholstered chairs. Another more casual seating area off to the side contained a coffee table, more comfortable-looking furniture, and a buffet with a tea set on top. Along one wall were bookshelves filled with volumes, some looking new and some very, very old.

"Finally," he said as I approached. "Did you get lost on the way?" he began, darkening my mood.

"You neglected to mention exactly where your office was," I sniped, bringing that piercing gaze down on myself.

"Did I," he intoned. It was not a question, and I didn't answer, even as he gave me a long stare. "Sit down, please," he commanded, gesturing to the chairs in front of him.

I did as instructed and folded my hands in my lap as he considered me. *Why did my dad think this was a good idea?* I mentally rolled my eyes at my father. He really did care about me and tried his best to give me every opportunity, but sometimes his efforts were *so* misguided.

"Respect," Elsmed barked, startling me out of my internal rant.

"Respect?" I parroted, when he didn't seem inclined to continue.

"Respect," he repeated, "will be our first area of study. But first, let me make a few things clear. Nothing—and I mean *nothing*—that you observe during your internship with me may be disclosed to any other individual. Not your father, your best friend, your boyfriend, or even another person with an office in these halls. Do you understand?"

I nodded. "Complete confidentiality. Got it."

He studied me for another minute, then continued. "Second, do not allow anyone to accompany you to these offices. They are seldom visited, and I expect them to remain so. You may come and go for the purposes of your study with me, but at all other times, unless I have directed you to do so, there is no reason for you to be here. Clear?"

"Yes," I agreed. *I certainly don't intend to be here more than absolutely necessary.*

"Third," he said, "I do not have time to repeat myself or answer unnecessary questions. If I deem your questions relevant, I will answer them at the appropriate time. Is that clear?"

"Um, I guess so," I said with less certainty. *How am I supposed to know what he deems relevant? I don't even know what this internship is about. And what happens if I ask an "unnecessary" question? I guess he'll just ignore me? Seems pretty rude.*

"Now we can start on respect."

He lectured me for half an hour on the importance of respect. Respect for my elders, teachers, peers—basically everyone. He told me that courtesy begins within, and that I should always keep my thoughts civil, so that my words and actions would follow suit. I tried—really tried—not to roll my eyes, and I thought I did a pretty good job of keeping a straight face, but as he went on (and on and on) I felt like he was becoming angrier at me. Finally, he gave me a task to do.

"Take this stack of papers and put them in chronological order," he said. "While you work, practice keeping your thoughts respectful."

Stifling a sigh, I took the papers from him. *Great, more filing.*

"You can work at the desk out there," he said, gesturing toward the doorway, "but be sure to keep the area tidy."

"Yes, Mr. Fairchild," I replied, and took my pile of papers into the next room.

I looked at the first page. All it contained was a date. *Huh, must be a cover page,* I thought, flipping to the next one. That page had only a date as well. I paged through the stack quickly. Every page was completely blank, except for the date.

Feeling ready to explode with rage, I slammed the stack down on the desk. *Busy work? What the hell kind of internship was this?*

"Remember to focus on respectful thoughts," came the pompous voice from the old man's office.

Taking a deep breath, I tried to calm myself. Maybe it was just a mistake. Maybe he'd given me the wrong stack. Chiding myself for being so quick to anger, I stood, gathering the papers, and went back to Mr. Fairchild's office.

"I think there's a mistake," I said, making sure to keep my voice friendly. "All of these pages just have a date, and nothing else."

"It should be easy for you to put them in chronological order, then," he replied, his gaze fixed on the file open in front of him.

"Yes, but why—" I began, but stopped when his eyes cut to me.

"*Why* is not your concern, Miss Long. This task, while dull, needs to be completed. It should leave your mind disengaged enough to practice respectful thought. If you don't do it, I will have to. And I have more important matters to attend to. So if you don't mind . . ."

I do *mind*, I thought. *I didn't want to be here in the first place, and this is just a waste of time.* Unable to bring myself to say something nice, I turned my back and returned to the desk.

After a lot of internal grumbling and shuffling of pages, I settled into a rhythm. Just as I was about to crack a smile as I neared the end of my pile, Elsmed brought another stack of papers out and dropped it on the desk, saying only, "These too."

I only just managed to keep the pouting frown off my face as he shuffled back into his office. I decided that putting up a fight wasn't going to get me out of there any faster, and kept sorting pages.

After about two hours of the most boring internship known to man, there was a knock on the door, followed by a woman's voice. "Elsmed?"

Without waiting for a response, she entered, stopping short when she saw me. "Celeste?"

"Mrs. Augustine?" *What was Gianna's grandmother doing here?*

"What are you doing here?" she asked me, clearly as taken aback to find me there as I was to see her.

"Chronologizing?" I replied automatically, since I had just been debating with myself whether that was a real word. "I-I'm doing some work for Mr. Fairchild," I stammered.

"Are those Court records?" she said, her voice rising in pitch as if she had asked if the chair I was sitting in was on fire.

"Calm down, Mathilde. Of course not. She can't read them anyway," said Elsmed, coming through the doorway from his office.

Now it was my turn to be incredulous. "Can't read what?" I snapped. "They only have dates on them!"

"See?" he said, turning to Mrs. Augustine as if that answered all the questions. "Now, would you care to join me for a cup of tea?" He motioned for her to enter his office.

What the hell? My rage came barreling back, and I felt my face heating even as I somehow managed to keep my expression mild. I reminded myself that my dad would be very disappointed with me if I blew up at this geezer, so I'd better keep a lid on my temper.

Still obviously flustered, but at least somewhat appeased, Mrs. Augustine sighed, nodded, and went through the door, giving me a sideways glance.

"Almost finished?" he asked me.

I looked down at the last page, then quickly filed it in its spot and straightened the stack.

"Finished," I answered, mentally patting myself on the back for doing a fair job of keeping the anger out of my voice.

"Good," he said. "We are done for the day. Please come by again after your lessons on Friday."

I sighed with relief. At least I would have a break tomorrow from the never-ending pile of blank pages.

"Thank you, Mr. Fairchild," I said, though it almost physically pained me.

He gave me a tight smile.

"You're welcome, child," he said, before turning, following Mrs. Augustine into his office, and closing the door.

I got out of there and scurried home as fast as I could before the sun dipped behind the mountains.

CHAPTER 4

JONATHAN

I was used to small towns. Before coming to Havenwood Falls, we had been hiding out in a village in Portugal, surrounded by olive groves and vineyards. But even in the secluded countryside there, the hunters found us. When we heard a stranger on the road had been asking after us, my mother and I fled, escaping with only the clothes on our backs and the treasure my parents had been tasked with keeping safe. We later learned that our home had been burned to the ground that very day.

Before that, we'd lived in the highlands of Scotland, where my father had relied too heavily on his skills of concealment—the same skills I now possessed—and paid for that mistake with his life. It was only a matter of time before the hunters tracked us here; I was sure of it.

I had asked my mother if we shouldn't hide in a city—if it would be easier to remain anonymous among the crowds and noise. She said that it might be easier to remain hidden for a while, but that that very anonymity made it a dangerous place for hunted fae such as ourselves—our hunters could come and go as easily, and unnoticed, as we could.

So I looked over my shoulder often, kept my shields up, and

used my enhanced glamour to make myself nearly invisible. This usually worked to keep us safe for a while.

I was used to small towns. But Havenwood Falls was *not* the average small town. It's hard to describe, but it felt like there was a delicate balance between the people here, as if one wrong step could throw everyone off kilter. I wondered if we'd stay long enough to assimilate into the town's population, or if we would be on the run again soon. My mom seemed to think that we'd finally found our safe haven. I was far more skeptical.

Being in detention for the fourth day in a row didn't bother me. I used the time to acquaint myself with the topics already covered in my assigned classes and with those yet to be covered. I found that, even though I had moved from school to school over the years, and they were generally small rural schools, I was already familiar with most of the material that had been covered. The only classes I was behind in were Government and English Literature.

I flipped through my Government book, keeping one eye on the other two students in the classroom and the teacher at the desk next to the whiteboard. She had been in and out of the room, clearly having more important things to do than babysit a few high school kids. Since the code of conduct was pretty strict, most serious infractions merited a suspension, and students in detention had done little more than arrive late for class or talk back to a teacher.

The aggressor who had landed me here was himself suspended for ten days, although I assumed he'd spend part of that time in recovery from his self-inflicted wounds. *Dumbass.* As far as I had heard, it was very rare to get off as easy as detention for being caught in a fight. I figured that somehow Mr. Friske was feeling charitable toward the new student, or he had concluded that I was blameless in the incident. I doubted it was the latter, so was busy pondering the likelihood of the former.

The teacher returned just as I glanced up at the clock. Only fifteen minutes left.

"Jonathan Burns? Is Jonathan here?" I heard her say when she got back to her desk.

Lowering my glamour's protection, I raised my hand. "Here," I said.

"A note for you," she said.

I strode to the front of the room to take it from her. As I did, she said more quietly, "You're excused for the rest of the day."

"Thanks," I said, opening the note as I went back to get my bag and books. It was from my mother, requesting that I meet her at City Hall on the town square. It went on to give directions to a particular office.

Pocketing the note and gathering my things, I raised my shield and slipped out the door.

City Hall was halfway across town, but I walked quickly and made it there in fairly short order. If we were going to stay here for any length of time, I needed to get some form of transportation. Passing by Havenwood Falls Garage & Tow, I noticed they had a few used cars for sale. I'd have to stop back and check them out when I had time.

I arrived at City Hall and found the office of Elsmed Fairchild, whom I'd met previously when my mom and I first arrived in town. He was apparently an old acquaintance of my parents. I knocked on the door with the elder fae's name on it, and stepped inside when I heard a faint, "Come in."

Closing the door behind me, I saw the girl sitting behind the desk, sorting through a stack of papers, and almost stumbled over my feet. The one who'd tried to save me from punishment earlier in the week, she was more than simply pretty, with delicate features, long wavy blond hair, and bright blue eyes that seemed to sparkle even in the dim fluorescent lighting.

"Hello," I said, keeping my cool.

She squeaked. Her mouth opened, as if she was trying to say something, but no words came out. She just stared at me as if I had two heads.

Clearing my throat, I tried again. "I'm Jonathan Burns. I got a note to meet my mother here?"

Shaking herself to her senses, she blinked delicate lashes and nodded rapidly. "Yes, of course. Through there," she finally got out, pointing to a closed door on my left.

"Thanks." I nodded, reluctantly turning to knock on the second door.

"Celeste," she said, still staring at me, like she was waiting for something.

"Nice to meet you, Celeste," I responded with a smile, then opened the door and went inside to see what was so urgent it couldn't wait another fifteen minutes.

∾

CELESTE

OH MY GOD. How much more of a fool could I possibly have made of myself? Did he ask you your name, Celeste? No. He didn't ask, and he doesn't care. And now he probably thinks you're an idiot.

I felt my face turn red, and just thanked my lucky stars no one else was there to see my humiliation. Shaking my head at myself, I continued putting pages in my stack. *Now at least I can put a name to that face, though.* I smiled to myself.

I wonder what he's doing here. Mathilde Augustine arrived a while ago, slightly less surprised to see me than she was two days before, followed a short time later by a middle-aged woman who introduced herself as Leah Burns.

I still had no idea what Elsmed Fairchild did, or what kind of internship this was supposed to be. My task for today was the same as the one earlier in the week, but today he lectured me on respectful speech, and told me to think on keeping my tone pleasant when speaking with others. I thought he just didn't like me talking back to him. *Ha! It's going to take more than a lecture and some paperwork to stop this mouth.*

∿

"HAVE you noticed an unusual amount of strange occurrences around you?" Elsmed said. He had spoken with the Burnses for about half an hour before they left, looking very serious. I wondered what sort of business this new family in town could have with an elder statesman such as Elsmed. After they had gone, he asked me back into his office for a "chat."

"Strange how?" I asked. Havenwood Falls was its own brand of unique, according to my extensive research consisting of books and movies. I wasn't sure what qualified as strange in Elsmed's book.

"Have you felt you were able to influence the outcome of events without doing or saying anything?"

My brows wrinkled. *What a thing to ask.* Did he think I was some sort of weirdo that believed in telekinesis and other psychic powers?

"No," I said slowly, wondering where he was going with this.

"So you haven't noticed that things always seem to go your way, even when logically they shouldn't?"

"No. I don't think things always go my way at all." *Take this conversation, for example.*

The old man harrumphed. "What about other . . . turns of luck, shall we say?"

I thought for a minute, trying to decipher what he could be getting at, all while those piercing eyes were glaring at me. "I've been fortunate enough to witness the effects of karma recently, but that's about it." I sighed. "It restores my faith in the universe to see people get what they deserve."

I thought I saw Elsmed shiver suddenly. It was a bit chilly in the office.

"Karma," he repeated.

"Yes, karma," I said. "Like when the school bully rammed his own face into the lockers after picking a fight with the new kid. Oh, and the other day, this woman was being totally nasty to my friends and me, and the next thing we knew, she was tumbling down the mountain sideways." I shrugged. "I guess it could have been bad luck, or a coincidence, but I like to believe things happen for a reason."

"Oh, there's a reason," Elsmed muttered. He got up to pour a cup of tea, and the expression on his face was one I hadn't seen there before, like he was worried about something. "Listen, Celeste," he began, "there is a reason these 'karmic' things happen around you. It's not karma. It's you. You're doing it."

"Doing what?" I said, trying to understand what he was talking about. Maybe the old man really was starting to go senile.

"You're giving them a push, making them do what you want."

"A push? I never touched that woman on the slopes. She just fell. I was nowhere near her!"

Elsmed was shaking his head. "Not a physical push, a *mental* push. Your mind is very powerful, Celeste, and you can influence people without even realizing you're doing it."

Now it was my turn to shake my head. "That's crazy. How can I push people with my mind? Is this some kind of joke?"

"No joke, unfortunately. It's very serious. You have an innate ability to influence people's minds directly, sway them one way or the other at a moment of decision. We were able to overlook it until now, as you were a child and your powers were not fully developed. Now that you're becoming an adult, they are getting stronger, and you need to learn to control them."

I couldn't believe someone could spout this kind of nonsense and still be such a highly regarded figure in town. "So you're saying I have been controlling people, and now you want me to learn to control them better?"

"You need to learn to control *yourself*. To stop yourself from exerting that power you have over people. The mind is very vulnerable, and if you're not careful, you can do permanent damage. Abusing a power like yours is a grave offense."

"What, there are laws against mind control?" I scoffed.

Fairchild was off his rocker, but I wanted to see how far he was going to take this foolishness.

"In this town, yes, there are."

I knew Havenwood Falls had some weird laws, but a mind control prohibition? That was beyond the realm of weird and into unbelievable.

"I would rather have waited to have this conversation with you, eased you into this idea, and given you time to adjust to it. But the truth is, it can't wait. You're a danger to others, and if you're not careful, Celeste, you won't just be doling out karma. You'll be facing your own. And you know what they say . . ."

"What's that, Mr. Fairchild?"

"Karma's a bitch."

CHAPTER 5

JONATHAN

*W*hat is it about small towns and their festivals? We had only been in Havenwood Falls for a few weeks, but it seemed like there was something going on every weekend. Last week, there was the Sweethearts Dance for Valentine's Day. I showed up, but I wasn't sure why, since I hadn't even been to school a single day yet.

Actually, I did know why. My mom. She insisted that it was important that I assimilate into the high school social scene, even though she kept reminding me to be careful who I made friends with. She was a bit conflicted.

This weekend, there was something called the Snowman Sled Races. I was too intrigued to stay away. My mom was huddled with Mrs. Walsh, doing some quilting or something.

Although it was at the other end of town, I walked there on my own, stopping in for a hot coffee at Coffee Haven about halfway there. Even though I'd lived in the mountains for the previous several years, Havenwood Falls was at a much higher altitude, and I sometimes became short of breath when walking around. As I got closer to Danzan Park, where the event was being held, I saw that plenty of other people were heading there, too. Almost all of them, from families with young children to older adults, dragged sleds behind them or carried one tucked under an arm.

I arrived to some kind of organized chaos. At the top of a gently sloping hill, people were milling about, walking around tiny plots of snow-covered ground that had been marked off with tape wound around stakes in the ground. At a table off to the side, they were handing out small cardboard signposts, which people were then taking to the plots to stake their claims.

There was a band playing on a small platform toward the back of the area, and tables set up with food and drink for sale. I approached the table where they were handing out stakes and picked up a flyer. "Snowman Sled Races," it read. "Claim your plot —Build a snowman—Race to win."

"Want to stake a claim?" a lady sitting behind the table asked, and I looked up, surprised to see she was talking to me.

"No, thanks," I replied. "Just here to watch. It's my first time."

"No problem, dear. There are some benches along the far side of the field where you'll have a great view of the races, but they aren't scheduled to start until two o'clock."

I nodded. It was only eleven thirty. I had thought I'd be fashionably late, but it looked like I was somewhat early for the spectator portion of the day.

I took my time strolling along behind the long plots, where people were scooping up the snow and forming it into balls.

"Jonathan!" I heard a female voice call. Looking around, I expected to see someone hailing a different Jonathan. It was a common name, after all. That was why my parents chose it. Instead, I saw the pretty girl from Elsmed's office making a beeline for me.

"Jonathan," she repeated. "Hey."

"Hey," I said. This wasn't awkward at all. "Celeste, right?"

"Right!" she beamed, obviously pleased I remembered her name. "Listen, I need your help. Are you racing a snowman?"

"No. No sled." I shrugged. "I was just going to watch."

"Perfect!" she cried. "Would you . . . I mean, if you wanted to . . . I need a partner," she finally got out in a rush.

"Oh, to help build?"

"Yes. I came with Margaret, Gianna, and Emma, but then Xavier came, and Margaret wants to pair up with him, which leaves me the odd woman out, so, well, if you wouldn't mind . . ."

"Sure," I said, seeing an expression of relief immediately brighten her face. "Lead the way."

I followed her to a little rectangular section of snow in the long row of plots. At the end of it was a rather slick-looking sled, painted pink and purple.

"Guys, this is Jonathan. He's going to help me with my snowman. Jonathan, this is Margaret and Xavier, and behind you are Gianna and Emma."

I waved at Celeste's friends, then looked down at our patch of snow. "So how big is this snowman we're building?" I asked.

"About man-sized," Celeste answered. "It has to be big enough to keep the momentum going all the way down the hill," she said, her cheeks already turning pink from the cold.

She pointed at what looked like some kids' beach toys—an assortment of pails and miniature shovels. "We can use those to scoop and pack the snow, so our fingers don't freeze off."

I grabbed a shovel and started scooping.

"So you're a junior too?" she asked, and I realized I'd just agreed to a two-hour interrogation.

"Yes." Maybe if I kept my answers short, I wouldn't have to reveal too much.

"When did you move to town?"

I doubted she really needed to ask. In a small town like this, everyone was sure to know when a new family arrived. Even a family as good at hiding as we were. "A few weeks ago."

"How do you like it so far?"

"It's okay." I could see the only way to stop the questions coming would be to go on the offensive. "How long have you lived here?" I asked.

"All my life," she said. "Never even been out of Colorado."

"Really? No family vacations driving across the country in a station wagon?"

That made her laugh. "No way. My dad is too tied to work to go away for more than a long weekend. And you watch too many movies."

I couldn't help my grin as I kept my eyes on the snow, scooping and dumping while Celeste formed the ice crystals into an ever-growing ball. "What does your dad do?"

"He's an accountant, has an office down in Miller's Plaza. How about yours?"

I stilled, taking a breath and letting it out. It still got to me after all this time.

"He's gone. Dead." I heard the wooden sound of my voice, followed by her small gasp.

"Oh, no. I'm so sorry. I didn't mean—" She looked into my eyes. "I didn't know. My mom, too. She passed when I was a baby." She took a step toward me and threw her arms around my shoulders. "I'm sorry."

The sudden show of affection stunned me, and I stood there like an idiot for a moment before I came to my senses and returned her hug. She was warm and smelled of cinnamon. "It's okay." We both turned back to our snow tasks.

"It must be hard to change schools in the middle of the year," she said, changing the subject. "Are you having an easy time catching up?"

"Mostly. I was living outside the country, so Government is the one I'm having the hardest time with."

"Oh yeah, I can imagine that would be difficult if you hadn't been raised here. I can help you if you want. I took it last year, and I still have all my notes."

"Thanks." I smiled. "That would be a big help."

"Where are you from, anyway? That accent is a bit . . . hard to place."

"Yeah, it's evolved over the years. Still a work in progress." I grinned, hoping to distract her from her prying.

She nudged me with a tiny shovel. "You didn't answer the question."

I chuckled at her persistence. I knew I wouldn't get off that easy. "We moved around a lot. I guess I picked up a little of the local accents all over Europe."

"I see . . ." she said, seeming lost in thought for several minutes while we silently worked side by side. We smoothed the surface of our snowman's bottom just as an announcer called out that there was one hour left for building.

"Are you copping a feel on our snowman?" Celeste asked, holding back a giggle.

"Who, me?" I put my most unbelievable innocent face on. "Nah, I'm more interested in the snow women," I smirked.

She let her giggle out now, turning a deep shade of pink. It was cute.

"You guys aren't going to finish on time if you keep standing there making eyes at each other," Emma said loudly from the plot next to us, flipping her light brown hair. I watched Celeste's expression turn from amused to decidedly not so, while her shade turned darker still. Neither one of us dignified the comment with a response, but got back to work and tried to ignore the giggles coming from Emma and Gianna.

After a few minutes, I noticed that Celeste was forming her snow into fist-sized balls instead of piling scoops onto the midsection of our snowman. I caught her eye and looked pointedly at the growing pile of snowballs, giving her an *Are you doing what I think you're doing?* eyebrow raise.

She replied with a *Yeah, what of it?* shrug, then added a *You in?* side-eye.

I responded with a *Hell yeah!* nod, and we quickly built up our arsenal of snowballs, hiding them behind the snowman's bottom, which we'd placed on top of the sled.

When we both silently agreed we had enough, I held up three

fingers, turning down one, two, and then all three fingers. Celeste, crouched with snowballs in each hand, sprung up with a roar and started pelting Emma and Gianna. As much as I didn't like the idea of fighting against girls, when they started throwing snow back in our direction, I had to back up my teammate.

As we lobbed snowballs over the top of the giant half-built snowman and ducked for cover behind it, I noticed that revenge really brought out the best in Celeste. She was radiant, and I'd never seen a smile so big in my life.

～

"AND THE WINNERS ARE . . . Everett Weston and Graysin Ravenal!" shouted Mayor Stuart, whom Celeste had pointed out to me while we put the finishing touches on our snowman. He had hurtled down the hill behind the winning sled, then crumpled in a heap at the bottom of the hill, which was now a huge snowbank of wrecked snowmen with sleds sticking out.

"In second place, Jace Edwards and Zane!" I glanced over at Celeste, next to me. Her bottom lip was sticking out in a little pout.

"And in third place, Remy and Roxy MacKinnon! All winners please come up to the stage to claim your prizes!" We watched as they all filed up onto the little makeshift stage. Everett jumped as Graysin pinched his butt. This sent Emma and Gianna into a fit of giggles.

"Racers, collect your sleds. The hill is now open for sledding! Be careful, everyone." The mayor placed medals around the necks of the winners while racers began trudging down the hill to retrieve their sleds.

"I'll go get your sled, if you want to wait here," I offered.

"I'll go with you, man," Xavier said. He gave Margaret a peck on the cheek and turned down the hill. Celeste gave a brief nod and stepped over to put her head together with her friend.

I caught up with Xavier and fell into step beside him.

LIZ FERRY

"Hey, nice job on your snowman today," I said. I'd never been good at making small talk.

Xavier laughed. "We barely finished it on time. We got a little . . . distracted."

I chuckled. I'd seen them stealing kisses when they thought no one was looking. "How long have you guys been together?"

"Just a week or so. I was so nervous she'd turn me down, I delayed four months before asking her out. Turns out she'd been waiting for me to ask."

"Sounds like you guys are meant to be," I said, almost choking on the platitude as it came out of my mouth.

He nodded and smiled. "I hope so, man. So what about you and Celeste?" he asked as we reached the sleds.

"Me and Celeste?" I said, surprised. I shook my head. "No, we're not together. She just needed a partner for the race."

"Dude, Celeste was bragging to us about how she'd out-build us on her own before you showed up. And I've never seen her blush so many times in one day. She's into you, man."

"Huh," I said, pulling out the purple-and-pink sled before brushing off the remains of the snowman and walking beside Xavier to the walkway with stairs leading back up the hill. "I don't really know her. I mean, we just met this week."

"Well, you may not know her, but it seems like you're into her a little, too," he said, looking pointedly at the sled tucked under my arm.

I didn't have a response to that, so I kept my mouth shut as we climbed back up the slope and made our way back to the girls. Celeste was certainly attractive and charming, but I'd never had the luxury of being able to fall for a girl. My life wasn't that of a normal teenager. Mom and I were on the run, and I couldn't ever forget it. Couldn't let my guard down for a minute.

We'd been living in Portugal for three years before they found us, but when they did, we'd had to run and never look back. We would never be able to contact anyone there, for fear they'd trace us to our new location. How long would it be until Havenwood

Falls was in our rearview mirror too, and we were looking for the next place to hide?

After a few sledding runs, we were all chilled and tired, ready to head somewhere warm.

"Napoli's for dinner?" Celeste proposed to the group.

"I'm in," Gianna said, dusting the snow off her sled.

Margaret and Xavier looked at each other and shared some kind of silent communication, after which Margaret announced, "Us too."

Five pairs of eyes turned to me. I froze. "Uh, sorry, I can't. Have to get home. My mom's expecting me for dinner."

Celeste's face fell a little, and I instantly felt guilty. Her words didn't betray a trace of feeling one way or the other, though. "Okay, well, thanks for being my snowman-building buddy."

"It was fun. Thanks for asking me to join." With a nod to Xavier and waves to the girls, I turned my back on the little group and began the long, cold walk home, mentally kicking myself the whole way.

It's best you don't form attachments here, I told myself. *You'll just have to break them sooner or later.* There were no hard feelings if you didn't have people to leave behind. There were no feelings at all.

CHAPTER 6

CELESTE

I was posing while Jonathan built a snow woman copy of me when a very loud and obnoxious horn started blaring just behind me. Actually, it was less like a horn, and more like—

My alarm clock. My eyelids fluttered open, and I rolled over to see an angry red 5:00 AM staring back at me. I silenced the assault on my ears and cursed Elsmed Fairchild.

He'd let me know before I left his office on Friday that he was signing me up for early morning Yoga in the Vines classes down at the Blackstone Winery on Tuesdays and Thursdays, for "training in meditation and mental focus techniques." I did not see how twisting my body into a pretzel was supposed to help my mental focus, not to mention doing it before I was meant to be awake on a school day, but he would hear no arguments.

When I appealed to my father about this ridiculous demand, he just said, "Yoga sounds like a great idea. You need to maintain your flexibility if you're going to keep skiing, you know. Just look at what happened to that tourist last week."

Thanks a lot, Dad.

I dragged myself out of the warm cocoon of my comforter and did the bare minimum to make myself presentable for a yoga class. I'd have to stop back home after the class to get ready for school.

If the alarm hadn't fully done its job of waking me up, the blast of freezing air when I opened the door to walk down to the winery certainly did. It was positively frigid, and the sun wasn't even up yet, though the sky was starting to lighten, coloring the wispy clouds in pastel purples and pinks.

While it hadn't snowed overnight, the sidewalks were icy, and it took a lot of attention just to keep from slipping and falling. With my head down, I picked my way around the slick patches and listened to the tree branches creaking under the weight of the ice that encased them.

This was probably the quietest I had ever heard the town. Even though it was small, Havenwood Falls never seemed to be completely quiet at night. There was often a rumble of motorcycles late at night, and people seemed to like going out for evening strolls after dinner, because I'd often hear footsteps outside long after dark.

One thing my dad was strict about, though, was my curfew. He really didn't want me out in the town at night. If I was safe in a friend's house, it was one thing, but I had to be inside by eleven o'clock. I wasn't sure what he was so worried about, but it was never a big deal, because most of my friends' parents were the same way.

I got to the winery and spotted a couple of ladies with yoga mats tucked under their arms heading for a cabin out in the vineyard. I had heard that Yoga in the Vines took place in the actual vineyard, but they cleared out one of the cabins to use as a yoga studio in the winter months. I followed them to the cabin, which had a sign on it reading, "Yoga in the Vines—Namaste."

I slipped inside and pushed the door shut behind me to keep the cold air out. There were a handful of ladies chatting as they put their shoes in cubbies and rolled out their mats.

"Namaste," said Letitia Blackstone, pressing her hands together and bowing slightly toward me. She looked to be about seventy years old, but was still limber enough to lead the yoga class. "It's nice to see a new face in class."

"Namaste," I responded, returning her bow. "I, um, don't have a yoga mat."

"Not to worry," she said, pointing toward the corner. "Just take a mat out of the bin there."

"Thank you," I said, and chose a mat, which I rolled out next to a beautiful woman with long wavy black hair, olive skin, and dark eyes.

"Hi," said the woman, "I'm Alina."

"Nice to meet you," I said. "Have you done this long? It's my first time."

"Oh, yoga? Yeah, I've had a few classes. Haven't got my poses perfect yet, but you can keep an eye on me, or Mrs. McCabe up there," she pointed to the woman in front of us, "if you need guidance. Letti doesn't do the poses herself, but she'll help you out, too."

I looked at Mrs. McCabe, who was flanked by Roxanne MacKinnon, a girl in my class at school, and Audrey Smith, Roxanne's older half-sister. Roxanne was super thin and had beautiful amber eyes. Her sister was more muscular and looked like she could be a dancer. All three moved with the grace of cats, and I guessed they had been doing yoga a while.

"Thanks," I said, feeling a little more at ease.

Alina turned to introduce herself to Sherry Grimes, who was setting up on the other side of her and eyeing the coffeepot in the back of the room.

Letitia put on some soft, nondescript music and started the class, reteaching us how to breathe for ten minutes before leading us through some simple poses that stretched my muscles and tested my balance.

"Beginners, please resume the child's pose. More advanced students, let's try the lord of the dance pose."

I curled myself in a ball and extended my arms the way Letitia had shown me earlier. The gentle stretch in my back became my focus as I breathed slowly and deeply, while she took the more advanced students through a few more poses.

"Everyone to easy seated pose."

I sat up slowly, tucking my feet in front of me, with my hands upturned on my knees.

"Close your eyes and focus internally," Letitia said as she walked around, straightening backs and nudging knees to get our positions right. "Listen to your breath," she said, pulling my shoulders back a fraction of an inch.

I closed my eyes and listened to my breath. I tried to tune out the other little noises in the room and the voice in my head reminding me of the assignments I had to turn in today. The darkness behind my eyelids was slowly emptying of afterimages and becoming deeper. The grainy colors disappeared until there were only a few points of light left. I counted them. Five stationary, and one that moved, floating above the others.

I watched the moving one and noticed its movements were not fluid, but it would circle around the others, stopping occasionally next to one or another. Curious. It stopped next to the point of light I estimated was closest to me, and I heard Letitia's voice nearby, speaking to Alina.

"Keep your back straight," she said.

I kept my eyes shut tight, focusing now on the remaining points of light that still wouldn't go away. As Letitia's footsteps moved on, the hovering point drifted away. Was my brain keeping placeholders for the people in the room? That would certainly be odd. I'd never noticed myself doing that before, but then again, I'd never tried any meditation techniques until then.

The hovering light came around again and stopped in front of me this time. I gazed at it, wondering what it would do next. As I did, it seemed to flash at me, just before a voice over my head said, "Chin down, Celeste."

My eyes burst open, and my easy seated pose fell apart. *Holy crap.* I looked up at Letitia, my jaw hanging open. She gave me a quizzical look.

"Something wrong, Celeste?"

I shook my head to buy time while I thought of something to say. Letitia glanced at the clock, then back at me.

"Savasana," she announced to the class, and I lay on my back, my mind racing. Did I really just *see* the minds of the other women in the room with me? I closed my eyes and tried to bring the vision back, but it was useless. My mind was full of unanswered questions.

What exactly was that, and was it real or something I just imagined? What if everything Elsmed had told me was true? If I could see people's minds, could I really influence them? How? And he said I'd done it before, but I'd never seen *that* before.

I couldn't process the words Letitia was saying, but I assumed they were supposed to be relaxing, wrapping up the session and giving us energy for the day ahead. All I could hear were the questions bouncing around my brain.

What was wrong with me?

"Namaste," Letitia said, and the other women started to stand up. I followed them in a daze as they rolled up their mats and put on their shoes and winter coats, readying themselves to brave the cold outside, except for Sherry, who made a beeline for the coffee machine.

"See you on Thursday?" Letitia asked me as I put my mat back in the corner bin.

I turned to her and nodded. "Definitely," I said.

Whatever I had just seen, I needed to know if it was a fluke or something I could repeat.

∾

JONATHAN

I KEPT my head down on my way to school Tuesday morning. If I didn't make eye contact with anyone, my protective glamour had a better chance of staying intact. After I'd taken a seat in English Lit, a long pair of legs walked by my desk, and I looked up to see Celeste passing by on the way to her seat. I worried she'd seek me out, but she paid me no mind, going straight to her seat and plopping down, a dazed look on her face.

Fortunately, the class had started a new segment, so I was no longer behind on my reading and lost in the discussion. As Mr. Zander droned on about the use of imagery and its deeper meaning, I kept watch on Celeste out of the corner of my eye. She was clearly on another plane.

"So who can tell me what the use of the color white represents in this chapter?" Mr. Zander posed, casting about the room for a student to call on when, inevitably, no one volunteered to answer.

Almost in slow motion, I saw his gaze land on Celeste, a twinkle in his eye as he prepared to embarrass her for spacing out. Before I knew what was happening, my hand shot in the air, and I was proclaiming, "It represents purity and innocence."

Mr. Zander looked startled as his head whipped toward me, almost as though he'd forgotten I was in his class. With my glamour, he probably had. He paused a moment before nodding toward me and conceding, "Correct, Mr. Burns."

As he went on to direct everyone to open their books to examine a passage of the text, I saw Margaret smile at me in acknowledgment and nudge Celeste to bring her back from whatever planet she was currently inhabiting. Celeste gave her head a shake and turned to get her book out.

Clearly something had her preoccupied, and she had me preoccupied. I just wanted to reach over and smooth out that crease between her eyebrows. I didn't know her well enough to even guess at what might be bothering her, and that had suddenly become a problem for me. I knew I should keep my distance, but it was like I couldn't help myself.

When class was over, I watched for her to come out the door as I switched books at my locker, which had been moved to this hallway.

"Celeste!" I called to snag her attention as she floated by, still focused on something other than the hallway in front of her.

Her gaze jumped to mine. "Hey, Jonathan. How's it going?"

"Good. I just— You look a little distracted today. Everything okay?"

I watched the blush creep up her cheeks. "Oh, I'm . . . I'm fine," she said. "I just woke up early to go to this yoga class, and I'm a little tired, I guess."

"Tired."

"Yeah, you know, from lack of sleep?" she said, raising an eyebrow at me.

"Nah, I'm not buying it."

"Excuse me?"

"It's cool if you don't want to tell me what's bothering you, I get it." I leaned in toward her, holding her gaze. "Just don't lie to me."

Her jaw dropped, and a cute little gasp came out. The warning bell rang, and I closed my locker.

"Better get to class, Miss Long," I said in my best Mr. Friske impression, hauling my bag onto my shoulder. I hid my smile as she huffed and spun on her heel, then stomped off down the hall.

I headed in the opposite direction to French class, without an answer, but with an image of a blushing Celeste to keep me entertained for the next seventy-five minutes.

AFTER SCHOOL, I arrived home to find my mother frantic, and Mrs. Walsh's house in disarray.

"I don't know how this happened," she said, lifting the couch cushions and sliding her hands along the inside seams of the furniture, before turning the whole couch on its back to search the carpet where it had been sitting.

Mrs. Walsh appeared to be trying to stay clear while also preventing her house from being totally trashed.

"What's going on?" I asked, but neither of the women seemed to hear me.

"It's gone . . . It can't be gone!" my mother exclaimed, falling into a panic all over again and bringing her hands up to claw at her collarbone.

Oh shit. The pendant. The one thing we were supposed to protect, the whole reason we've had to hide for my entire life, was a pendant hanging from my mother's neck. It was there always, and I'd never seen her without it. Until now.

It was a tiny thing and looked like a gold filigree butterfly to most people—people who didn't look close enough to see it was a fairy. More than just a piece of jewelry, though, this was an ancient artifact of the Seelie fae. It had some mysterious power and was sent away from Faerie for safekeeping during the war. If the Unseelie got their hands on it, they could turn the tide against us, putting our people at risk.

It was given to my family to protect, and we had managed to do so for decades. My father's life had been sacrificed to keep this thing safe. Hell, my mother had never even wanted to tell me what the thing did, because she was so afraid I might let something slip that would lead our pursuers to us.

And now, in this supposed safest of safe havens, it had disappeared within weeks of our arrival. Never in my life had I seen my mother misplace the pendant. Could it have been taken? Had we been lured here under false pretenses? Or let our guards down too far?

My mind was spinning out of control, and I was about to lose my shit, when I heard a booming voice say, "Stop!"

Elsmed Fairchild strode out from the bedroom hallway, taking a cell phone from his ear and ending a call. "Everyone please take a seat and calm down, as best you can," he said, lowering his voice to a more reasonable level.

My mom and Mrs. Walsh righted the living room couch and sat on it, though I could see my mom still surreptitiously sticking her hands between the cushions to continue her search.

"The artifact is no longer in this house," Elsmed said.

My mom started sobbing.

Elsmed eyed her as he continued, "But it has not left Havenwood Falls. I can still sense its presence within our boundaries."

My mom's head shot up, renewed fire in her eyes. "Where? Can you tell where it is?"

"Not precisely," the elder fae answered. "Only that it's within about a five-mile radius. I've already alerted the Luna Coven to notify me of any movement across our wards. Why don't you tell us how this happened, Leah? Maybe that will give us a clue where to start looking."

"I was just reading here on the couch, and I guess I dozed off. I woke up, and it was gone."

"Do you often nap during the day?" Elsmed inquired. I looked at his face, but didn't see any traces of judgment there. My mother was still looking for work in this little village, but she wasn't anyone's definition of lazy.

"No, not really," my mom answered. "I don't even remember feeling tired."

"What else do you remember?" he asked.

Mom thought for a minute, her brows furrowed. "There was something . . . no, someone. I think?" She shook her head as if to clear it.

"I went out for some groceries," Mrs. Walsh said, "and she was in a panic when I came back. I was gone for less than an hour."

"Addie will be here any minute," Elsmed said, glancing at the door. "Perhaps she can help clear your mind."

I helped Mrs. Walsh put away her groceries while my mother paced and Elsmed glared at the door. After a few minutes, a knock at the door announced a young woman with long brown hair, black-framed glasses, and a diamond piercing in her nose. I recognized her as Addie Beaumont, the witch who had given us tattoos as part of the town's registry process when we first arrived.

"It's about time," Elsmed said, casting a stern look at the newcomer.

She ignored his comment. "How can I help?"

"Mrs. Burns has had something of great value stolen from her person, but she doesn't recall the incident," Elsmed explained. "Could you please see if she has a memory block and remove it?"

"Of course." Addie smiled, turning to my mom. "Let's have a seat, and we can get started." She led my mom to an armchair beside the couch. "Now just close your eyes and try to relax," she said.

My mother closed her eyes and took a few deep breaths while Addie stood in front of her and began chanting in a low voice. After a minute, she stopped and nodded to Elsmed.

"What happened after Helena went to the store?" Elsmed inquired.

"I-I was here in the living room, reading the paper. There was a knock at the door. I looked out the window and saw a woman with . . ."

"Take your time," said the older fae in a surprisingly gentle voice.

"Sorry, it's still a bit fuzzy. She was holding something—a potted plant or . . . a flower arrangement? I remember thinking it looked unwieldy, so I opened the door and stepped outside to help."

"What did the woman look like?"

"She had fair skin, dark hair—I can't quite get a grasp on her features," my mother said, frustration creeping into her voice.

"What happened when you opened the door?" Elsmed continued.

"She shoved the plant at me and said something I didn't understand. It might have been Latin? I don't remember the words now. After that . . . I don't remember anything before I woke up on the couch, when Helena came back."

"Hmm. She must have knocked you out. Was there anyone else with her?"

My mom thought a moment and shook her head. "I don't think so."

"It was definitely a witch's spell on her mind," Addie volunteered.

"All right," Elsmed said. "I want immediate reports on anyone crossing the town borders. You and Saundra should take account of any members of the Luna Coven matching the description, and I'll talk to the sheriff about setting up surveillance on the other witches in town."

"Wow, it's a literal witch hunt," I heard myself mutter.

Elsmed's cold eyes swung to me. "You didn't tell anyone about the pendant, did you, boy?"

"Of course not," I answered.

"Good," he said. "I want you to stay with your mother until this is all sorted out. Make sure there are no aftereffects of the spells. If you see anything out of the ordinary, call me or Addie. Helena has our numbers."

"We'll call Mr. Friske," Mrs. Walsh added, "and let him know your mom is keeping you out of school for the time being. Maybe your teachers can put together some assignments for you so you don't fall behind."

I doubted that would be necessary, but didn't contradict her; she was just trying to help. I was fairly sure we'd be leaving town once we tracked down the pendant, whether it took a day or five weeks.

We all wanted to get on with the search, so Elsmed and Addie left. Mrs. Walsh tried to distract my mom by enlisting her help with dinner preparation.

I wanted nothing more than to be out there hunting down the perpetrator of this theft, but knew there was not much I could do with the little knowledge I had of the town and its residents. I set up camp in the living room and tried to focus on my homework.

CHAPTER 7

CELESTE

I wandered through my day in a haze. There had to be a rational explanation for what I had seen. Maybe my mind was playing tricks on me. I woke up too early, and the lack of sleep was messing with me. I came up with a dozen explanations, but none of them seemed to ring true. Instead, over and over, my mind kept repeating Elsmed's words back to me.

"You have an innate ability . . ." *Ridiculous. If I had an innate ability, wouldn't I have noticed it by now?*

". . . to influence people's minds directly . . ." *If that were true, I would have everything I ever wanted. Was this his way of saying I'm spoiled?*

"We were able to overlook it until now . . ." *Come to think of it, my dad is kind of a pushover. But that's not my fault, is it?*

". . . your powers were not fully developed . . ." *So maybe that's why no one noticed before? Has anyone noticed now? Besides Elsmed, of course.*

". . . they are getting stronger, and you need to learn to control them . . ." *What will happen to me if I can't? Will I go to mind control jail?*

I shook my head. This just sounded crazy. Maybe Elsmed was just an old kook who got his kicks tormenting teenage girls. *I should talk to Dad and get myself out of this weird internship.* Then I imagined the look on his face when I told him I didn't want to continue. He would be disappointed. Tell me he only wanted the best for his little girl. *Ugh.* Who was the controlling one after all? For that matter, he'd think *I* was the crazy one if I told him I thought I had some psychic power. I didn't think I could endure the therapy he would surely insist upon if *that* came out. Better to just suffer through a month or two with Elsmed.

Still, I kept coming up with new questions, all of them unanswered. Where did this ability come from? Why me? Was I the only one? Did my dad have any idea about this? Did he have abilities himself? What about my mom? Or was there a radioactive spider to blame? I turned the questions over and over in my head, going through the motions at school and walking home on autopilot. I vaguely registered Margaret trying to flag me down as I headed for the main door of school, but it was like I was stuck on a track, unable to deviate from my path or turn my eyes toward her, just as I was unable to turn my mind from its problem.

Once home, I took out my books to study, but no amount of staring at them and turning pages could help me concentrate on what was in them. Instead, I sat cross-legged on my bedroom floor, closed my eyes, and focused on my breathing.

My dad was still at work, and the house was empty. I saw nothing but darkness behind my eyelids. I waited, clearing my mind of any thoughts that popped into it. I concentrated on the in and out of my breath, the filling and emptying of my lungs. I waited.

I don't know how long I sat there like that, focused inward, before I saw a tiny light, like a faraway star. It floated down below me, from far away, but coming closer. I watched as it bobbed along, moving more or less in a straight line, slowing as it approached. It came to a stop nearby. If I'd pointed myself directly at it and opened my eyes, I'd be looking at the sidewalk in front of my house.

But I didn't dare open my eyes. I watched as it floated there for a moment, then made a right turn and moved a little closer. It paused again. I held my breath.

Ding-dong!

I won't lie, I screamed a little. My doorbell had me almost jumping out of my skin. "Oh my god." I got to my feet and raced down the stairs, my heart pounding in my chest. "Oh my god, oh my god, oh my god." I peeked through the peephole and saw Margaret fidgeting on my doorstep. I opened the door and greeted her with "Oh my god."

"Celeste?" She looked surprised, and a bit worried. I waved her inside, looking up and down the street behind her. Empty.

"Oh my god, Margaret. You are not going to believe this."

"What's up?" she asked, definitely confused now.

I closed the door behind her and lowered my voice, though no one was around to hear us. "I *saw* you coming."

"Uhhh . . . okay," she said slowly.

"But not with my eyes," I said, watching the look of confusion grow on her face. "With . . . my mind." I shook my head. "It sounds so stupid when I say it like that."

"Why don't you start from the beginning?" she said, taking my hand and leading me to the sofa. She thought I was going crazy. I thought I was going a little crazy too.

"Okay," I began. "So I was meditating—"

"Wait, what?" she interrupted. "When did you start meditating?"

"This morning." Her eyebrows rose. I pressed on. "So I was meditating, and I saw you coming closer, and then you rang my doorbell."

"Like a vision?"

"No, it was like a little light."

"Uh-huh." She looked at me expectantly, waiting for more.

"And it happened this morning, too."

"You saw me this morning?"

"No, I saw the other people in my yoga class."

"And where were you?"

179

"In my yoga class. But with my eyes closed."

"I see. And when did you start taking yoga?"

"This morning."

"So let me get this straight. This morning you started a yoga class, learned to meditate, and started seeing—"

"Lights."

"Lights that you think are people—"

"I think maybe it's like a representation of other minds? Like their consciousness?"

"Uh huh. So you see other people's minds when you close your eyes."

"Just if I'm concentrating. And I think they have to be close to me. Or maybe it only works if I know them? I don't know, but I don't see a lot, only a few. Or one, just now."

She still had a look of disbelief on her face. "Are you sure it's not your imagination? Or, I don't know, a hallucination?"

"Did you tell me you were coming over here today?"

"No, I just saw you in school looking like a zombie, and decided to check on you. Maybe it's lack of sleep?"

"When you came over just now, you stopped—hesitated—on the sidewalk before coming to the door."

Her eyes shot to mine. "Yeah."

"I saw that."

"With your eyes closed."

"With my eyes closed."

"Did you know it was me?"

"Not until I got to the door."

"Huh."

I just nodded. I could see she was starting to believe.

"So is this why you were a zombie today?"

"Yeah, I guess. I kind of can't stop thinking about it."

"Hey, I don't blame you. If I had a superpower, I'd be a little zoned out at school, too," she said.

"It's not exactly a superpower," I said.

"So what is it, exactly?"

"I'm not sure." I shrugged. I wanted to tell her about what Elsmed had told me, about an ability to not only see minds, but to influence them. But I remembered his warning about keeping our chats between us, and I had a feeling I did *not* want to piss him off. "I just need to get my mind off it, or I think I'll go crazy wondering what it is, and where it came from."

"Okay. Want to study for the history quiz?"

I grinned. Margaret really was the best kind of friend. "Absolutely."

THE NEXT DAY, I had regained my focus. As I sat in my morning math class, I started a list of questions for my new mentor. *How does this mind control thing work? Are the lights I see really other people's minds? Is that vision related to the power to influence? Why do I have to meditate to see the lights?*

So many questions. I wondered how many of them I'd actually get answers to. Ms. Wells was talking about logarithmic functions, and I wondered if I could put myself into a meditative state with her droning as background. She really didn't like people sleeping in her class, though, so I thought I'd better not test it.

I looked around surreptitiously for Jonathan. I had spotted him in this class before, though he often snuck in somehow without my noticing. I didn't see him. I started paying attention and taking more detailed notes. It never hurt to have good notes. And if a certain someone who, say, missed class asked for them later, then I'd be able to help him out.

During my last class of the day, the office sent a note saying I should meet Mr. Fairchild at an address in Creekwood Estates after school let out. My mind started going in circles again, wondering what was up with the change in venue, and what he had planned for me today. I was fairly certain it wouldn't be paperwork, and for that I was grateful and excited.

When the final bell rang, I headed straight for Creekwood

Estates and found myself standing in front of a house with the address matching the one on my paper. I approached and knocked on the door, then I thought I heard scurrying before Elsmed's voice came through, saying, "It's all right. It's just Celeste."

Elsmed opened the door. "Good afternoon, Celeste."

"Good afternoon, Mr. Fairchild."

"Please come in."

I stepped into the house and looked around. A woman I recognized as Mrs. Walsh, Makenna's mom, was standing in the kitchen, with one hand resting nonchalantly next to the knife block. Makenna was a couple years ahead of me in school, but in a small town like ours, it seemed like everyone knew everyone else, at least superficially. Mrs. Burns, whom I'd met in Elsmed's office the other day, was standing in the living room behind Jonathan, who was looking quizzically at me. In fact, they were all staring at me, as if waiting for me to sprout wings or something.

"Hi," I said meekly, giving the room a little wave of my hand.

The women seemed to relax a bit, and Jonathan waved back at me. "Hey."

"Have a seat, Celeste," Elsmed said. "There's a lot to fill you in on."

I sat on the edge of the armchair he gestured at. "O-okay." *Fill me in? Yeah, 'cause I've got no clue what's going on here.*

"You are—" He paused, shook his head, and started again. "We need your help."

"What kind of help?"

"Mrs. Burns has been robbed."

I gasped. "Oh, no! Are you okay?" I automatically asked.

She just shook her head, looking like she was unable to speak.

"We need to keep her safe until we track down the perpetrator," Elsmed continued, bringing my attention back to him.

I felt my brows crinkle together. "Safe?"

"Yes, it seems that the . . . artifact that was stolen has a . . . key of sorts, and we expect the thief will be back once he or she figures that out."

My eyebrows tried to climb up my scalp. "Oh. I haven't . . . I mean, I'm not that strong, and I wouldn't know how— I'm no bodyguard, Mr. Fairchild. How can I help?"

"You remember that gift we talked about before? Your mental ability?"

Uh, yeah. How could I forget? I nodded.

"I hope you don't mind, but I discussed it with Mrs. Burns and Mrs. Walsh, and we agreed it would be very useful for keeping away unwanted visitors that might be a threat. I need you to turn away anyone who tries to approach the house. Everyone but those of us here and Addie Beaumont."

Now my head was shaking of its own accord. "Not possible. I don't know how to do that."

"You do. You've just never done it consciously before. Try it."

I looked at Elsmed. *Go upstairs*, I thought at him, focusing all my willpower.

"It won't work on me," he said with a chuckle. "Try someone else."

I rolled my eyes. "I *told* you I can't."

"Try again," he said sternly, those steely blue eyes growing even colder.

I looked around the room, my gaze settling on Mrs. Walsh, who was staring at something on the kitchen counter, pretending not to listen to our conversation. *Pick up a pencil*, I mentally commanded her.

She looked up at the bulletin board hanging on the wall and reached up to grab a pencil that was balanced on the top of the frame.

My eyes went wide.

Put it behind your ear, I silently told her. She did.

"What the—"

"Watch your language," Mrs. Walsh called absentmindedly, as if she was used to scolding a child.

I looked at Elsmed in wonder. "How?" was all I could manage.

"That is a question I do not have time to answer right now, unfortunately," he sighed. "I have to go speak to a potential witness. Time is of the essence in this matter."

"Wait, what if . . . what if it doesn't work?" I asked, nervous to be entrusted with this responsibility.

"If there is any problem, call me." *With your mind*, I heard his voice add in my head.

I shrieked, my eyes going wider than I thought they could. "What was that?" I squeaked.

"A reliable communication system, better than cell phones," he answered with a rueful smile. "Call if you run into any problems. Stay here, all of you," he broadened his address to the room. "Jonathan's been on guard all night and day, and he needs a rest."

So that's why he was nowhere to be seen at school today.

"I have questions," I said. *Even more now than before.*

"And I will answer them, later," he said. "I really must be on my way now. Call your dad and let him know I'll be keeping you late, but you'll be home before curfew."

I nodded again, too overwhelmed to say anything.

He waved to Mrs. Walsh and Mrs. Burns, then disappeared out the door. Mrs. Walsh hurried over to lock it behind him.

I looked from Mrs. Walsh to Mrs. Burns, not sure what to do or say.

"My, you look terrified, darling," Mrs. Walsh began, and reached out her hand to me. I took it, and she led me to the kitchen. "How about a hot cocoa?"

Polite Celeste kicked in. "Thank you, Mrs. Walsh, that would be lovely."

She started some milk heating on the stove.

"Jonathan, honey, why don't you head up to bed?" Mrs. Burns said quietly to her son. "Celeste will watch over us while you get some sleep."

Jonathan studied me as if seeing me for the first time. It seemed like maybe he didn't trust me, or wondered about my capability to keep his mother safe. I didn't blame him. I wasn't all that confident in myself as a security measure, either. But Elsmed must have had a good reason to choose me for this task, I supposed. I would try my best. Jonathan finally nodded his head and trudged up the stairs to take a nap.

Mrs. Walsh and I pulled an armchair from the living room to a spot right in front of the window facing out onto the street. From there, I could see anyone approaching the house from the front.

"Now you just sit right here," Mrs. Walsh said, pulling the curtains back to give me a good view of the street, "and I'll get your cocoa."

"Thank you, Mrs. Walsh," I said, and made a quick call to my father, letting him know I'd be home a little late.

After a few minutes of fussing in the kitchen, she brought me a steaming mug topped with marshmallows. There were even a couple of cookies on the saucer.

"You are too kind," I said.

"Nonsense," she replied. "You're the one doing us a favor."

I smiled and took a sip of my cocoa. "Delicious."

"Okay, I'm going to take my knitting and go keep an eye on the back of the house. If you need anything, I'll just be straight down that hall in the sunroom." She pointed toward the back of the house.

"Okay." I nodded.

"Don't you worry," she called as she made her way down the hall. "Elsmed will be back before you know it."

I settled into the chair and stared out the window, afraid to take my eyes off the street. Since Creekwood Estates was a residential development, there wasn't a lot of activity out there, and I wondered how long it would be before I dozed off.

Mrs. Burns pulled up a chair across from me, out of sight from the window. "Thank you for doing this, dear," she said. "I'm afraid we're all a bit shaken up."

I gave her a warm smile. "It's no problem."

"So, do you know my Jonathan?"

"Yes, we have a few classes together, and we hung out on Saturday, at the Snowman Sled Races."

"Oh, yes, he told me that was fun. Thank you for making him feel welcome."

I shrugged, turning my head to hide my blush. "He's cool."

We both sipped our drinks and sat in silence for a few moments before Mrs. Burns said, "Tell me about your family, Celeste."

"Oh, it's just my dad and me. He's an accountant; he does the books for a lot of the businesses in town. My mom died when I was little. I don't really remember her."

She nodded. "We lost Jonathan's father some years ago now, but Jonathan was old enough to remember him, and miss him." She started to tear up.

"I'm so sorry," I said, keeping my eyes fixed on the street so she could regain her composure. "Jonathan said you moved around Europe a lot, but your accent is different from his." I tried to change the subject.

"Yes, well, Jonathan's lived here his whole life, but I grew up in Faerie, and lived there many years before coming here."

"Faerie?" I shook my head. "Where is that?"

"Why, it's our homeland, dear. Has no one ever told you about it?"

"N-no . . ."

She clicked her tongue. "You're young yet, and there's been so much turmoil, I'm not surprised you haven't been, but I would have thought you'd at least heard of it." She had a perplexed look on her face. "Faerie is where our people come from. My family, yours"—she considered me—"or at least one of your parents, the Walshes, the Fairchilds. All the fae."

"Fae?" This woman was making less and less sense the more she talked.

She looked at me as if I were the crazy one. "Yes, of course. Fae come from Faerie. Did you think we were native to the earth realm?"

"Uh, yes. Are you saying you—we—are some sort of aliens? Is that why I have this ability?"

"In a way, I suppose you could say that," she said, tilting her head. "You didn't know?"

"No, this is all news to me. As far as anyone ever told me, I'm human. My dad's human. I thought everyone in this town was human, but you're telling me there's an alien—fae—population living here too?"

"Oh, there's a lot more than fae and humans in this town. There are shifters—humans that turn into animals—vampires, angels, demons, witches . . . Well, you don't need the complete list. Suffice it to say there are a number of supernatural species in town, and all living side by side." She shook her head. "It's amazing, really."

Vampires? Demons? People who turn into animals? This was insanity. I looked at Mrs. Burns again, but she didn't seem as though she were joking or trying to trick me.

"How do you know all this? Didn't you just move here?"

"Oh, yes, dear. But that's my ability—species identification. I can tell by looking at a person what they are, even if it's hidden from human eyes."

I turned my attention back to the window, trying to process what she'd told me. I would ordinarily think she was off her rocker, but this did give me an explanation for what was happening to me. Was it possible I'd been in the dark my whole life about not just who I was, but *what* I was?

"So is my dad fae too, then?"

"I'm not sure; I'd have to meet him. You definitely are, but you're also a bit human, so he could be human, if your mom was fae."

"Why didn't he tell me?" I said aloud, though really I was talking to myself.

"Maybe he was waiting until you were older. Or if he is human, maybe his memory was altered. They seem to be pretty strict in this town about keeping humans in the dark." She seemed to realize something, her face draining of color. "Oh, my. I think maybe . . . I shouldn't have said anything to you. I was warned not to speak of supernatural affairs to humans, but, well, you aren't human, are you?"

I shrugged. I didn't know what I was anymore. "Don't worry, I won't tell. Does Jonathan know?"

"He knows about you, just because of your position. Elsmed is an elder of our people, and he would not likely be mentoring you unless you were fae as well. And Elsmed did tell us about your ability, as it's pertinent to our security situation. It's so kind of you to help us like this. We have been running for a long time, but I didn't imagine they'd catch up to us again so quickly, not here."

I nodded, even though I had no idea what she was talking about. Why were they on the run? Had she done something wrong? Had Jonathan? Questions were bouncing around in my head so fast, I almost didn't notice the teenage boy on the sidewalk, eyeing the house as his steps slowed. I did a double take and recognized him as Remy MacKinnon, a boy I knew from school, though he had only moved to town a few months ago.

I focused on him, tuning out everything else jumbling my mind. *Go away*, I commanded him with my mind. *Keep on walking.*

His steps picked back up, still slow, but he was moving. *Go home*, I directed him, putting every ounce of my willpower into pushing that idea on him. *You have to be home, you have to be there now, and there is nothing here to stop you.* His head turned away, looking across the street as he passed the Walsh property and picked up his pace again.

I heaved a sigh of relief.

CHAPTER 8

CELESTE

*R*emy was back. He came from the other direction now, from what I guessed was his home, somewhere here in Creekwood. About an hour had passed since his first pass by the house, and this time he was headed straight for it.

"Go upstairs and call Elsmed," I said to Mrs. Burns, before calling out to him myself. *Help!* was all I could manage before turning my mind to pushing this boy away. I heard Mrs. Burns running up the stairs.

Turn around and run, I commanded him. He seemed unfazed, crossing the street diagonally. *You need to be at Danzan Park*, I pushed on him. *You're meeting someone there.* He didn't even flinch.

Just as he approached the front porch, I heard a woman's voice behind me. "What's going on?"

I turned to see Addie Beaumont standing in the living room, looking around at the empty space. *How did she get in here?* I pointed to the front door. "Someone is here. I couldn't turn him away."

She nodded her understanding as a knock sounded on the door. "Stay out of sight."

I tucked myself behind the wall next to the stairs while Addie answered the door.

"Hello, can I help you?"

"Uh . . . is this the Walsh residence?"

"Yes. How can I help you?"

"I-Is Mrs. Burns here?" he stammered. "I have a . . . message for her."

"I'll take it," Addie replied.

"No, I have to give it to her personally," the boy said.

"No, you don't." Addie's tone said she was brooking no argument.

"If she's out, I can wait—"

"Oh, to hell with this," Addie muttered before she unleashed a string of what sounded like Latin. After a moment, she called, "You can come out, Celeste."

I came back into the living room to see Remy looking straight ahead, vacantly, while Addie pushed him into a chair. "Watch him, but he should stay put for a while. I'm going to call someone to come pick him up," she said, then went into the kitchen to use the phone.

I moved to the front window again, keeping one eye on the street outside the house, and one on the boy in the chair. He didn't even blink; it was as if he were sleeping with his eyes open. Creepy. I also saw he was wearing a jagged black stone on a leather cord around his neck. I wondered if that could be the reason my pushes didn't work on him.

Addie finished her calls and proceeded to start pulling things out of her messenger bag—candles, jars, and bundles of herbs.

"I'm going to refresh the wards on the house," she told me. "Help should be arriving momentarily."

After a few minutes, I saw Elsmed arrive out front, at the same time as Mike McCabe. They shook hands and exchanged a few words, then approached the house and opened the front door without knocking. Surveying the living room with a frown, Elsmed finally settled his gaze on me.

"Celeste, thank you for your help. I'll cover the front door. Why don't you go and check on Mrs. Walsh and Mrs. Burns?"

I nodded and proceeded to the sunroom to fill Mrs. Walsh in on what had been occurring in her house since she'd left us. I arrived in the bright, chilly room to find Mrs. Walsh slumped over in her chair, eyes closed, her knitting fallen to the floor.

"Mrs. Walsh," I exclaimed, running over to her. "Are you okay?" I shook her shoulder gently, but she didn't wake up. Quickly checking her pulse, like we'd learned in health class, I found it steady and strong.

But I was sure Mrs. Walsh hadn't just passed out for no reason. I scanned the room, and my gaze snagged on the side door—unlatched. Otherwise, though, the room was empty and undisturbed.

If someone had taken out Mrs. Walsh, it was likely they were still in the house. Instead of yelling for help, I crept noiselessly back to where Addie was chanting over a crystal in the corner and told her what I'd found.

She gestured for me to follow her up the stairs. I did, trying to make as little noise as possible. When we reached the top landing, we heard muted voices coming from behind a closed door. To the left, the hallway led to a bathroom and a bedroom, both with open doors. To the right were two closed doors and one open doorway nearer the stairs.

"Let him go!" we heard Mrs. Burns cry.

"Give me the key, and he's all yours," said another woman's voice; I didn't recognize it. Addie pointed at the nearest closed door, and I slunk along behind her as we approached it.

"You're not even fae! What could you possibly want the key for?" Mrs. Burns stalled.

"It's not for me, you idiot; it's for the Collector. And I don't care why. All I ask is how much I'm getting paid." This brought Addie up short, and she cocked her head as if confused.

"And how much is that?" Mrs. Burns asked.

The woman laughed. "Much more than you could ever hope to scrape together, if you're thinking you can outbid on this job."

I peered in through the open doorway as we passed it; it looked like Mrs. Walsh's bedroom.

"Please, just put down the knife, and we can talk about this."

A knife! Fear crawled up my throat, and I pushed it back down. If we lost the element of surprise, it could be disastrous for Jonathan and his mom. I put a hand on Addie's shoulder, tilted my head toward the open bedroom, then tiptoed in. She stayed in the hall.

"There's nothing to talk about. Give me the key, or I'll slice this boy's throat. Even your kind don't heal that quickly," the intruder sneered.

I dropped to a seated pose on the plush beige carpet and closed my eyes, trying to tune out her threatening words. With all the tension, I was afraid I wouldn't be able to bring myself to a meditative state. My mind raced, and my heartbeat thundered in my ears.

"You'll never get away," Mrs. Burns said.

I tried to focus my mind, but it felt like a whirlwind of emotion. I put my hands in my lap, palms together, and imagined the whirlwind as a tangible thing. Once I saw it in my mind, I tilted the funnel cloud out slowly, pushing it until the center pointed away from me. I took a deep breath and blew out slowly, releasing the whirlwind as the air left my lungs.

All the emotion—the fear, self-doubt, and worry—was sucked away, and my mind was left clear. Within moments I was looking at a small constellation of stars—two clustered together, one nearby, and one slightly farther away. Jonathan, the attacker, Mrs. Burns, and Addie, I placed them. But of the two close together, I wasn't sure which was who.

"Clueless woman. Getting in was the hard part. I can portal out of here in seconds," the stranger said.

I had to take a chance. I didn't know if trying to influence a mind from this state would work, or if I had to see the person. I had a fifty-fifty chance of choosing the right light to focus on. But

I didn't have time for deliberation. I chose the one farther from what I thought was Mrs. Burns.

Drop the knife! It's burning your hand! Open your hands! I threw a few commands out, hoping one would stick. I heard a scream, then a scuffle. I kept shooting commands at my target. *You can't close your hands. In fact, you can't move. Your muscles have all gone stiff.* A couple of thumps preceded a strangled cry of pain.

I opened my eyes and rushed through the hall and into the next room. Jonathan had his arms wrapped around a woman with dark hair, fair skin, and bright red lips. Mrs. Burns was standing on the blade of a knife, flattening it against the floor, and Addie was chanting again, her hands pointed at the stranger.

Footsteps thundered up the stairs and down the hall. Roman Bishop burst into the room, followed by Sheriff Kasun. The sheriff took one look around and calmly slapped handcuffs on the woman, who was standing stiff as a board. I smiled to myself.

"Where is it, witch?" Mrs. Burns cried. "Where is my pendant?"

The woman smirked at her but said nothing.

"Why don't you leave the questioning to us, Mrs. Burns?" Sheriff Kasun said. "We'll find out what she's done with it."

"Not to worry," Roman said. "It won't take us long." He flashed a truly frightening smile at the woman, who seemed to go even paler at his statement.

Having turned the woman over to the authorities, Jonathan crossed the room to put his arm around his mother, who was shaking uncontrollably—whether with rage or fear, it was hard to tell.

The sheriff and Roman filed out of the room, the woman between them, leaving me and Addie with Jonathan and his mother.

"Are you both okay?" I asked, looking them over.

Mrs. Burns took a shuddering breath. "No real harm done, dear. Thanks to you, I presume."

I felt a blush creep up my face as Jonathan looked at me in

surprise. "She just dropped the knife all of a sudden. That was you?"

I nodded sheepishly. "I didn't know if I could, but I had to try. And, somehow, it worked."

Addie shook her head. "She was foolish to come in here unprotected. I guess she thought that boy would provide enough distraction to allow her to get to you, Leah."

"Well, she was right about that, I guess," Mrs. Burns said. "She was in here waiting for me when I came up. Is Helena all right? That witch was gloating about knocking her out."

"Yes, I think she'll be fine," Addie said. "I asked Elsmed to check on her, and he's probably already called Dr. Underwood."

Mrs. Burns turned to Jonathan. "Are you sure you're okay? She didn't—" She broke off, tears coming to her eyes as she realized what could have happened.

"I'm fine, Mom. Go check on Mrs. Walsh. I want to talk to Celeste for a minute."

"Okay," she said, looking at me, then back at her son. "We'll see you downstairs in a bit, then."

Addie put her arm around Mrs. Burns's shoulders as they left the room and went downstairs, leaving me alone with Jonathan.

"So . . ." I said to fill the awkward silence. It just made it seem more awkward.

"So I wanted to thank you. I don't know how you did it, but . . . thank you."

I shrugged off his gratitude.

"No, really." He put a finger under my chin and lifted my face to meet his gaze, sending a shiver through me. "I don't know what would have happened if you hadn't stepped in. My mom was going into panic mode." He sighed, dragging fingers through his longish hair. "We've had to leave our life behind so many times; all we have is each other. She can't give up the artifact, but she isn't willing to give me up for it either." He took my hand in his.

"What is it? The artifact, I mean."

"Mom won't tell me exactly what it does. I just know

that if the wrong people get their hands on it, well . . . it could turn the tide of a war that's been going on for generations. It could mean genocide," he said, making me gasp.

"Well, you're welcome," I said quietly, unsure of what else to say.

He chuckled and leaned in, pressing a soft kiss to my cheek. "You're special, Celeste."

"So are you." I was blushing so hard now, I felt my hair was about to catch fire.

"Oh, really?" he teased.

I nodded vehemently. "Yep. It's not just anyone I rescue from wicked witches," I said with a sly grin.

He rewarded me with a deep belly laugh, then composed himself and bowed low, still holding my hand. "I am honored, my lady," he said, eliciting a giggle from me.

"So I guess you'll be out of school for a few days?"

"Yeah, at least until they find the pendant. I can't leave my mom alone while it's out there. They could send someone else to —" He broke off, and I nodded.

"Well, I know this is far from over, but in the meantime, I can bring you notes and assignments to get your mind off things while they search. Help you study?"

He hesitated, and I guessed he hadn't considered keeping up with his schoolwork, but in the end he smiled. "Sure, that would be great."

We exchanged cell numbers to keep in touch.

"Come on, we'd better go downstairs before they come looking for us," I said.

Elsmed was talking to Mr. McCabe when we reached the living room, and through the window I could see the sheriff helping the dark-haired witch into his truck, with Roman Bishop impatiently tapping the toe of his expensive-looking shoe on the sidewalk.

"You'll have to keep a close eye on him," Elsmed was saying.

"Addie will clear him of the compulsion, but he's susceptible. We don't want him caught up with this thief again."

"You have my word, Elsmed," Mr. McCabe said, giving the older man a firm handshake. "I have no intention of letting him out of my sight except to send him to school, and I'll make sure Friske has a tight leash on him as well."

"Thank you, Mike," Elsmed said. "Now let's get you back home."

As if on cue, Addie appeared from the hall to the sunroom. After nodding to Elsmed and Mr. McCabe, she proceeded to stand in front of Remy, who was still sitting in a chair, staring vacantly. She held her hands out toward him and started a low chant that went on for several minutes.

When she finished, Remy blinked rapidly and looked around with alarm, seeming as if he'd just been startled awake.

"What— Where— How—" he uttered in obvious confusion, his eyes darting from one person to the next, before landing on Mr. McCabe.

"I'll explain on the way home," Mr. McCabe said, extending an arm to rest around the boy's shoulders as he rose to his feet. "Let's leave these folks to their business." He nodded to Elsmed as he opened the front door, revealing Dr. Underwood with his hand raised to knock on it.

Once McCabe had left with Remy, Addie escorted Dr. Underwood back to the sunroom to check on Mrs. Walsh.

"Jonathan, why don't you go help your mother and Dr. Underwood," Elsmed said. "I'll see that Celeste gets home safely."

Jonathan looked to me as he nodded, touched my hand in goodbye, and disappeared down the hallway.

"Why?" I asked.

Elsmed peered down at me as he walked me home. "Would you care to expand on that?"

"Why didn't my dad, or you, or anyone tell me I was fae?"

"Well, your dad didn't—doesn't—know, and I'd like very much to keep it that way. I was . . . getting around to it."

"He doesn't know? How is that possible? My mom was fae, right?"

"Yes, and your dad is human. We have rules in this town to protect the humans from knowing too much about the supernaturals. I can't say how much your mother told him about her nature when she was alive, but after she was gone, the Court ruled that he would be better off not knowing."

"The court? What court would rule a man should be kept in the dark about his own wife—and daughter?"

"The Court of the Sun and the Moon. It's not your average civil court. It's the ruling body of this town and decides all matters of importance affecting supernatural residents and visitors. It is made up of certain members of the founding families of this town, and I am one of them."

"So we have an extra court that enforces its own rules? Is that legal?"

I could swear he rolled his eyes. "It's for the good of the town and everyone in it. What do you think would happen if someone let slip that there were supernaturals living here? Do you think we would be safe if word got out there were fae in Havenwood Falls? Or vampires? Or witches? We've learned from our past, even if the rest of the world refuses to." He fixed me with a glare that indicated that was all he was saying about that subject.

I decided to get back to the point. "How could my dad be better off not remembering my mom?"

"Oh, he remembers her. It's just that his memory is fuzzy on a few details. Humans are used to that."

"But . . . I still don't understand why."

"It's a . . . delicate issue, Celeste. Your mother's death was very . . . unusual. Violent. It would have been traumatizing for your father to know the truth. We decided it was for the best to let him forget some of the supernatural elements, but let him retain the essence of his relationship with his wife. Trust me, it was kinder this way."

"I see," I said, my voice sounding small. "So it wasn't . . . the accident?"

The old man just shook his head.

"Will you tell me what happened to her?"

Elsmed eyed me. "Perhaps. But not tonight."

We both fell silent, our footsteps on the sidewalk reverberating through the freezing evening air.

"So what about me?"

"What about you?"

"Well, am I just left to figure things out on my own? Don't I get a faerie godmother or something to help me?"

This started in Elsmed a chuckle that soon grew into a hearty laugh, which almost seemed to threaten his breathing. "A . . . faerie . . . godmother!"

I couldn't help the smile that crept across my own face.

Once he'd caught his breath, Elsmed continued walking. "I've kept an eye on you from afar. Your abilities were mostly benign until recently, but I monitored you to make sure they didn't get out of hand. I stepped in once it became clear your awakening was beginning and you would need guidance to control your gift."

"What else can I do? I mean, is what I did in there the extent of my ability? Or is there more?"

"Each person's ability is their own. We will continue to explore the nature of yours. In addition, I would like to get you enrolled in an evening class at Sun and Moon Academy that will help you develop and hone your skills. It's a private school for supernaturals, and they specialize in helping young people master their abilities."

"*Another* class?" I whined. *First yoga, now this. I'm going to have no social life at all if he keeps signing me up for all these classes.* "I don't think— I mean, isn't that expensive? My dad isn't exactly private-school rich."

Elsmed regarded me out of the corner of his eye. "Don't worry about tuition; just tell your father I applied for a scholarship on your behalf. I'll take care of the enrollment. You just make time in your *busy social schedule* to attend class on Thursday evenings."

"Do you listen in on everything that goes through my head?" *I sure hope not.*

Elsmed chuckled. "No, certainly not. But keeping a civil tone in your mind is good practice for maintaining one on your tongue. Respect will get you far in this town, but it must be given before it can be received."

"I'll keep that in mind," I promised.

When we arrived at my house, I was dismissed to my room while Elsmed chatted with Dad, probably about my new classes. I, for one, was exhausted, and starting to come down from the adrenaline rush of the afternoon's events.

I settled in to do homework, but found myself replaying the day in my mind. Havenwood Falls had been my home my whole life, but suddenly I felt like I didn't know anything about my own town. A town filled with supernaturals, who apparently had their own school even, and I'd been completely oblivious. What else was I blind to?

CHAPTER 9

JONATHAN

*I*t was lucky we hadn't accumulated much since we got to town, because we were moving again. Mom said she couldn't continue to put Mrs. Walsh in danger, and even though Mrs. Walsh protested, I could see the fear in her eyes. Her parents lived in the apartment above the garage; if anything happened to them because of us, my mom would never forgive herself.

Havenwood Falls wasn't the idyllic place it purported to be. I'd heard rumors in the short time I was in school that for some time now, valuable items had gone missing and more than one person had even been kidnapped. It made me wonder why my mom thought this was a safe place to come to begin with. No place was safe for us anymore. It was pretty clear to me, so I didn't know why she couldn't see that truth.

Of course, we couldn't leave town until we'd gotten the Seelie key back. My mom had finally filled me in on what exactly we'd lost. More than the simple piece of jewelry it seemed, the key would grant access to one of the most sacred places in Faerie, a source of power for the Seelie fae. If the Unseelie army infiltrated it, they could cripple the Seelie army and topple the Seelie Court. We could not let that happen.

Fortunately for them, but unfortunately for us, the key would not work on its own. It needed a password—a key to the key—to work. My mom said she didn't have the password, but she must know who did. The most important thing right now was getting that pendant back and getting on the road. If we kept moving, it would be that much harder to find us.

To be honest, though, I was getting a little tired of living constantly on the run. I felt an unexpected pang of sadness at the thought of leaving, and not for the first time, wished we could settle down somewhere for good. We hadn't been in town long enough for me to really grow attached to much, but there was one person I didn't want to say goodbye to yet: Celeste.

For now, Elsmed was moving us to one of his properties in town. There were no guarantees we'd be any safer there, but at least we wouldn't be putting anyone else in danger. I finished packing all my worldly belongings into my backpack and a single duffel bag just as my mom came into the room.

"All set?" she asked.

"Yeah, this is everything."

A sad look crossed her face. I knew this wasn't the life she imagined for me, for her family. But it was the life we got. Sometimes there were circumstances beyond your control, and you just had to roll with it. I knew it, and she knew it.

"Okay, let's go say goodbye."

My mom thanked Mrs. Walsh for her hospitality and apologized for the trouble our stay had caused her, while I waited by the door. The two women had become fast friends, and while we weren't leaving town just yet, I could see in my mom's slumped shoulders and tearing eyes that she was pulling away from the friendship in preparation for our eventual final departure.

When we finally made it out the door, Elsmed Fairchild was waiting to take us to our new temporary home.

"Good afternoon, Burns family."

"Good afternoon, Elsmed," my mother greeted him. "Thank you for giving us a place to stay until the key is found."

We loaded our meager possessions into the waiting car and piled in.

"The new house will be more secure until this all blows over," he said, as the driver pulled away from the curb. "I still think Havenwood Falls is the safest place for you both to stay, even after we've found the key and returned it to your care."

"How can you say that?" my mom blurted, earning a glare from Elsmed. She cleared her throat and ducked her head. "Respectfully, Elder, the key was stolen within weeks of our arrival here. It doesn't seem the safest place for us or it."

"By all appearances, the perpetrators of the theft are not associated with Unseelie elements. The woman who attacked you is just a money-hungry witch, and we'll get to the bottom of what brought her here. She'll forget about this place as soon as she leaves it, and won't be able to enter again. The wards on the town offer you a layer of protection you won't find anywhere else. Not to mention the residents who are able to help."

"How did she find out about the key in the first place? It's not exactly common knowledge outside fae circles."

"That's one of the questions we're trying to answer with our interrogations. Trust me, the entire Court is focused on eliminating any threats to our town's residents and visitors. It's better to be inside than out."

"I'll keep that in mind, Elsmed," Mom said, still sounding skeptical.

The car pulled up to a small Victorian house just a block from the town square. It looked well maintained, if plain, with white siding and a covered front porch. Elsmed got out and waited while we gathered our things.

"This is one of the most protected spots in town," he said, walking ahead of us toward the front door. "Addie lives only a few blocks down that way"—he pointed to one side of the house— "and your neighbor on this side, Everett Weston, is a gargoyle protector." *Wow, this town really does have one of everything.* "Across the street, of course, is the police station. Anyone would be mad to try to attack you here."

Mom looked up and down the street, anxiety still apparent on her face.

"Don't worry, Leah," Elsmed said. "We'll get all the information we need out of that witch soon enough. Roman is questioning her right now."

She pursed her lips, saying nothing.

Elsmed continued the realtor routine. "The place is furnished —two bedrooms—and there are linens in the closets, but I haven't had a chance to stock the icebox. The grocery store in Miller's Plaza should have everything you need."

"Thank you, Elsmed," my mom said. "We'll get settled in on our own. I'm sure you have a lot to do."

He nodded once and handed over the house key. "You know how to get in touch with me should you require anything else. I'll let you know when we have any news."

~

CELESTE

It was Thursday, and I was fidgety all day. Even though I knew the witch was locked up, I kept waiting for her to jump out at me from around a corner. On top of that, I would be attending my first Awakening Lab class that evening, and I'd never even been to Sun and Moon Academy before. I didn't know what to expect.

The halls of Havenwood Falls High seemed so different now that I knew they were populated by not only humans, but other supernatural species. I was still wrapping my head around the fact that I was one of them. It felt silly, but for a second I wished I had Mrs. Burns there with me to identify the kids I'd known all my life.

After school, I visited the teachers whose classes Jonathan was in but I wasn't to pick up assignments for him. As I was leaving the last one, books and folders piled high in my arms, I ran into Margaret.

"Hi, Margie."

"Celeste! There you are. Where did you go after class?"

"I'm just getting a few assignments to keep Jonathan caught up while he's out." I was also anxious to learn if they had any news on the search for the pendant, but I couldn't tell her that.

"Oh, is he okay?" Margaret said, looking concerned.

"Yeah, he just had to stay home to deal with some family stuff for a while. I'm going to go study with him now."

"Oh, I see," she said, a smile creeping onto her face. "I enjoy *studying* with Xavier, too."

I bumped her shoulder with mine, making her curls bounce. "I'm not sure if he wants to *study* like that with me."

"Of course he does," she said. "He seems like he's into you. And he wouldn't have asked you to study with him if he didn't want to spend time with you."

"Well, I kind of offered. And there was a definite hesitation before he agreed."

"Hmm, okay, well, has he made any other moves?"

"Well, he did kiss me . . ."

"*What?* Why are you—"

"On the cheek."

"Oh."

"Yeah," I said. "I felt like . . . I don't know, like his little sister or something. I mean, it was sweet, but . . ."

"But not much heat."

"Yeah."

"Well, maybe he's just shy. Give him a minute to get to know you. He won't be able to resist that charm for long."

"You think?"

She looked at me over her glasses. "I know. Now go take those books to your *study buddy,* and I'll see you tomorrow."

❧

TRUDGING down to the town square from school was different with two loads full of books and folders. On my internship days, I'd been able to drop my things at home on the way to City Hall. By the time I got to the corner of Stuart Street and Eleventh, I was cold and wobbly on my feet, not to mention distracted by thoughts of the witch and the pendant.

Just as I was stepping onto the sidewalk from the crosswalk, my foot landed on a patch of ice. Time seemed to slow as books and papers went flying, my arms windmilling futilely for balance, and my bottom landed hard on the pavement.

"Ow."

"Are you okay?"

I looked up and into the face of arguably the hottest guy in town, Everett Weston. I mean, he was taken and probably a dozen years too old for me, but he was perfectly suitable as eye candy. I looked into his bright green eyes and tried to catch my breath.

"I-I think so," I stammered, tearing my eyes away from his to survey the damage. I was surrounded by a circle of books and papers, and my bag had fallen into the street.

Everett turned in a circle, evidently looking for a place to set down the two Coffee Haven cups in his hands, when another voice came from farther down the sidewalk.

"I've got her," Jonathan said, making my breath catch in my throat once more.

Everett and I both looked up to see him strolling down the sidewalk toward the site of my calamity, eyes fixed on mine.

"You okay with him?" Everett muttered under his breath.

I nodded. "Yeah, he's my study date," I said, a smile forming as I levered myself up to my knees so I could start gathering my things. "Thanks, Everett."

"Sure thing. Be careful," he said, then nodded to Jonathan and headed for the steps of his office and home.

Jonathan reached me and stooped to help me gather his

schoolwork, then hoisted my bag onto his shoulder and held out a hand to me. I took it, the way his grip enveloped mine with warmth giving me a thrill as I pulled myself up, careful not to bump into him and knock us both to the ground again.

"Well, I almost made it," I joked.

"A valiant effort." He smiled. "Thanks for bringing all this. It's making me a little crazy sitting around waiting for something to happen."

I laughed nervously. "I know what you mean. I don't know that your Government textbook will make you any less crazy, but at least it's something to do."

We reached the door, and he held it open for me to go inside.

It was a cute space, with blue-striped furniture in the living room and a little white wooden table in the kitchen area. Mrs. Burns was on the phone in the living room, pacing back and forth nervously.

"Let's go upstairs to study," Jonathan suggested. "Mom's likely to be on the phone a while."

"Okay," I agreed, and followed him up the stairs to a sparsely decorated bedroom with a bean bag chair and a low table opposite the bed.

"Please, take the chair," he said, gesturing to the bean bag. "I imagine your behind's had enough of hard surfaces today."

I blushed, but took the offered chair. "Given my behind a lot of thought, have you?"

Now it was his turn to blush. "No more than it deserves," he said with a smile.

Someone's feeling flirty today. "So, any word on the pendant?"

He sat down on the floor beside me. "No—well, yes. They think they've got an approximate location out of the woman, but they haven't found it yet. From what I could tell, it sounded like she'd buried it in the forest somewhere. Mom's on the phone with the sheriff, and they've got a couple of wolf shifters trying to sniff out the location."

"Wolf . . . shifters," I repeated.

"Yeah, you know, they shift from human to wolf, and back."

"I see." *Wow.* My head was starting to spin again.

"Someone named Rusty, and Conall Kasun, I believe, are doing most of the tracking."

"*Deputy* Conall Kasun? Is a wolf?"

"A shifter, yes. The whole Kasun family is. They were going to ask the mountain lions for help, but they've got their hands full with making sure the boy doesn't get sucked back in."

"The boy?"

"The one that was at the house yesterday? At Mrs. Walsh's?"

"Remy. He's a . . . mountain lion?"

"Shifter."

"Uh-huh."

"You really had no idea about any of this, huh?"

I shook my head. "No."

"How is it no one ever told you? Didn't you feel . . . different?"

"Different from what? I've always felt like myself. Apparently, my mom was fae, but my dad is human. She died when I was young, and the powers that be decided it was a good idea to wipe my dad's memory, so who was there to tell me?"

"Okay, I get that. But even before your awakening, you should have had some tendencies toward your ability. Didn't anyone notice?"

"I don't think so. It's not something even I knew I was doing. I just figured I was skilled at getting people to do what I wanted. I attributed my powers of persuasion to my sweet smile and impeccable reasoning. Obviously."

He laughed at this.

"One of my first memories is of my father apologizing to my kindergarten teacher. He said I was a 'willful child,' and that he was at the end of his rope with me. Apparently, I had convinced one of the other kids in my class that he was the appointed pencil sharpener for me and my friends, and he got in trouble for spending twenty minutes at the pencil sharpener. When the teacher had the audacity to tell me I was responsible for

207

sharpening my own pencils, I gave her the silent treatment. For the rest of the month."

"Wow. That's commitment."

"Sometime along the way, my dad and I came to an understanding, and I made my peace with school eventually, but I still don't respond well to being slighted."

"All hail Queen Celeste." He chuckled.

"Hey, I'm not so terrible," I said, pushing his shoulder. "I'm a benevolent ruler."

"Just don't get on your bad side."

"Exactly," I said with a smile.

"You're cute," Jonathan said, and touched my cheek.

"*Cute* is not a word used to describe a queen."

"Oh, of course. My apologies, Your Majesty. I meant to say, of course, delightful."

"Divine?"

He tilted his head as if considering this, then leaned closer and said, "Demure."

"Delicious."

His eyebrow quirked up at this, and his pale blue gaze held mine, only inches away now.

"How would I know if you're delicious?" he said quietly.

I shrugged. "I guess you'd have to take a taste."

Who am I right now? I was like a runaway train; the words came out of my mouth without asking my permission first.

His gaze dropped from my eyes slowly, landing on my lips, which parted at the attention.

"May I?" he asked softly, looking back into my eyes.

I nodded once.

He inched closer and gently pulled me in, his hand on my cheek moving to cradle the back of my head. I closed my eyes and felt his long lashes brush my cheek just before soft lips pressed to mine. Kissing Jonathan was like being wrapped in a warm, cozy blanket after the craziness of the last few days.

"Delectable," he said, pulling away.

"Mm" was all I could manage.

Footsteps on the stairs alerted us to company, and we sprang apart, each picking up a random book. Mrs. Burns stopped at the threshold.

"They've found it."

CHAPTER 10

JONATHAN

*C*eleste and I scrambled to our feet.

"Where was it?" I asked, relieved and worried at the same time. If the key was still out there, unguarded and uncovered, it could easily be lost or taken again.

"Buried in the forest near Mount Alexa," Mom said, her face scrunching in contempt. "I guess the witch figured no one would find it out there." She shook her head at the phone still in her hand.

"So should we go out there to meet them?" We followed my mom down the stairs.

"No," Mom said, "they're going to bring it in to the police station. Ric said we should meet him there." She finally put the phone down and headed for the coatrack by the door.

We all bundled back up in our winter jackets and headed out the door to the police station, just on the other side of the street. I held on to Celeste's hand, mostly so she wouldn't slip and fall again, but also because it felt right being connected to her. She didn't seem to object.

As we neared the door to the station, we met Elsmed Fairchild and Mathilde Augustine heading toward us from the direction of City Hall. I held open the glass door as everyone filed in, the five of us nearly filling the small waiting area just inside. While Mrs. Augustine spoke with the secretary, Elsmed pulled my mom and me aside to a corner of the room.

"We need to discuss the future plans for the safety of the key." He looked at my mom. "I think it's time to pass the mantle on."

She shook her head, her eyes going wide.

"It's all right, Leah. He's old enough."

She looked at me nervously.

My eyes darted back and forth between them. "You . . . me? You want me to guard it? Why not Mom?"

Elsmed put a hand on my shoulder. "You're of age now, son. And it seems too many people know of your mother's guardianship. Time to pass the torch, and perhaps you can stop running for a while."

I laughed out loud at this, causing Celeste to turn her head toward us from where she stood next to Mrs. Augustine.

"Stop running?" I said to Elsmed. "We haven't stopped running my whole life." I glanced at my mom and saw her cast her gaze to the floor. "Now that we've lost the key once, we've got to run even farther and faster than before."

"Slow down, Jonathan," Elsmed said. "I heard your mother yesterday, and we've been working on a plan to throw any pursuers off your scent. The unique thing about Havenwood Falls is that anyone who comes here and leaves again won't remember this place, or what occurred while they were here. We can send out a false key with the witch. She'll think she's got the real thing, and once she leaves our borders, she won't have any recollection of you or how she got it."

"Won't they come looking for us again? What's to stop the process from repeating?"

"We'll send her on a wild goose chase for the password. It will keep her busy for some time and give us a chance to make progress on finding out who her employer is, since she's lied about that. By the time they discover the key's a fake, we'll have put an end to all this trouble."

"And if you don't?"

"If we don't, you're still in the most protected place in the earth realm. No worse off than you were when you arrived here."

Mom looked at me with worry in her deep blue eyes. "Are you ready for this responsibility?" she asked.

I nodded, amazed that she was even considering this plan. I was ready, though. Happy, even, to take this burden from my mother, to take on the duty that my father carried before me. Before he died, he had explained to me that the burden of protecting the pendant would fall to me someday. "I am."

Elsmed nodded. "We can disguise the real key so that it is unrecognizable to anyone who saw it before. Mathilde is skilled in such magic, and it will be further hidden by your glamour, Jonathan."

"All right," I said, putting an arm around my mother, who was still shaking with nervous energy.

We looked up as the sheriff came into the police station, a small iron box in his hand. A slight wave of nausea swept through me. Being close to iron had that effect on me, and I could tell the other fae were feeling the signature weakness as well, though less than we would have felt outside the protection Havenwood Falls afforded us. The sheriff told the secretary he needed "the big room," and tilted his head to indicate we should follow him. We did, along with Mrs. Augustine and Celeste.

We all entered a space that looked much like a conference room, with a large table and several chairs. Sheriff Kasun closed the door behind us and invited everyone to take a seat.

"Well, it took us a little while, but we found it. Is this the item that was stolen from you?" He opened the box to reveal my mom's pendant inside, nestled on a velvet cushion.

Mom broke out in tears, nodding her head and reaching for the pendant.

"Yes, that's it," I responded, because she was clearly unable to get words out at the moment.

Mom lifted the gold pendant to her chest, clutching it so tightly in her fist I thought she might crush the thing.

"Thank you, Ric," Elsmed said. "The box should be processed for evidence right away. It did not belong to Mrs. Burns, but might hold a clue to identifying whoever really hired the witch."

"Sure, I'll hold on to it. Why don't you all keep the room a few minutes, until you're ready to leave," he said, looking at my mom, who was still racked with sobs.

"And please call Wieland Manos and have him meet us here right away."

"Okay," Ric said, clearly not understanding the purpose behind the command, but not about to question Elsmed Fairchild.

"Give our appreciation to Rusty and Conall, please, Ric," Mrs. Augustine said as he opened the door.

He nodded his acknowledgment and left, closing the door behind him. Elsmed and Mathilde quickly put their heads together and started discussing something I supposed we weren't meant to hear.

I leaned over to Celeste, who had taken the seat on the other side of my mother, and whispered, "Manos?"

She turned her head and whispered in my ear, "Jeweler."

Aha.

We waited for Manos, my mom slowly recovering from her crying bout and releasing her vise grip on the pendant. Celeste laid a comforting hand on Mom's shoulder.

About ten minutes later, the sheriff escorted a man into the room. Wieland Manos was medium height, with green eyes and blond, almost white, hair. He smiled as he entered, though it was obvious he had no idea why he'd been summoned.

"Wieland, thank you for coming," Elsmed said, rising to shake hands with the man. "I don't know if you've had the pleasure of meeting Leah Burns and her son, Jonathan?" He waved a hand in our direction.

"Ah, no. It's nice to make your acquaintance," he said.

I rose to shake his hand, and my mother managed a smile.

"Please, sit," Elsmed said, taking his own seat again. "We have need of your services—and your discretion," he continued, sharpening his gaze at Manos to make his point. "You are skilled with gold filigree, are you not?"

Manos puffed out his chest a bit. "Yes, it is a specialty of mine," he answered.

"Excellent. We need you to replicate this piece exactly," Elsmed said, gesturing to my mother to show the pendant.

She reluctantly opened her hand and laid it on the table, its surface shimmering in the fluorescent lights.

"Oh, that is exquisite," Manos said, reaching out to pick up the piece of jewelry. My mom gasped and reached out as if to take it back, but Celeste held her hand and put an arm around her shoulders to calm her.

Manos took a jeweler's loupe out of his pocket and examined the necklace closely, turning it over in his hand. "Do you want a chain like this too?"

"Yes, exactly the same."

Manos bent his head to study the chain again, then nodded. "I can do it. No problem. I'll have it ready in two days' time."

"That will have to do," Elsmed said. "I'm afraid we cannot let it out of Mrs. Burns's possession, though. Can you craft it from memory?"

Mr. Manos looked less sure of this proposition. "Can I take some pictures?" he said.

Elsmed considered this, exchanging glances with Mathilde before answering.

"Yes, you may photograph the piece, but all images must be destroyed once the piece is finished. No copies, Wieland, digital or otherwise. Understood?"

"Yes, sir. No problem."

We all waited and watched in silence as Manos took out his phone and photographed the necklace, turning it this way and that to capture every detail. I felt myself growing wistful. After seeing the necklace on my mother every single day of my life, I would miss seeing its delicate form.

Once Manos was finished, he stood to go. "I'll give you a call when it's ready," he said.

"Thank you, Wieland," Elsmed said, standing to shake hands again and close the door behind the jeweler.

"Now there's one thing left to do," Elsmed said, turning to Mrs. Augustine.

"May I?" Mrs. Augustine asked my mother, who gave her a nod and looked sorrowfully at her pendant.

Mrs. Augustine picked up the key and closed her hands around it, holding them close in front of her and bowing her head. She looked like she was praying, eyes closed and speaking words too softly for us to hear. After a minute, she looked up at me.

"Do you want a magical tracker on it?" she asked.

I looked to my mom, who gave me a slight nod of acceptance. We both knew this could be dangerous if the tracker was compromised, but could save us if anything like what had happened over the last few days were to transpire again.

"Yes, please," I told Mrs. Augustine.

"Come here," she said.

She bowed her head and mumbled some more words over the key as I came over to stand beside her, then stood herself and placed her still-folded hands against my chest. Now that I was standing close to her, I could hear the words she said, but couldn't make sense of them. Suddenly, she stopped speaking and looked up, opening her hands.

As I looked down into her open hands, I saw a completely different piece of jewelry. It was a tarnished silver disc with a Celtic knot design embossed on it, strung onto what looked like a leather cord. And I could feel it. It was not uncomfortable, but it felt like a string had been pulled taut between my heart and the pendant, and I knew I could find it with my eyes closed.

"The feeling will go away once you put it on, and return if you take it off," she said.

"He won't take it off," Mom said.

"No, you won't need to," said Mrs. Augustine. "The cord looks like leather, but it's not. It's stronger than steel and resistant to water. And the disc won't polish if you rub it, so don't bother trying." She smiled.

"It's perfect," I said, lifting it over my head to rest around my neck. "Thank you, Mrs. Augustine."

"My pleasure, dear," she said, backing away and brushing imaginary dust from her skirt.

I looked to my mom, whose eyes were tearing up again. I rounded the table again to stand beside her. "Don't worry, Mom. Nothing is changing, except I'm wearing it now. Everything stays the same."

"Oh, honey," she said. "Nothing's the same. I knew this day would come, but I didn't imagine it would be so soon. We will be okay, though. We will be okay." She sounded as if she was trying to reassure herself.

Elsmed cleared his throat, drawing everyone's attention to him once again. "All right, we've done all we need to for now. Ric will keep the witch locked up until the necklace is ready, and then we'll drop her off well outside the border and let her lead us to this person she called the Collector. Then we can find out what brought her here, and prevent it from happening again."

"I'll walk back with you to get my stuff," Celeste said. We all made our way out of the police station.

"Don't forget your class tonight, Celeste," Elsmed warned as we parted ways. "You're already registered, and I've asked Gianna's mother to give you a ride home from class."

Celeste blanched. "Gianna's . . ."

"A witch, of course, like me," Mrs. Augustine finished for her.

I saw the light dawn on Celeste as she put it together. "O-of course," she managed to get out. "That sounds great, thanks."

We turned to go our separate ways.

"I don't know that I'll ever get used to finding out that people I've known all my life are not . . . people."

"Oh, we're all people, dear," Mom said. "Just different kinds."

"I guess so," Celeste mused, still looking a bit dazed.

"What class are you taking?" I asked to try to snap her out of it.

"It's called Awakening Lab. It's for practice, I guess, to learn control of your abilities. I thought it was just for fae, but I guess not."

"You know what they say, dear," my mom said.

"What's that?" Celeste asked.

"It takes all kinds to make a world."

∾

CELESTE

THE WALK to Sun and Moon Academy was just as far from the Burnses' place as Havenwood Falls High, and I was worn out from a long day when I arrived at the Academy. Somehow, even though I'd lived in Havenwood Falls my whole life, I'd never been on the Academy's campus. It was beautiful, even though I couldn't see much of the grounds because by the time I arrived, full dark was descending.

I passed through a stone arch into a courtyard surrounded by stately buildings. It felt almost as if I'd wandered onto a college campus, though there were few people around at this time of the evening. I followed signs to the Falls Campus, where my class was being held, and found myself trailing behind a few other students headed the same way.

Luckily, they knew where to go, so I didn't waste time searching for the classroom. I should have been dead on my feet after the day I'd had, but somehow I felt more energized the farther I ventured onto the campus. My footsteps echoed in the courtyards. The nearby waterfall was mostly iced over from the winter's cold, and only a slight trickle could be heard.

As I took a seat, I again found myself wondering what species were in the room. To my surprise, Gianna's mom—Ronya Augustine, Mathilde's daughter-in-law—entered the class a moment later and introduced herself as the instructor. My jaw almost dropped to the floor. I supposed I should just get used to being astonished.

After a few preliminary announcements and ground rules (no active practicing on your classmates unless specifically requested to do so by the teacher), we were split into small groups—shift control, harnessing energy, appetite management, mental exercise, and physical exercise. I went up to Ms. Augustine after the assignments, while the other students rearranged themselves into groups.

"Excuse me, Ms. Augustine?"

"Welcome to class, Celeste. I'm so excited to get to work with you," she said.

"Me too. But I think I was assigned to the wrong group."

"Oh, let me see." She looked at her list. "No, I have you in appetite management."

"Shouldn't I be in mental exercise, though? I mean, I don't have an appetite problem"—I looked at my group and gulped—"not like other students might."

"No, of course," Ms. Augustine said. "Every student here is unique. We rotate you through groups as you gain proficiency in the study areas, but we have to take things in order or there could be repercussions. Right now, the first priority for you is appetite management."

I shook my head, still not understanding, but let her shoo me back to my group. She gave us an assignment to take a few minutes to identify our most pressing desires before we started to brainstorm ways to manage them. The other members of my group introduced themselves. Otis was a tall boy with longish dark hair and brown eyes. I had seen him around Havenwood Falls High, but didn't have any classes with him. Delia was a petite blonde with green eyes whom I'd not met before. We pulled our desks into a circle to talk.

"Blood," said Delia, conspicuously looking everywhere but at me. "Always blood." *I guess she didn't need a few minutes for that one*, I thought to myself, and made a mental note to keep my distance from her.

"The hunt," said Otis. "I dream about hunting, and now I'm even starting to daydream about it. It's distracting me from school, friends, everything."

They looked at me. *My turn.* What could I say? I didn't have any uncontrollable urges that I knew about. I had become aware of certain strong feelings about Jonathan, but I wasn't about to share them with these practical strangers, and certainly not in front of Ms. Augustine.

"I-I don't know," I said.

"Think about it," Ms. Augustine said, walking up to our group from behind me. "If not for yourself, what do you most want for someone else, right now?"

Other than to be not here? I closed my eyes to shut out the looks Delia was giving me. I was suddenly feeling a little unsafe. *Like poor Mrs. Burns. How awful it must have been to be violated that way, to be attacked not once, but twice.* I started getting angrier the more I thought about it. *How dare that witch prey on innocent people like that! And for what, a little money? She just attacked Mrs. Walsh in her own home!* The events of the past couple of days were finally catching up to me, and I was so enraged I forgot what question I was even supposed to be answering.

"What is it you want, Celeste?" Ms. Augustine said quietly.

"Revenge," I blurted out, surprising myself, and judging by their expressions, those around me.

"Whoa," said the hunter.

"Dark," said the bloodthirsty girl.

I looked at Ms. Augustine. "Good work," she said. "Now brainstorm ideas for managing your desires." She looked at each of us with a smile and turned to go speak to another group.

"Do you drink animal blood?" Otis asked Delia.

"Yes," she said, "but it's not exactly . . . satisfying. I'm trying to get off the human blood bank supply. I don't like the idea of feeding off my friends and neighbors, you know?"

"Yeah, totally," I said. *Wow, maybe this girl isn't so bad after all.*

"How about you?" she said to Otis. "Don't you get to hunt with your family?"

"Yeah," he said, "when the weather's nice. But my mom won't let me go out in the cold. She says she's afraid of finding a pup popsicle in the morning."

"Have you talked to the coach at school?" I asked. "Maybe some other kind of physical activity could help out."

"No, but you're right, I should. There are a lot of shifters on the football team. I bet he has some sort of regimen worked out with them."

Huh. I guess that makes sense.

"So what about you?" Otis said.

"Me, well," I said, "I've started yoga. I've heard meditation helps with . . . I guess, keeping my cool. I just get so *angry* sometimes at the injustices I see."

"My dad always says, 'Empathy is the best prevention for anger.' Maybe that's something to work on?" Otis suggested.

"I *do* have empathy, though," I rebutted. "I have empathy for the victims, the ones who deserve it."

"Everyone is a victim of their own circumstance," Ms. Augustine said, circling back to us. "And everyone is deserving of empathy. Once you accept that, you may find you are better able to use your ability for positive purposes. It is not a tool for punishment but for empowerment."

"Empowerment," I parroted, turning the idea over in my head.

"Yes. Think about whom you could lift up with your ability, and you'll be surprised, I think, at the positive impact you can make."

CHAPTER 11

CELESTE

*S*chool on Friday felt like an eternity. I was hopping with nervous energy, and couldn't stand the thought of another attack. There was no chance of me focusing on what my teachers were actually saying. At least it gave me plenty of time to think on what Mrs. Augustine had said the evening before. There had to be a way I could use my anger and turn it to a positive purpose.

In English Lit, I resolved to do something to help get rid of the witch once and for all. Even with the return of the key, the threat to Jonathan and his mom still lingered. I just didn't trust that the witch would go straight to the mastermind of the theft if she was driven outside of town and dropped off by the authorities. Something told me she was a little smarter than that. She needed an extra push.

In Bio, I began to hatch a plan that would either be an amazing win or a spectacular failure. If I could use my ability to make her think she was getting away clean, we might have a better chance at tracking down the person who was really behind the theft, and maybe prevent it from happening again. Maybe it would even convince Jonathan's mom that they could stay in Havenwood Falls and stop living on the run. By the final bell, I couldn't wait to get out of school, and practically ran to City Hall to meet Elsmed and run my plan by him.

"Absolutely not," Elsmed said when I explained my idea to him.

"But—" I started.

"What makes you think we need your help tracking this witch, Celeste?" Elsmed thundered. "We've been protecting this town for many more decades than you've been alive, and I think we know what we're doing by now." His stare had turned angry, and my excitement shriveled up and turned to a sour ball in my stomach.

"I just . . . I thought . . . maybe I could help, and then the Burnses wouldn't have to worry about another . . ." I trailed off, realizing I probably sounded idiotic to him. A teenage girl helping the supernatural protectors of the town? It even sounded ridiculous to me, once I really thought about it.

Elsmed's expression softened slightly. "And how do you think you can help, exactly? We have expert trackers ready to follow her to whoever is behind this. What do you think you can add to our efforts?" His voice took on a tone of condescension, as if he were speaking to a child. I supposed, to him, that was exactly how it felt.

"Well, what if she opens a portal when you let her loose? How will you track her then?"

"The same way we'll track her if she opens a portal from Havenwood Falls. Our witches can detect the approximate location of the portal's destination if they are there when it's opened. How is your way any better?"

"Because I can control where she intends to go with her portal. She found her way into Havenwood Falls, so she's smarter than the average hunter. Who's to say she won't portal to another location first to put us off her trail?"

"Why would she? She won't remember anything about the town once she passes the border. She wouldn't recognize Sheriff Kasun if he were standing right next to her, once she's outside the boundary."

"Well, she clearly had a plan to find Havenwood Falls before she got here. There's no reason to think she doesn't have one for getting out—one that takes the memory spell into consideration."

Elsmed gave me a long look. "Why shouldn't we have one of our witches compel her to give up the location of her employer?"

"So you haven't already had them questioning her about that? Using compulsion and any other techniques at their disposal? It took a day of interrogation just to get her to give up that it was in the woods somewhere, and it took the shifters' tracking to do the rest. She must have some protection against compulsion. But she's already given up her protection against my ability."

The look on his face told me I had hit a nerve. He glanced to where the black stone on a cord Remy had worn still sat on his desk, undoubtedly protected by some spell or another. "I'll take your comments under advisement," he said, "and discuss the matter with the Court."

I nodded, knowing enough to hold my tongue after that small victory.

For the remainder of the afternoon, he helped me practice quickly reaching a meditative state, locating other minds in proximity, and even let me push a few harmless thoughts into people's minds. It was hilarious seeing the maintenance man at Elsmed's door, completely confused by his unexplained appearance there.

We learned that while I could sometimes maintain my concentration through Elsmed's speaking directly into my mind, often it broke my focus, so we stuck to audible communication for the most part.

The next day, though, I heard Elsmed's voice in my mind. Unfortunately, I was "studying" with Jonathan at the time. I had to excuse myself to have a mental chat with my mentor about what the Court decided. He didn't give me any details about their deliberations, of course, but said they agreed that the witch seemed to have protections against their interrogations thus far, and that they had nothing to lose by trying my idea.

Tomorrow, he told me, they would arrange for me to be there when they transported the witch out of town for banishment, in human handcuffs so she could escape without suspecting they were letting her loose when I pushed her in the direction they wanted. Addie would be there to trace the portal to its destination. If my influence didn't work, there was a chance the witch would escape without anyone being able to track her. But if it did, they might gain a clue to whom the witch worked for and how they came to target the Seelie key.

The pressure of keeping the artifact—and the Burnses—safe didn't descend on me until I tried to sleep that night. Then, my mind raced through all the possibilities of how the plan could go wrong. My heart started racing and my stomach was in knots. I didn't sleep a wink.

ON SUNDAY, I met Elsmed at City Hall, and we walked over to the police station together. I was still nervous as hell, but a little comforted to know that at least Jonathan and his mom were safe at home, and wouldn't be bothered by the criminal witch again.

"Everything ready?" Elsmed said by way of greeting Sheriff Kasun when we entered the station.

"Yes, sir," the sheriff replied. "She's cuffed for transport with the regular human cuffs, and I've got the box already processed for evidence and ready to go. You have the necklace?"

"Here it is," Elsmed said, pulling out of his pocket a gold chain with a pendant that looked exactly like the one Mrs. Burns had worn.

Sheriff Kasun took the piece of jewelry from Elsmed, examining it. "Manos does good work," he said, shaking his head. "I'd never be able to tell the difference by looking at it."

"Let's hope it fools the witch and her employer," Elsmed replied.

The sheriff nodded and placed the necklace in the box, closing it again.

"Where is Addie? She was supposed to meet us here," Elsmed said, though it sounded less like a question and more like a complaint.

"Sorry I'm late," Addie's voice preceded her through the front door.

"Good of you to join us," Elsmed said, giving her some serious side-eye.

Addie glanced at me with a reassuring smile. It was only then I realized I'd been wringing my hands and probably looked every bit the nervous wreck I was. I took a deep breath to calm myself and then kept at it when it didn't do a damn thing.

"Do you need to do any preparation before we set her loose?" the sheriff asked.

"I need a minute," I said, looking for a decent place to focus, when a thought occurred to me. "Won't she recognize me?" I asked. "She saw me at the house the other day."

"Sit down and face toward the wall," Elsmed said. "I'll block her view of you."

I did as he said, taking deep breaths and forcing my pulse into a slow, steady rhythm, which I used to put myself into a meditative state. Against the darkness of my eyelids, three lights hovered nearby, while a few others glowed somewhat farther away.

"Ready," I intoned.

"Addie, need anything?" the sheriff asked.

"No, I'm good. Anything I did would tip her off, anyway. I can read portals without any prep."

Addie went to a spot around an interior wall, where she would be able to see the portal, but the witch wouldn't see her.

"All right, showtime," the sheriff said, leaving the box on the counter and going through a heavy door, where I guessed the jail cells were.

"Focus," Elsmed said quietly. "They're coming."

I concentrated on the lights moving around in the station.

There were a few that remained relatively stationary, but I saw the sheriff and the witch moving together toward the door he'd disappeared through a moment before. I heard the door open, then Elsmed muttered under his breath, "She's in front."

I focused on the light that was jerking back and forth, probably trying to free herself from her restraints.

"We found your little treasure, and we're returning it to its rightful owner," Sheriff Kasun said. "The Court has ruled that your punishment for your misdeeds is banishment, though if you ask me, it should have been much harsher."

The woman cackled, just like I'd imagined a witch would when I heard fairy tales about them as a kid. "You can't keep me out," she said. "I can come back here anytime I like."

"We can, and we will. There's nothing here for you anymore, anyway," Elsmed broke in. "The poor family you attacked fled as soon as you were captured, and where they've gone, your kind can't follow."

"Is that so?" she said. "I'm sure the Collector will pay handsomely for that information. Thank you." I thought I could hear Elsmed rolling his eyes.

"Cuffs!" Sheriff Kasun called, and I prepared myself to strike.

"Now," I heard Elsmed whisper, and I sent the first message to the witch.

"*Take the box with the key,*" I shoved into her mind. "*Steal the iron box, the one where you hid the key.*" The scrape of the box being swiped off the counter reached my ears.

Suddenly, my lungs filled with fire and my concentration fell apart. Coughs racked my chest. I struggled to breathe, wondering what the hell was going on.

The witch's laugh rang in my ears. Clearly, she was unaffected. What had she used? Pepper spray? A spell to make the air unbreathable? Whatever it was, it was working. I looked up at Elsmed and panicked when I saw him coughing too.

"You think you can confine me with ordinary handcuffs and concrete walls?" the witch asked no one in particular. "It's a wonder you all have lasted this long. You lot are clueless. Or maybe just powerless."

Crouching low as if to get under the cloud of invisible smoke, I saw Addie, seemingly unaffected, pulling items from her pockets, her lips moving nonstop. I couldn't hear what she was saying, but it must have been some powerful magic, because the witch appeared to be rooted in place, and after what seemed like several long minutes, but must have been only seconds, the air began to clear.

"Brought your own witch, did you, fools?" she screeched. "No matter. I have more spells at my disposal than she's ever heard of."

In between gasping breaths, I peeked over the police station's front counter and saw the witch pulling beads off her necklace. In her hands, they twisted and flattened, turning into gleaming throwing stars before my eyes. I ducked as she started flinging them around the room, while Addie started frantically waving her hands, presumably doing something to prevent the weapons from meeting their targets.

Holy crap. This woman was a walking arsenal. We needed to get ahead of this quickly. Addie was holding her off, but if she missed any one of those stars, we could have a serious problem. I needed to get my head together and finish what we started.

Fear rose up in my throat and threatened to choke me again. I sat cross-legged, closed my eyes, and imagined myself pushing that fear back down with both hands. *Now is not the time for doubt,* I told myself firmly. *Jonathan needs you to put an end to this.* With that thought lodged in my brain, I took four deep breaths— ignoring the blades whirring above my head—and saw the lights corresponding to each mind in the room.

"Focus on the one in the center," Elsmed said. "We've got her surrounded."

I found her light, and everything else fell away. "*Make a portal to the last place you saw the one who sent you after the pendant,*" I pushed at the witch, with every ounce of willpower in me.

There was a pause in the assault. I no longer heard the *thunk* of metal lodging in walls or the *whoosh* of near misses. After a moment of silence, I repeated the command, pleading with the universe to make this plan work. Nothing.

"*Make a portal to the one who sent you after the pendant.*" I pushed it at her over and over, repeating it like a mantra, until I heard a strange ripping sound, and I knew she had done it.

"Your feeble spells have no hold on me," the woman gloated. "Better luck next time!"

There was a shuffling of footsteps, followed by the sound of one person running, and then the ripping sound again. The witch's light disappeared from my vision. I opened my eyes and rose to look around, not believing she was actually gone.

"Got it," Addie exclaimed.

"Was that—" Sheriff Kasun began.

"It was indeed," Elsmed cut him off. "I will inform the Court of this development. We will convene soon to discuss next steps."

The sheriff nodded and went about folding up his cuffs and tucking them away, as if we hadn't just released a money-crazed evil witch into the world.

"She won't remember this place to come back here, Celeste," Elsmed said. "And if by chance she does, the wards have already been set to cast her out and alarm us immediately. There's nothing more to worry about."

"But . . . the person behind this? Did you see where they were?"

Elsmed looked at Sheriff Kasun. "We got a solid lead, and the professionals will follow up on it. It definitely wasn't fae, Unseelie or otherwise. Your part in this is over, and very much appreciated. Thank you, my dear."

I let out the breath I hadn't realized I had been holding. It worked, and I didn't screw up and put the Burnses or the whole town in danger.

"You're welcome," I said. "I'm glad I could help."

"If you could do me one more favor?"

"Sure," I said.

"Would you inform the Burnses that the attacker is safely out of Havenwood Falls, and they are out of danger? I'll expect to hear from them about their permanent residency status by the end of the week."

"I'll let them know."

"Good girl. Run along now. I've got important business to attend to."

~

JONATHAN

SOMEONE WAS EITHER USING a jackhammer on the front door or urgently wanted to see us. I ran to the door to see which it was and saw Celeste standing there, her cheeks flushed as if she'd been running.

"Hey," I said.

"Hey, can I come in?" she said, out of breath.

"Sure." I stepped aside so she could fly by me in a flurry of excitement.

"What's going on?" Mom asked from the kitchen as I closed the door and helped Celeste out of her coat.

"It's done," Celeste exclaimed, a smile splitting her face. "The wicked witch is gone. Our plan worked."

"Plan?"

"Yeah, Elsmed's and mine. I made her open a portal to the location of whoever sent her here, so the authorities could make sure they don't send someone else."

"Oh, and where is that?"

"Well, I don't know. I had my eyes closed."

Mom's face fell.

"But don't worry! Addie and Elsmed and the sheriff saw, and they're working on pursuing it. They said it definitely wasn't Unseelie. But the important part is, she's gone."

"And the necklace?" I asked.

"Yep, she took the fake with her."

"Oh. Well, good," Mom said. She looked like she couldn't decide whether to be relieved or worried.

"It's all going to be fine," Celeste reassured us, nearly tripping over her own words. "Elsmed said the wards are set to make sure she can't come back, and if she even tries, it will send up an alarm."

"Sounds good," I said. "And thank you."

"I'm so happy I was able to do it. I was nervous I wouldn't get the timing right, and she would get away, but I did it. And it worked! Wow."

I laughed. She was clearly excited about using her ability, and her energy was infectious. I pulled her in for a hug.

"Oh, there's one more thing," Celeste said, her words slowing and her face dropping.

"What's that, dear?" Mom said.

Her whole demeanor changed, and she glanced down, as if she couldn't look us in the eyes while she delivered this next message.

Shit, this must be bad.

"Elsmed said he wants to hear from you by the end of the week about whether you'll remain in town as permanent residents."

"Oh," Mom said.

Celeste looked up at her now, worry crossing her face.

"I know it's not my decision to make, Mrs. Burns, but I really do hope you decide to stay. It's such a nice place to live, and usually very safe. And, well, I haven't known you for very long, but —" She blushed. "I just don't want you to leave."

My mom smiled for the first time since Celeste had walked through the door. "We like you too, Celeste. We will discuss it, and we'll let Elsmed know. Thank you for your bravery today, and for being such a good friend to us. It must be a very special place to have people like you in it."

Celeste rushed to my mom and enveloped her in a hug. "You are very special to me, too," she said. "Who knows how long it would have taken Elsmed to tell me the truth if you hadn't spilled the beans?" She laughed.

My mom laughed with her and invited her to stay for dinner, but Celeste wanted to get home to her father.

"I'm afraid he's been working too hard. I haven't been around much these past couple of weeks, and someone's got to make sure he's eating and sleeping and stuff," she said with a smile. I got the sense she was only half joking.

"Okay, go ahead home. Jonathan will keep you updated."

I walked her to the door and gave her another hug as I helped her put her coat back on.

"Talk soon," I whispered in her ear, and gave her a quick peck on the cheek.

She winked at me and disappeared into the frigid afternoon.

CHAPTER 12

CELESTE

TWO MONTHS LATER

"*M*argaret! Finally," I said, opening the front door to find her there, looking perfect, her curly hair in a complicated twist and her new glasses daintily perched on her nose.

"That's what you're wearing?" she said.

I didn't think it was *that* bad.

"No, no, no. Come on, we still have time," she continued, marching up the stairs, dragging me along behind her.

"What's wrong with this one, exactly?" I looked down at my blue A-line dress made of raw silk and studded with silvery beads. I thought it was lovely.

"What are you, a nun? That one says, 'Admire me from a distance, but don't touch.'"

"Well, yes, that's what my father wanted it to say."

"Where's that black dress we found last week at Callie's?"

"The one with the plunging neckline—I mean waistline? It's behind the closet door," I admitted.

"Yes! That one is hot. The gossamer sleeves are so perfect. And the slit up the side? Epic."

"But my dad is downstairs, and he insists on pictures," I reminded her.

"Okay, okay," she said. "We can do this. We are two intelligent, resourceful ladies, and we are kicking this prom's ass." She bustled around my room, opening drawers and cabinets until she found what she was looking for. "Aha!" she exclaimed.

"My underwear drawer is not going to help with this problem, Margie," I said, rolling my eyes.

"But this will," she said, lifting a black camisole from the drawer. "Put it on under the dress now and lose it when we get to the dance."

"Oh wow, I forgot I had that. Great idea. I'm so glad winter is over," I sighed, "but the coats did make it easier to dress."

"Okay, change quick. Xavier will be here soon."

I changed out of the lovely pale blue and into the racy, flowy, swirly floor-length black silk.

"Hand me those strappy shoes, would you?" I asked.

She helped me put the shoes on and touch up my makeup, then we were both tromping down the stairs, her in frothy pink, and me in fluttery black.

"How do we look, Dad?" I said, clutching Margaret's hand.

"Stunning, of course. But what happened to the other dress?"

"It just wasn't right for prom, Dad. I'll wear it another time, I promise."

"Okay, well you are lovely either way. Let me take some pictures before you go."

We posed for my dad and then a knock on the door announced our ride. My dad answered the door, and Xavier came in, greeting Margaret with a hug and a kiss on the cheek. Behind him, in a tuxedo that made him look scorching hot, was Jonathan.

"Come in, come in," my dad said. "I need pictures before you head out."

We all crowded together and grinned for more photos.

"Now you take care of these girls, and treat them like the princesses they are," my dad said.

"Yes, sir," the boys said in unison. Jonathan caught my eye and winked, his blue eyes twinkling in the light.

I couldn't help the grin that crept across my face and stayed the rest of the night, fixed there by the boy who couldn't hide his heart from my will.

∽

ABOUT THE AUTHOR

Liz Ferry writes stories so they stop bouncing around the inside of her head and keeping her up at night. This novella is her debut long-form fiction work, but she plans to write more. When she's not writing, Liz typically occupies herself with reading and editing other authors' books. She lives in sunny Miami, Florida, with her husband, two boys, and a herd of cats.

ACKNOWLEDGMENTS

Writing this book has been an incredible experience. First thanks go to my husband, Scott, for supporting me in everything I do, and my parents, for being perennial cheerleaders. Special thanks go to my boys for being my inspiration and constant source of new ideas.

Many thanks to Kristie Cook, who came up with this amazing plan to get a bunch of talented authors together to create something fantastic. I'm so happy to be involved in this ambitious project. Thanks also to Kristie and SF Benson for polishing this story with their editorial eyes.

To all the Havenwood Falls authors, it has been an absolute delight to work with each and every one of you. I have been so impressed with the collaboration and joint world-building in our little group, as well as the kick-ass stories you all have written.

Thanks to E.J. Fechenda, Morgan Wylie, Susan Burdorf, T.V. Hahn, Kristen Yard, Belinda Boring, R.K. Ryals, Nadirah Foxx, Victoria Escobar, Victoria Flynn, Amy Hale, and Kristie Cook for allowing me to use your characters.

Special thanks to Randi Cooley Wilson, not only for use of her characters Everett, Graysin, and Roman, and not only for giving me the push I needed to pitch this story, and then again to keep at it when I got bogged down, but also for introducing me to the Havenwood Falls project, taking a chance on me as an editor, and being an awesome client who made me realize work could be fun.

Finally, thank you, dear reader, for taking a chance on me as an author, for joining us on this journey, and for loving our characters and stories as much as we do.

CAST IN MOONLIGHT

ALI WINTERS

HAVENWOOD FAILS HIGH

Cast in Moonlight

USA Today Bestselling Author

ALI WINTERS

~ A Havenwood Falls Young Adult Novella ~

ALSO BY ALI WINTERS

THE HUNTED SERIES

The Reapers

The Exodus

The Moirai

The Fallen

Flirting with Death

Sound of Silence

A Sky of Shattered Stars

Army of the Winter Court

Favor of the Gods

For Michelle Fritz,
Your friendship is worth more than
all the books in the world.

CHAPTER 1

I crack open my eyes and instantly regret it. Bright florescent lights flicker above, accompanied by the harsh glare of sunlight through the window, and an annoying, constant beep. I squeeze my eyes shut before I can focus on anything and groan, trying to roll over. I can't. It hurts too much. Every inch of my body aches, and I think every part of me must be bruised.

Voices murmur nearby. I can't make out what they're saying. One belongs to a man, the other to a woman. I don't know who they are. The talking stops as I reach up to place a hand over my splitting head.

There's a tug on my hand, and I realize I'm attached to something.

What happened? Where am I?

I force my eyes open again. White walls, a soft blue knitted blanket draped over my legs, and a railing on either side of my bed. I'm in the hospital, or at least something like one. The room is small. There's not really much to it.

Before I can fully get my bearings, a woman approaches. The one who must have been talking to the man in a white coat just outside the door.

"Oh good, Clarke, you're awake," she says.

It takes me a moment, but I recognize her from pictures Mom showed me years ago. The two of them on a road trip in the nineties, the summer before college, taking selfies before it was even a thing.

Looking at her face is like looking into a mirror where I've aged, though only slightly, perhaps only by a few years. But unlike me, she has a sense of style. I swear she has hardly changed since those pictures were taken. She's slender, with brown hair just past her shoulders. Where hers is wavy, mine is straight, but her brown eyes match mine perfectly. I know she's family. Considering I've only heard stories about one distant relative, there's no one else she could be.

"Aunt Michelle?" I manage to croak out. My throat is sore and dry. I'm so thirsty.

I push myself up to a sitting position, and I hate every second of moving. But I don't think anything is broken. My aunt holds onto my arm, giving me extra support.

"You can call me Auntie, or Michelle. You don't need to be so formal." She bends down to fluff my pillows, then hugs me gently, if not a little awkwardly.

Her voice is almost familiar. Then I remember why. A month before Mom and I moved, we got a call. I'd answered the phone, and hers was the voice on the line. She called me by name then, but I was too distracted running out the door to wonder about it until later. I wonder why Mom hadn't told me it had been her. I would have liked to talk to her. Then again, I suppose after that call, Mom had been quieter than normal. I didn't want to press her when she seemed to have so much on her mind, so I just never asked. I forgot it soon enough.

"What happened?" I ask. I don't know what hospital this is or how I got here. There's a fog surrounding my mind, making it hard to think.

Michelle frowns, and the fingers of her hand gripping her purse strap tighten until her knuckles lose color. Then she looks up at the doctor as he walks into the room. She doesn't answer my question. I stare at her, waiting for one anyway. But she keeps her gaze locked on the doctor.

My head hurts too much to think clearly.

The doctor—my eyes flick to his name tag: Dr. Underwood—starts talking to my aunt Michelle. After a few seconds, I tune them out, resting my head back against the pillows. I close my eyes, and when I open them again, I'm unsure if several minutes have passed, or just several seconds.

He fusses, and I barely give him a passing glance as he checks my pulse, eyes, throat. He's average height, with salt-and-pepper hair and blue eyes that I'd normally drool over. But not today. Today I just want to keep my head from splitting open from the pain.

Michelle puts her purse in her lap as she sits down on the chair next to my bed, waiting for the doctor to do his thing.

"How do you feel, Miss Price?" he asks.

I hate that my last name is different from Mom's. Always have. I never understood why she gave me my dad's name and not hers, when he hasn't been around since before I was born. Even hyphenating would have been preferable; then at least I could request people use Baker.

I purse my lips and want to give a smart-ass answer, but I hold my tongue. He's only doing his job. Besides, it's only the drumbeat of my pulse pounding at my temples that's making me irritable.

"Not great. My head hurts," I mutter, and because I still want an answer, I add, "What happened?"

"You and your mother were in a car accident, sweetie," Michelle says. The quietness of her voice doesn't suit her.

I jerk up to sit straighter and wince at the pain. "What? Where's Mom? Is she okay?"

My heart thumps, and I can feel each beat hammering in my skull.

Michelle looks to the doctor like she's afraid she's said too much. That look has me worried. *What isn't she telling me? Whatever it is, it can't be good.*

"Can you remember anything about what happened?" the doctor interjects. He must have perfected his bedside manner, because he doesn't look the slightest bit concerned.

I think back. I remember Mom wanting to move to some small town in Colorado I'd never heard of for her job. We were going to stay with an aunt I'd never met before, who is obviously Michelle. I remember packing my things into the car and hoping the movers wouldn't get lost, the vast hours of straight road with next to nothing to look at once we left Oregon, how it was even worse after we crossed through that small corner of Utah, and it was pitch black out with only the blinding headlights from other cars . . . But that's it.

I shake my head, then instantly regret the movement. I hope a nurse comes by with pain meds soon. I don't think I can rest until this pain dies down.

"Don't worry too much about it. You just woke up. Sometimes temporary amnesia of the event can happen. You're very lucky— no broken bones, just some bruising." Dr. Underwood writes on my chart as he talks.

And aching muscles that feel like I've been deadlifting a moose, I think.

"What day is it?" I ask.

"It's the ninth," the doctor says, his pen not even pausing.

It's been two days since we left.

"When can I go home?" I ask. If I have to lay around and be in pain, I'd much rather it be somewhere less sterile looking.

"I would like you to stay the night, but barring any issues, you should be able to go home in the morning."

"What about my mom?" I push. Panic presses down on my chest.

His face is neutral. Not happy, but not the face of having to deliver *really* bad news. "Ms. Baker is stable, but she isn't awake yet, which is for the best. She has quite a few injuries, so we are isolating her for the time being. It will allow her to heal faster without risk of infection. I am confident she'll wake up in the next few days." A strange look passes over his face.

I sit back and breathe. The tightness in my chest eases. Just a bit. She's not in critical condition, so I'm glad for that, though this is far from what I'd hoped to hear.

The doctor puts my chart back at the foot of my bed and says, "I'll be back to check on you later. Visiting hours are only for another few minutes."

Then he leaves the room.

I just want to go home, to sleep in my bed in good old Boring, Oregon. I don't know where we are, but I know this isn't home. "What town are we in?"

Michelle—because even though she's my aunt, I don't know her well enough to think of her like that. Not yet—stands and looks at the clock as she slides the purse strap over a shoulder.

"You're in Havenwood Falls." I must make a face, because she clarifies, "Colorado. The car crashed just outside of Grand Junction, a few hours from here. I had you both brought here when I heard what happened."

I stare dumbly at her. I guess I don't remember *anything* after somewhere in the middle of Wyoming. Did I fall asleep? Mom must have been driving for hours while I was unconscious.

"Get some rest," she says, hugging me again. "I'll be back for you in the morning."

Then she leaves, and I'm alone. I scoot down into the bed, pull a pillow from behind my head, and hug it tightly to my chest.

I don't want to be here, away from my home, my things, and without my mom.

CHAPTER 2

$\mathcal{I}$ wake up feeling heavy, like I slept a long time but somehow still not long enough. I push myself up to sit, thankful my body isn't nearly as sore as yesterday. I wish there was a TV in the room, or at least a halfway decent book. I'd even settle for a school-assigned novel. Not that those have ever been bad—I secretly enjoyed them in the past—they just weren't my preferred taste.

I've already taken one nap since a nurse woke me up this morning to check my vitals.

A nurse or volunteer comes in—I'm not really sure which, because I'm staring at a phone on the wall outside of my room. She drops a tray of food off, then leaves without a word. By the time my brain puts things together enough to say thank you, she's already gone.

I glance at the clock. It's noon, and Michelle isn't here yet. I want to call her, but . . . even if I could get to that phone across the hall, I don't know her number.

I adjust myself to look at the tray. The food doesn't look nearly as bad as people complain about in hospitals, but I don't feel all that hungry. I pick up the spoon and cup of gelatin and frown down at it. Lime. The color reminds me of fresh grass clippings, and though it smells more appetizing, the color is pretty weird. I poke my spoon into it and stir it around. Maybe if I don't look while I eat, it won't be that bad?

I take a bite.

Not great, but I've had worse.

"Sorry I'm late!" Michelle enters in a flurry of movement. She's wearing a pretty pink dress, with knee high boots that don't look like they should work but do, and her hair is pulled back into a cute updo.

I quickly set the toxic-looking food down and push the tray away.

"I got caught up at work and then had to fill out your discharge paperwork." She plops a bag down on a chair. My bag. "I had no idea it would take so long."

"It's okay," I say. She looks at me expectantly. So I blurt the first thing that comes to mind. "Did you know hospitals serve green gelatin because the red flavors are too close to the color of blood, and they need to tell the difference if they need to do emergency surgery?"

She blinks.

Great. She's known me for all of five minutes, and she already thinks I'm weird. Spouting weird facts has always been a mostly bad habit of mine. Mom says I started when I was about five, though even she doesn't know where I picked it up from. I usually do it when I first meet new people or I'm stressed, or really, anytime I'm slightly uncomfortable. Either that or I completely shut down and have a hard time speaking. It always made making friends difficult. That was the one good thing about moving every year or two—I was never in one place long enough to make too much of an impression on anyone.

"I brought your bag for you," Michelle says.

"When can I see Mom?"

A look crosses her face that I don't have time to decipher before it's gone. "I'll go talk to the doctor about that while you get dressed."

If I didn't know better, from the strain in her voice, I'd say there was something that she didn't want me to know. But before I can ask, she's out the door, heading down the hall.

I drop my feet off the edge of the bed and stand. My legs are a little weak, though it's the same feeling I get when I've forgotten to eat all day, so it's manageable.

Opening my bag slumped on the foot of the bed, I rummage around, passing up my jeans for a pair of dark leggings and my Darth Vader sweater. The back of my hand catches the corner of a box I didn't pack. I dig down and pluck it out. It's small, teal, and made of the standard cardboard used for some types of jewelry.

I remove the lid, attaching it to the underside. Inside is a simple, silver bracelet. A tiny star charm, with a chunk of raw amethyst embedded into the center, dangles from one of the links. Mom must have snuck it in my bag as an early birthday present. I clasp it onto my wrist, admiring the glint of light off the polished metal, then shuffle my way to the bathroom to change.

When I look into the mirror, my appearance makes me cringe. My dark brown hair is in tangles, so I work my fingers through, combing it back as best I can.

Michelle is back when I emerge from the bathroom. She's smiling and holding my bag. "The doctor says we can visit Angela in a few days. He just wants her to heal a little more first."

It's not bad news, I tell myself. I'll be able to see her soon enough. We've been apart for longer periods of time than that when she goes on her business trips.

Michelle leads me out to her car. As we exit the building, a blast of cold air hits me. It's the middle of the day, with a little wind and full sun, yet I swear my breath froze before it even had a chance to exit my body. I crinkle my nose, rubbing it with the back of my hand to rid myself of the odd sensation. I was not built for this kind of weather.

The drive is mostly silent. Sleep weighs on me even though I've been sleeping for days.

I look at Michelle from the corners of my eyes. But she

continues talking, not leaving me with an opening, telling me about the bakery she owns, Daily Knead. I'm too tired to really focus on her words or respond with more than grunts and nods anyway. Instead, I watch the town pass. Everything is so close together.

Michelle turns onto a street leading up to a small neighborhood.

"Welcome to Havenstone," she says as we pass a sign stating as much.

The houses are cute and remind me of a ski resort you'd see in TV shows. The roofs are steep, and the wood has been sanded and polished to accentuate the lines and knots of the trees they were made from. Michelle puts the car in park in front of one with dark-stained wood.

Inside, her place is warm and cozy. An overstuffed couch sits under a window, the fireplace is on the far right wall, and two very comfortable-looking chairs, with thick fur-like blankets draped over the backs, sit near the back wall of the room. The floors are hardwood, a light honey color with rugs strategically placed. That will be nice in the mornings.

It surprises me a little that she doesn't live in a bigger place. Not that she needs one, but with her corporate hairstyle and heels, I'd expected her home to look like it came out of a magazine. You'd think she lived in a bubble of spring while the rest of the world is in the middle of what has to be an unusually arctic winter.

Looking out the window, I frown at the snow. I much prefer rainy winters.

I wander into the dining room on the left. It's small and simple, with a round wooden table pushed against the wall. There's a swinging door that I assume leads into the kitchen.

"Your great-grandfather made that," Michelle says to me from behind. She nods toward the table. I smile and move back into the main living area. She walks around me, motioning down the hall, and shows me to my room. "I've made up the guest room for you until your mother gets out of the hospital. Then we can go house-hunting together."

I just nod.

We pass a closed door, which I assume is Michelle's room, and an office with a large desk and shelves of books lining one wall.

Once we get to my temporary room, I drop my bag at the foot of the bed and plop down onto my back, ready to take a nap. *How can I still be so tired?*

"Don't fall asleep just yet. I'm expecting company soon, then I'll make lunch." And with that, she is off down the hall. Again, I can't shake the feeling that there's something she's not telling me.

My eyelids droop. This mattress is too comfortable. I could curl up and hibernate straight through the rest of winter. Somehow, though, I manage to find it in me to roll off the bed and stand before I fall asleep. I stretch, then make my way out into the hall. My feet stop in mid-stride when I see a painting.

There's nothing remarkable about it, though it has a Bob Ross feel to it. The image is of a forest, but one seemingly out-of-place detail sticks out. I squint at the figure. A man standing in the distance. He looks like he doesn't belong, like someone added him years later, only with paints that weren't nearly as vibrant. The style in which he's painted is more detailed, and less free-flowing than the rest.

"Mason, your father, painted that years ago, before you were born," Michelle says.

You mean, before he left us, I think bitterly. My reply dies on my tongue as I jump, startled by the knock on the door.

AN HOUR LATER, I'm sitting on the couch, staring at my aunt like she's grown two extra heads. Which, given what just happened, would be slightly less weird. When she said *company*, I didn't expect to get a tattoo. I'm a minor, for crap's sake. I side-eye Michelle. Last I checked, that wasn't exactly legal. Something about wards and protections. I don't know. It doesn't make much sense to me still.

"So your mother didn't tell you?" she asks, gripping the back of a chair. Though her expression is calm and slightly confused, her knuckles are white from the strain.

I shake my head slowly. Either I'm insane . . . or she is. Either way, I'm stuck here in a tiny town in the middle of the Rocky Mountains with no one to save me.

"Nope," I say, hoping I'm doing a decent job at hiding my worry. My eyes are wide, so probably not.

Michelle paces the room for a minute, then sits down next to me and takes my hands in hers. "We are witches. The tattoo is to help keep your powers under control as they come in. I know it's hard to believe, but . . ." She trails off and studies my face for a moment. "I think it will be easier to show you."

She waves her hand at the fireplace and snaps her fingers. Instantly, a roaring fire starts up.

I jump up on the couch, pulling my knees to my chest. The skin on my right shoulder, where I got my tattoo, stings a little from the movement. "What. The. Crap!"

Try as I might, there's no explanation I can come up with to explain how she did that—not any that doesn't involve magic. I blow out a breath. Magic . . . witches . . .

"Does Mom know?" I ask.

She laughs and moves to sit next to me. "Of course. Your mother is a witch, too. We tend not to use our powers like that, and never in public."

"So what? Is this town some kind of witchy sanctuary?" I ask.

Michelle reaches for my hand, but I jerk it back. She takes the hint and scoots away, giving me a little more room. "Not exactly. There are a lot of different supes in this town. Shifters, witches like us, some witches with vastly different types of magic, fae, and more."

I think she stopped at *more* to spare me further insanity.

"Shifters? Like . . . werewolves?"

"Wolves, dragons, and—"

"Dragons?" I snort. "You know this sounds absolutely insane, right?"

"I know. It will take some getting used to. But there are also humans in town, though most aren't aware of us."

"Is it even safe to go outside?" I can feel my eyes about to pop out of my head.

She laughs. "Of course it is. We live here because it's safe." Michelle lowers her voice. "I'm sorry. I never realized Angela didn't tell you. That's why the two of you moved here, because your powers will be coming in on your birthday, which also happens to be on the night of the supermoon. And because our power is drawn from the moon, your powers will be the strongest our family has seen in generations."

"I think I'm going to be sick." This has to be a joke. I mean, there's no such thing as witches like she's trying to get me to believe.

Yet, I saw her light that fire. No hidden button, no remote. Just a snap of her finger. This is crazy, and what's worse is that I find myself starting to believe her.

"I will help you as your powers manifest," she goes on.

All I can do is nod, hugging my knees to my chest as she keeps talking. But I've stopped listening. Her voice is just a muffled buzz in my head. I'm feeling completely overwhelmed, and I can feel myself shutting down. The emotions are too thick and they steal my words, my voice . . . and I don't know how I'll ever find either again.

This cannot be real.

CHAPTER 3

"Are you okay?" Michelle asks. I startle at her touch, and she quickly withdraws her hand from my shoulder.

I dig deep, and try for something simple.

"I think so?" I manage to say, though it's more question than confirmation. My head is caught in a fog. It has to be shock.

She looks at me. "Are you sure? You've been sitting there staring at the wall for a good twenty minutes."

She sets down a tray on the coffee table in front of me, with two cups and a teapot with steam swirling up from the spout.

I drop my knees, bringing my feet to the floor. "So the town is full of witches . . ."

"And shifters, fae, angels, and—" She cuts herself off when she sees my incredulous expression.

My emotions have calmed some, so I think of something to say . . . anything. But what comes out is, "Did you know that no one knows where the word *witch* originated from?" I nod as if she answered. "Yeah, there are several words that could have led to it. There are three Old English words it could have come from, meaning 'female sorceress,' or the word meaning 'divination' or the one meaning 'idol.' There's also the Germanic word that means 'one who wakes the dead.'"

Apparently my report on the Salem witch trials back in the eighth grade stuck with me more than I thought.

Sorceress . . . divination . . . idol . . . waking the dead . . . These words are too heavy for me, and suddenly I'm overwhelmed again. I press my lips in a tight line.

Michelle is silent for a minute before she shakes her head and laughs as if I told a joke. "I didn't know that. Why don't you unpack, and I'll make you something to eat—"

"I think I need some air." I stand up a little too fast. My head spins, and I have to grab the arm of the couch.

"You probably shouldn't. You just got home from the hospital." She jerks her chin toward the kitchen. "And lunch will be ready in a few minutes. I'm making enchiladas."

The warm smell of seasonings and chicken wafts through the room, making my mouth water. Food is the last thing on my mind right now. And though I am hungry, what she told me has formed a pit of nerves in my stomach, and I'm not sure I could eat a single bite.

"I'm fine," I say as calmly as I can. Though really, this is too much to take in all at once, and I just need time, *alone*, to let it sink in.

Maybe she sees something in my eyes, because she says, "All right, I can drop you off in town for an hour or so."

"Nope, no. It's only a few blocks. I can walk." I'm being rude. I know I am. Mom raised me better than this. Guilt creeps in, but I push it away.

"Normally, I would let you, but considering your head injury, I'd feel better taking you. Besides, Angela would kill me if I let you walk. Here's a cell. I programmed my number in there. Just call when you're ready to be picked up. You'll also need a jacket."

I think about refusing, only for a moment. She's family, and insane or not, she's only tried to help me and take care of me so far. "Thanks," I mutter.

Michelle stands. "Clarke, I know this is probably a lot to take in, but we can talk more about it later."

More? How much more could there be?

She hurries to the office and is back in seconds with a warm wool jacket with large pearl buttons and knee-high boots that somehow are both practical and stylish. Maybe I should have her help me pick out a winter wardrobe, because I'm going to need it. None of my winter clothes are made for winters below an average of forty-five degrees.

~

AFTER MICHELLE DRIVES OFF, I turn in a slow circle, looking at my surroundings. There are a few people out running errands or walking leisurely with friends. I scan the businesses, and my eyes catch on the coffee shop across the street. Coffee Haven.

Good, I could use something to warm me up. I'm practically an ice cube from standing outside for less than five minutes. I cross the street and head in.

Instantly I'm surrounded by warmth and the heavenly aroma of freshly ground coffee. I take a deep breath and savor the bright scent. The setup is similar to most coffee shops, but it has a much friendlier vibe than those chain stores. Art lines the walls, some of them watercolors. The use of brush strokes and how the artist mastered using each color in a variety of ways make me wish I had a fraction of their talent. My eyes linger on the portrait of a platinum-blond-haired woman near the bar. I wonder who she is to be given such a prominent place.

Hanging plants and crystals spread around the place give it a personal touch and make it feel homey. It reminds me of Oregon. I think I found my new favorite place.

There isn't much of a line, so I stride over to the long marble counter that reminds me of an old-timey ice cream shop. I take my time scanning the menu. In the end, I settle on the same thing I get every time I'm at any coffee place.

"Next."

I blink and realize it's my turn. A girl about my age, with

shoulder-length dark-sand-colored hair and honey eyes looks at me expectantly. She's so skinny, and I have the urge to knit her a massive scarf. She doesn't say anything else, but I know she's waiting on me. Her name tag reads *Roxanne*. There's a book on the counter next to her, and I try to peek at the title, but can't see it from where I stand.

"One large hot chocolate with extra whipped cream—" My stomach growls loudly. I give Roxanne a sheepish look and add, "and a blueberry scone, please."

She rings me up, and I dig through my bag until I find my wallet, then hand over my cash. My fingers drum on the marble.

"Here you go," she says and hands me my change. "You can get your order when it's ready over there." Roxanne points down the counter. As my gaze follows where she points, I can't help but notice some scarring peeking out from the cuff of her sleeve. I wonder what happened. I feel rude for staring, so I push it from my mind. It's not my business.

"Thanks," I say, taking a step back.

The heel of my boot slides on melted snow I'd managed to drag in. As I stumble, my back collides with something hard. Two large hands come down on my shoulders to steady me. I freeze, not moving. The hands push me forward a step, and I nearly stumble again. *Would* have stumbled if he'd let go right away. Tilting my chin up, I look over my shoulder and up the massive chest to a painfully handsome face. Heat rises up my neck.

"Sorry," I say slowly, with a hint of a question mark thrown in. Slow enough to make me come across as slightly unhinged. My brain has gone slack from just looking into his eyes. *My* eyes are brown—these are something in another league altogether. An amber, *almost* brown, only with too much gold to be called something so . . . normal. They remind me of the setting sun.

I know I'm staring, but I've never been so attracted to a total stranger before in my life. It's textbook romance novel, and even in my half-drooling state, I know it's the ultimate cheesefest. I probably have little cartoon hearts over my eyes.

When he finally removes his hands from my person, I notice he's frowning at me, almost sneering. "You should watch where you're going" is all he says. He lets out an annoyed huff I don't think I was meant to hear, then moves around me, all but pushing me out of his way like I was a stray dog.

The cartoon eye hearts pop, and my attraction to him curdles like milk. *What a jerk!*

The barista places my order on the counter, and I snatch it up and storm over to a free table in the corner near a window.

Great first impression. I hope not everyone is as rude as he is. I already hate being here. Picked up in the middle of the school year and dragged to a place with winters that would make a polar bear hate life, with an aunt who was clearly losing her mind . . .

No, that's not fair. I know what she showed me was real, but it's still hard to wrap my mind around. And there was that tattoo lady . . . So maybe I'm stuck in a nightmare, losing *my* mind, and have created this white hell for myself. A cute little suburb that looks peaceful and sweet, but nothing good is waiting for me.

As much as I want to be mad at Mom for moving us to a tiny town in the middle of nowhere, I can't. Not when she's still in the hospital.

I twist a strand of hair around my finger and tug. I hope she wakes up soon.

That guy's voice breaks through my thoughts. I chomp down angrily on my scone, staring out the window and still seething. I force myself to keep my gaze on the world outside, refusing to give him a second's attention. Who says *watch it* when a stranger clearly accidentally bumps into them? It's not like I meant to do it, and I even apologized.

A chair at the table next to me scoots out with a screech, drawing my attention away from the snowy town. I nearly choke on my bite when I see his face.

Did he seriously sit down in front of me just to openly glare? Another guy, his friend, I'm guessing, takes a seat in the chair next to him, but I don't notice much more than that with those amber eyes bearing down on me. Why won't he look away already?

I take an angry sip of my hot chocolate and sputter when I burn my tongue. He's smirking now. It's childish, but I'm in such a foul mood that I don't care. I stick out my tongue and make a face, which only makes his smirk grow bigger.

I sniff, catching the scent of pennies, but it's gone before I can be sure. It's probably my insanity catching up with me.

I look away and eye the shops across from here, pausing when my gaze passes an old man standing directly across the street, staring right at me. I shake my head. No, from the look of him, he's probably just cold and hungry and staring at the café itself. His clothes are the kind of dark that happens to previously bright colors when they are covered in dirt and stains, and aged from wear.

Reaching into my pocket, I look at my change. I don't have enough left to buy him anything, but he might appreciate what I do have to give.

With Mr. Glares-a-lot so close, there's no way I can sit and enjoy my scone and hot chocolate anyway. I stuff the pastry in my mouth as I get to my feet, snatching up my drink and throwing my bag over my shoulder, then storm out into the chilly afternoon air.

The man is gone now. I scan the street and don't see him anywhere. I guess I was wrong.

As distracting as the rude guy was, I'm still not ready to go back to Michelle's place. Everything she told me is still swimming around in my head.

Shoving the change back into my pocket, I take the pastry hanging out of my mouth and hold it in my hand, then wander up and down the street for a while, window shopping, as I finish my scone. My hot chocolate cools off way too fast. I pass Summit Jewelers, ogling their window display and the array of beautiful designs.

When I move on, I manage to find a bookstore on the far side of the square. I look behind me, trying to remember the name of the bookstore next to Coffee Haven. I make note of them, planning to visit when I have more money. I'm almost finished with my current book and will need a new one soon. I stand in front of Into the Mystic New Age Books and Gifts, and I wonder if they have anything on witches.

I feel a pull to go in. My hand hovers inches away from the door handle, but just before I move to go in, a wave of . . . something hits me. It's a lot like being dizzy, only not. I don't know how to explain it. Something more overwhelming than that, something with a deep unidentifiable emotion attached to it. I shiver, suddenly feeling like I'm being watched.

Looking around, I don't see anyone, other than a few people running in and out of stores from their cars.

I check the cell Michelle gave me. I've been gone for a few hours. Even I can admit I've calmed down enough to go back. Even if I haven't, the cold is enough to make me call it quits. The cold air might hurt my face, but walking around in it certainly helped clear my head. Though I can't see how this witch thing will sort itself out in my mind for some time, I think I am ready to talk about it more.

So I shoot Michelle a text.

Clarke: I'm ready to be picked up.

A few minutes later it dings in my hand.

Michelle: I'm stuck at work, there was a minor emergency. Just got a last minute order. I can pick you up in an hour or two.

Michelle: Unless you want to walk here?

Clarke: Is it close to where you dropped me off?

I wait a few minutes before it pings again with directions. It doesn't seem as close as I would have liked, but I've walked farther over the past few hours, so it isn't a big deal.

Ten minutes later, I am freezing my toes off as I walk up to the storefront. A wooden sign is mounted above the door made of polished wood with simple deep blue lettering. I push open the glass door with my backside, rubbing my arms with my hands. A bell rings above my head. I don't see my aunt anywhere . . . but I do see *him*.

My hands still. His are splayed across the countertop, and Mr. Glares-a-lot is looking down his nose, giving me an expression I interpret as him feeling superior.

A blush crawls up my neck and burns my cheeks.

"Are you following me now?" he asks.

CHAPTER 4

"What? No, of course not!" I hiss, approaching the counter and barely keeping my voice from raising. The last thing I want to do is draw the attention of everyone in the dining area to the scene I'm sure we're making. "This is my aunt's store."

As soon as those words leave my mouth, he cringes before he can school his features. I note it with a little more satisfaction than I should.

There's a smear of flour on his cheek. He must have been working in the back. He looks at me for a few seconds longer, head cocked to the side, then goes back to work wiping down the counter and cleaning up, effectively ignoring me.

I fiddle with the bracelet around my wrist. It's strangely warm against my skin. Then again, I'm so cold right now, I'm not surprised the metal is doing a better job of holding heat than I am.

"Will you please let my aunt know I'll be waiting outside?" I ask through my teeth, trying to keep my voice as pleasant as possible.

He looks at me in a way I can't decipher, then goes into the back room without a word. Closing my eyes, I count to five and take in a slow, measured breath. I tried to be nice. I really did. It's a mystery why Michelle would want to hire someone with such a sour disposition.

The frigid air hits my face with an icy blast as I go back outside. I end up pacing the parking lot of the shopping plaza in an attempt to keep warm. It doesn't work as well as I would have liked. The light from the sun is fading fast, thanks to the towering mountains swallowing up a good bit of sky.

That guy's face flashes in my mind. I don't know why I let him get under my skin like this. I don't know how he can when we've never even held a conversation. He's a total stranger I had no idea existed before a few hours ago. I'm going to be eighteen in a few days. Yet somehow he manages to make me feel like a cranky child who missed her nap.

A shiver works its way down my body. I continue pacing and rub my hands up and down my arms. When I look up from the ground, I see the old man again, across the street in front of the high school. I glance around. This is definitely a different street. What an odd coincidence.

It's strange that he'd be out here when the temperature is quickly dropping. Then again, so am I. The difference is that I have somewhere to go, where I can only assume he doesn't.

Remembering the change in my pocket, I decide now is as good a time as any to give it to him. I rub my nose, trying to get the sudden sharp tang of copper out of my nostrils. I'm pretty sure the cold is somehow messing with my sense of smell.

The street is quiet, so I take a step toward him, my foot just touching the asphalt of the street when I am jerked back into a hard body. A car drives by a second later, kicking up a small wave of snow slush.

"Are you *trying* to get yourself killed?" Mr. Cranky grunts. I really should learn his name, but it doesn't really matter, I suppose. I don't exactly plan on becoming BFFs with him.

When I don't say anything, he lets me go, crossing his arms over his chest. He shifts his weight and cocks his head. Waiting.

It takes a few seconds before I can get my brain and mouth to sync up enough to answer him. I blink. The man is gone, and the car that nearly hit me is driving down the road, snow sloshing beneath the tires.

"I-I didn't see it! There weren't any cars around a second ago."

His liquid amber eyes narrow. I'm not sure he believes me. "Michelle asked me to come get you. She said she was going to be too long and doesn't want you to freeze."

His tone is softer than I expected, so I let him guide me back inside. I can't help but notice his hand stays on my lower back the entire time. He's so warm, it's hard to avoid leaning into him. Part of me is relieved he came to get me. I don't think I would have lasted much longer outside.

His hand doesn't leave me until he pulls out a chair at a small table in the back and motions for me to sit. Then he's gone, and I'm left to entertain myself until Michelle is ready.

I trace the lines of wood on the table with my finger for a few minutes before pulling my book out of my bag and opening it. I flip through the pages, removing the bookmark, and get lost within the words. The murmur of other patrons' conversations surrounds me in a sea of white noise.

A white ceramic mug with a mountain of whipped cream on top jolts me out of the story. I slam the book closed and look up, startled to see *him* of all people.

"Here" is all he says. But he doesn't leave. We just look at each other for a long moment. Then he rolls his eyes and lets out an exaggerated sigh, setting a cookie down next to the mug on top of a folded white napkin.

Perhaps this is a peace offering? Either that or my aunt is making him be nice. I look from the cookie to his face, meaning to say thanks, though what comes out instead is, "The average American will eat thirty-five *thousand* cookies in their lifetime."

I can't believe I just said that. I reach up and tug on a strand of hair. If I'm not mistaken, the corner of his mouth twitches in what I can only assume is an attempt to hide a smirk. When he doesn't move or speak, I say, "I'm Clarke."

"I know," he says, then, "Seth."

There's no offering of a handshake from either us. I suppose we'll take this one baby step at a time then. The smear of flour from earlier is still there on his face.

"Do you want to sit down?" I ask hesitantly. Though I'm not sure I actually want him to.

Using the toe of my boot, I scoot the chair across from me out as much as I can. His gaze bounces from the chair to my face a few times. He opens his mouth, and I think he's about to accept, but there's a clatter in the back room that draws our attention away from each other.

He shakes his head and jerks a thumb over his shoulder. "Looks like I might be needed in the back, then I need to start the prep for the morning shift."

It's the most words he's said to me since we met. And the nicest. I look at him, not sure what to say to that. And when I take too long, he walks away.

Great. He's trying, and I ruin it by not speaking.

I finish my drink and cookie while pretending to read. I can't focus anymore and keep stealing glances at him from the corner of my vision as he mans the register and cleans between customers.

By the time he leaves, jacket in hand, the store is otherwise deserted. I think about running over to apologize. He's too fast, and before I can make up my mind to actually do it, the door is closing behind him. I'll thank him for the peace offering the next time I see him.

A few minutes later, Michelle finally comes out of the back room.

"Sorry that took so long," Michelle says as she approaches. She pauses in the middle of the dining area and looks around as if she expected something completely different.

The drive home is mostly silent. The cold has zapped any energy I'd had, and I'm ready for bed. I trudge up the steps into the house behind Michelle. She has a lot of energy still, and I'm super jealous.

"I can have dinner ready in about an hour," she says as she unlocks the front door.

"Thanks," I say, "but I think I just want to head to bed."

She nods understandingly. "There will be a plate in the fridge if you wake up and decide you're hungry."

Then she flits off toward the kitchen while I make my way down the hall. I pass the painting and look at the faded man with an arm raised, as if he were caught jumping up and down.

"Even you seem to have more energy than I do right now," I mutter to him.

My exhaustion must be getting to me because I could have sworn he was a little smaller and just standing when I'd looked earlier.

I shake it off and then make my way to my room, dropping facedown onto my mattress. Though I'm exhausted, the events of the day swirl though my mind. How could I have missed that car? I'm lucky Seth was around, otherwise I'd be frozen roadkill right now . . . then there was the peace offering. What could that have meant? Am I reading too much into a cookie?

But underneath it all, I find myself believing what Michelle told me is true, despite not having witnessed any sign of magic since she demonstrated hers for me.

I am a witch.

CHAPTER 5

*L*ight filters in through the window. I crane my neck to look at the clock on the nightstand next to my bed. It's almost half past eight, which means I've been sleeping for over twelve hours. I force myself to sit up. The thick pink blanket, which Michelle must have draped over me, slides to the floor.

I'm still a little achy, though not nearly what I felt like yesterday or the day before.

Walking like a zombie, I fumble my way to the dining room to find Michelle fully dressed and drinking tea as she reads the paper. I've never met anyone more put together than this woman.

"Good morning, Clarke, would you like some tea or coffee?"

I shake my head and spot a box of cereal on the counter. "No, thanks, I'm just going to have some of this," I say, grabbing it and setting it on the table before I go into the kitchen to grab the milk.

When I get back, a bowl and spoon already wait for me on the table. Michelle is tidying up the counters, and when I finish pouring my cereal, she takes the box and milk away. After skipping dinner last night, I am famished. I start shoveling spoonfuls of cereal into my mouth while she washes her mug.

"I was thinking about going for a walk later," I say between mouthfuls. "I'm still a little sore, but I think moving will help."

"That's a good idea. Be sure to take your phone in case you need anything. I'll be at the bakery for most of the day again."

Lifting the bowl to my mouth, I drink the leftover milk, then walk to the sink and wash my dishes while my aunt dries them.

"I can drop you off in town," Michelle offers, leaning a hip against the counter.

"That would be great, thanks."

She wipes her hands on a dish towel and folds it. Setting it down, she turns to face me. "I almost forgot. I had your car towed and am having the windows replaced. The mechanic said there wasn't much damage, so we'll be able to pick it up soon."

I swallow, not entirely sure I feel like getting into that particular car again anytime soon. "You don't have to do that," I protest.

"Nonsense, you will need a car to get around while I'm at work, and when Angela gets home, she'll need it as well."

I smile at her practicality. "Well, thank you."

Michelle crosses to me and kisses the top of my head. "Okay, go get ready, then."

I hurry down the hall back to my temporary room to get dressed. I pull out an outfit from my bag. I'll need to unpack when I get back. There's no telling when Mom and I will have our own place. That, and living out of a suitcase sucks.

Picking an oversized gray sweater and some colorful leggings that match the boots Michelle let me borrow yesterday, I make my way to the shower, throwing my hair up into a messy bun.

I turn the water up as high as I can stand, soaking up as much of the warmth as possible. I could stay standing under the water all day as the practically scalding temperature soothes my muscles, but Michelle is waiting for me, so I force myself to hurry.

By the time I get back to the front room, I realize I've taken longer than intended. Though there's not an ounce of impatience in her, I apologize. She brushes it off, saying she doesn't mind, and we head out.

The car is already running as we walk outside. I appreciate the warmth blasting from the vents.

"Most people will be at work or school, so if you get bored, you can come by the bakery and hang out," Michelle says as I buckle myself in.

"Would it be okay if I went there with you before I go into town?"

Michelle smiles knowingly. "Seth isn't working today."

Heat prickles at my chest and works its way up my neck to my face. I push my mortification from my mind. That isn't what I'd meant at all. I clear my throat.

"Do you think we can visit Mom soon?" I ask quietly.

She taps her palm against her forehead. "Oh, I meant to tell you earlier, Dr. Underwood said we could visit her Wednesday of next week."

"Really?" I ask a little louder than I meant to. While I'm glad I will get to see her, it's not as soon as I had hoped. Wednesday was the day after my birthday. It will be the first birthday without her. I shake away my sad thoughts and tell myself that we can celebrate it another time together.

Then I turn and watch the neighborhood go by, covered in snow and decorated with pink and red hearts and cupids. With the move and the car wreck, I've completely forgotten about Valentine's Day.

Beautiful aspen trees are nestled into the landscape, and fit so perfectly with everything it almost looks as if someone placed each and every one of them in a specific spot. Not even a fake town could look half as perfectly put together.

The drive is shorter than it felt last night. I probably could have walked, but I think I'd like to get to know Michelle a little better. Even though I have about a million questions, I appreciate that she's not pushing the witch thing on me. I want to talk about it, but the idea is just so . . . unbelievable. I feel like Darrin did in that classic TV show Mom and I used to watch together when I was growing up, *Bewitched*. Except I guess, in this case, I'm Samantha.

We walk into Daily Knead, and there is a short line and several people sitting at various tables, eating.

Michelle walks straight toward the back, greeting everyone as she walks past them. It's the kind of thing I've only seen in Hallmark movies. Everyone seems to know everyone. I look around at the faces and wonder how long it will be until I know every face by heart.

A woman with a blond bob is at the register, helping the short line of people. I get in line, and it's not long before it's my turn. I order a large tea, then head to a small two-person table along the back wall. I dig out my book from my bag and open it to where I left off, getting lost in the words.

Flipping the last page and reading the conclusion I had been hoping for, I let loose a contented sigh. I close my book and stand, stretching my back, then glance at the clock. Nearly noon. I've been reading for most of the morning.

The sun shines brightly outside and reflects off the snow, making the day brighter than normal. With the breakfast crowd gone and the lunch crowd not yet starting, the place is nearly empty. Walking toward the counter, I lean over. Michelle spots me and waves. I motion toward the door indicating that I'm heading out for my walk, and wave my phone. She smiles and nods.

I take off and look at Havenwood Falls High School in the distance. I think I'm actually looking forward to starting school. While I enjoy my alone time, I miss being around other people as well. It would be nice to know others my age, and maybe if I'm lucky, I'll have time to make some friends before summer break.

I cross the parking lot and head farther into the city, ending up at the town square across from City Hall. Covered in snow, it looks like a postcard. The cold sucks big time, but this town still manages to be beautiful, even with the pink and red Valentine's Day decorations that are everywhere.

Pulling my cell from my bag, I snap a few pictures. I'll show

Mom once she wakes up. I pause and suck in a shuddering breath, suddenly filled with overwhelming uncertainty. It takes several inhales before I calm my anxiety and remind myself that Michelle will be calling the doctor today, and we'll get an update.

I continue walking the parameter of the square, snapping pictures of the town and the mountains surrounding it. In the distance, I hear the sound of a bell ringing. The high school must be out for the day.

Just shy of completing my first round, a wave of dizziness washes over me, and for half a second, I'm not sure which way is up or which is down. The tang of copper twinges in my nose. I stumble as my foot catches on a small chunk of hardened snow. I grunt, barely regaining my balance in time to avoid falling.

Snow crunches underfoot, like I'm stepping on piles of tiny bones. It's a morbid thought, not the type I tend to gravitate toward. I screw up my nose and brush off the thought as a side effect of the dizzy spell. A shudder skitters along my skin as I try to shake the thought away while I make my way to the nearest bench. I dust the thin layer of snow off and take a seat, super glad it's not made of metal.

That was so weird. I rub my temples with my fingers. I'm probably pushing myself too hard without realizing it. Or the cold is getting to me more than I thought.

Deciding to stay on the bench for a few minutes before I try to get up again, I scroll through the pictures I took. After going through the first few, I squint, taking a closer look at them. There's a man in the background of several of them, always looking toward the camera.

I snap my head up and scan the park in that area. He's there, across from me, near the gazebo, leaning on a tree and smoking a cigarette. I'm overcome with self-consciousness because I swear it seems like he's watching me. In reality, I'm sure he's waiting for a wife or girlfriend to show up . . . but it seems strange to meet someone so early in a park. Of course, it's a possibility he's just on a break.

Or maybe, I think, letting my imagination run away, *he's a spy waiting for his secret informant, who may or may not be hiding in the tree like the spy from my favorite sixties TV show,* Get Smart.

I laugh to myself and stand, feeling more stable than I was a few minutes ago. I think I'll call it a day on this walk and just head back to Daily Knead.

I don't manage to take more than five steps before I slip on black ice. I'm falling and hitting the hard ground before I know what's happening. And my ankle is screaming.

"Frick, frick, frick!" I say through clenched teeth, as I clutch at the throbbing pain.

Somehow, I manage to hobble around the patch of ice and back to the bench, swearing up a storm the entire way.

"I don't know why Michelle lets you go off without a babysitter," a warm voice says close behind me. There's a hint of annoyance in the teasing words. Warmth brushes across my skin, making several hairs that escaped my bun move, tickling my neck.

"Excuse me?" I seethe, turning to face Seth. He's much closer than I thought, and I swallow.

"Look at you." He waves a hand toward my leg, smiling an ever so slightly crooked grin. Seth folds his arms along the back of the bench, hovering over my shoulder. His face is only a few short inches from mine. Close enough that when he talks, I can feel his warm breath brush my cheek. I snap my face forward, looking straight at the ground. "A few hours on your own, and you slip and fall on the smallest patch of ice in this town."

He's teasing me, but I feel so overwhelmed with everything. A new place, a new school, no friends within a thousand miles, my mom still in the hospital, and I can't even visit her yet . . . and I keep bumping into this jerk. His attempts at humor are falling wide of their goal.

"Just go away," I mutter. I don't want to look at him. I don't want him to know that if I blink, I might just start crying. This vulnerable feeling snuck up on me. Though I suppose it's been there this entire time. The pain in my ankle and his pathetic attempts at humor seem to be the final straws.

The more I think about it, the more I find myself unable to speak. And the fact that he's here right now, bugging me and forcing me to tell him to leave me alone, infuriates me.

Everything is too much. The emotions in me are too strong, making me want to close my mouth and never speak again.

I hate that I shut down. But even more, I hate that he's forcing me to fight it. It keeps the emotions too raw. My hands ball into fists on my knees.

Then I feel him sidle up to me on the bench.

"Get up," he says.

"Go. Away." I fold my arms over my chest, twisting away from him.

"Come on, I'll help you walk back."

Why won't he just take a hint? It's like he's trying to push all my buttons.

"No, thank you," I insist.

He waits a few beats, then takes my arm and lifts me by the elbow with a gentle but firm grip. "You can't just sit here all day. Your aunt would be pissed if I didn't take you back."

"She can't fire you for that." I snort derisively at him.

"I know," he says. "That's not what I'm worried about."

I narrow my eyes at him for a long moment, debating how stubborn I feel like being today. I try to distract him. "Did you know one of Saturn's moons has an ice volcano?"

"No. That's . . . *weird*." He clears his throat. "Are you ready to go now?"

He holds out a hand. I stare at it like it might bite me, then grudgingly, I take it and let him loop an arm around my waist while I stretch mine to get it over his shoulder. I don't even try to talk to him on the way back. If I didn't need his help, I would have stayed on that bench until he went away.

Being so close to him feels strange. I kind of hate that I *don't* hate it. He has this relaxing woodsy scent, something like wood smoke and dark chocolate. As we walk, I occasionally test out my ankle. Each time, a stabbing pain shoots up my leg, and Seth practically growls, snapping at me to stop doing that.

We don't reach the bakery fast enough for my liking.

As soon as we enter Daily Knead, I remove my arm from his shoulder and push his arm from around my waist. I hobble to the counter and get in line. Lucky for me, there's only one person ahead of me. I use the counter for support as I advance. Seth is standing inches away. He probably thinks I'm going to fall.

"Welcome to Daily Knead." A girl's chipper voice calls my attention away from Seth. Her name tag reads *Meghan*. She's slender, with her dark hair pulled back into a ponytail. Meghan gives me a broad smile that reaches her dark eyes.

"Can I get a hot chocolate with extra whipped cream?" I ask.

"Sure thing!" Meghan rings me up while I fish for my wallet in my bag. "You're new here, aren't you?"

"Yeah, I'm registering at Havenwood Falls High later this week." Then after a moment I say, "I'm Clarke."

Meghan's smile broadens. "Really? Maybe we'll have a few classes together! I'm Meghan." She points to her name tag, then her smile falters for half a second, and she asks, "Clarke? Michelle's Clarke?"

There's something incredibly infectious about her attitude. I can feel the stress of starting at another school start to melt with just a few words.

"Yeah." It's a strange feeling to be recognized for a change.

"Are you going to the Sweetheart Dance?" Meghan asks, her eyes flicking toward Seth.

Warmth blooms across my face. "Probably not. I don't start school until next week." The words come out in a rush. I can almost feel Seth's eyes on me.

Seth's arm reaches between us and hands Meghan the cash for my drink. I scowl at him, then look past, realizing I'm holding up the line. So I keep my comments to myself. Meghan hands me my drink and says, "Well, hope to see you around!"

"Yeah!" I agree. "I look forward to it."

Seth grabs my drink before I can and stretches out his arm toward the tables. I hobble to one and plop down in the chair. He sets my drink down, then leaves without a word, my "thank you" dying on my lips. I just don't understand that guy at all. He's both helpful and annoyed at the same time.

I sip my hot chocolate, nearly burning my tongue. I can feel his eyes on me from a few tables over. But I do my best to ignore him.

CHAPTER 6

I shift, making the tissue paper crinkle on the exam table. My hands are folded in my lap, and I lace and unlace my fingers. My aunt is in the chair in the corner, reading a magazine. My hands feel clammy, and I don't know why I'm so nervous. The only sound in the room is the ticking of the clock and the sound of pages turning.

The room is as nondescript as it can get. It looks like every other examination room in every other medical facility. White walls, table and furniture with blue faux-leather material, a blue privacy curtain . . . Just once, I wonder what it would be like to see a daffodil yellow curtain, a mural of a forest along one wall . . .

Bored, I swing my legs, and wince. As long as I don't move my ankle, it feels fine now. I hate to admit it, but I'm glad Seth found me when he did and helped me back to the bakery. I didn't realize how cold it was until he held me to his side. I feel heat bloom across my cheeks thinking about it.

Dr. Underwood walks in, grabbing my chart from the back of the door.

"How are you doing today, Ms. Price?" he asks, sitting down on the cushioned rolling stool. He flips through the intake form, scanning the information.

"I'm okay, I guess," I say. "I slipped on some ice and twisted my ankle." It even feels stupid saying it. But it could be worse. I could have fallen on my face and cracked a tooth. Just the idea of breaking a tooth sends a shudder along my body.

Setting the paper down and taking notes, he says, "Why don't you take off your sock and shoe and roll up your pant leg."

I oblige, setting the single shoe next to me.

"All right," he says, scooting over to me and lifting my leg by the back of my calf muscle. His gloved fingers test the skin around my ankle, then the ankle itself. "Does this hurt?"

I shake my head no. He rotates my ankle, and I hiss through my teeth when he fully extends it.

Then he gently sets my ankle down and tells me I can put my sock and shoe back on. He scoots back to the desk and makes a few notes in my chart before turning back to me.

"There's not much swelling, but try to avoid walking on it as much as you can for the next few days. Keep it elevated and ice it a few times a day for twenty minutes each. Just give it a few days, and it will be good as new again."

"Thanks," I say, fixing my pant leg.

"Before you go, how's your head feeling?" he asks. He gets up from the rolling stool and gently feels my head.

"Fine," I say.

"No headaches, trouble sleeping, blackouts?"

"Nope."

He checks my eyes and ears. "Disorientation, nausea, or vomiting?"

"No, nothing like that. But I get a little dizzy sometimes."

"That's normal, but if it continues much longer, I'd like to see you back here." The doctor returns to his seat and makes a few more quick notes. "You are all set to go. Just take it easy for the next few days."

I hop down from the table, landing on my uninjured foot, keeping the other high enough from the ground to avoid jostling it. "Doctor, I know you said we could see Mom on Wednesday next week, but since we're here now, can I please see her? Just for a moment?" I clasp my hands and hold them to my chest, looking at the doctor with the best puppy dog eyes I can manage.

"Clarke—" Michelle starts.

"Pleeeeease?" I beg her, drawing out the *e* sound in the word.

They look at each other as if silently communicating. I wish I could read minds. But there's definitely something they don't want to tell me. I hold my breath, waiting for an answer. Then Dr. Underwood gives the briefest of nods to her before addressing me.

"She still has a few open wounds that haven't healed as much as I would like, but you can see her through the window. She only needs a few more days."

Michelle visibly relaxes. It's weird. I have no idea why Mom would need to be confined for her wounds. It's not like I wanted to lick her face or sneeze on her. But what do I know?

I narrow my eyes at him and wonder if he's human . . . or supe. If he is a supe, I doubt he'd go around advertising it. That thought makes me wonder. Mom is a witch, like Michelle and me. Could her quarantine have to do with some magic . . . something or other?

Those thoughts leave my mind as quick as they come, and all that remains is that I get to see Mom!

Michelle offers me her arm, and we follow the doctor out of the exam room and down the hall. I barely pay attention to where we are going, trying to walk fast and still avoid putting too much weight on one foot.

Not soon enough for my liking, we get to a hallway with several doors, each with their own large window looking in. Dr. Underwood stops in front of one room, and I limp closer, letting go of Michelle's arm. The tangy smell of copper fills my nose. I rub the back of my hand on my nose, trying to make it go away as I hop toward the window.

The window on the outside wall has the blinds drawn, but enough sunlight filters in, bathing the room in the warm glow of the late afternoon sun. Mom is sleeping. She looks pale, but peaceful.

I touch the glass, longing to hold her hand. But I'm just glad I can see her face. Even if her lips are pale and dry and cuts mar her face and arms. But I can see with my own eyes that she's healing. The steady rise and fall of her chest and the steady pulsing of the machine next to her both fill me with comfort. I can feel my stress ease quite a bit.

I'm not sure how long I stand there, but I know my good leg is starting to ache from supporting twice as much weight as normal.

A hot hand touches my arm, drawing my attention from Mom. "We should go soon, Clarke. The doctor has a lot of work to do." Then she turns to him and says, "Thank you for this. Seeing her helps."

"Not a problem."

I know he's busy, but still his voice is warm and friendly as if, standing here, watching me stare at Mom, is just as important as anything else. I look back toward Mom. There's so much I want to tell her, to ask her . . . I turn to the doctor, my hand still pressed against the cool glass. "When can I go in and see her?"

He checks her clipboard. "When you come back next Wednesday."

"Thank you," I say.

He smiles and gives one nod. "Of course."

I take a deep breath and let it out, and relief washes over me for the first time in three days.

CHAPTER 7

I flip through the list of shows and movies on the to-be-watched list I made three nights ago, after twisting my ankle, determined to stay in and binge a few shows. With doctor's instructions to ice my foot and stay off it as much as possible, I'm glad to take advantage of being stuck inside, where it's warm and decidedly not icy. After three days, though, it is beginning to wear on me.

We're going to visit Mom on Wednesday. I can't wait. Looking at the calendar pinned next to the door, I note it's been five days since I woke up. Only six more days until I can finally see Mom. It will be a late birthday present, but it's the only one I want or need. Maybe this time she'll be awake. If not, just being next to her will be enough.

The doctor told Michelle he would prefer we wait, just to give her time and peace to heal. It's still been hard. I understand their concern, but it still sucks. At least I got to see her through the glass window.

Michelle kisses me on the top of the head. "I'll be home early today to take you to the school to register for classes," she says as she heads out the door to work.

The day passes slowly, and I switch to reading when a headache starts to form after a little over an hour of watching TV, though I suppose it's been more like listening to it as I stare out the window, watching the barest amount of snow fall continuously. Between chapters, I doze for a few minutes here and there, then switch back to listening to the TV. I'm not used to being cooped up like this without being sick. It's terribly boring, and I still haven't managed to make it back to either of the bookstores yet.

It's a relief when Michelle comes home. I limp toward the bedroom, using the wall for support. My ankle doesn't feel too bad anymore, just a little stiff. And though I could probably walk without the limp, I don't want to push it. I tested it out last night and can move with a minimal amount of soreness. I don't want to be limping my way to class when I finally start school.

During the drive, a swarm of butterflies flutters in my stomach. After as many moves as I've been through, I shouldn't be feeling like this. I suppose it's the not knowing that gets to me. Each school was different. Some were great, others run of the mill, but then there were the terrible schools where bullies sought out the new kid and made my life hell.

I reach for my bag to get my wallet, and the strange scent of copper fills my nose. My wallet snaps into my open palm. I stare at my hand for a long moment. *What the crap was that?*

"Be careful." Michelle looks at me. "It's fine when it's just us. But you need to learn how to control your powers. They'll be erratic at first, but as long as you keep your emotions in check, you'll be fine." I blink, staring at her with my mouth open. She keeps talking like what I just did wasn't crazy. "And *never* do that in front of a human. Maybe I'll look into enrolling you in some classes to help you learn to control your powers."

"Okay . . ." is all I can manage to squeeze out. *More classes? I guess I'd better enjoy my down time while I have it. Doesn't seem like I'll be getting much over the next several months.*

"With the supermoon coming up on the nineteenth, you'll need to practice."

"Okay," I say again. I look at my hands and wonder what magic will feel like. Will it be mentally or physically taxing, or will it be easy—just have to will something to happen and . . . poof?

By the time we get to the school, my nerves are humming. I can feel my heart beating hard in my chest. Michelle waits for me to collect myself before we get out and walk up to the large brick building.

I follow behind Michelle as she leads me through the arched entryway and down the hall to an office with "Principal Friske" written across the glass door in bold, black lettering. She does most of the talking for me, but I make sure to introduce myself to the woman behind the desk and give her the best smile I can. It's strained, and I hope she doesn't take offense.

Michelle continues to talk with the woman behind the desk, and I excuse myself. "I want to check out my locker before we go, if that's okay."

"That's fine. I'll be waiting in the car whenever you're ready," she says, then goes back to talking. She's collecting a stack of papers. I nod, then close the door quietly behind me.

I exit the office and look around. Gray lockers line the halls, and I try to study the room numbers as I look at my schedule. I want to get a feel for the halls and the way the classrooms are numbered before I start. Nothing is worse than being late to every class because you have no idea where anything is. Or worse, get bad directions from a student who pretends to be helpful.

I make it to my locker just as the bell rings. The hall floods with students talking and lockers opening and slamming shut. A group of athletes passes, wearing their blue and silver letterman jackets. No one seems to notice me. Why would they? My face is about six inches from my locker. I stare at the locker combination in my hand and turn the dial.

It doesn't open. I double check the locker number, then try again, rolling my shoulders for good measure first. I take two deep breaths to push down my nerves and try again.

I reach for the dial and spin it a few times before attempting my combination again. It doesn't work. I frown, then look at the paper with my locker number to make sure I have the right one.

My face heats as I scoot over one locker. *Nope.* I look around and hope no one saw me. If they did, no one has said or done anything. I try again.

It opens, and I do a celebratory dance—on the inside. I breathe deeply.

The locker is clean and empty, but it will be full of books and school supplies soon. I close the door and turn the handle. When I turn around, Meghan pauses mid-stride.

"Clarke, you're here!" she says excitedly and gives me a brief hug.

"Yeah! I finally registered for classes. I start Tuesday."

"Oh, really? Can I see your schedule?" I pull the paper from my pocket and hand it to her. "Sweet, we have third and fifth periods together."

I can't help the inner sigh of relief. At least I'll see a friendly face in a few classes.

"That's great," I say.

Meghan shrugs her bag over her shoulder. "Well, I should get going. I have an afternoon shift to work today. But I'll see you next week."

"See you next week," I echo, waving as she takes off down the hall, her dark hair flowing behind her.

The crowd has thinned a lot now, so I head back the way I came, weaving through the few students taking their time. I earn a few curious stares from others, but so far, no intimidating glares. I'll take that as a win for now.

I head for a side door, toward the parking lot. Thankfully I don't run afoul of any more patches of ice and make it to the car in one piece.

"How does pizza sound to you?" Michelle asks as I slide into the car and buckle myself in. "I called in an order while I was waiting."

"Sounds fantastic!" I say. My stomach gurgles a little at just the thought.

She backs out of the parking spot and drives down Main Street, turning toward the town square. "Your mom's car will be ready tomorrow."

"Already? That was fast."

"We have some of the best mechanics here," Michelle says as she puts the car into park.

I wave my hand, stopping her from getting out. "Don't get out. I'll run in really quick and grab the food."

Michelle reaches into her purse and hands me some cash. "The order will be under my name."

I jump out and hurry inside, making my time in the rapidly chilling air as short as possible. There aren't many people here. It seems we managed to beat the dinner crowd.

It's a low-lit restaurant, with a comfortable atmosphere: booths made of dark-stained wood, the seats of worn leather, and red-and-white-checkered table cloths adorning the surfaces of the tables. The smell of garlic and tomato sauce fills the air, and I'm nearly drooling.

I hurry to the counter and bounce on my toes while I wait for the cashier to ring me up. I can't wait to get home and eat! He slides the pizza box to me—*large*—and I thank him as I turn away.

I can't help the small jig I do as I push the door open with my rear and step outside. The cold air blasts me in the face, and I can't help uttering, "Yuck."

By now it should feel familiar, expected even, but I'm still surprised when, as soon as I walk through the door, I'm jerked backward into a hard body. I nearly lose my grip on the pizza box.

Without looking, I know the chest at my back belongs to Seth. Ice falls and shatters at my feet. Exactly where I'd been standing. I blink and look around. I think I see a shadow pass by a tree, but when I blink again, it's gone. It was probably nothing.

"Why am I not surprised?" He lets me go, throwing his hands in the air as I spin to face him.

I open my mouth to say thanks, though what comes out instead is, "Why are you always around everywhere I go?"

"Not that it's any of your business, but I like to eat food on occasion. Is that all right with you?" he snaps.

Apparently, his snarky tone hit a nerve, because now I'm angry. "Why do you bother saving me if you hate me so much?"

Seth's eyes grow large. He looks taken aback, then after a moment, he says, "I don't hate you."

"Well, you obviously don't like me. And what I can't figure out is why you are nice to me one minute, and then the next, you act like you can't stand being in the same town." I wave my free arm around as I rant.

He takes my wrist and lowers my arm to my side, his other hand helping to steady the food in the other. "First, just put that away before you hurt someone." Seth pats me on my upper arm, like it'll go crazy and smack him—which I'm not entirely sure I wouldn't have if he hadn't pointed out my flailing. "Second, I'm sorry. I don't mean to be rude. It just worries me that someone can be so accident-prone and live to the ripe old age of . . ." He draws out the last word and raises his brows like he expects me to answer.

"Seventeen," I grunt.

"Seventeen. It's like you're always getting hurt or trying to get yourself killed. How did you even survive until now without a personal bodyguard?"

"I have never been accident-prone. This is just a coincidence," I say, pointing to the shattered ice at our feet. "Maybe you're just bad luck?" I try to keep a lightness to the jab, but he frowns. "Sorry," I mutter.

How can I chastise him for being rude when I'm rude as well?

"What about that first day?" I ask after what feels like several long moments. "You were rude then, and that was the first time I ever saw you."

He looks sheepish. "Sorry, you caught me on a bad day. I just got some . . . bad news."

There's something about the way he says *bad news* that keeps me from prying further. It sounds too personal, too painful. So I keep my lips pressed shut and twist the end of my ponytail around my finger.

He jerks his chin toward Michelle's running car. "I think someone is waiting on you."

"I-I should go," I say.

"I'll walk you to the car."

I don't even argue. I wouldn't win, even if I did. We walk the short distance in silence and without the anger or attitudes that have been present since I first bumped into him. I suddenly feel awkward around Seth.

I reach out for the door handle, and I feel his hand wrap around the top of the arm clutching the pizza. Only the fact that his gentle hold is steady is keeping me from the sin of dropping the box at my feet. His fingers are warm against my chilled skin even through my jacket. I turn slowly and look up at him. My heartbeat speeds up as he takes a step closer to me. The cold metal of the car presses against my back.

"Uh," he starts and seems to have trouble holding my gaze. "Let me make it up to you. Burger Bar has the best burgers you'll ever have."

Is he asking me out on a date? I scrunch up my nose. If he is, then I'm not sure. It might just be an apology. I think on that for a minute, stealing a glance at the pizza box, then say, "Tarantulas can go two years without eating."

Seth's eyes narrow slightly. "And are you a tarantula?" he asks teasingly.

I shake my head no.

"So . . . is that a yes?"

I lick my lips, nodding dumbly, and his smirk comes out to play across his face. My stomach flips, and it's not unpleasant. Seth leans forward and musses the top of my head playfully, then he turns and leaves, shaking his head and laughing softly to himself.

I look down at my hand to find a small slip of paper with a

number written across it. *His* number. I feel heat rise to my cheeks as I climb into the car.

Wow . . . that was completely unexpected.

"What was that all about?" Michelle asks as I buckle myself in.

"I think . . ." Again, I look down at the slip in my hand. "I think I have a date."

CHAPTER 8

*H*olding my phone above me, I stare at the screen, rereading my message and debating if I should send the text or not. I roll over and hit send before I can talk myself out of it completely.

Clarke: hey, just texting so you have my number, too - Clarke

Lame . . . so lame. I smack the palm of my hand against my forehead. It could be worse, but it still feels cringeworthy. I am so *bad* at this stuff. Maybe I should have waited a few days—or a week, but now it's too late for what ifs. Though honestly, what would waiting prove? Waiting would have meant anxiety. And I already have more than enough of that to go around. Then there's the fact that he works for Michelle, so he already knows more about me than I know about him. I kind of want to even the score.

Seth: I didn't expect a text so soon

Crap. Double crap. I waited a day. I knew I should have taken longer before sending the text. Maybe I shouldn't have sent one at all. He probably thinks I'm some desperate loser now. Who would want to be friends with that?

Seth: You haven't changed your mind about going on a date with me, have you?

I swallow the ball of nerves working its way up my chest.

Clarke: It's a date?

Seth: What did you think it was?

Clarke: I don't know?

Seth: How does tomorrow sound? Around six?

Clarke: I guess I'll probably want to eat tomorrow

Seth: You're funny

Seth: Gotta run, something just came up

Seth: Pick you up at six?

Clarke: Okay

Seth: See you tomorrow

Clarke: Yeah. See you then

Two minutes later my phone dings with another message.

Seth: Good night, Clarke

I smile, then set my cell down on the nightstand and click off my light. When my head lands on my pillow, my eyes refuse to close. I will not be sleeping much tonight. I'm nervous about tomorrow, though I'm not sure why. It's not as though we haven't spent time together before.

But this was different. Those times were never intentional, and our conversations were mostly snarky. This feels weird. But in a good way.

CHAPTER 9

T sit on the couch nervously chewing on my thumbnail until I hear the rumble of a car outside. Jumping to my feet, I'm at the door, my hand hovering over the handle, waiting for him to knock.

I listen and hear his footsteps approach, then stop. He clears his throat. "Are you going to open the door?" Seth asks.

My eyes widen, but I stay quiet. This is already awkward, and we aren't even in the same room.

"I can see the top of your head through this little window." He taps gently on the glass pane right above my head.

Blowing out a breath, I pull open the door and motion for him to come in even though his car is still running. It's going to be nice and warm, which is good, because that blast of air that came in with him was enough to make me want to hibernate.

Seth smiles, and it's nice. One corner of his lips lifts a little higher than the other, showing off part of his eye tooth. There's something almost animalistic about the look. And it sends butterflies swarming in my gut.

I step away. "Shall we?"

He nods, and once I close the door behind us, he guides me to his car with one hand on my lower back. Part of me thinks it's because he's afraid I'll fall and break something, but another part wonders if he might be looking for an excuse to touch me.

Seth opens the car door for me, then closes it gently as I buckle myself in. The heat feels amazing, though as soon as he slides in next to me, I almost want to roll the window down, just a bit. Because with him so close, the heat is almost too much, as if the temperature went up twenty degrees the second he got in.

As if he can sense the overload I'm feeling, he reaches over and turns the dial down. I twist a strand of hair around my finger, again and again.

"It's okay," he says with a hint of laughter. "You can relax. I'm not going to bite."

There it is again, that smile that is both sweet and innocent, and dark and dangerous at the same time. The one that says he *could* bite if I wanted him to. I look away and out the side window, watching the town pass, trying to memorize where everything is. It only takes a few minutes to get to the restaurant.

He parks, and I look around. We're in Miller's Plaza. Daily Knead is straight ahead, and to our left is Burger Bar. I lick my lips. I scan the rest of the plaza, something I hadn't even bothered to do until now. Serendipity Dance Studio, VIP Nails, and . . .

"What is that place?" I ask, pointing.

Seth pauses halfway out of the car. His eyes travel in the direction I'm pointing.

"Sakura Buffet?" He gives me a strange look. "It's a Chinese, Vietnamese, and Japanese buffet. Why?"

I can feel my eyes growing large. I had given up all hope of there being a Japanese restaurant in this part of the country, but all three in one? I think I might be in heaven!

I get out of the car to find him still watching me with that look. Seth laughs lightly. "I was going to take you to Burger Bar, but we can save that for another day if you'd prefer to go to Sakura."

"Really?" I clasp my hands and can't help but do a body wiggle.

He laughs again, this time not bothering to try to suppress it. Seth walks around the car and offers me his arm. I take it, letting him lead me across the parking lot.

"If you like this place"—he gestures toward Sakura Buffet—"you'll *love* the Tacos for Daze food truck. I can take you there when it's warmer."

"Yes, please!"

We walk in, and the delicious smell of the food nearly knocks me over. I was too nervous to eat breakfast, so now I'm starving. My stomach lets out an embarrassingly loud growl.

"If you're not hungry . . ." Seth starts, a large grin plastered across his face.

"Don't even joke about food right now," I mutter.

There are twelve tables inside that would fit four people each and three booths along the large window facing out. The buffet is along the back, with a view of the kitchen behind it. In front of the buffet is the cashier.

I follow half a step behind him to the counter. While he gets the plates, I can't help but ogle the large variety of food. I am tempted to get a bite of everything. Glancing at the back of Seth's head, I frown. He might think I'm overly gluttonous. So I'd better stick to one or two things. But everything looks and smells so delicious.

We pick the booth along the window farthest from the door. I drop off my bag and drape my coat over it before heading to fill my plate.

I scan the buffet and am almost overwhelmed with the choices—chicken lo mein, boneless spare ribs, tempura shrimp, sashimi, and curry chicken! And so many more options. Ugh, how's a girl to choose?

I can always come back, I remind myself. So I settle on Kung Pao chicken with peanuts and a boneless spare rib. I load up my plate and head back to the table. A minute later, Seth joins me, somehow balancing two drinks in one hand and his plate in the other. He sits down next to me rather than across. I'm pinned between him and the wall, though I don't feel trapped.

We angle our bodies toward each other so we have a little more elbow room and chat between bites. He's easier to talk to than I expected. He has this way of asking me questions that don't feel invasive but have me revealing more about myself than I normally would to someone I just met. Seth's manner is relaxed. He's so different from the guy I met a week ago. Smiles come easy to him. And I want to know more about who he is.

Seth was right—the food here is really good. Before I know it, my plate is empty, and I'm tempted to go for another round. Instead, I pick up my drink and sip. He is watching me. More observant than most people, he almost seems like he's studying me. There's something not exactly human behind his gaze, and it makes me wonder . . .

Putting down the soda, I lean forward. He mirrors my movement, a conspiratorial smirk gracing his lips. I look around, and when I'm sure there is no one within hearing distance, I whisper, "What *are* you?"

I can tell that's not what he was expecting me to say. The grin slips from his face, and he looks half upset and half like I've grown a second head.

"What do you mean?" Seth asks slowly. His nostrils flare slightly.

It occurs to me then that he might just be another human. "Uh, I mean . . ." I stumble, looking for something to cover up my slip. "What's your sign?"

Oh. My. Gawd. I cringe visibly, and it's obvious he knows that isn't what I meant. Not even close.

He leans in a little closer and says, "Look, I will tell you this because I *know* your aunt." He puts an emphasis on *know*, as if it means more than *I'm her employee*. "You can't really go around asking people that here. There are people—humans—who don't know about supes, and there are some supes who would wish to remain unknown."

I struggle to get my tongue to form words. Of course it's rude to ask that. "Do you know what I am?"

He nods, slowly.

"How?"

He licks his lips. "I can smell the magic on you. It's faint, but it's there." I'm not even sure what that means. Seth leans back against the booth. "Besides, I do work for Michelle, and she already told me about your family."

I'm still leaning forward.

"So you know that I'm a—" I cut off. I don't know if I should say the word out loud. It's still unbelievable. After what happened in the car on the way to register for classes, I tried starting the fireplace for three hours straight. But nothing had happened, and I'd felt nothing.

"A witch?" he says in a normal speaking tone, though after whispering, it sounds more like shouting to my ears.

My eyes go wide, and I can feel a tingling in my chest, burning its way up my neck and scorching my cheeks. I can't believe he said it so loud!

"What are you doing?" I hiss.

"I'm just playing with you. Trust me, no one heard."

I cut my eyes to a man eating alone, with his back toward us only a few tables away. Seth just laughs. Of course, he's right. The man made no move to indicate he'd heard.

As soon as my heart climbs back down and out of my throat, I ask, "So, you know about me. Don't you think it's only fair for me to know about you?"

Maybe I'm imagining it, but I think he's a little embarrassed. "Shifter . . . wolf," he mumbles.

Finally, I lean back as well. I cross my arms and consider him, then I nod and say, "That explains a lot."

Seth cocks his head as if to tell me to go on.

"You do seem to growl an awful lot when you're annoyed," I clarify, eyeing him up and down.

He almost spits his drink out. Now it's my turn to laugh.

"No, I don't," he says defensively.

"I'm kidding," I say. "It's your eyes. They look almost golden in some light. It's not a very common eye color, and then . . . even when you hated me—"

"I never hated you," he says flatly and very seriously as he cuts me off.

I reach out and place one of my hands on top of his. "You still had a protective quality about you."

He says something, but I don't hear it. A ringing starts in my ears and grows louder and louder until I have to grasp the edge of the table to keep upright.

Seth grabs my arms and holds me up, talking to me, but the words are muffled and distorted by the ringing. I try to look up at him, and my eyes snag on a dark shape as it stands. I can't make out who or what it is. The lines are distorted, like bad reception on an old television set. I try to point it out to Seth, but I don't know if my words are coming out as more than gibberish or if they are only thoughts in my head.

Then the shadow is gone, and so is the ringing. I slump in my seat and try to catch my breath. My skin is like ice. The metal of my bracelet feels like it's burning in comparison.

"Clarke? Clarke!" Seth's worried voice breaks through my fog.

I snuggle closer to his warmth. This cold is nothing like the cold outside, but something deeper, something darker coating my bones.

"Clarke," he says again. More firmly this time.

I force myself to move, to straighten my spine, and look at him. Sharp pain pierces my temples. "I'm fine," I say weakly. "I just have a migraine."

His lips pinch together, and I know he doesn't believe me, but he won't argue here.

The drive home is silent. Thankfully my headache is mostly gone, only a residual pain remaining. And I'm so tired.

When Seth parks the car, he turns to me. At first I think he's angry, then I realize that's wrong. He's concerned.

"What happened back there?" His voice is soft, but the words are demanding.

I shake my head. "I don't know. I've been getting headaches a lot since I've been here. I don't think I've adjusted to the altitude yet, or maybe it's the concussion from the accident."

He considers me for a long moment and must believe that I'm not hiding anything, or at least not *trying* to hide anything. Though now, I think he might have a better idea of what's causing my headaches than I do.

I don't wait for him to open my car door, and by the time I get to the front of the car, he's at my side, linking his arm in mine as he walks me up the steps. Whatever bothered him about my dizzy spell seems to have dissipated.

I've never had a boy walk me to my door before. I've only seen things like that in movies, right before he kisses the girl. My pulse races.

"Clarke, I . . ." Seth takes his arm from mine and reaches into the pocket of his leather jacket. Then he's handing me a small dark blue box. My heart hammers as thoughts of what it could be and why he's giving it to me race through my mind.

I take it, running my fingers over the textured surface.

"It's nothing special, so don't read too much into it. It's more of a welcoming gift." He looks away, refusing to meet my eyes, and if I'm not mistaken, his face is a little flushed.

"Thank you," I say.

Before I can open it, he's running his hand over the top of my head. It's a strange gesture, almost brotherly. But it quickly changes into something more when his hand pauses at the nape of my neck, pulling me closer. I think he's going to kiss me.

He swallows hard, the knot on his throat bobbing. I lean forward into him. My hand rests on his chest, the other clutching the box at my side. Seth could melt snow with the heat that's radiating off him.

I try to control my breathing as our faces inch closer and closer.

And just when I can almost feel his lips on mine . . . Seth backs up and walks backward down the steps. "I'll talk to you later, Clarke. Feel better."

I am a little disappointed but also relieved. Because I think I might spontaneously combust if we kissed.

Clutching the box in my hand, I unlock the door and close it behind me. The sound of Seth's engine roaring to life doesn't come until I turn the lock on the front door.

CHAPTER 10

I slip off my boots and pad down the hall, pausing to say goodnight to the painting. There's just something about it that feels familiar. I squint at the man, and I swear he looks a little bigger than the last time again. Clearly that's impossible, so I laugh it off and continue to my room.

It's not until I shower and change into my nightclothes that I sit on the bed holding the blue box. There's something about prolonging opening up a gift that makes it even better. I lift the lid to reveal a glass ornament wolf. A gold string is looped through a hook in its back. It's beautiful. I set it next to the bedside lamp and pick up my cell.

Clarke: Thank you. I love it

Seth: I'm glad

Clarke: I'm sorry about tonight. I want to make it up to you

Seth: There's no need

Seth: You didn't do anything wrong

Clarke: Come to dinner tomorrow

I wait a few minutes, wondering if he even wants to, or if he'd only asked me out as a friend. But he'd said it was a date. And then there was that almost kiss. The longer he takes to respond, the more my mind wonders if I read him, and the date we had, all wrong.

Seth: So . . . is this a date? ;)

A large, almost painful grin spreads across my face at his response.

Clarke: Do you want it to be?

Even I'm surprised at my uncharacteristic confidence and ability to tease.

Seth: I look forward to it

My heart flutters in my chest. I click off the light, tuck myself under the blankets, and turn on my side to admire the wolf. The moonlight streams through my window, dancing through the cut glass facets and creating a beautiful rainbow of faded colors along the wall.

I LOOK in the mirror and frown. Strip off the thick pink knit sweater and try on another. I really need to go shopping. Most of my clothes are too casual. The movers should have been here days ago with our things. We'll have to wait until Mom is home to find out what happened to them. At least the car arrived this morning, so now I have what was in my other suitcase in the trunk.

I sigh and go back to the first sweater I tried on, a thin knit the color of azure blue to match the sky.

There's a knock at the front door as I pull it over my head and smooth it down. I take a deep breath in and let it out, twice, before hurrying to the door. A glance at the clock tells me he's twenty minutes early.

Seth hurries inside as soon as the door opens, closing it quickly behind him against the wind and snow that blow in after.

"You look nice," he says, as if he's surprised to find that I did more than brush my hair.

"Thanks." We stand awkwardly for a moment. He's so close, I'm tempted to reach out and grab his shirt, pulling him even closer, to start where we left off last night. He quirks a brow, and one corner of his mouth ticks up, as if he knows what I'm thinking and knows I can't help it. I push the thought down until later, then add, "I still need to set the table. You can relax on the couch if you want."

Hurrying to the dining room, I put down the two plates and napkins. I forgot to ask him what he wants to drink, so I just set down empty cups for now. I push my way through the swinging door into the kitchen and load up a tray with everything, then return to the dining room and set it down in the center. I take a second to make sure everything is straight.

"Okay, dinner is ready!" I call out to the other room and spin around when I hear laughing right behind me. "How long have you been standing there?"

"The whole time," he says. There's that arrogant smirk again.

"Sit down." I point to a chair with a jerk of my chin. He's looking from me to the food.

"What?" I ask.

"I don't know what I expected, but it wasn't tacos."

I gasp in mock horror, pressing a hand to my chest in melodramatic fashion. "It's your fault, you know. You were the one who mentioned Tacos for Daze."

Seth crosses the room, but instead of sitting down in one of the chairs, he stops less than a foot away. He lifts a hand and skims a lock of hair with one finger. "Tacos are great, but I really just came for the company."

Before I get a chance to attempt to formulate a response to that, the front door opens and slams quickly. "Clarke? Are you here?"

"In the dining room!" I call out.

It suddenly dawns on me that I invited him over without asking Michelle first. What is with me lately? I'm never this inconsiderate.

"Oh, Mr. Cooper, I didn't know you were coming over." Her eyebrows shoot up in surprise.

"I invited him over for dinner. I hope that's okay?"

She waves my concern away. "Oh, that's fine, dear." Her eyes graze the table then, before she walks into the kitchen. I can feel my eyes nearly bulge out of their sockets from the look she gives me. What does that woman *think* is actually going on here?

From the devilish grin on Seth's face, he knows exactly what Michelle is thinking. I make a slashing movement across my throat with my hand just as she returns with a pitcher of water.

"Why don't you join us?" I offer.

Michelle hesitates. "I don't want to intrude."

"We insist," Seth says.

"I'll go get an extra plate," I say, running off to the kitchen.

I stop on my way back to the dining room, my hand just shy of touching the swinging door when I hear them talking.

"You didn't need to come over to watch her tonight. She's been home all day. It's safe here," Michelle says.

Adrenaline spikes, and I am pissed. *Watch me? Watch me!* I'm not some helpless princess. And to ask me on a date to just—what? Keep an eye on me? The realization stings a lot more than I expect.

Who are these people, treating me as if I were a child? A minor slip on the ice isn't all that uncommon for someone not used to this kind of winter. It feels like a betrayal that Michelle had him follow me. No wonder he was there when I slipped. That's why he's always around.

"I don't mind, and this was—"

I don't wait to hear another word before I burst through the doorway. They both turn to face me, and from the look on their faces, they know I heard.

A tear falls down my cheek. *Traitorous body!*

"Who the hell do you think you are? I'm not—" My voice breaks. "You had him follow me, watching me? I'm not some invalid incapable of taking care of myself!"

They both stand at the same time. Seth takes one step forward, hand reaching out for me.

"Sweetie, it's not like that—" Michelle starts, but I don't let her finish before I round on Seth.

"And you . . ." I seethe. "How could you? I don't need or want your pity dates!" I'm shaking now. Rage races through me in an icy wave. I'm crying, and I don't care anymore. "You made me think you liked me."

He recoils like I slapped him. "Clarke, please just listen. It's not—"

"No. Just get out and leave me alone."

I turn on my heel and storm off before either of them have a chance to say another word, before they have a chance to make up some lie to try to make me feel better, to try to justify having him follow me. I slam the door to my room behind me.

A few minutes later, the front door opens and shuts, and I wait for the roar of his car's engine, but there's only silence.

I've never felt more alone in my life than I do now.

CHAPTER 11

*a*n annoying buzz drags me from sleep, and I peel my eyes
open. They feel swollen from crying. I groan and roll over
to my side.

The glass wolf is staring at me from the night stand as if
pleading with me to listen to Seth. *Fat chance.* I don't want to hear
what he or Michelle has to say. I feel betrayed, like I'm the butt of
some twisted prank. I avoided them both all day yesterday. I just
can't see myself being ready to talk to them yet.

I glance at the calendar. Tomorrow is the nineteenth, so I'll at
least get to see Mom in two more days.

My phone buzzes again. I pick it up and glare at the name
across the display. Seth. I hit ignore and place it face down. I can't
believe I wanted to kiss that jerk, *almost* kissed him. And just as I
promised myself I wouldn't do, I was rushing into something.
Letting my heart lead the way instead of my brain.

Throwing my covers off, I get up and move into the living
room to watch whatever happens to be on TV, flipping blindly
through the channels.

The vibration of the cell on the wood surface echoes down the
hall, so I turn up the volume to drown it out.

"Take a hint," I mutter.

Though I lay on the couch with my eyes pointed at the screen for several hours, I don't remember a minute of anything I've "watched." I've played what happened last night over and over in my head, wishing they'd tried saying something different, wishing they'd tried to give me something better than excuses . . . wishing I'd said more to let them know that what they did was horrible. But alas, I don't have the skills required for time travel.

My stomach growls loudly, and I realize it's already the middle of the afternoon, and I haven't eaten yet. Maybe walking to the burger joint will help clear my head.

Standing inside the doorway to my room, I listen for the vibration of my phone. Thankfully, it's silent. I quickly throw on a pair of leggings and an oversized faded red sweater that clings to my form. I wonder what kind of shopping this town has and if I'll have to go to the next town over to have a selection.

For a brief moment, I debate taking the car. It would be warm for sure, but I think I need the exercise to clear my head. And it doesn't seem too chilly out today. The fact that I'd rather face the cold than use a nice warm car doesn't escape me.

As I finish slipping on the knee-high boots, my phone buzzes. My stomach forms into a knot. That's it. I am not going to walk there and back with the constant buzzing. I just want a few hours of peace. For a moment, I'm tempted to look at the number of missed calls and messages, though that passes quickly.

Instead, I march out of my room, snatching up my jacket on the way out, pausing to grab the house key—now attached to our car keys—from the bowl next to the door. I pause at the bottom of the steps and look back at the townhouse, wondering if I *should* bring my phone after all. No, if I get lost, I'll just ask someone for directions. I'll be home long before Michelle.

The sun shines, and I'm glad for its warmth, but the glint off the snow is nearly blinding. I look around me as I walk. The birds sing, and as I focus on their song, I find my muscles release their tension. It's peaceful, and more beautiful than I gave the town credit for, with the snow-covered pines and the mountains in every direction.

By the time I reach Burger Bar, a super cute drive-in straight out of the fifties, I've warmed up. It's right across from my future school and in front of the plaza where the Daily Knead is.

I knew Burger Bar looked retro from the outside, but inside is a whole other level of epic. Black-and-white-checkered flooring, with just enough wear and tear that I know it's original. Booths with the classic red-and-white leather, stools at the counter to match. Polished tin ceiling tiles. I haven't seen anything like that since Mom took me to Salem, Massachusetts, when I was twelve. There is definitely some history to this place. The only thing that doesn't quite fit is the TV in the back.

I sit down at a table to peruse the menu. I quickly settle on a cheeseburger and fries. It's always been my belief that you can tell a lot about a place by how well it does the basics. It doesn't take long for me to shed my jacket. After being out in the crisp air, I'm a little warm.

The Beatles play from a jukebox, and I tap a finger on the metal table while I wait for my food. Staring blankly out the window, I let my mind wander. My eyelids grow heavy as I sit alone at this little table, content and surrounded by the scent of delicious food. My mouth waters, and my stomach growls loudly in response. I must be hungrier than I realized.

I hear a chuckle, warm and inviting enough to send a tingle along my skin. My spine straightens as a knot forms in my chest. Slowly, I turn and look over my shoulder. My heart stutters, and I struggle to breathe as two amber eyes lock onto mine.

Seth takes a few steps toward me and hesitates when I shake my head, but continues to approach regardless. I command my body to move, though it ignores me and stays right where it is.

I feel like a caged animal.

Trapped.

I stand, ready to bolt.

"Wait, please," Seth says quietly. The tips of his fingers rest on my wrist. I curse how much I want to sink into his touch.

There's something in his eyes that makes me want to sit back down. Something that looks so sincere, almost so heartbreaking it makes my knees weak.

"What?" I ask through clenched teeth. I don't want him to know how I feel. It's stupid, but I don't care. There's still too much hurt, and it hasn't even been a full day yet.

"Please sit," he says, and when I don't, he adds, "Give me two minutes, and then you can leave, or I'll leave. I won't bother you again."

I don't know what I want. Do I never want to see him again, or just not for a while? I haven't thought that far ahead. Neither option is ideal. What I *want* is for him to have not played errand boy for my aunt, for him to not pretend to like me because it makes keeping an eye on me easier for him.

So I sit and agree to give him two minutes.

Seth's shoulders slump, and he lets out a breath. "I'm sorry, Clarke. I should have told you the first time."

"Yes, you should have," I snap. Crossing my arms, I avert my gaze, glaring at the floor. "You made me think you liked me," I say, the words almost too quiet.

He reaches out until his fingers brush the material of my sleeve, then he withdraws, curling his fingers into his palm. "That wasn't an act. I really do like you."

I want to believe him. My heart speeds up, happy to hear his words, but my brain is shouting *idiot,* and telling me not to listen to the lies. Grudgingly, I meet his eyes, though I stay silent.

"I really am sorry." His brows pull together. "Michelle only asked me to keep an eye out for you *if* I saw you. That's all. She didn't ask me to follow you. She was just worried."

"But you did follow me?"

"No, that was all a coincidence." Seth slashes a finger in an X motion over his heart. "Promise."

"But she said you didn't need to watch me last night, like you were supposed to watch me some other times," I insist.

"I think when she saw me at the house, she assumed I misunderstood what she'd asked and why I was really there." Now he reaches out and takes my hand in both of his.

"And why were you there?"

He looks at me with a rueful smile. "For you. To spend time with you. I never told her I'd asked you out on a date. I don't think she even knew I liked you. She knows now."

"Oh." Well, that certainly gives me plenty to think about. I did only hear her say he didn't need to watch me, and I don't actually know what he'd been planning to say when I walked in on their conversation. He could be lying now, but I don't believe he is. There's something so sincere in his expression and in the way he spoke. Michelle isn't a bad person, and I doubt she'd hire someone who was underhanded.

Seth lets my hand slide out of his grasp and onto the table. It's cold in comparison to the heat of his hands. Then he gets up and turns. And I know what I want.

"Wait." It comes out louder than I intend. "You can stay."

When he faces me, I smile nervously. "Are . . . you sure?" he asks.

"Have lunch with me, my treat."

He scoffs lightly and sits down just as my food comes. He orders a strawberry shake, which doesn't take long to arrive.

It's awkward between us, though I'd rather have that any day than avoid him. I hate being upset with people. It sends my anxiety through the roof. I eat my fries from the basket and debate how to tackle the massive cheeseburger next to them while he drinks his shake. Neither of us say anything for a long time, and I can feel the awkwardness grow thicker by the second until I'm practically squirming in my seat.

"Strawberries aren't actually berries," I say between bites of fries when the silence becomes too much to take any longer.

"Oh? What are they then?" Seth snatches a couple fries and downs them before I can protest.

I take a sip of my Coke. *Fine. I can share.*

"They are still a fruit but not a berry, since berries have their seeds on the inside." I take a huge bite of my burger and have to consciously stop myself from moaning out loud. *Holy fish sticks, Batman, that is good.*

Seth laughs, though I can't tell if it's my weird knowledge of strawberries or the face I must be making.

He raises a hand and waves at someone over my head. I turn to look and see a girl with long golden brown hair standing next to a very tall guy with dark brown hair, both waving back. They approach the table, and I hurry and set my burger back down in the basket while I try to finish my bite before they reach us. I wipe my hands on my napkin.

"Eris, Rylan, what are you two doing here?" Seth asks in a cheerful voice. I can tell by the way the three of them regard each other that they have a close bond.

"Not much, just grabbing a bite to eat," Rylan answers.

The girl, Eris, smiles at me, her honey-colored eyes sparkling. She's a little taller than me, but much more athletic. She reaches a hand out toward me. "Eris Blaekthorn."

Her grip is firm.

"Clarke Price," I say, feeling a bit awkward.

Rylan shakes my hand next, and we exchange pleasantries. He's even larger close up. I see what I think is the corner of a tattoo peeking out from the hoodie he's wearing. Seth and Rylan immediately fall into a conversation. So I turn my attention back toward Eris. She's wearing minimal makeup, but it brings out her natural beauty.

"You're new here, right?" Eris asks.

I nod. "Yeah, I'll be starting Havenwood Falls High Tuesday."

"Great! I'll probably see you around. Look for me during lunch."

"I will," I say.

"Well, we should get going. See you around, Seth," Rylan says. They turn and head to a less crowded area.

Seth settles back in his chair. "Eris is a senior, so you might have a few classes with her," he explains.

I jerk my chin toward them. "Isn't he in school?" I ask, wondering why Seth would assume I'd only have classes with one of them.

"No, he graduated last year." Seth helps himself to another fry.

I take a bite of my burger. That makes sense.

"Eris is the daughter of my alpha," he adds in a little quieter tone.

I nearly choke on the food in my mouth and peer over my shoulder. Eris waves at us from across the restaurant. "What about him?"

"Same as me. Sentinel and hunter."

"Oh" is all I can think of to say, so I stuff my mouth full of fries. Though she's soft-spoken, there is something about Eris I can't put my finger on that makes her command attention when she speaks. I hadn't even thought about the possibility of a pack for shifters, but I suppose it makes sense.

I'm only half finished with my food when he looks at his watch. "I have to run to work. I didn't realize how late it got."

I'm disappointed that he has to leave. Seth pulls out his wallet, but I shake my head and try to swallow my bite as fast as possible. "I said it was my treat."

He smirks as if he's trying to be good-natured, but I can see he doesn't like that I'm buying him a shake. I barely hold back the urge to roll my eyes at his well-meaning but dated view on food. Then his eyes sparkle mischievously. "Fine, but only if you let me take you out again. Soon."

"Okay." I can't stop the smile that forms across my lips. I've forgiven him completely. And it only took two minutes—maybe less—and a strawberry shake. It might be a mistake, and as many times as I tell myself to keep my heart guarded, I fail to listen. The risk will either pay off, or someday I'll learn. Maybe. Probably.

He leaves, and I find sitting alone no longer feels as peaceful, now that it's tainted by the touch of loneliness. The afternoon has ended with me feeling completely different than how I started the day. I hurry and finish my food, ready to go home. I think I need to talk to Michelle as soon as she comes home. I'd like to clear the air.

After paying, I bundle back up and head out the door, holding it open for an older man who's coming in for a late lunch. His shoulder bumps mine, and I am knocked slightly off balance, but manage to catch myself.

"Excuse me, miss," he says at the same time as the automatic sorry leaves my mouth.

My heart thumps hard against my chest once. He looks familiar, though I can't place where I would know him from. He probably just has one of those faces.

And then he looks back at me, his voice dark when he says, "You should stay away from that one." His head jerks toward the table where Seth and I were sitting. "Bad things will happen if you continue to let him cling to you."

Cling? Bad things? I frown, not understanding this stranger. Is Seth into something I don't want to know about? Who is this old man? My vision tilts for a few seconds, and when it settles again, the man is already inside. I twist the bracelet around my wrist a few times. He probably thought I was someone else.

When I make it home, I pull my keys from my pocket and unlock the door as I stomp the snow from my boots. The cold combined with my now full belly have made me sleepy.

A yawn rips itself from me as I drop the keys in the bowl next to the door. My boots are soaked, so I toe them off, too lazy to bend over and remove them by hand. It takes me a few tries, but if I sit down to remove them, I won't be getting up anytime soon.

Maybe a little nap would be nice. I glance at the painting as I move down the hall. The man standing in the forest has both hands in the air. Now, I *know* he wasn't doing that before. Either I've gone insane or my memory for detail is worse than I thought. Because paintings don't move. And anyone who thinks they do would have to be certifiable.

Tired. I am definitely tired if I'm this confused over a painting.

CHAPTER 12

J run. The forest flies by in a blur as I struggle to catch my breath. I'm barefoot and only wearing my flannel night pants and my worn Tea-Rex shirt. Snow has matted my hair to my head. It's cold, but I don't seem to feel it through the sickening panic coursing through my veins.

I don't know how I got here. I don't even know where *here* is.

But I can't stop. Something is chasing me. I can hear it crashing through the branches, its feet crunching against the snow, drawing closer and closer behind me. Its panting and snarling grow louder.

My aunt's house looms up ahead, and I push my body faster, though I'm not sure my legs can keep up this pace for much longer.

What is happening?

I can see someone standing on the porch. I open my mouth to call out, but my lungs are struggling as it is. *Almost . . . there . . .*

I slip in the mud at the foot of the stairs, and I can feel the shadow of whatever is chasing me crash down. Too close. Somehow, I manage to scramble up the steps, and Michelle pulls me inside and slams the door.

She's asking me what happened. I know this because I read her lips, but I can't hear anything other than the ringing in my ears. Then my body crumples to the ground, and darkness consumes my consciousness.

I sit up, panting. A dream. It was only a dream, even though it felt so real.

Letting out a loud breath, I fall back onto my pillows.

Dim light filters through my window. I look to the alarm clock. It's barely five a.m. It's way too early to get up on my first day at a new school, but after that nightmare, I don't think I could fall back asleep. When my heart rate slows enough that I know it won't explode, I get up and walk down the hall. The hardwood floor almost feels warm under my cold feet.

Michelle is in the kitchen, making jam. Does this woman even sleep? She looks like she's been up for hours.

The sugary sweetness fills the air. She stops humming and looks up, startled to see me standing there. I appreciate that she gave me space and didn't try to force me to listen. I didn't even hear her come home last night.

"I'm sorry about the other night," I blurt out. "Seth told me everything. I should have listened to you and not just assumed the worst."

Michelle smiles and continues to pour red mush into mason jars. "Don't worry about it, dear. It was a miscommunication on all our parts. Let's just forget all about it."

I wonder if her willingness to brush it off is because in her mind it isn't a big deal, or because we still don't know each other all that well and she doesn't want to do anything that might be seen as taking my mom's place. But if she's okay with letting it go, then so am I. Besides, now that I'm up early, it's the perfect chance to talk to her about this witchy stuff.

"Sounds good to me," I say, walking to the cabinet to get a bowl. I snatch the box of cereal from the top of the fridge on my way to the table and pour myself a big bowl.

I step on something dry and crusty. Moving to the side, I look down. It seems to be a small bit of dried mud. My vision wavers as

I try to examine it, and I stumble. A shower of rainbow colored flakes scatter around me. I shake my head, falling to my knees to clean up the mess. "I'm sorry!"

"Clarke? Are you all right?" She stoops to place a hand on my shoulder.

"Yeah, just dizzy. I think I slept too long."

Michelle lifts me by my arms and tells me to sit in the wooden chair at the table while she sweeps up. I feel bad letting her take care of my mess, but if I'm being honest, my legs feel a little too unsteady right now.

"Has this happened before? Do you need to see the doctor?" She asks this casually, but the lines around her mouth are drawn tight. Michelle brings a broom to where I spilled.

"No." I wave my hands. "No, it's nothing like that. I want to say it's something else. But it's hard to explain. I just feel overwhelmed when it happens. It's probably just because I fell asleep so early."

She's quiet for a while as she finishes sweeping up the cereal. "Is it a surge of energy one second, then a drain the next?"

I nod that it is.

"I thought so," she says. She places the broom and dustpan back where they belong, then leans against the counter. "Your powers are starting to come in. Being so close to your birthday, that is to be expected. If you don't know what to expect, they can catch you off guard." She walks over, pulling out a chair and sitting a few inches in front of me. "I'm going to call the school, and tell them you'll be starting on Wednesday instead."

"No," I start to protest. Starting in the middle of the week is the worst.

"I insist. I don't want you fainting from these surges and getting hurt. It's only one more days."

After the wave I experienced, I know it would be safer to wait, especially after and being told these episodes would continue to get stronger until my powers fully come in. Though I've been looking forward to seeing Meghan again, and maybe getting to know Eris a little more, but they'll still be there later this week.

"What will it be like?" I ask when Michelle gets off the phone. I keep telling myself to think about it, to talk to Michelle about it, but it's just not something I want to face, not for longer than a few seconds at a time, anyway. It feels like a fantasy, and it's too much with everything else—the accident, the new town, and Mom still in the hospital.

"You will feel it more than most because the supermoon will enhance your magic tenfold. For most of us, though, we hardly notice it."

This doesn't make me feel good. I almost feel like a freak, even among my own family. "But what will happen?"

"It's different for everyone. It all depends on how *you* feel about it, how open you are, and of course, the strength of your powers. You will be the most powerful Price woman in generations." Michelle says this like it's something to be proud of, or excited about.

"Is it like this for every witch?"

"No. Most witches are born with their powers. Our line doesn't develop them until our eighteenth birthday."

I frown. "Why?"

Michelle shrugs. "For as long as I know of, even further back when our family first moved to Salem—"

"Salem?" I blurt. "You mean we were Salem witches?" I've always found that part of history fascinating, if not terrifying and heartbreaking. But to know my family had been there . . . I'd always thought my family was from the Northwest. I was way off!

"Yes, our family line has always been dependent on the moon. Strongest during the full moon, and weakest during the new moon. However, the sect of lunar witches our family comes from is small. Like the majority of witches in Havenwood Falls, most are born with their powers."

Then something strikes me as strange. "So why haven't I ever seen Mom do any kind of magic?"

"Angela was born with her powers, raised right here in Havenwood Falls, where she met Mason. When she was young, she chose to wear an amulet to suppress her powers. She had dreams of traveling the world and didn't want to feel dependent on them. And when Mason disappeared . . ." She trailed off.

"Who's Mason?" I ask slowly, though deep down I am pretty sure I already know.

"Mason was my brother . . . and your father."

"My father?" I think my mind is imploding. *My father!* "Do you know where he is?"

Michelle shakes her head. "No. No one has seen him since that night."

I knew my mother had me right after high school, but she's never spoken of my dad. He was gone before I was born. Maybe he isn't the deadbeat I've always assumed he was. Or maybe he is. For all I know, he took that opportunity to run and avoid the responsibility of a kid straight out of high school. I came into this conversation with a handful of questions, but now a million more pop up in their place.

"This just feels so crazy. I feel like I'm losing my mind. Stuff like this only happens in movies or books, not in real life."

She pats my hand, and I think she means it to be comforting. "I know, dear. But it *is* real. This is why you and your mother moved here, and . . ." She trails off. Michelle's eyes cloud over, and she stands abruptly and goes back to pouring jam as if we'd been talking about the weather.

There was something else. Something she started to say that she doesn't want me to know. A spark of annoyance flickers in my gut. I understand that she cares about me and wants to protect me, but it doesn't excuse deciding what I can and can't handle or keeping things from me.

"And what? What aren't you telling me?" I stand.

Michelle sets down her jar and wipes her hands on a dish cloth. Her chin drops to her chest as if the towel she's using is the most interesting thing in the world. Her body is turned away, and the light through the window silhouettes her profile. "Your father's twin, Tamsin. Your mother called me saying she'd felt his presence last month and was worried for you. We both decided that it would be safest to bring you here. She knew I could protect you in Havenwood Falls."

"How do you know?" I have an uncle I've never heard of before. Normally, I think that finding more family would be a good thing. Why would Mom and Michelle fear him? The thought of someone related to me being a danger makes me feel sick. I wrap my arms around my middle.

"There are wards around Havenwood Falls. Any resident gone longer than a month starts to forget about it, and visitors forget immediately. And he's never been here." She raises her brows. "Haven't you ever wondered why your mother needed to take monthly trips for work?"

I hadn't. I just assumed she had particular clients. "So what does this have to do with my uncle?"

Michelle walks over to me and grips my shoulders with her hands. She is stronger than she looks. "He wants to take your powers."

"I don't understand," I say. He's my uncle. Why would he want to take something from me?

"Your uncle turned to black magic when his powers never developed to the same strength as the rest of us. He tried to kill your father and take his powers, but our sister, Sarah, got in the way. She died protecting Mason that night."

What if my uncle did something to my dad?

My eyes go to the spot on the floor where I thought I'd seen the mud. It's gone now. I don't think I saw her scrape it up, and I don't know if Michelle would have said anything to me about tracking dirt inside.

I don't know what else to say. Michelle doesn't seem to know either, so I excuse myself and curl up on the couch, covering myself with a thick faux fur blanket, and stare out the window, trying to process everything. I think I'd almost prefer to be insane than face the fact that all of this might actually be very real.

CHAPTER 13

I yawn and stretch the seatbelt away from my neck as I let my head lull to the side. The falling snow streaking by in the dark, lit by the headlights of our car, is hypnotizing.

My body grows heavy, and my breathing slows. I think I've been here before. Some cheery song from decades before I was born plays on the radio softy in the background. Mom is humming along, her hands quietly tapping along to the beat of the music on the steering wheel.

We've been driving since long before the sun rose. I don't know why we couldn't make this a two-day trip. But it's been nearly a full day of nonstop driving.

I already miss my home, my school, and the few friends I had. The farther we go, the more I can feel the distance grow between me and the small town of Boring, Oregon—which really isn't as boring as the name suggests. It was actually named after the city founders.

I pull my jacket over my lap and use it as a blanket. Even with the heat on, the cold seeps in through the glass of the windows.

My eyes droop, half closing as I struggle to stay awake. I watch the headlights skim along the winding road.

I blink, and there's a dark shape ahead in the middle of the road. A shadow the light cannot penetrate. I blink again. Then my eyes widen as my entire body lurches forward. Mom swears and slams on the brakes.

Screeching fills the air, drowning out my mom's shouts . . . and I think my screams as well.

Time slows for a single heartbeat, and I can see the shadow—a man. His face remains shrouded in darkness. He lifts his arm, then my world is in chaos. The car skids on ice, flipping over and over.

There's a loud crack, then I feel a sharp pain in my head and damp warmth. When the world stops again, I am upside down. I reach to undo my seatbelt and free myself, but I can't lift my arms. I'm too tired, and everything hurts too much. The darkness is rushing in, swallowing up the light of our headlights against the snow.

I blink. And I hear sirens. I try to keep my eyes open, but I think I'm fading in and out because the next things I see are blue-and-red flashing lights. Then strange voices surround us. I try to speak, to call out for help. I don't know if my voice is broken from screaming or if my mouth didn't even open.

Rough hands are grabbing me. Gravity pulls on me, and I'm lifted into the air.

Then the dark comes again.

I gasp for breath as if I haven't been breathing for a while. It's painful. My body jerks up, and there is nothing but silence everywhere.

It wasn't an accident after all.

I'm sitting in the middle of the forest floor. Snow falls everywhere, except on me. When I look down, my hands are covered in something dark. At first I think it's mud, but it's warm and sticky. *Blood*, I realize.

I strain my ears, listening for the slightest clue to where I am.

A branch snaps behind me, and a shout echoes through the trees. Another voice joins the first. Two men are arguing, I think. I get up and run toward them. Fronds reach out like arms, trying to hold me back, roots and uneven ground working to trip me, to slow me. But I push on until I reach the edge of a clearing.

I can't make out their faces, but they have their hands on each other, as if almost to the point of striking, but holding back for some unknown reason. One shoves the other, forcing him to stumble away to avoid falling. He doesn't stay back for long. In two long strides, he runs and jumps. His body flies through the air, and he transforms into a . . . wolf.

It's so unexpected, I stagger, tripping over a tangled vine or some other plant. I don't take my eyes from the two men.

The other man is lifting his arm. Moonlight catches his face, and I know him now. He is the man in the street, from when Mom and I crashed. And he's the same man I've seen around town. The younger one in the town square, the homeless man, the old man from Burger Bar—he was always the same.

At the time, I thought they were all different, their ages impossibly too far apart. But now as I remember them, the veil of whatever had made me see differently has lifted, and my memories are crystal clear.

The wolf lunges. Something dark and sharp flies from the man's hand, striking the wolf through its massive neck.

It falls to the ground, dead.

I scream.

MY EYES FLY OPEN. I'm breathing hard, drenched in sweat, and tangled in my covers. Another dream? I don't understand them, but I know deep down that they mean something. The soft light of predawn is breaking through the window. I don't think I can get back to sleep now, even if I wanted to.

Dropping my feet off the edge of the bed, I look over to see the glass wolf is knocked over. I reach out and set it back up. I must have hit the nightstand in my sleep during that awful nightmare.

My phone dings. Picking it up, I check the display and see Seth's name across the top.

Seth: I know you're sleeping, but do you want to come over and watch a movie after school?

The haunting feeling of my dream lingers and pushes down on my heart, squeezing it. I know what I want to say, but do I dare? The man from my dream, the one who'd warned me to stay away from Seth—what if he wasn't crazy after all? What if the warning he gave me to stay away from Seth wasn't a warning . . . but a threat?

I quickly type my response, then silence my phone, setting it face down on the nightstand. Tears sting my eyes, and I make my way into the bathroom, turning the shower on as hot as I can stand.

Seth is the first guy I've really liked since my ex, Jordan, broke up with me a year and a half ago. But if my dream really was a warning, and I continued to see Seth . . . I would never forgive myself if something happened to him.

As the hot water rains down over me, I lean my back against the cold porcelain wall and cry.

CHAPTER 14

I make my way out to the living room. My days are starting to bore me, and I can't wait until tomorrow, when I can finally start school and talk to Mom. I've already read the few books I brought with me, and I'm bored of all the TV shows. I should make an effort to get to the bookstore in town soon.

There's a pink envelope sitting on the coffee table with my name on it. I open it and read the card inside. In Michelle's neat handwriting is a note that reads:

Happy birthday! Relax and sleep in. We'll celebrate tonight when I get home. I shouldn't be any later than three.

P.S. Give Seth a call and see if he'd like to join us for dinner.

Today is my birthday, and I didn't even realize it. The smile on my face falls when I read his name. I want to invite him, but I can't take that chance. That dream was way too real.

Still, I go back to my room and grab my favorite book to reread. Pausing in the doorway, I regard my cell, then snatch it up, taking it with me. I'm not mad at him, though this would be so much easier if I was.

I trot back out into the living room and huddle on the couch. A few texts from him have already come in.

Seth: If you can't, that's okay. But why don't you want to see me anymore? Is it something I did?

Seth: I thought things were okay?

Seth: Clarke? Tell me what happened.

I read his messages, but I don't respond. Instead, I curl up on the plush white couch, draping a blanket over my legs, and open my book. My phone is tucked between my side and the couch. After one or two more messages, it goes quiet.

It's snowing, which makes the world feel like a sleepy, quiet place. Like I'm the only one around within miles. I stare into the snowy morning outside, admiring the beauty as the sun finishes rising, while I get to stay inside, warm. Then I get lost in my book.

A few hours later, a buzz against my side jolts me, and I nearly jump up. Letting out a quick breath, I check my phone.

Seth: I don't know what's going on but please talk to me.

Seth: Don't shut me out.

Seth: Do you need help? Are you in trouble? Your text has me worried.

I should message him back. My fingers hover over the screen for a long moment before I push the side button and darken the display. I *want* to respond. I just don't know what to say. I doubt "My dream and some crazy old guy told me to stay away or you'll get hurt" would suffice. Even I wouldn't believe that, and it was my dream, my experience.

Casually I drop the phone to the far side of the couch and go back to reading. I don't know how long it's been when the sound of a loud engine breaks my concentration. I look up to see Seth's dark blue car pulling around the corner, headed for my driveway.

I dash off the couch and run to the front door, making sure it's locked. His footsteps are heavy with snow as he walks up the few steps. I press my back against the door and crouch down. He knocks and calls out to me.

If I let him in now, I know my resolve to avoid him will break. But it's so tempting to give in. He sounds worried. I just don't think I can risk it.

"Clarke? Please talk to me. You don't even have to let me in. Just let me know you're okay."

I clench my fists on top of my knees to keep from reaching up and unlocking the door.

"Please. I know you're home."

I hear him sigh. I wait two beats, three . . . four. Then I can't take it anymore, and I start to straighten my legs. But now he's turned and is walking back to his car. I lift myself up on my toes and peek out the small glass window at the top of the door in time to see him pull away.

My stomach turns leaden. I need to talk to Michelle. I need to find some way to make it so he's not in danger just from knowing me. My mind flashes back to the glass wolf knocked over and to the dream with the wolf leaping and being struck down. I've never believed in omens before, but I know those two things combined are some kind of warning. Something in my gut is telling me to listen to the signs.

I go back to the couch and read until my stomach growls. I look out the window; the sun is already starting to set. I know it's winter, and sunset comes early, but Michelle should be home by now. I bend over, picking my phone up from the ground, and look at my missed messages.

There's nothing. Michelle must have lost track of time at work. I can't help but feel disappointed. It's her business, and I get that. As far as I know, she only has a handful of people working for her —Seth, Meghan, and a few others. But loneliness still creeps in.

I wish Mom was out of the hospital. I just want to see her. I want her to tell me everything will be okay. I just need to be in the same space as her. To talk to her, even for a few minutes.

I suppose I could drive to the bakery, but then Seth might be there. And if I see him, I know I'll spill everything, even if it makes me sound like a crazy person.

No, I'll just wait until Michelle comes home.

~

THERE'S A CLATTER OF METAL, and my head jerks up. My book falls to the floor. I rub my forehead. I must have fallen asleep reading. The sky is pitch black against the bright supermoon drowning out the stars just over the edge of the horizon. The light reflects off the snow, making the night feel eerie. The tire tracks from Seth's car have faded a little, so I know it snowed an inch or two while I slept. My aunt's car isn't outside.

I rub my eyes, then do an inventory of how I feel. Michelle said my powers would come in tonight. But I feel the same as I have every other day of my life. Should I be able to feel them? Doesn't matter. I will ask her about it in the morning.

I check my phone. No new messages. It's late, almost ten. She has to be home. So I walk quietly toward her bedroom. She must have come in and seen me sleeping and just let me be. I shiver. She might have parked on the side of the house.

The door to her room is open, and her bed remains untouched. There's not a single light on in the house.

The sound comes again, and if I'm not mistaken, it sounds like something knocked the lid off the garbage can outside. Probably just a raccoon. I should pick it up so Michelle doesn't have to deal with it after her long day.

I don't know if Michelle has to work tomorrow, but I bet she's barely going to get any sleep tonight. She's never up this late, let alone at work past six. I yawn and pull on my jacket and boots.

Wow. I didn't even get out of my nightclothes today. Talk about a lazy day. I'd be embarrassed, but other than Seth knocking on the door, I haven't been around another person all day. *Happy birthday to me.*

I grab my phone and stuff it in my flannel pants pocket in case I need a flashlight and unlock the door. I stick my head out and listen. It's silent. The kind of silence only heard in the winter with snow muffling the usual music of the night.

Closing the door quietly behind me, I venture onto the porch. My feet stop at the edge of the top step. For half a second, I debate leaving it until morning, but I'm already outside. My breath comes out in white plumes before dissipating into the night.

The night is clear and bright. Now that I'm outside, I can see stars glitter faintly across the sky. If not for the light pollution of the moon, it would be perfect for viewing constellations, if I knew what any were besides the big dipper. I rub my arms against the cold. Maybe I will learn more this summer.

I go down the four steps and walk around to the side of the house. Just as I thought, a beat-up old metal trash can has been knocked over. There aren't any bear tracks in the snow, so I take that as a good sign as I straighten it back up.

I turn to go back inside when I see a footprint in the snow just off to my right, somewhere I hadn't stepped, and much too large to be mine even if I had. My heart crashes against my chest.

The faint smell of cigar smoke wafts past me.

Someone's arm snakes around my waist. I open my mouth to scream, but a hand clasps a cloth around my mouth and nose. It smells like chemicals and is sickly sweet. It makes me want to gag. And then I feel my body go limp as I am swallowed up by darkness.

CHAPTER 15

$\mathcal{M}$y head is splitting as if someone tried to cleave it in two with a large rock. Every muscle hurts, and I am freezing, not yet numb. It's only a relief because I know it means I haven't been outside long. I try to move into a more comfortable position, but I can't. My body won't move. My eyes fly open, and I am staring at the starry sky, a rounded clearing with large trees framing the edges of my vision. A light dusting of snow is drifting down.

I pull on my arms, and for a second, I think I am paralyzed. But when I drop my head to the side, I see my wrist and ankles are tied by rope, and I am on a large, flat rock.

"W-what?" I jerk on the ties. *How did I get here?* There's the eerie familiarity from my dream again, only this time it is real.

Snow crunches near my other side, but I can't see who it is. I don't know if I should pretend to be unconscious still and hope whoever it is hasn't seen me move or heard me, or . . . All thoughts leave my head when the man comes into view.

He pulls in a large lungful of smoke from the cigar he's smoking and exhales slowly before flicking it to the ground, where it extinguishes in the snow with a hiss. He's the old man from

Burger Bar. Only, as impossible as it seems, he can't be much older than thirty.

I realize now how stupid I was to go outside tonight. The ultimate in stupid. It was first-person-to-die-in-a-horror-movie-because-the-dumb-girl-ran-up-the-stairs-instead-of-out-the-open-front-door level of stupid. I literally out-stupided the entire planet.

"Who are you?" I demand. Though, even as I say the words, I think I know exactly who he is.

The neutral expression on his face twists up into a sneer, which is thankfully somehow less creepy than the blank veneer he wore seconds before. He stalks closer to me until he stands at my head, and I have to straighten my neck to look up at him.

"Let me go!"

He leans over, his face only inches from mine. I try to scoot away, but the rope tying me down to this cold boulder prevents me from moving. "What's the matter, Clarke? Don't you recognize me?"

I tug hard on the binds at my wrist. The harsh rope twists against my skin until it's raw.

"What do you want?" There's a tremor in my voice now that I wish I could blame on the cold, but I know it's from fear, because I went numb the second I saw him.

"Happy birthday, Clarke," he says darkly. I hate the way he says my name.

And from the gleam in his eye, he knows it, too.

"I don't care who you are, let me go!" I was wrong. I preferred the creepy doll face. Now he is angry, and I swear red sparks just flickered in his eyes.

"This is exactly why we are here." He trails a hand up my arm, across my shoulder, and over my head then down the other side.

His touch makes me want to retch. I don't know what he's going to do to me, but I know it's worse than anything I could imagine. I inhale a breath to scream, but he is gripping my chin hard enough to leave a bruise. The inside of my mouth is pinched hard against the sharp edges of my teeth until I can taste copper.

"Don't even think about it." He lets go with a painful shove. The back of my head scrapes against the rough-hewn stone. He paces from my head to my feet and back again, stopping once to look at the moon cresting over the trees, making its way directly above us. "Most people call me Tamsin," he says, pressing his hand to his chest as if we were having a formal meeting. "But you, my dear, may call me *Uncle*."

I can barely catch my breath, and it feels like I've been running for miles. "W-where is Michelle?" I ask.

He smiles, and it feels like a thousand spiders are crawling all over my skin, making my nearly frozen muscles clench painfully.

"They thought they could keep you from me," he continues, as if I hadn't spoken at all. "But we are family, and I'm not about to let them keep me from what rightfully belongs to me."

"I don't belong to you, or anyone!"

He laughs. "I am talking about your magic, girl. *That* does belong to me."

I am insulted and angry and scared beyond what I thought possible, though I glare like I am not. His thought process is insane, and completely stupid.

My skin is burning from the cold now. I continue to strain against my ties, but the ropes are too thick and refuse to give even an inch of slack. Pain like pins and needles stabs along the skin of my exposed arms. My jacket is gone, and so are my boots.

"You shouldn't have even been able to get into town," I spit out.

He huffs, then leans his side against the stone and looks down at me. "And why on earth would you think that? You know residents can come and go as they please. The real trick was how I found ways to use magic that wouldn't alert the Court of the Sun and the Moon to what I was doing. The last thing I needed was their interference."

Keep him talking, I tell myself. *Keep him talking. Michelle will find me.* "What do you mean?"

"I mean that I couldn't outright attack you, so I had to get creative. A harmless cloaking spell, a touch of telekinesis . . ." He waves a hand in a circle. "It was all so troublesome. I would have preferred to use magic outright. Of course, that mutt who's been sniffing around found a way to ruin all my attempts and save you like he was your personal knight in shining armor."

Save me? Then it hits me with a hard kick of clarity. The car I didn't see, the incident with the icicles . . . those accidents I had were *not* accidents. My heart speeds up.

"Why am I tied up?" I try to keep him talking. I would rather freeze to death than endure whatever sick plans he has in store for me. I hope Michelle can find me in time, or—

I could kick myself for sending Seth away. He would have kept me from going outside like an idiot. Maybe he could have helped stop this from happening in the first place. And I hate that. I despise that I've put myself in a position to be helpless and in need of rescuing.

"You have your father to thank for that."

I don't know what he's talking about. "My father? He left before I was born. I've never even met him. I have nothing to do with him!"

Whatever worry I had for my dad dissipates and is replaced by anger. Whatever he did to this psycho before I was born, I am being held accountable now. Hate like this couldn't possibly come from something so stupid as not being born as powerful. Then, I remember—Michelle said they'd fought, and Mason hadn't been seen since then.

Tamsin laughs as if I've said something funny, then he disappears out of my line of sight. I strain my neck, trying to see where he went, but the rock prevents me from moving too much.

Something vibrates against my leg, and I nearly jump out of my skin until I realize what it is. My cell. I pull on my arms, and twist my hip toward my hand, slowly, trying to keep my movements as small as I can. Trying to reach my phone, my fingers brush against the material of my pants, but I can't get my hip close enough to reach in and grab it.

I freeze when Tamsin walks into view again. This time, he's holding a painting—*the* painting from the hall at Michelle's. Why would he bring it out here? I glance from his face to the painting and back, and he's looking at me like I should know what it means.

Tamsin pushes it closer to my face when I don't say anything. Two figures stand in the woods . . . *two*. Much closer than before. One that looks exactly like Michelle and the other like the man in front of me, only younger . . . kinder.

My stomach gutters out, and I finally understand.

My dad *didn't* leave. He'd been trapped by his brother.

CHAPTER 16

$\mathcal{T}$amsin tosses the painting over his shoulder, and my heart skips a beat as I hear a sound I can't identify. I don't know if it ripped or landed paint down in the snow. I hope it's not damaged, because I don't know what would happen to Michelle or my dad if it was ruined.

He looks up at the moon, now almost directly overhead.

"It is nearly time!" he announces with childlike glee.

I don't like the sound of that. "Time for what?"

Tamsin drops his chin to look at me with disgusted disbelief. He sighs in exasperation, folding his arms and rubbing his forehead as if I'm an idiot for not knowing his plan. "For your powers to come in. Didn't they teach you anything? You will be the most powerful—"

"That's stupid." I snort. I take pleasure in the shocked, almost hurt expression he gives me. "There's no way—"

Like a flash of lightning, his arm soars through the air, striking my cheek with the back of his hand. I see stars, and a metallic taste touches my tongue. I can feel the inside of my cheek swell from being cut on my teeth.

"Do you see that bracelet?" He runs a finger over my wrist. "It isn't just a tracking device. It also monitored your powers as they started to emerge, so I know *exactly* how powerful you could be. And once all that power is mine, I can finally be rid of *them* once and for all." He throws a glance over his shoulder toward the discarded painting.

Tracking device . . . so that's how he'd found me, how he managed to be in the same places I'd been. I thought Mom had put it in my bag as an early present. But if my dream was really a memory then when he flipped our car that night, Tamsin would have had the perfect opportunity to plant it in my things. He had known where I was all along.

Tamsin lifts his arm and checks his watch. "It is time to begin."

My phone vibrates against my leg again.

"You don't have to do this!" I nearly shout. "I didn't even know you existed until yesterday."

"That is most unfortunate," he says, but his tone says he couldn't care less.

"Look," I try to reason with him, slow him down until I can get my phone. "If I'd known, I would have looked for you. They tried to keep me in the dark." I take a stab at telling him what I think he might want to hear. "I don't know why you're all fighting, but—"

"Don't lie to me," he bites out. For a second, I think he'll hit me again. He certainly looks like he wants to. Instead, he picks up an old leather-bound book at his feet.

I stretch until I think my left arm will rip from its socket. Finally, I manage to get my right index finger into my pocket and begin swiping at my phone, hoping that somehow I'll be able to reach Seth. I'm so focused on trying to hit the right spots on the screen that I think will send him a message, I don't see Tamsin has noticed me until it's too late.

The book slams shut.

"What are you doing?" He reaches over and grabs my wrist, twisting it in his vise-like grip. I cry out. His icy hand reaches into my pocket and rips my cell out. He throws it to the ground with a loud crack. Then I hear his boot stomp down on it with a crunch. Once. Twice. "We'll not have any of that now."

I go limp. Defeated. Pretty sure this man is going to kill me and there's nothing I can do, nothing anyone can do, because the only people who know where I am are stuck in a painting, and my only hope of getting help is now in a shattered and broken heap on the ground.

Tamsin cracks open the book, the cold leather binding groaning in response. He places it down on the stone slab, and when he raises his hands, he's holding a long knife with a slightly rounded blade.

I panic, afraid he's going to drive it into my chest right here and now. The adrenaline makes it hard to draw in a breath to scream.

Moonlight glints off the sharp point. He plunges the knife down, and I stare in horror as it penetrates his own palm. With a quick jerk, he rips it from his flesh without the slightest hint that he even felt it. The knife clatters to the stone top, forgotten, yet out of my reach.

Tamsin stalks toward me. My screams come out as nothing more than whimpers. He dips the fingers of his other hand into his wound and then grabs my chin painfully as he smears his blood across my forehead, drawing symbols. My teeth cut into the already wounded side of my cheek. The warm sticky feel of his ichor makes me gag.

"Gross," I manage to say. I take pleasure in the look of disdain he's giving me, as if *I* am the one being unreasonable and completely nuts.

He picks up the knife again with his wounded palm. Crimson drips off his hand. I feel like an experiment for a mad scientist. Tamsin tugs on the end of my tee and slices, shredding a piece off and wrapping it around his hand.

Then, in a move I didn't anticipate, Tamsin cuts the rope holding my left hand, and for a second, I think sense has returned to him, but then I scream as he slices my palm through with the knife.

I scream again as he jerks the blade away. He picks up the book again and starts to read.

Strange words make my vision vibrate. And even with one free arm, I am unable to move. My mind buzzes with the maddening noise like a swarm of wasps. The sound scrapes my bones.

Black smoke forms above me and settles on my chest as if it has a consciousness. My breath is controlled by the dark thing sitting on me, and I swear it's a demon. I can feel it reach its rotting hand right through me.

The pain is too much, and I feel my magic for the first time. I feel it awaken and wind its way up, pulled forcefully from its sleeping depths until I gasp from the overwhelming pressure of it.

My eyes roll back. I think this is it. He is going to take my magic like he wanted to take my father's, and he will kill me to possess it.

My thoughts fade into shadows, and I feel everything about who I am start to disappear. I think I hear the song of a wolf crying somewhere far in the distance, but that is soon overpowered by the sharp and ugly words dripping from my uncle's mouth. The intense scent of copper—*the scent of blood*—fills my nose. . . my mouth, and I am drowning in it.

CHAPTER 17

I gasp with the sudden cessation of Tamsin's words as the dark power vanishes in a puff of smoke. My own magic snaps back like a rubber band, but it is not fully part of me anymore. It's more like fog that hovers around me, and I can feel that it has been injured.

Tamsin cries out as the wolf from my mind materializes out of nowhere, slamming its body into him. It is the wolf from my dream. I try to reach out, but I'm weak, and no sound makes it out of my throat. My hand falls limply onto the rock.

There's a familiar scent. Woodsy. Like fire and wood smoke—and something rich and bittersweet. My vision comes and goes as I watch the wolf. It hunches and grows tall and lean, changing its skin to that of a human.

Seth?

"—won't let you hurt her!"

He's standing in the shadows with his back to me. I can barely make out the top half of his shirtless form. Spots dance before my eyes. I reach out toward him, but he can't see. Then he's gone again, and the wolf is standing in his place.

Slowly I regain some feeling in my body, and I realize the tie on my other hand has slackened. I lift my bloody hand to my forehead to stop the spinning and grimace. *How did Seth find me?* How did he know?

My mind is clear now, but still I don't move. Not yet. Seth is moving, trying to block Tamsin's view of me so I can get loose.

Seth growls, and Tamsin lunges, grabbing the knife before I can get to it. Metal scrapes against stone, kicking up sparks. Seth jumps back from me, leading Tamsin farther away.

"Nooo!" I scream.

But they move too fast for me to see, and all I hear is a deep thunk. Limbs and fur blur with unnatural speed. I roll to my side and loosen the tie around my right wrist until I can slip my hand through. My skin is raw and bloody, but I don't have time to see how much damage has been done. I'm fine. I'm fine as long as I can still move.

I scoot toward my feet, fumbling with the rope. My fingers are numb from the cold, and I can barely get them to do what I need. I claw at the binding. My gaze keeps jumping to the two of them as they continue to fight. Tamsin is slashing at Seth, and he barely leaps out of the way in time.

The ties fall away just as the knife plunges into Seth's shoulder. Or is that his chest? I can't tell from this angle. But Seth falls to the ground. He doesn't change back, his wolf form lying still in the snow-covered ground.

"No!" I scream again, my voice straining, burning my raw throat.

Tamsin pauses and meets my eyes with his.

"No?" The question is soft, as if he's actually considering my request. "You care for this . . . *beast?*" He delivers a swift kick to him. I can hear the sound of his boot connecting to Seth's ribs right before the wolf lets out a whimper.

I lick my chapped lips, and I know my protest has given away too much.

Tamsin stalks toward me. I scoot back until I'm on the edge.

"You would betray your own kind, your own *family,* for that abomination?" He's so close that I think he will grab my bruised face again or hit me. But he doesn't touch me. Instead he leans in close until I can feel his rancid breath brush across my cheek. "Don't worry. I will dispose of it when I am done with you."

He makes no move to tie me back down. Perhaps he can see how weak his magic has already made me. Tamsin picks up the book and turns his back to me. He doesn't think I can get away. Maybe he's right, but I'll still try.

I push my legs to the edge of the rock slab, and it's too much. I can feel my own magic wrap around me. I tilt my head back and watch as the moon hits its perfect zenith.

Time slows, and I feel overly full, like a cup, ready to spill over.

The moon's light grows brighter until it swallows up my entire field of vision. It pulls on me like a tractor beam. The world shifts as inch by inch, my magic clicks into place. Strange and foreign and beautiful and familiar all at once. None of it makes sense, but it feels right.

Then there are those words again. Tamsin's harsh grating voice as he begins to read once more, not caring that I managed to get loose. His dark magic scrapes along my own and scrapes bitterly.

My body is no longer my own as I slide off the slab to the frozen ground covered in white. My power is fending off the black magic spewing from Tamsin, but just barely. I rip the silver bracelet from my wrist, and I feel the bindings that muted my magic break. And it's as if I can finally breathe clearly for the first time.

I try to look for Seth, but my muscles won't move. I am paralyzed again by the warring magics. I manage to catch a glimpse of him from the corner of my eye. He is unmoving on his side, his eyes are closed, and red darkens the snow around him.

My dream has come true, and there is nothing I can do about it. Then I fall, slipping away from my magic as it hangs in the air like something tangible that only I can see. Tamsin has finished reading and sets the book down on the stone.

I don't move. I wait for him to turn his back on me. He grabs the knife, walks over to Seth, and kicks him hard, rolling him over onto his side. Seth grunts, and I am glad he is still alive. If only I could get to him and protect him from my uncle.

Tamsin lifts his hand, hovering the knife over Seth as he straddles him, lifting him just slightly off the ground by his neck.

I use the stone for support and push up to my feet as his arm sails through the air, down toward Seth's heart.

CHAPTER 18

I will my power to come back to me. Demand that it obey. I want to scream at Tamsin to stop, to not touch Seth, but my voice is gone.

Tamsin's arm falls. Once again, time slows, and my heart slows with it. I watch the knife fall closer to Seth's chest.

My magic has listened. It's building up inside me, waiting for my command. I reach out, not knowing how to stop what's about to happen. But my magic knows. And it crests like the wave of a tsunami pouring over the edge, spilling up and out and flying in a blinding streak toward them.

I can hear Tamsin screaming. Then there's a painful snap as my power returns to me, knocking me back as if it were a demolition ball. Then there is only the moon and the stars. I gasp, clawing at my chest as I try to catch my breath. It takes a long moment before my lungs remember how to work.

The ground is biting beneath my hands and legs as I am forced to stay seated; my legs are too weak to stand or even crawl. The cold from the snow, soaking through my clothes, is stinging my skin.

Tamsin falls to the ground next to Seth, quiet. I can't tell if he's dead or not until his hand moves, swatting at something I can't see, swinging across his body again and again, until his movements become frantic and he is hysterical.

Black oily smog rises up, swirling around him, forming a lanky beast with a small body and many arms.

The air wavers like heat rising from asphalt. It makes me feel ill, as if I were swallowing bitter poison. He's screaming now, rolling around on the ground, while dark smoke continues to billow around him.

Then his cries go silent, and the air around him clears.

He's not moving. The beast looks me in the eye and hisses before wrapping itself around Tamsin and disappearing behind a dark plume of black. When the air clears, the thing is gone. And so is Tamsin.

I blink, and a weight is lifted.

There's a loud hissing behind me, the sound of a hot poker slowly doused in water. I spin in place where I'm sitting in the mud and slush. The painting Tamsin tossed to the ground is melting though the snow, and more of the same darkness grows out of it, thick and impenetrable.

Then there's a loud crack from the stone I'd been tied to. The connection between my brain and body jumpstarts, and I can move again. I jump and scramble away. More fissures snake their way through the rock. It crumbles into fine rubble, kicking up a thick mass that swallows everything.

Coughing and rasping come from within the dust cloud. Then the billowing blackness crumbles into a thick, fine dust, and the air clears, exposing two figures. The altar is gone, completely, leaving no trace that it had ever been there.

Michelle is standing at the base of the tree next to a man who looks so much like the one who tried to kill me only minutes ago. But he looks a little younger, clean shaven with evident smile lines.

The man has to be Mason . . . *my dad.* So many thoughts and emotions tumble through me. I've been angry at him for so long for walking out on us. But he didn't.

They spot me, and Michelle rushes to my side, gathering me in her arms, hugging me and kissing the top of my head. She pulls back.

"How did you escape?" I ask.

"When he died, so did his curse and everything his dark magic created," Michelle says. "I knew you could do it."

I still. Was she implying that *I* killed him? I'd only wanted to stop him from hurting Seth. I look back over my shoulder, not nearly as fazed as I would have expected. I mean, nearly being murdered . . . a demon . . . shock. It has to be shock. When it all hits me, it is going to be ugly. I already know that much.

A shudder walks down my spine, echoing through my entire body. Tamsin disappeared. Though Michelle just said he died, I have to know if he'll find some way to come back and get me. I have to know he won't be back for my family.

"Where did he go?"

"He made a deal with a demon, and when he failed to deliver, the demon took him as payment." Michelle explains, angling her body and waving Mason over. He hesitates. "Mason, come meet your daughter."

At that last word, he brightens and rushes to close the distance. He scoops me up, hugging me tight and spinning me in a circle. It should be weird and uncomfortable. But as he crushes me to his chest, I find all those feelings I'd had growing up—being mad at him—melt. He'd been trapped in a piece of art.

My father takes my face in his hands and examines me with a look that's a cross between pride and sorrow. "You've grown so much," is all he says, then he's hugging me again.

"Seth," I say. "He's hurt—" I pull away from my dad and somehow manage to amble over to Seth's side. He's lying on his back, the barrel of his chest heaving. I drop down next to his side, covering my mouth with one hand, stifling a sob and stroking his large wolf head with the other. "I thought he killed you."

Seth lifts his head at my voice and rolls to his belly. I swear he's smiling at me in wolf form. Part of his lip is lifted slightly on one side to reveal an elongated canine. Then he sits up.

I push his big head out of the way and examine the wound. It's much too small an injury for the size of the blade.

"Clarke," Michelle's voice draws me away. "You're shaking—You're not wearing any shoes! We need to get out of here before you lose your toes to frostbite."

"What about Seth?" I protest.

Michelle waves a hand. "He'll be fine. He will heal in a few hours."

"How?" I ask.

Michelle smiles. "There's plenty of time to discuss that when we are somewhere warmer."

Mason picks me up in a sudden sweeping motion. I let out a surprised squeak, and if I didn't know better, I'd say Seth was laughing. I still manage to stick my tongue out at him.

I am exhausted and so cold that everything hurts, but I'm determined to stay as strong as everyone else. To keep from giving in to the sudden lack of strength as the adrenaline leaves my body.

It's a longer walk than I expected, but Seth leads the way, following a set of large footprints. His paws step over them, erasing the last marks Tamsin left behind. A set of two uninterrupted lines trail next to them. I study them for a second only to realize that monster had dragged me through the snow instead of carrying me over his shoulder!

Michelle walks next to us, her hand coming up to stroke my hair every few yards. I don't know where Seth is leading us, but he seems to be sniffing out a trail. After several long minutes, Mom's car comes into view. My eyes widen.

"You drove?" I ask loudly.

Seth cocks his head and snorts. Michelle laughs. I get the feeling I missed something, but I'm pretty sure that whatever Seth implied was wolfy-sarcasm.

"It seems Tamsin wasn't strong enough to use magic to get you all the way out here," Michelle says, answering the question I meant to ask.

"Where exactly are we?"

This time, it's Mason who answers, "We have to be at least twenty-five miles outside of town. Tamsin would have to be outside of the wards to attempt—" He cuts himself off, his grip on me tightening.

We all understand the words he doesn't say.

Michelle opens the car door and slides into the driver's seat. The engine roars to life. And only then does Dad put me down so he can open the back door for me.

I climb in, grateful to have my feet in something other than snow. I reach for the door and stop to look at Seth. "Why haven't you changed back yet?"

"Well, probably because he'll be naked, dear," Michelle says from the front seat.

I can feel heat try to rise up my face at having nearly seen everything earlier. I like him, but it's way too soon for that. "If you pop the trunk, there should be a blanket there."

A minute later, the other door to the back opens, and Seth is standing there, wrapped in nothing but the blanket. His grin spreads wide, and I realize I've been staring.

I look away, and he climbs in next to me. Michelle drives off the path where we'd been parked to the road.

Finally, I look at Seth, making sure to only look him in the eye. "Are you hurt badly?"

"I'm fine. It will be fully healed in a few hours, just like your aunt said—"

He wouldn't tell me if he was bleeding out. I pull the blanket away from his chest to look.

"Are you always so rough?" he asks, wincing.

It's hard to believe, but no one else is worried. "Wha—"

He wiggles his eyebrows, and his smile grows even larger. Finally getting the double entendre, I swat gently at his uninjured shoulder, then shove more blanket at him.

Seth puts his hand on the back of my head and pulls me to him, resting his forehead on mine.

"Thank you for worrying about me," he says quietly. Then he

kisses me. His fingers tangle in my hair. He pulls me closer, refusing to let me go until his fear passes completely. I think my lips will bruise, but I can feel his relief that I'm okay. After a moment, the pressure lightens, but he continues to kiss me.

Mason coughs loudly, followed by Michelle shushing him, telling him to let us be.

The cold has filled me down to the marrow of my bones, and I am mostly numb. Slowly, Seth's warmth penetrates my skin, thawing me.

He finally relinquishes my lips, and my mind goes blank. My breath is quick, though truthfully, if I didn't need to breathe, I would still be kissing him.

I look into his amber eyes. I don't know if I believed he was a wolf shifter until I saw him change.

"Did you know the ancient Greeks invented the spiked collar to protect their sheep-herding dogs from wolves?" The words spill past my lips. I can't believe I just said that. I clamp a hand over my mouth, horrified.

"What?" He laughs at me. And then that crooked smile appears on his face again.

I shrug. "I'm sorry. That was rude," I mutter.

He shakes his head and hugs me closer, placing a kiss on my forehead. "You and your random facts." He looks me up and down, no doubt noting how inadequately dressed I am. Soaked flannel pants, bare feet, and a tee. "You're freezing."

My skin is red from the cold.

"I'm fine," I say. Though I think he knows I'm full of it.

He scoffs, then wraps me up in his arms. He's stronger than he should be. It's awkward, but I don't fight it, because he's warm. I wrap my arms around him and nuzzle my face into the crook of his neck. The steady sway of the car along the road and the absence of the stark cold relaxes me.

The car ride is long and silent. I think we are all trying to process the events. Either that, or Michelle and Mason—*Dad*—think I'm sleeping. Regardless, I'll take it.

Seth insists on carrying me from the car to the house, even though I tell him I can walk, and I'm worried the blanket will slip. He only presses me tighter against him, giving in when he can set me down on the couch. I grab his hand, and he turns to go.

I don't want to be alone. Not right now. I want as many people here with me as I can get. The idea of being by myself makes my throat tight.

Seth's hand squeezes mine. "Let me get dressed, and I'll be right back."

"You have clothes here?" I ask.

"When I came to check on you again, I saw the door open. I knew something had happened. I stripped before I shifted." He nods to the pile of discarded clothing on the floor.

I nod, then let go, watching him walk into the other room. He's not gone long, and just seeing that cocky smile eases me. He crosses the room and sits next to me, pulling me into his side.

"I'll get the first aid kit and wrap your hand," Michelle says and walks from the room.

I look down. I'd nearly forgotten about it. Flexing the muscles slightly, I hiss through my teeth. Now it hurts. To get my mind off it until Michelle returns, I look up at Mason. It's weird to think of him as my dad. But that's who he is. He didn't desert us. He was imprisoned. "You were here the whole time?"

He nods, then takes a blanket off the back of one of the chairs and drapes it over me. I worry I'll get it filthy, but quickly dismiss that thought. I'm freezing and happy for the added warmth.

"I tried to get Michelle's attention for years, but she would never look."

"Mason!" Michelle scolds playfully from behind him. He flinches as he laughs. Then her features soften. "I kept it because you made it . . . but looking at it only reminded me that you were missing." He puts an arm around her and gives her a hug, only to be pushed away seconds later. "You smell to high heaven. Go shower."

"You wouldn't smell that great if you were stuck in a painting for eighteen years—"

"Go now. We'll talk more when you're out."

Dad slinks off to the bathroom, looking back at me as if he doesn't want to let me out of his sight.

"You'll have all the time in the world with her." Michelle points toward the bathroom. "Now."

He listens, leaving Michelle to tend to my hand. She sits on the coffee table in front of me. Her fingers move deftly, cleaning and bandaging the cut on my palm. Her eyes flick to Seth a few times, as if she's unsure of him. I know she trusts him, but I think him liking me was not something she'd expected.

"And what about you?" she asks him when she finally relinquishes my hand.

Seth shakes his head.

"Fine." She sighs. "Then I'm going to make some food. I'm sure Mason is starving." She pushes up and heads to the kitchen.

Seth and I are alone now. I turn to him, and before I can utter a word, he grabs my face and kisses me, hard. His tongue grazes my lips, and I lean into him, melting as his fingers brush against my jaw and down my neck.

I groan when he pulls away, not entirely ready for the kiss to end.

"I'm sorry," Seth says.

I list my head to the side and frown. "Why?"

"For not coming sooner."

I shake my head. "How could you have known? I didn't exactly make it easy for you to be here. How *did* you know where to find me?"

"I was in town." He shrugs as if it isn't a big deal. Then, more seriously, he adds, "I was worried when I saw Michelle's car still at the bakery, even though she'd left hours before. I knew something was wrong. Then you wouldn't respond to my calls or texts. I knew you were home." He gives me a frown. Not an angry one, more sweet, like he can't help but pout about it. "I smelled your scent here, but something just didn't feel right. It was different than usual, so I went scouting to see if I could find the source, but he was too far ahead of me. Then I scented you."

"Ohmygawd, what?" I ask, horrified. He can *smell* me? What on earth do I smell like? My face burns from the embarrassment, heat climbing up my chest and neck to my face.

"Your magic, I mean." He laughs as he clarifies. I relax a little. Still not overly thrilled that the guy I like can scent me. This might lead to a complex. "The rest, you know."

"Well, thank you for saving me." I lean back into the cushions of the couch, pinning Seth's arm under me. I don't want him to leave, but I am so tired, I can hardly keep my eyes open.

"I'm just glad you're safe," he murmurs quietly into my hair as he kisses me on the top of my head and wraps an arm around me. "Does this mean you'll let me take you out for your birthday?"

I snort but nod as I mumble something I mean to be a yes but is probably more of an unintelligible noise.

By the time my dad and Michelle rejoin us, I'm too tired to keep my eyes open, so I let the quiet lull of their voices comfort me as I finally let sleep take me.

CHAPTER 19

I wake to Seth's arm around me. I feel safe. I honestly don't think I could have slept at all if he hadn't been here. I snuggle deeper into his side, pressing my ear tighter against his chest, listening to the steady thump of his heart.

The door opens, and in comes a blast of cold air and flakes of snow fluttering everywhere. My eyes shoot wide open. Every trace of the sleepy peace I had seconds ago has vanished. I rub my bleary eyes, clearing the sleep from them. When the door closes, Mom is standing there, grinning down at me.

It takes several seconds for reality to hit me. Then I'm rolling off the couch and onto the floor as I scramble to my feet and run to her. She wraps her arms around me and squeezes me tight.

"Mom!" I cry. There's not a scratch on her. "I thought you were still too hurt!"

"What is going on out—" I hear Michelle start.

"Angela?" Mason says softly.

Michelle joins our hug, but Mason hangs back. Mom and Michelle are talking at the same time, crying happy tears. I am squished and uncomfortable, but it is still the best feeling in the world.

"Mason," Mom says, finally realizing he's here. The look on her face is a mixture of happiness and pain. She shakes her head. "Why? How?" She motions around the room.

Michelle cuts him off before he gets the chance to speak. "He never left. Tamsin trapped him in the painting. It was never his choice."

Mom sniffs and looks from Mason to the wall where the painting used to hang. Countless feelings I couldn't even begin to guess flitter across her face. Then she says, "You were stuck in that ugly thing this whole time?"

Mason blinks a few times before laughing. Mom runs into his arms, pushing him back a step, and he doesn't hesitate to hold her. "I'm still mad at you."

But I can tell there's no real anger there. It will take time, but I know from her reluctance to let him go that she's already forgiven his absence for the last eighteen years, just as I have. Of course we all have a lot of adjusting to do, but I think the love they have always had for each other will make our family fall into place in no time.

It takes several minutes for everything to quiet down and break apart. We each take a seat, either on the couch or in one of the plush chairs, and talk. I tell Mom about everything that happened with Tamsin in the woods, with Mason and Michelle, and even Seth, adding details here and there.

"How are you out of the hospital?" I ask again.

Mom nods and gives me a tight-lipped smile. "After the car crashed on the way to Havenwood Falls, I knew Tamsin had found us. I was hoping we'd be able to make it to the safety of the wards before he could reach us. But before I could do anything, he struck. He poisoned me with his magic. I was conscious the whole time, but I was unable to move." Mom's voice hitches. She looks up in Michelle's direction then back to me. "I'm just glad your aunt brought us to Havenwood Falls. I tried fighting the effects of his magic, but I'm not very strong." She drops her chin and looks down at her hands for a long moment before balling them into a fist. "I shouldn't have shut out my magic like I did when I was younger. If I'd learned how to control it better, I might have been able to wake up earlier, and you might never have been taken." She cups my cheek and meets my gaze, her own eyes filling with tears. "I'm so sorry, Clarke. But as soon as he died, his magic died too, and I was able to wake up."

"I'm sorry, but . . . what?" It wasn't that what she was saying didn't make sense. I remember the sharp smell of copper and realize now it was Tamsin's magic I'd sensed that day. I shudder, realizing how clueless I was, . . . how close I was to losing her to that monster. "It might have helped to know about him and magic and everything else before we moved here," I say, picking at my nails. I'm not mad. I know Mom did what she felt was best.

"Oh, Michelle, really!" Mom scolds gently. "You didn't tell her anything?"

"I told her some of it, but in my defense, you did tell me that you wanted to do this together." Michelle averts her gaze. "I had no idea Tamsin was so close."

Mom puts a hand on her leg and gives her a comforting squeeze. "It's okay. It's really my fault. I should have thought everything through. I was just so worried, I couldn't think straight." Then she turns to me once more. "Our powers are at their strongest when the moon is full, but are also most vulnerable when they first come in. That is why your uncle needed to try to steal your powers last night. He was at his strongest, and you, your most vulnerable."

I already knew about the moon thing, because Michelle explained that. But . . . "Would he have killed me?" I ask.

She nods solemnly. Then, after a moment's hesitation, she leans forward and hugs me. It must be hard for her to admit it, but I appreciate her candor. "We will start training you as soon as you're ready."

I frown at this. I'd struck Tamsin when I'd meant to. My magic had known what I wanted. I assumed this is how it works. "What do you mean? Don't I already know how to use my magic?"

I move back to the couch, to Seth's side. The warmth radiating from him is soothing.

"You do at the most basic level. I believe it worked as well as it did on Tamsin because of the moon's position and because your will was so strong in that moment." Mom looks back over her shoulder at Michelle and Mason. "You're powerful, the most powerful Price in generations, but without training, there is a chance your magic could turn dark."

That thought is terrifying. My hands grow ice cold and clammy. If a lack of training equals power possibly going to the dark side of things, then . . .

"You said Tamsin wasn't very powerful," I accuse my aunt.

She looks down. "He wasn't. But it was his heart that twisted his magic." They all have that look that says there is way more to this than they are saying. "We worry, because his dark magic touched you. He was partway through the ritual, which opened your magic up to his darkness."

"Oh," I say. "Why didn't anyone tell me about any of this before?" I blurt out, hurt that so much was kept from me. Mom should have told me everything years ago. At the very least, she should have told me when we left to move here.

Mom opens her arms and motions for me to come to her. And I do, because I'm relieved that she's okay. That she has been this entire time.

"I'm sorry, sweetie. We didn't tell you because we thought that the less you knew, the safer you'd be."

I lean back, scrunch up my face at her, and say, "That's stupid logic." Then I pull back. "We?" I look to Michelle, but she's avoiding my eyes and looking at Mason.

Mom laughs. "I thought if you knew about it, then you'd be tempted to experiment with your magic and draw attention to yourself. I didn't want your uncle to find you."

Seth has been quiet the entire time. Nothing about his expression tells me any of this surprises him or is in any way new to him. If it is, he's doing an excellent job of hiding it. I rub my hands over my face and wince from the pain in my palm. "Just promise me one thing—from now on, if there's anything I need to know, please tell me. Don't try to hide it to *'save'* me."

They all agree without a fight. That was much easier than I expected. I let her go and lean back into Seth's side. Everyone looks relaxed and happy . . .

Except for Mason. He's fidgeting with his hands in a way that doesn't fit his stature and looking at Mom like she is the sun and the moon, like she is his entire world. He drops to one knee and pulls out a small box from the pocket of his slacks.

"I was going to propose to you the next day. I carried this stupid thing around in my pocket for a month before, just wondering if we were too young." Mason looks at me and smiles before focusing on Mom again. "I wasted time then, and I don't want to spend another minute without you as my wife." He pulls back the lid to reveal a thin gold band with a single diamond on top and a simple white gold flourish. "Angela, will you—"

"Oh, get up, Mason!" Mom says. Her cheeks grow a bit pink. "We have a lot to talk about before we get to anything of the sort." Sheepishly, Dad stands and puts the ring away. Mom swats at him, missing. "There's plenty of time for that."

Then he laughs. It's not the response I expected. He runs a hand through his hair. "You're right. It's hard to remember that even though it only feels like a few months for me, it's been nearly two decades for you." He gives a slight shake of his head. "Time moved differently in there."

Mom hugs him tight, then plants a big kiss on his mouth. I look away. That was borderline embarrassing, but I see why they were together. They're both slow to anger and have a lighthearted view on the world. It might not be today, or tomorrow, or even next week, but our family is becoming whole.

I bite my lip. I've never seen her so happy before. Group hugs and happy tears commence once again, though not nearly as crushing.

Michelle manages to disengage, and I follow suit, letting my parents have their moment. Seth stands for the first time and wraps an arm around my shoulders.

It has always been just me and Mom. It's so overwhelming now, but in the best possible way. I have a father and an aunt. I never expected I'd have a family. Not like this. But I do, and I would do everything again a thousand times over to keep it.

Mom and Mason—*Dad*—pull apart just slightly, and each hold out one arm to me. I rush to their side and hug them again for possibly the hundredth time since Mom walked through that door.

And everything finally feels complete.

WE HOPE you enjoyed this story in the Havenwood Falls High series of novellas featuring a variety of supernatural creatures. The series is a collaborative effort by multiple authors.

Stay up to date at www.HavenwoodFalls.com

ABOUT THE AUTHOR

Ali Winters is a USA Today bestselling author as well as an Amazon and international bestselling author. She was born and raised in the Pacific Northwest, where she developed her love of nature, animals, and all things green.

For as long as she can remember, she's been mesmerized by the extraordinary world of books and fantasy. There has never been a time when stories were not begging to be told, either by drawing, photography, or writing.

With encouragement from one of her favorite authors, she jumped in, head first, to pursue the career that had been calling to her since the day she opened her first book.

She has a deep love for coffee, tea, warm blankets, dogs, creating art in any medium she can get her hands on, and family.

Connect with Ali online at
www.aliwinters.com
www.facebook.com/authoraliwinters
www.instagram.com/authoraliwinters
www.twitter.com/aliwinters_

ACKNOWLEDGMENTS

Ever since I discovered the small town of Havenwood Falls, I've wanted to be part of the family. I want to thank Kristie Cook, the creator of this magical and amazing little town, for welcoming me into the Havenwood Falls family. It has been a *blast* to write alongside the others. This has been a wonderful challenge that has allowed me to grow and stretch my wings.

Thank you to Michelle Fritz for your constant support and friendship. For letting me come to you with questions, ideas, and feedback. I hope you love your namesake in the story.

And lastly, to the readers. Authors would be nowhere without you—I would be nowhere without you. You mean the world to me. Thank you for joining me on this journey to Havenwood Falls.

AN EXCERPT

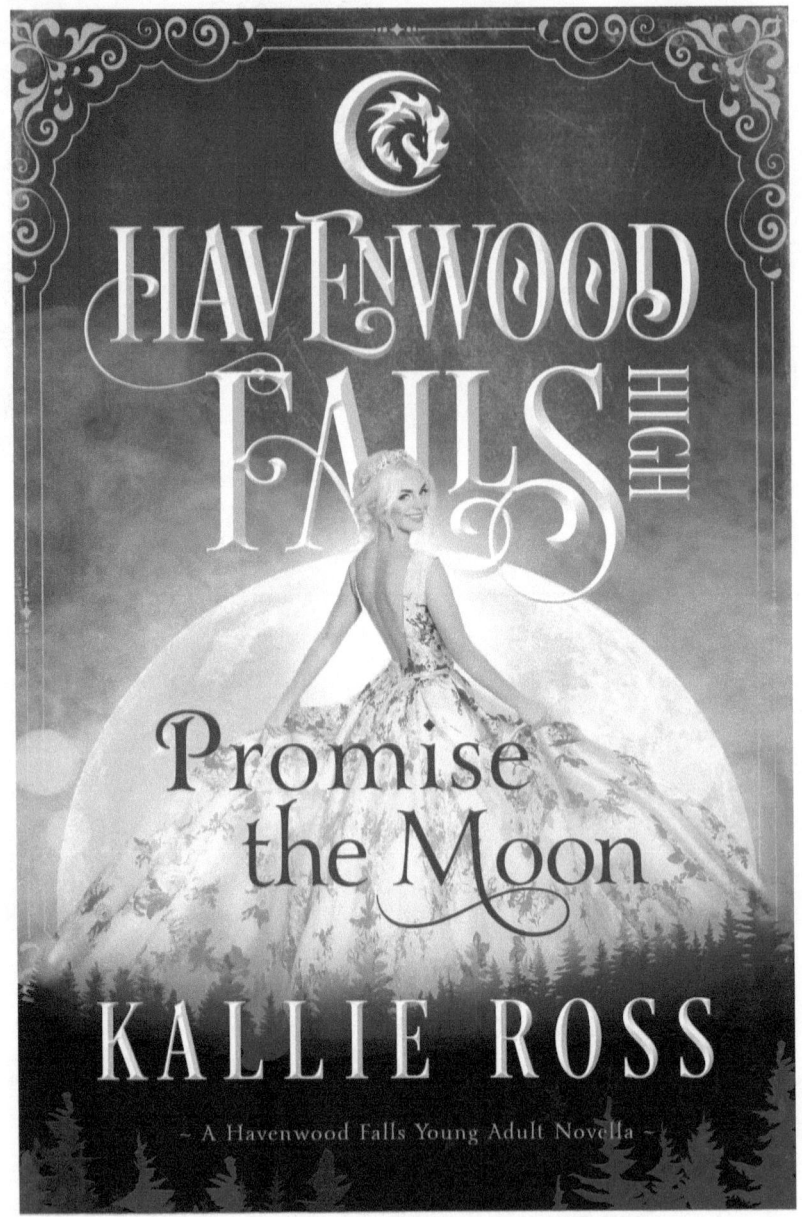

Promise the Moon (A Havenwood Falls High Novella) by
Kallie Ross

**With her future already fated by others, vampire-hybrid Elle
makes the most of her present—but a friend's betrayal could
end it all.**

Seventeen-year-old vampire-dryad hybrid Elle can't live up to
her parents' expectations. She's snubbed by her dad's bloodline-
obsessed vampire family while her mom's dryad side has
determined her fate—to return to New York City and protect
Central Park.

Unsure of her place in the world yet held to promises her
family made, Elle dreads leaving her friends as well as breaking
things off with her wolf-shifter boyfriend, Kase. With her destiny
out of her hands, Elle is determined to control what she can.

Even though Kase Kasun has spent his life living in the
shadows of his family name and the weight it carries, he's
embraced his role as a protector of Havenwood Falls. Everything
had been worked out, until Elle started distancing herself. Kase
knows the space she's creating between them will only make room
for trouble.

Intent on savoring every last minute together, Elle, Kase, and
all their friends plan an epic Spring Break camping trip. But when
one of Elle's so-called friends turns out to be an enemy intent on
taking her out of Havenwood Falls, her life may come to an
untimely end. Promises are made to be broken, and only the moon
has the power to save her now.

PROMISE THE MOON

KALLIE ROSS

The Havenwood Falls High bell rang sharply, alerting me to the end of the school day. Finally, spring break. Lifting my head from the pages of my assigned reading, *A Tale of Two Cities,* I watched the rest of the class hustle toward the hallway. Normally, I loved losing myself in a good book, but even with two years of French, I had a hard time keeping up with Darnay and the Defarges.

The thick novel didn't fit in my backpack, so I secured the tattered paperback in my coat pocket, shouldered my bag, and made my way to my locker. There was no need to carry thirty pounds of books, since I'd only need one of them to complete my homework. The weight didn't bother me, because I had super strength. Being a vampire half-breed had perks; for example, I didn't have to deal with bloodlust like my father did. Dryad blood pumped through my veins, powerful enough to subdue any unbecoming urges a young vampire would have. Only problem was each half-breed benefit came with inconveniences, like being able to hear every thought from every mind in the building. Over the last year, with the help of my parents, friends, and night classes at the Academy, I'd mostly learned to control each of my abilities, including the ones I hadn't expected.

The school's hallways always buzzed with the latest gossip and hormones. Tuning out self-conscious teenagers had become second nature. Disregarding arrogant and even lustful thoughts took a little more concentration. And the weirdest part of mind reading wasn't all the jumbled thoughts, but it was seeing them in my mind's eye. My ability was similar to reading a book and visualizing the story like a movie.

So when I heard Ana Novak's thoughts about Kase Kasun, I not only caught a few details about what a good kisser he was, but I envisioned Kase's lips so close I could feel his warm breath brush over my cheek.

I pressed my palm to my forehead to clear my thoughts.

When I looked up, the two were at the end of the corridor across from my locker. Ana was leaning against the old blue-painted metal facing Kase, and she grinned up at him and giggled. Then, as if she sensed I was watching, she nudged his shoulder playfully. Her touch lingered a second too long. He glanced down at the spot she'd touched and shook his head. Her bottom lip pouted out flirtatiously, and he ignored her attempt to win him back and turned to walk in my direction without a word.

As his eyes met mine, he frowned. We'd both been trying to ignore the spectacle Ana made of herself on a daily basis, but somehow she'd found out I called things off romantically with Kase during the holiday break. Ever since, I'd been trying to avoid both of them. Kase had known from the beginning, since his split with Ana, that I wasn't staying. My family had always expected me to move back to New York after graduation. Not to mention, I'd die if I didn't bond with a tree in Central Park by my next birthday. After I'd gained control of my strange powers, and the rumors about the mysterious death of my ex-boyfriend were replaced by who wore what at the latest gala, I'd had to beg my parents to allow me to stay in Havenwood Falls to graduate. Neither of my parents were biological, but they'd been looking after me since the night they found me. I'd been no more than a few months old, and I'd been laid at the foot of my mother's tree in the park.

Kase and I had agreed to stay friends after the holidays, but seeing him through Ana's thoughts made me want to vomit. Every day, the love I felt for Kase grew heavier in my chest. For the last few months, when I knew he had a class in one hallway, I'd go down another so I wouldn't have to face him. Lugging love around, instead of giving it to Kase, made me realize sadness isn't a void. True sorrow is a weight.

Behind him, Ana gave me a death glare. I shrugged and turned toward the exit. Avoiding Ana had become essential for both of us. She had a way of making me crazy, and I couldn't risk losing control in a school filled with humans who didn't know about our supernatural world.

Thirty pounds wasn't that heavy anyway.

Kase walked faster to catch up with me, and I could feel him getting closer. Eluding him had been impossible. The warmth he radiated had to be because he was a wolf shifter; at least, that's what I'd convinced myself. It couldn't be anything more. We couldn't be anything more than friends. It would be easier the next time I saw him. The truth was I'd be seeing him more this next week than I'd allowed myself for months.

Kase cleared his throat, and when I looked over at him, one corner of his mouth pulled up, revealing a dimple.

"You have mean girl cooties," I teased, and wrinkled my nose when he tried to hold my hand—again. It was partially my fault he kept trying. The few times we found ourselves alone, usually because I'd been hanging out with his sister, I felt drawn to him. He had to feel it, too.

When Kase frowned, disappointed at my rejection, my heart ached.

Kase Kasun was everything I'd wanted in a guy when I was wishing for the perfect boyfriend in middle school. Back then, I was just a normal girl, my powers hadn't been triggered, and I'd attended an all-girls prep school in New York City. There was something dreamy about ending up with the All-American athletic good guy. Only, this good guy had gotten himself caught in the claws of an evil, power-hungry she-wolf before I'd arrived.

Kase's steps synced with mine, the rhythm echoing slightly in the emptying hall, and he reached in front of me to open the door leading to the parking lot. My backpack brushed against his forearm. In an effort to avoid knocking him over, I shifted the weight and nearly tipped myself over from being so top heavy. Kase used his wolf-like reflexes to catch me.

I stiffened in his arms.

"Come on, Elle," Kase whispered, and I melted. His olive skin was smooth and his dark eyes warm and inviting. Kase had been the star quarterback of our high school's football team the last two years, and there was no mistaking the muscular build under his letterman's jacket.

He brushed some of my long blond hair over my shoulder to get a better look at my face. He'd discovered all of my tells while we dated, and I could feel him analyzing me. Forcing myself to remain indifferent, I relaxed my jaw, released the inside of my cheek from between my teeth, and loosened my grip on the straps of my backpack.

"How about I take you out for coffee?" he asked. The simplicity of his invitation didn't imply anything more.

I gave him a tight smile, determined to stay strong and let him down easy. "I could use one, but you know I have training."

"Will you stay with me? Please. Even if it's only for a few minutes." Kase's voice croaked, and he gently pulled me a little closer. "We can just talk out here. I miss being with you."

My body betrayed me and leaned into him. Why couldn't we sit at Coffee Haven all afternoon and hang out with our friends? I thought after pushing Kase away for so long, it would be easier to turn him down. Last month, on Valentine's Day, I'd stayed home and claimed to be sick, all in an effort to keep Kase out of sight and out of mind.

My wall was crumbling.

"How about we get that coffee," I agreed with some hesitation, and quickly scrambled to rebuild my façade. "But as friends."

Kase slowly released me, careful to make sure I had my balance.

"I'll take what I can get." His mouth formed a tight smile, and he waved a hand in front of himself, allowing me to lead the way.

Our cars were parked side by side at the back of the lot. His blue truck made my black smart car look like a toy. He and his twin sister, Willa, shared the truck, but Willa always had archery practice after school. Her boyfriend, Tarron, also on the team, always gave her a ride home.

"Wanna ride together?" Kase asked and chuckled as he looked from his truck to the car. "I'll even try to squeeze into your car if you want to drive. Maybe you can open the sunroof so I can sit up straight."

Before I could stop myself, my hand flung out and backhanded his chest. Kase was over six feet tall, and while I was considered average height, he still towered over me. He'd always teased me about my car, and it almost felt normal to joke about it. Only, our normal had been being *together*, and we would have to figure out a new normal. My goal the past few months had been to avoid running into him altogether. Since his sister was one of my best friends, it proved more difficult than I'd anticipated.

"Haha." My fake laughter was filled with a good dose of sarcasm, and I rolled my eyes as I rummaged through the front pocket of my backpack for my keys. Kase moved around my car to open the driver's side door, and I pushed one of the buttons on my key fob as he rounded the front.

A loud honk blared, making him jump, and I couldn't contain my real laughter. The surprise on his face morphed into a genuine grin.

"That's what you get." My chest filled with warmth, even though it was freezing outside. Being with Kase made me happy, so why couldn't we ride to Coffee Haven together without it being *together*? My lips twisted as I thought, and I made my decision.

"Let's just take your truck," I said and reached for the handle of the passenger door. Kase beat me to it, and opened the door for me. Always the gentleman, he took my backpack and tossed it into the back. Pulling *A Tale of Two Cities* out of my coat pocket, I set it in the middle of the bench seat. Kase climbed into the driver seat and looked down at the novel, with its dog-eared pages and worn cover.

"Is that one for class or for fun?" he asked as he started the truck.

The novel was not what I'd call fun, but Kase was really trying. His friendship would be the one I'd miss most when I moved back to New York.

"Definitely class," I answered. "It's been too long since I've read a book for fun."

Kase put his truck into reverse and backed out of the space. He'd started to put his arm along the back of the seat when he looked behind to check for other cars, but stopped himself. He sounded easygoing, but his posture was rigid, and he almost seemed nervous. After maneuvering out of the parking lot, he relaxed a little.

"So what have you been doing for fun?" he asked softly, keeping his eyes on the road.

When I shifted to face him, the seatbelt threatened to decapitate me. Wrapping my hand around the stiff fabric, I pulled it under my arm and answered, "Mostly training and hanging out with Scarlet and your sister. My parents are still back and forth to New York on business. I almost think they feel bad about being gone so much. Last week, my dad brought a telescope home and said I needed a hobby."

"Soon you'll have track and field season to keep you busy," Kase said, and he shrugged sheepishly. "But until then, astronomy sounds cool."

"Yeah, I guess," I agreed half-heartedly.

"No, really, the sky can tell you so much, especially at night. Knowing the phases of the moon and the different constellations can help you navigate by the stars. You can even tell time by connecting Polaris to the Big Dipper."

Squinting at Kase, I wondered who the imposter was, and asked, "Who are you, and what have you done with Kase?"

He smiled and rubbed at the back of his neck with one hand. "It's me, I promise. There's a lot more that goes into patrolling the town borders than racing against Joe from one ridge to the other. And, in the state he's in, we haven't done much racing. It's not like I have to worry about the phases of the moon because I can control when I shift, but I've had to use the constellations a time or two to stay on course. And I've used the moon to help tell time. Did you know the moon has no light of its own? It's how the sun shines on it that makes it useful."

"That's cool," I said and placed a finger on my chin thoughtfully. "Maybe I'll actually tilt the telescope up and take a look."

"Tilt it up, huh?" he asked with a mischievous grin.

"You may patrol the borders, but somebody has to keep an eye out for the people in town." A giggle escaped me.

Kase slowed the truck down as we approached the four-way stop at Main and Eighth Streets. He looked over at me and asked, "And who exactly do you feel like you need to keep an eye out for?"

"Oh, no one in particular. Think of it as a neighborhood watch," I said with a smirk.

"Sounds more like stalking to me," he mumbled with a chuckle. The truck moved through the intersection, and Kase was on the lookout for a parking space.

"I don't like your tone." So I decided to flip the script. "What have you been doing for fun?"

Kase pulled into a space across the street from Coffee Haven. He kept the truck running, with the heat on, and unbuckled his seatbelt. "Hanging out with Joe mostly. He's missing Infiniti. It's kind of making him crazy. I know you're going to find this cheesy, but kind of like the moon needs the sun to be useful, I've discovered I don't have much fun without you in my life."

Shifting in my seat, I faced forward. He'd gone there. My head pressed back into the seat, and I sighed.

"I can't—no, I won't let you talk me into *this*." I waved my pointer finger between us back and forth a few times. Pausing to gauge where his mind was at, I heard nothing. Kase had blocked me. He'd learned to veil his thoughts from me by the end of our second date.

"I know you're trying to protect me—" he started.

"Don't think I'm some saint. I'm also trying to protecting me." My hand covered my heart.

"I promise to never hurt you." Kase scooted closer, and the paperback between us pressed against my thigh. He lifted his hand and cupped my jawline.

Leaning into him, I closed my eyes and whispered, "That's like promising me the moon, Kase. It kills me to see you every day in those hallways, and a few weeks ago I even stayed away, thinking it might be a little easier. But not seeing you was worse. I thought a half vampire, half dryad dating a wolf shifter was trite, but the fact that I don't know how I'm going to live in New York without you feels pathetic."

"You are anything but pathetic," Kase muttered, his warm breath caressing my cheek. "Elliot Martin, the only I question I have for you is are you doing all of this—keeping me in the friend zone, moving back to New York—for you or for your parents?"

Pulling away, I felt weak. He was the only person in town I'd ever explained my past to, and he was partially right. I wanted to press my lips against his more than anything. Even though I'd been training for over a year to build my strength, to learn to control my power, I was completely vulnerable when it came to Kase.

Purchase *Promise the Moon* where books are sold.